The Angel Maker

MARCIA CLAYTON

For Bryan, Stuart and David
and, of course, in memory of Paul

Reviews

"I couldn't wait to start this book and I wasn't disappointed! The story carried on from the first book and just flowed. I loved all the characters especially Sabina and Sam. I'm looking forward to more stories from Hartford Manor! If you liked Upstairs Downstairs and Catherine Cookson's books, you'll love this one! I would definitely recommend this book and I'll definitely be looking out for Marcia Clayton's books."

"Having thoroughly enjoyed The Mazzard Tree, I was ready for a return visit to Hartford to find out what happened next. The Angel Maker continues Annie and Robert's story beautifully, but there is more. Alongside the absorbing detail of country life and the budding village romances, dark forces are at work which ultimately test the bravery and resourcefulness of the community. I can certainly recommend The Angel Maker to anyone who wishes to pull up a stool at The Red Lion ready for a cosy pint and a cracking good tale!"

"What a lovely story! I enjoyed 'The Angel Maker very much, and enjoyed learning about the ways of country folk in the 19th century. What a hard life people had. Marcia Clayton has a knack of getting into her character's minds and bringing them to life. I would recommend both of her books to anyone who loves a good story with wonderful characters and a good knowledge of the times. Once again, thank you Marcia."

"Carried on lovely from the first one. Enjoyed all of the characters. I was born and live in North Devon so recognised the surroundings. I hope there will be book 3 to carry on the story."

"Did not want the book to finish. More please..."

"Well worth five stars, thoroughly enjoyed, I would strongly recommend this book to any lover of local North Devon history."

"A truly addictive read. Cannot wait for the sequel. How did Annie continue her life as a lady? Was she ever accepted by Robert's family?"

Enthralling story following the lives of characters who are skilfully crafted to show how individuals can be affected by seemingly trivial events. I enjoyed following characters from " The Mazzard Tree" because I wanted to learn more about Annie and Robert. This is a real family saga and I am looking forward to reading the next book in the series.

Also by Marcia Clayton

The Hartford Manor Series

The Mazzard Tree

The Angel Maker

The Rabbit's Foot

Acknowledgement

Thank you to my husband, Bryan, for his patience and encouragement, and also my sons Stuart, Paul and David for their help along the way.

To Bryan, my sister, Gill, and my nieces, Sharon and Marilyn, for being the first people to read my book and provide constructive criticism and support.

To my talented daughter-in-law, Laura, for producing a fantastic cover for the book, and to Stuart for helping me to publish this book on Amazon.

Last, but not least, the biggest thank you goes to my readers. I have received some wonderful messages from readers who have told me how much they have enjoyed my books. Each and every review and message encourage me to continue writing. A simple message, particularly from a stranger, saying they loved my story helps to dispel my doubts over my ability as an author. I can't tell you how much those lovely messages mean to me. Thank you.

THE ANGEL MAKER

The Main Characters of Hartford

The Carter Family

EDWARD CARTER (b1812)
Married **BETSEY LOVERING** (b1814)

Their children:
1. **EVELINE CARTER** (b1837)

2. **GEORGE CARTER** (b1840)
   Married Alice Brown (1840 - 1880)

   Their children:
- Harriet (b1860)
- Francis (b1862)
- Alfred (1865 – 1869)
- Theresa (b1868)

George's sister-in-law: Mary Ann Brown (b1848)

3. **FREDERICK CARTER** (b1841)
   Married **LUCY FULLER** (1843 - 1881)

   Their children:
- Llewellyn (b1872)
- Rosella (b1876)
- Alfie (1877 – 1877)
- Grace (1879 – 1879)
- Eddie (b1880)

4. **TOM CARTER** (1841 - 1880)
   Married **SABINA BAILEY** (b1846)

   Their children:
   - **ANNIE** (b1864) married Harry Rudd (1851 – 1881)
   - Mabel (1866 – 1866)
   - Willie (b1869)
   - Mary (b1871)
   - John (b1872 - 1880)
   - Emma (b1874 - 1880)
   - Edward (b1876)
   - Stephen (b1878)
   - Helen (b1880)
   - Danny (b1880) Foundling (Son of Charles and Eleanor Fellwood)

5. **WILLIAM CARTER** (1845 - 1881)
   Married Lottie Chang (1850 – 1880)

   Their children:
   - Identical twins Joseph (b1875) Matthew (b1875)
   - Amelia (b1876)

   Married (2) **SARAH MARTIN** (b1845)

   Their son:
   - Bentley (b1882)

The Fellwood Family of Hartford Manor

LORD CHARLES FELLWOOD (b1825)
Married: **ELEANOR CHICHESTER** (b1838)

Their Children:
- David Fellwood (1861 - 1881)
- Lily Fellwood (1862 – 1864)
- **ROBERT FELLWOOD** (b1863)
- Victoria Fellwood (b1863)
- Sarah Fellwood (b1870)
- Danny (b1880) (Adopted by Sabina Carter)

The Hammett Family

Isaac Hammett (1806 - 1880)
Married: **LIZA JONES** (b1810)

The Cutcliffe Family

John Cutcliffe
Married (1)   Hannah Matthews (1846 - 1880)

Their Children:
- Daisy (b1873)
- Mary (b1874 - 1880)
- Rachael (b1876)
- Tommy (1879 - 1880)

Married (2)   **Noeleen Gubb**
Her children:
- Clarice (b1867)
- Ruth (b1869)
- Susanna (b1872)

The Chugg Family

ALFRED CHUGG (b1815)
Married **JANE WATTS** (b1820)

12 children - one son still living at home: Jimmy Chugg
(b1855)

Brother of Alfred Chugg: **CHARLIE CHUGG** (b1835)

The Rudd Family

Benjamin Rudd (1815 - 1881)
Married **Matilda Yeo** (b1820)

Their children:
- **Harry Rudd** (1851 - 1881)   Married Annie Carter
  (b1864)
- Jacob Rudd (b1855)
- Francis Rudd (b1860)

The Webber Family

Peter Webber (b1815)
Married Mary Jane Watson (1818 – 1866)

Their son:
Arthur Webber (b1836)
Married Drucie Reynolds (1840 – 1866)

Their children:
- Christopher Webber (b1856)
- Dudley Webber (b1858)
- Elsie Webber (b1863)
- Maria Webber (b1866)

CHAPTER 1

Charles Fellwood glared up at his son from his wheelchair. The left side of his mouth drooped slightly, and his withered left arm lay uselessly across the thick blanket draped on his knees. His thin brown hair had receded from his highly domed forehead, and he looked older than his fifty-nine years. His eldest son, David, had died fighting in the Boer War, and that devastating news had brought on a severe stroke leaving his left side paralysed and his speech impaired. Since that time three years ago, he had used a downstairs room as his bedroom, no longer sharing a bed with his wife, Eleanor.

The wealthy Fellwood family had owned Hartford Manor for generations. The estate covered over two thousand acres, divided into four farms. The home farm was the largest, with around eight hundred acres, and the other farms were smaller and rented out to tenant farmers. Many of the local men were employed as agricultural labourers or lime burners and lived rent-free in tied farm cottages. Since the death of David, his second son, Robert, had managed the estate, and it was this son who now stood angrily before his father.

His face ashen, Charles was almost incoherent with rage, and spittle flew from his lips. "You will not marry her! I forbid you. She's a common servant."

"I don't care what you think, Father. I shall marry Annie and soon."

"I'll never give my permission, and I'll take the estate back off you."

"You forget the estate's already been signed over to me, and there's nothing you can do about it. Anyway, you will agree to our marriage when you hear what I have to tell you."

The young man went to the double doors that led into the garden and ushered in a young woman carrying a child. She was slightly built with pale white skin and freckles. Her vivid red hair hung in ringlets almost to her waist, and her eyes were a deep green. She looked extremely nervous. The little girl in her arms was about two years old. Her hair was brown, with auburn highlights which shone in the sun, and she had her mother's green eyes. She buried her head shyly into her mother's neck.

"Father, this is Annie. I expect you remember her, from when she worked here? And this is her daughter, Selina." Robert crossed the room to the washstand where a blue and white pitcher stood. He picked up a bar of white soap, and put it to his nose and inhaled deeply. He turned to smile at his father, but the smile did not reach his eyes. "Mmm, Sandalwood, I believe it's called, is that right? I know you buy it in London. Nice, isn't it? Annie, come here. Do you like the perfume of this soap?"

Charles Fellwood looked at his son as if he had taken leave of his senses. "What has my soap to do with anything?"

"Quite a lot as it happens."

Annie regarded the soap as if it was evil. She raised it cautiously to her nose and sniffed.

"Is it the same smell?"

She nodded, and Robert turned again to his father. "When Annie worked here, she was attacked and raped. She was grabbed in a dark corridor when she was clearing up after a New Year's Eve party. Someone put their hand over

2

her mouth to keep her quiet and carried her to the West Wing and into the cellars. As you know, that part of the house is unused and the perfect place to be undisturbed."

Even more colour drained from his father's face. "So, what has it to do with me?"

"Annie didn't know who attacked her because she was also beaten. She was stunned, and it was dark. The only clue she had was the perfume the man wore, and now it seems it's the same as your soap."

"There were many guests present that night, and several must have used that same soap. It's not uncommon, and as you've said, we'd had a party. This doesn't prove I had anything to do with it."

"No, it doesn't, but it is significant, especially when you take into account the other evidence. You see, Annie was left pregnant by the encounter and was then sacked by Miss Wetherby for her loose morals. This little girl is the result of what happened that night."

Charles Fellwood still looked puzzled. "So why are you telling me all this?"

"Annie, would you be so kind as to undress Selina and let my father see her shoulder, please?"

Annie nodded and started to undress the child. She slipped off her blue cardigan, dress, and bodice and stood her before the old man. An ugly purple birthmark marred her shoulder. It was a strange shape, almost like a crescent moon. Charles Fellwood pursed his lips.

"Yes, that's right, father. It's the same birthmark that my sister, Victoria, has, isn't it? I see you recognise it. Our old nanny used to say it runs in the family. Now how could that have got onto Selina's shoulder? Let me see." Robert scratched his head theatrically. "Well, my brother, David, was fighting in the Boer War at the time, getting himself killed, and I was at boarding school in Exeter, so you were the only Fellwood male in the house at the time. Do you still deny this child is yours?"

3

The old man hung his head miserably. Annie drew Selina to one side and stepped forward. She spoke sharply. "Look at me. Was it you? Was it you that raped me?"

"Well, what if it was?" Charles Fellwood suddenly looked up at her defiantly. "You'd been flaunting yourself in front of me for weeks. This sort of thing happens all the time to servants, and it was only a bit of fun, you must know that. I'd no idea you were with child or that you were dismissed, but what good is this to you now? I'll never let you marry my son."

"I've never flaunted myself at anybody, let alone an old man like you. I'll never forgive you as long as I live, and I hope you rot in hell!" Annie hissed at him furiously and then slapped him hard across the face.

Robert gently led her and the shocked child away from the old man. "If you don't give your consent to our marriage, I will tell Mama about this. I'll be twenty-one in May and then I can marry whom I like, but it would look better to have your approval."

"Surely you wouldn't tell your mother, Robert? Think how much it would upset her."

"Oh, I'm afraid I would. You didn't worry how much you hurt Annie, did you? Just in case this is not enough to convince you, though, I have another surprise for you today." Robert went to the doors again and called out. "Willie, are you there? Can you bring Danny in, please?"

Annie's younger brother, Willie, appeared, leading a little boy by the hand. The child was about four years old and had dark curly hair and big blue eyes, which looked around in wonder at the grandeur of the room. His top lip was split up to his nose, and both feet turned inwards, one worse than the other, giving him a strange lopsided gait as he walked.

Charles Fellwood's eyes narrowed as he looked at Robert. "It's not …? It's not …?"

"Yes, it is, father. I've brought your youngest son to see you. This is Danny. The son you didn't want. Or, perhaps to be fair, the son that Mama didn't want because he wasn't perfect. As you can see, he's doing well, considering the difficulties he has to cope with. See how well Annie's mother is looking after him; your money is being well spent. Say hello to your son."

"Your mother; she might come in." Charles sounded breathless as he looked anxiously at the door.

"No, it's all right, don't panic. She's visiting one of her friends this afternoon and won't be back for a couple of hours yet. Now look, I know this is blackmail, and I'm not proud of myself, but if you don't consent to our marriage, then I'm going to ask Annie and Selina, Willie and Danny to stay here and meet Mama when she returns home. We might as well get this over with. I wonder what she'll say."

Charles Fellwood lowered his head for some moments, then raised his eyes and looked coldly at his son. "I don't have much choice, do I? I've no idea how your mother will ever understand my apparent approval for your marriage. You do realise that the gentry will shun you if you go ahead with this?" He turned to Annie. "And you young lady, you may think you are making a good marriage and will never want again, but I can assure you it will not be like you think. You won't know how to behave or dress; you won't be accepted in society, and quite frankly, life will be very difficult for you."

"That's our worry, Father, not yours. I don't care if the aristocracy ignores me; to be honest, that would almost be a bonus. I hate all the dressing up and pretence that surrounds our life. As for Annie, well, I'm sure we can find someone to help her with the correct etiquette and dress sense, though as you've already pointed out, we're unlikely to be asked anywhere socially anyway. If people want to come here, then they'll have to accept our marriage. As for Mama, though, you're right; I have no idea what she will make of this, but I do know she won't like it. That is a pity, but I love Annie, and she loves me, and I will not ruin our chance of happiness for the sake of appearances."

"Go, please go, now, before your mother comes home; please take these people away. She must not see them. Seeing these children, and knowing what I have done, would destroy our marriage. If only David was still alive, none of this would be happening."

"No, it wouldn't, and I wish he was here too, but I would still want to marry Annie." He smiled at his father. "We will go now. I would say I'm sorry to have upset you, but given what you did to Annie, I'm afraid I can't even pretend that I am. Just be aware, though, that I intend to announce our engagement at mine and Victoria's twenty-first birthday party in a month. I'll need to tell Mama before that, so just make sure you support me when I do. I can easily bring Selina and Danny back if I have to."

His father nodded and waved them away wearily.

As they left the Manor House, Annie and Robert walked on ahead of Willie, who was leading Danny and Selina by the hand. Willie took his time, allowing his sister some privacy, for he knew she was upset. He had to walk slowly anyway as Danny couldn't walk very fast. It was early April, and he helped the children gather primroses for his mother, Sabina. Willie was fifteen, and a farm labourer on old Mr Houle's farm where he lived in, but today was his weekly half-day off, and he was happy to help Annie and Robert.

Robert was delighted that the awkward meeting with his father was over and pleased they were one step nearer to marriage. However, Annie was anxious. She still didn't believe she would ever be allowed to marry Robert, the son and heir of the Lord of Hartford Manor.

Robert grinned at Annie. "Well, that's the hardest part over. Let's go and tell your mum and Liza now."

Before his death, Annie's father, Tom Carter, had been a labourer on the Hartford estate, living in a small cottage with his wife, Sabina and their seven children; one child, Mabel, had died soon after birth. Tom suffered from consumption, and as his illness progressed, it became ever harder for him to hold down his job.

There were seven cottages in the hamlet where they lived, all tied cottages with the inhabitants working on the estate in one way or another. Liza Hammett, and her husband, Isaac, a childless couple in their seventies, lived a few doors from the Carters. Isaac just managed to eke out a living as a rat catcher and handyman on the estate to enable him to keep a roof over their heads. However, one night during a violent storm, a large oak tree had blown down in the wind, crushing their cottage roof and trapping Isaac in his bed as he lay sleeping. Somehow, the tree had missed Liza, and she crawled to safety and summoned help. Annie's father, Tom, and other neighbours did all they could to save Isaac, but although they managed to free him from the wreckage, he died the next day. Unfortunately, exposure to the icy elements that night caused Tom to become seriously ill with pneumonia. With his body already weakened by consumption, within days, he too had died, leaving his wife Sabina bereft.

In the days that followed, Sabina had been beside herself with worry. The cottage they lived in was dependent on Tom's job, and she knew it would be needed for a new worker. Soon to be homeless, and with no income, she feared they would all have to go into the workhouse. However, Liza Hammett had suggested a solution that she thought might help them all. She offered to move in with Sabina and look after the children to allow their mother to continue working on the estate and so keep a roof over their heads. The arrangement had worked well, though the work had been incredibly hard for Sabina, especially when she had discovered she was pregnant with her ninth child.

Sabina and Liza were surprised to see Robert openly accompany Annie home, for they knew nothing of the recent encounter at the Manor House.

"Hello, Mum, Robert and I need to tell you something. Could you send the children out to play for a while? They shouldn't hear this yet."

Robert smiled at the children. "I'll tell you what; I've got a few spare coppers in my pocket. How about Willie takes you to Mrs Scott's shop in the village to buy some sweets?" He was rewarded with wide smiles all around, and Annie's siblings went off happily with their elder brother.

Liza reached for her shawl. "I'll go for a little walk and give you some time alone with your mother."

Annie put her hand on the old lady's arm. "No, don't go, Liza. We're happy for you to hear what we have to say. We'd all be in the workhouse by now if it wasn't for you."

She turned to her mother and bit her lip nervously. "Mum, we know who raped me and who Selina's father is."

Sabina and Liza looked surprised and her mother voiced what they were both thinking. "How have you found that out after all this time? She'll be three in a few months."

"Actually, we've known for some time, Mum. It was Robert's father, Charles Fellwood."

"What! No, surely not. You must be mistaken." Sabina's voice was incredulous.

At this Robert joined in. "No, there's no mistake, Sabina, the birthmark on Selina's shoulder runs in our family, and my father was the only male Fellwood at home at the time of the attack. We've just taken Selina to see him, and when we confronted him, he admitted it."

Annie smiled at her mother. "We waited until now because I wanted to leave a respectful time after Harry's death. I didn't love him, but I was fond of him, and it was so good of him to marry me considering my condition. I'll always be grateful to him for that, and I'm so sorry he died in the way that he did."

Sabina sat down unsteadily. "Your parents will never allow it, Robert; I've always said so."

"They've no choice, Sabina. The estate was formally signed over to me recently, and it's too late for my father to change that. That's also why we've had to wait until now. I've told him that if he doesn't give his blessing to our marriage I'll show Selina's birthmark to Mama and tell her where Danny is living. Father is horrified, but there's nothing he can do about it. My twin sister, Victoria, and I are twenty-one next month, and after that, we can marry whom we like anyway. I know my mother will be furious, but it will help if my marriage has father's approval."

"I don't know what to say, Robert. You know I think the world of you, and any mother would be proud to have you as a son-in-law, but how could this work? Where would you live?"

"Annie and I will live at the Manor House, of course. It would be awkward, but that's a small price to pay for us to be together; we've waited so long. I'm glad you mentioned living arrangements, though, because you will no longer be able to live here." He turned to face Annie. "I'm sorry, I haven't even told you this yet."

Sabina gasped and looked even more worried. "What do you mean? Surely you won't turn us out?"

Annie too looked anxiously at Robert.

"No, of course not, but I can hardly have my future mother-in-law working on my estate, milking the cows, and living in a farm worker's cottage, can I? I've given this a lot of thought, and I think the best thing is for you all to move into the old Lodge House at the entrance to the Manor House drive. Do you know the place, I mean? It was used as a gatehouse in years gone by. It's rather dilapidated because it's not been lived in for years, but we can get it repaired, and that would be quicker than building a new house. What do you think? Would it be suitable?"

Sabina's mouth had dropped open, but Annie had a wide smile on her face. "That would be incredible. Mum you'd love it there. Say something."

"I … I … don't know what to say. I'm just so shocked by all this. I can't take it all in. The Lodge House is huge and so grand. We couldn't possibly live there. What would people say?"

"I think most people would be delighted for you, and the rest of them don't matter. Look, just think about it. I'll get the key from Jack Bater, and we'll have a look around and see if it's any good. Just keep all this to yourself for now and get used to the idea. I'll have a word with Jack and tell him he'll have to find someone else to do your job." Robert smiled at the three women. "It will all be fine, you'll see, though things will never be quite the same for any of you again, that's no bad thing as far as I can see."

CHAPTER 2

A few days later, Robert met with his parents in the drawing-room. His father was in his wheelchair, and his mother, Eleanor, was sitting on a sofa doing some embroidery. She was a handsome woman with dark brown curly hair and brown eyes. As tall as her husband, she was of statuesque build, but still slim despite having borne six children. She wore a light blue dress, elegant in its simplicity. His father looked ill with worry, but his mother smiled as her son entered the room.

"Ah, there you are, Robert. This is rather intriguing. What do you want to talk to us about? Is it about your birthday celebrations because I have been giving that some thought, and we do need to make plans?"

Robert smiled back at his mother and went to sit beside her. "Yes, it is about my birthday, but I have some other news I need to tell you first. Mama, Papa, I intend to marry soon and I want to announce my engagement at mine and Victoria's birthday party in May."

His mother looked taken aback. "That truly is a surprise, Robert; I had no idea that you were even seeing any young ladies. Whom do you wish to marry?"

"I'm afraid this is going to be a big shock for you, but I've fallen in love with a girl in the village. In fact, before her first marriage, she was a servant in this house."

Eleanor gasped. Charles looked uncomfortable, and his already pale face lost yet more colour and took on a ghastly sheen.

Robert put his hand on his mother's arm. "I'm sorry, Mama, I know this is a surprise, but I do hope you can be happy for me, and give us your blessing."

Eleanor looked at her son in amazement. "Don't be ridiculous, Robert. You are the heir to the Hartford estate, and there is no way you can marry a common village girl. Have you taken leave of your senses? Charles, say something for goodness sake."

Her husband shuffled uncomfortably in his chair. "It would be rather unconventional, Robert, and not something I would encourage. Far better to marry someone of your own class. I'm sure there are plenty of young ladies who would be interested."

Eleanor looked at her husband in disbelief. "Is that all you have to say? That it would be unconventional? The marriage is out of the question. Tell him you will not allow it."

"I'm sorry you feel that way, Mama, and I rather thought you might, but you see, once I'm twenty-one, I can marry whom I like. I don't need your permission, though I would like your blessing."

"You'll never get it. And as for the estate, well, if you persist with this foolishness, it will have to pass to Victoria instead of you."

"It's too late for that, Mama. The estate has already been signed over to me, and neither of you can change that. I'm sorry, I really am, because I don't want to upset you over this, but I love Annie. If you would just meet her, I'm sure you would like her too."

"I am not receiving a village girl in this house. It's out of the question, and particularly a former servant. If it's the girl I'm thinking of, didn't Miss Wetherby sack her for some reason? Charles, I can't believe you have nothing to say. You surely can't approve of this?"

Charles Fellwood looked sadly at his wife. "I'm afraid Robert's right, my dear. The estate is now legally his, and once he's twenty-one, he can marry whom he likes. It's not what I would have wished for him, but there is nothing we can do. Perhaps we should meet the girl and make the best of it?"

Eleanor could not believe what she was hearing from her husband. He had always been so strong-minded, even since his stroke, and this was not like him at all. "I can't believe you are willing to accept this, Charles. Wait, did you already know of this? You don't seem surprised."

"I had mentioned it to him, Mama, and I know he's not happy with the situation, but he knows there is nothing he can do about it."

She glared at her son. "We'll see about that. I shall visit Mr Billery at the bank at the very first opportunity to see if the estate can pass to Victoria instead of you."

"Do that if you must, but I've been managing the estate since Papa's stroke, and as I come of age in a few weeks, Mr Billery has already completed all the necessary paperwork, and it's been formally signed over to me. If you remember, you signed the forms yourself, a few weeks ago. It was dealt with early as there was no reason not to."

Eleanor was furious, not only with Robert but also with her husband. She simply could not believe he was accepting this. "I don't know where you intend to live with this girl, Robert, but it will not be in this house."

"I'm afraid it will be in this house, Mama, because it's mine now, and if you want to continue to live here, you must agree to receive her."

Charles quickly intervened. "Robert, please leave us now, and let us discuss this between ourselves. It's been a great shock for your mother. Give us some space before we all say things we might later regret."

"Very well, but I'll be bringing Annie to this house soon, and I will not have her upset. If you feel you can no longer live here after our marriage, then you must consider moving elsewhere, though I hope it will not come to that. I'm going to tell Sarah my news now, and I'll write to Victoria later. I might as well also tell you that I'm going to move Annie and her family into the Lodge House. It's stood empty for years, but it would be ideal for them. I'll get the key from Jack later to have a look at it and see what work needs doing. I'm sure you can see that it's hardly appropriate for my future wife's family to be living in a farm worker's cottage. I will also tell you that Annie was married before, and her late husband died in a fire. She has a small daughter called Selina, who is nearly three, and I hope she will also be living here eventually." He held up his hands before either parent could speak. "All right, I'll leave you now because I know you're upset, but we will need to arrange a time for you to meet Annie, and soon."

As Robert left the room, Eleanor rounded on her husband.

"I can't believe that you are just going to accept this, Charles? It's not like you."

"As I said, unfortunately, there's nothing we can do about it. Robert has chosen his timing carefully, and he knows he has the law on his side."

"If only David had not been so stupid as to run away and join the army, none of this would have happened. He would have inherited, and that would have been that."

"I'm sure David didn't plan to get killed in South Africa, but even if that had not happened, I think Robert would still have wanted to marry this girl. If you remember, we sent him back to school early because we could see he was infatuated with her when she worked here. He's been keen on her for a long time."

"He should know that a man in his position can't always have what he wants. There are standards to maintain, and people in our class seldom marry for love. Indeed, I hardly knew you when we married."

"Well, it's not worked out so bad, has it?" Charles looked at his wife worriedly.

"No, of course not, and that's just my point. He could easily marry a more suitable girl and come to love her."

"Talk to Tom Billery at the bank, by all means, but I think you'll find our hands are tied. I was always reluctant to let Robert run the estate because he has such a soft heart, and I thought he would run us into debt, but I understand from Jack that he's making a good job of it. Apparently, we made an impressive profit last year."

Before his stroke, Charles had taken little interest in the estate, preferring to leave the day to day running of it to his manager, Jack Bater. David, too, had not wanted the responsibility of his inheritance as he had always longed to join the army. However, Robert took after his late grandfather, Joshua, and knew and loved every inch of the countryside and house and took a keen interest in everything. Following David's untimely death, Robert had left boarding school and taken over the management of the estate, despite the fact he was only eighteen. He worked well with Jack, and together they had made many improvements. The tied farm cottages had been in a shocking state of repair. The roofs needed thatching, and the windows leaked. Charles Fellwood had refused to spend any money on them for several years, but they were now fully refurbished. The farm workers had been given a small wage increase, again something that had not happened for many years. Robert had reaped the benefit of these actions, for the workers appreciated what he had done for them, and they worked hard in return. Their health improved once the cottages were no longer so damp and draughty, and there had been fewer deaths.

Leaving his parents, Robert went in search of his youngest sister, Sarah, who, at fourteen, was becoming quite the young lady. She was taught at home by her governess, Jane Leworthy. Not having any school friends, Sarah had missed the company of her sister, Victoria, since her marriage, and she now spent a lot of time with her friend, Mabel, who lived nearby. Robert found Sarah in the stables, just dismounting from her pony, Jenny. She was a plain girl with long brown hair, which she wore in plaits. She smiled when she saw him.

"Hello, Robert, are you going for a ride? I've just been for miles over the moors, and it was wonderful. The gorse is in full bloom, and it looks amazing. You should get out there."

"Yes, I might later, and I'm glad you've had a good ride. I hope you told someone where you were going though? I don't like you going out on your own."

"Oh, rubbish. I'm a good rider, but yes, I did tell Dodger where I was going, didn't I, Dodger?"

The stable boy took the horse from the young girl to rub it down and smiled at her. "Yes, she did tell me where she was going, sir, and she is an excellent rider."

"Well, make sure she always tells you, Dodger, good rider or not, accidents can happen."

"Aye, sir, I'll be sure to ask her." The young man led the horse away.

"I have some news to tell you, Sarah. I'm going to get engaged on my birthday, and I plan to marry soon."

Sarah looked just as puzzled as her mother. "Are you? I had no idea you were even seeing anyone. Who is it?"

"This has been a huge shock for Mama and Papa, but I'm going to marry Annie Carter. She used to work here. Do you remember her? She has bright red curly hair and green eyes, a pretty girl."

Sarah looked stunned. "My goodness, yes, I do remember her, but wasn't she sacked for getting pregnant?"

"Yes, she was, and she married Harry Rudd, but he was killed in a fire at the smithy a couple of years ago. She has a little girl called Selina."

"I can't see Mama and Papa ever agreeing to you marrying a servant, Robert. Are you sure about this?"

"Fortunately, they'll have no choice once I'm twenty-one, so I've only got to wait until May. The estate is already legally mine so there's nothing they can do, but you're right, and they are furious. What do you think? Do I have your support? I love Annie, Sarah, so I hope you'll be nice to her?"

"Hey, if you love her, that's good enough for me, but I can see lots of problems ahead. Yes, of course, I'll be nice to her and if there's anything I can do to help, just tell me, though I expect it will get me into trouble with Mama and Papa. Congratulations though, I'm pleased for you, now come here and give me a hug."

Robert embraced her warmly. "You have no idea how much that means to me. You're the first person I've told who is pleased for me." He grinned at her. "If I tell you a secret, will you promise to keep it to yourself?"

His sister looked at him impatiently. "Of course; when have I ever let you down?"

"Do you remember that day, in the nursery, when we looked out of the upstairs window and saw a boy crawling along the path dragging a sack of vegetables behind him? He thought by keeping low, no one could see him over the hedge."

"Yes, of course. It was pouring with rain, and he was covered in mud. We kept watch for days, but we never saw him again."

"Well, not long after that, you broke your ankle and were out of action, but I lay in wait in the grounds for a couple of mornings to see if I could catch him, and I did."

"Oh, you meanie, you never said. I'd have liked to know that."

"I know, and I did feel bad not telling you, but the thing is, it wasn't a boy, it was a girl, and it was Annie."

"What! So not only do you want to marry a servant, but she is also a thief? This just gets better and better."

Robert grinned. "No, she's not a thief. Well, technically, I suppose she is, but she was only stealing vegetables because her family was starving. Her father had died of consumption, and her mother had seven children to feed, and another on the way."

"Fair enough, though, I doubt Papa would see it that way."

"No, I know he wouldn't, and that's why you have to keep it a secret and tell no one. Anyway, I've been friendly with Annie, and her family, ever since. I would have liked to marry her before, but then she married Harry Rudd, and it was impossible. Sadly, for him, he died, but at least I can marry her now."

"Well, it's certainly going to be interesting around here. I can't wait to meet her. When is she coming here?"

"As soon as Mama and Papa can bring themselves to meet her. I'm giving them some time to get used to the idea, but I'm going to write to Victoria now to tell her. I'll see you, later." He kissed his little sister on the cheek and made his way to the library.

Robert's sister, Victoria, was his twin, though they did not look at all alike. Whereas Robert had brown hair like his mother and younger sister, Victoria had raven black hair and was something of a beauty. She was not as tall as Robert, and since motherhood, had put on some weight leaving her a little plump. Robert had been a skinny youth when he left school. However, the hard physical labour of working on the farm every day had honed his body, and strong muscles were now visible beneath his shirt.

Victoria had been married to Frank Eastleigh for a couple of years. He was a rich and handsome young man and they lived in London. They had one daughter of eighteen months, called Caroline, and Victoria was now pregnant again with her second child. She was to return home to celebrate her joint birthday with Robert in May and planned to stay at Hartford Manor to await the birth in July. Robert and Frank had been friends since childhood, but on a visit to the Manor when Annie was working there, Frank made a pass at her, and he and Robert fought. Things had been bitter between them ever since, and, at first, Annie had suspected it was Frank who had raped her. However,

Robert had gone to London to confront him about the attack, and Frank was so adamant it was nothing to do with him, that Robert believed him. The relationship between the two men remained strained, though both had made an effort since his marriage to Victoria.

Robert sat in a chair by the window and selected some notepaper. He started to pen a letter to his sister. He had no idea how she would react but fervently hoped it would be in a positive manner.

CHAPTER 3

After breaking the news of his forthcoming marriage, Robert kept out of his parents' way for the next week or so. He thought it best to give them time to become accustomed to the idea, though he wondered if they ever would. It would not have surprised him if they had chosen to leave the house and turn their backs on him. He took his meals in the kitchen, where, in truth, he was more comfortable and enjoyed the easy company of the elderly cook, Mrs Potts, who had always spoilt him. The servants wondered what was going on, but of course, dared not ask.

Finally, he decided he must find out whether his parents would meet Annie and presented himself for the evening meal. As he entered the dining room, he could immediately sense the hostile atmosphere, and it was clear his parents were barely speaking to each other. He sat down quietly and allowed the servants to serve the meal in silence, and then asked them to leave the room.

"Mama, Papa, I know you are both upset, but we do need to talk about this. Have you come to terms with my news?"

His mother looked at him haughtily. "I'll never come to terms with your marriage plans, Robert, and I simply can't understand why your father does not have more to say on the subject. If it was practical for us to leave this house and live elsewhere, I would do that tomorrow, but unfortunately, it's not so easy. Your father is disabled and needs full-time nursing, and it would be difficult to arrange that elsewhere. I've been to see Tom Billery, and he has confirmed that the estate does now formally belong to you, and you will be free to marry whom you choose after your birthday. I'm extremely disappointed in your lack of compassion where we are concerned."

"You may not believe me, Mama, but I am genuinely sorry this is so difficult for you. However, I have been giving this some thought. This is a large house, and I think day to day, we would need to see little of each other. I, too, went to see Mr Billery the other day to go through the accounts, and he was pleased to tell me that the estate is doing remarkably well and showing a good profit, so some of my ventures are working. I suggest we refurbish the West Wing of the house, and Annie and I live there. We would keep mostly to ourselves, and you and Papa would notice little change. What do you think?"

Charles looked hopefully at his wife. "That may be a compromise. What do you think, Eleanor? This is not what we would have chosen for Robert, but we need to find a way forward, so we can all live under one roof. I don't want to leave the house. I was born here, and the Fellwood family has lived on this land since before the Domesday Book was written."

"I suppose it might be one way to make the best of a bad situation, though I suspect many of our friends will suddenly find they have other engagements and not want to come here once that girl's background is revealed."

Robert encouraged that his mother was even willing to talk to him, smiled at her. "Good, that's settled then. I'll survey the West Wing and see what needs doing, then we can get the work started. I must ask though, would you please both meet, Annie? I'm sure if you would just get to know her, you would like her, but that's not the reason. The servants are going to find this situation surprising, and one or two are going to be uncomfortable. Your housekeeper, Miss Wetherby, for one because she unjustly sacked Annie for becoming pregnant, when in fact, she had been taken against her will by someone in this house."

His mother looked surprised. "I didn't know that."

"I think there are probably quite a few things that go on in this house that you are unaware of, Mama." He glanced at his father, who was shuffling uncomfortably and staring intently at the ground. "What's important is that as far as the servants are concerned, everything is fine. We don't want them gossiping."

Charles grimaced. "I think that will be impossible to avoid, but I agree we must at least meet the girl. Eleanor, my dear, can you bring yourself to do that? It needn't be for long, and if we include Sarah, that might make it a bit easier."

His wife bit her lip and looked dismayed but nodded. "Make it as short a meeting as you can, Robert, and tell the girl to keep out of my way in future."

"Thank you, I'm sure we can make this work if we all try, and who knows, in time you might come to like her." Robert beamed at his parents, for this was more progress than he had expected to make.

He left the Manor House in high spirits and went to tell Annie the good news. However, Annie was horrified. "Oh no, I can't. I can't meet your parents. They must hate me."

Robert calmly took her hands in his. "Annie, if you want to be my wife, things will have to change, and you must do this. There will be things you won't want to do and will feel uncomfortable with, but if you want to spend your life with me, that's what you'll have to do. You don't need to worry, though, because I'll be there with you every step of the way and Sarah is looking forward to your company. It will be all right. Now, do you have anything suitable to wear?"

"Goodness no! The only nice dress I have is the one I wore to the Christmas party when I worked at the Manor, and that once belonged to your sister, Victoria, so I can't wear that one. All my others are far too tatty."

"It doesn't matter. I'll take you to Exeter to buy some. We could go on the train tomorrow if you like?"

Annie looked at him in amazement, for she had never been on a train, nor ever expected to. She had also never had anyone want to buy not just one dress for her but several, and she suddenly realised just how much her life was going to change. She smiled at him. "That does sound exciting, and I would like to do that one day, but for now, could we just buy some material and ask my Aunty Evie to make me a dress? She's a good dressmaker, and I expect it would only take her a week or two. Would that be too long?"

"No, if that's what you want. Shall we go to your Uncle George's shop and buy some material?"

Annie laughed. "It would certainly surprise him if I turned up there with you, but shouldn't we keep this a bit quiet until after I've met your parents?"

"It's going to get out soon enough, but yes, I suppose so. Shall I give you some money, and you can go there with your Aunty Eveline?"

"Yes, that would be better, but I'll have to tell her. Is that all right?"

"Yes, of course. Right, here is some money, but just let me know if it's not enough. Ask her to make you two dresses, and they will do until we can get to Exeter."

The Carter family had lived in Hartford for generations, many of them running The Red Lion Inn where Annie's grandparents, Ned and Betsey were now the innkeepers. They had been blessed with five children; one daughter called Eveline, and four sons, George, Fred, Annie's father, Tom, and William. Eveline, the eldest was now in her late forties, and had never married.

George Carter ran the grocery and drapery store in the village. As the eldest son, he had been set up in the business by his father, Ned. At first, he had sold only groceries, but in recent years he had expanded his range to include clothes and shoes. Until recently, Eveline had worked in the shop with him and had been a real asset, coming up with many ideas to improve the business. George was a hard worker, intent on making money. He was strictly religious and taught in the Sunday school at the Baptist Chapel. He was on the parish Board of Guardians and heavily involved in the management of the workhouse and the distribution of poor relief. He was teetotal and abhorred drunkenness, which was somewhat at odds with his father's profession of running the local inn.

George had three surviving children from his first marriage, Harriet, Francis, and Theresa. His first wife, Alice, had died of diphtheria, and though he missed her, it had not taken him long to turn his attentions to his wife's younger sister, Mary Ann, who worked in the shop with him. After a respectable length of time had passed, they married. Young Nellie was now eighteen months old, and Mary Ann was due to give birth to her second child in August. In truth, George would have preferred not to start a second family at his age, but his attempts to avoid this had been unsuccessful, and at least Mary Ann seemed to enjoy motherhood.

Eveline was amazed at the news of her niece's forthcoming engagement, though she knew Annie and Robert had been fond of each other for years, and she was more than happy to make the dresses.

"I hope it works out for you, Annie, but it won't be easy. The dresses might take me a while, though, you know how busy I am looking after Fred's and William's children."

"Yes, I know. I don't know how you manage with six of them."

"I can't pretend it's easy, but they are getting older now. I love them all to bits, so it's not a problem. Besides,

Fred is as good as gold and helps out a lot, and what else could we do under the circumstances?"

"No, I know. With Fred's wife, Lucy, I suppose she couldn't help becoming mentally ill, though it was awful that she smothered two babies, but I think what William's wife, Sarah, did was even worse in a way."

"Yes, I feel the same. Lucy couldn't help herself, and she died a terrible death in that asylum, poor girl, but Sarah, well, I'd still like to give her a good hiding for abandoning William's children in London. If that friend of William's hadn't happened to call at the inn to see Mum and Dad, we would never have known what had happened to them. Have you seen the way she struts around the village now, with William's baby?"

"Yes, I've seen her. Bentley's a lovely little boy, though, isn't he? I think he looks exactly like William."

"Yes, he does, though I tend to ignore her whenever I see her. Anyway, about these dresses, I only have Eddie at home with me now that all the others are at school, so it should be all right as long as we pick a fairly simple style. Shall we look for some material tomorrow? Your Uncle George is going to be surprised at us spending so much money."

Annie couldn't help smiling to herself about the prospect of buying so much material in her uncle's shop. As she left Eveline's house and walked up the path to the front gate her Uncle George's second wife, Mary Ann, was passing by pushing her daughter, Nellie, in the pram.

Annie smiled at Mary Ann because although she was not keen on her Uncle George, she had nothing against his wife. "Hello, Mary Ann, how are you keeping?"

"Very well, thanks, Annie, though I must admit pregnancy is more tiring the second time around when you already have one child to run around after. This young lady keeps me busy."

"Yes, I can imagine. It's the same with Selina though, of course, I only have her to worry about. Anyway, glad to see you looking so well; bye for now."

CHAPTER 4

There was a dense early morning mist on the first day of May and a distinct chill in the air. However, the hot sun soon burned the fog away, and it promised to be a glorious day. Many villagers had been up since sunrise, for the custom was to gather flowers and branches, to decorate their houses, in the belief that the greenery spirits would bring them good fortune. Young girls would make a point of washing their faces in the morning dew, for this was said to make them more beautiful the following year.

During the week, the children in the village had been following the tradition of garlanding. At school, they made hoops of thin pliable branches and decorated them with flowers, greenery, and crepe paper. The garlands would be displayed at the May Day celebrations, and the vicar would pick the winner.

On the village green, Sam Symons and Richard Bedworth, were using a horse to pull the maypole into a vertical position, before dropping it into the hole, dug ready to receive it. They quickly filled the earth around the pole and stamped it down hard. The hole was deep enough for the pole to be secure. They walked away from it and stood at a distance to check that it was upright and admire their handiwork. The pole had been freshly painted with white paint, and long streamers in red, white, and blue hung from the top and flapped gently in the breeze.

"I think that's it then, Sam. We'd better get the trestle tables out of the inn cellar next."

"It looks good, doesn't it? The children will like dancing around that later. Yes, we'd better give Ned a hand; he'll never manage it all on his own."

Richard nodded his head towards one of the cottage gardens, where Clarice Gubb was carefully collecting dew from the rhubarb leaves. "I think it's going to take more than a drop of dew to make her beautiful, don't you? I think Mother Nature needs all the help she can get there."

Sam chuckled and nodded.

"Now, don't be unkind, Richard; she's a nice girl by all accounts, and they do say beauty is only skin deep."

"Aye, that's true, and I hear they're pleased with her at the Manor House."

Clarice's mother, Noeleen Gubb, had married John Cutcliffe a year or so before, and she had two other teenage daughters, Ruth and Susanna from her previous marriage. Of the three girls, Clarice, the eldest at seventeen, was the least good looking, or had been behind the door when the looks were handed out as was the local saying. She had recently started work as a kitchen-maid at the Manor House, and apart from her terrible acne, she was not a bad looking girl. Noeleen was John's second wife. His first wife, Hannah, had died a few years before in the diphtheria outbreak that had decimated the population of the village. He had also lost his young daughter, Mary, and toddler son, Tommy. His other two children, Daisy and Rachael, now aged nine, and six, had survived, but with no one to look after them whilst John worked, had ended up in the workhouse.

Hannah and John had been poor parents, and the diphtheria outbreak had started in their house with the death of Mary. They had spent what little money they had on cider, and the children were half-starved, filthy, and in poor health. Just before the epidemic, their neighbours Sabina and Annie Carter had tried to clean the family up, bathing the children, and putting them in clean clothes and scrubbing the house. Unfortunately, though, it had all been too little, too late, and John was left a broken man. To the amusement of the villagers, John had turned over a new leaf. His second wife was a religious woman and regular churchgoer and would not tolerate drink in the house. So far, John was abiding by the new rules and attending church every Sunday.

John and Hannah had lived in a tied farm cottage in the hamlet near the Hartford Estate, where John worked. However, he had given up this cottage and moved in with Noeleen following their marriage for her house was bigger and had become her own since her husband's death. Daisy and Rachael had been brought home from the workhouse and were overjoyed to be back with their father. They had been reduced to little more than skin and bone, for the regime in the workhouse was harsh, and food was scarce. They soon noticed a difference with Noeleen looking after them. She was a good cook, scrupulously clean and tidy, and kept a tight rein on their father so they had never had it so good. They began to put on weight, and the roses returned to their cheeks.

Clarice, Ruth, and Susanna carefully let the dew from the rhubarb leaves, trickle into a small bowl until they thought they had enough.

"Do you think this will work, Clarice?" asked Ruth. "It seems an awful lot of trouble to go to."

"That's what they say, isn't it? Anyway, it can't do any harm, and it might get rid of these awful spots. It's worth a try anyway. I'm going to use this rag to put the dew on my face; here's one each for you two."

The girls carefully dabbed the water on their faces, and Susanna grinned at her two elder sisters.

"Who are you two trying to impress then? I know it's Christopher Webber for you, Clarice, but I'm not sure about you, Ruth?"

Clarice's damp face flushed. "I don't know what you mean."

"Yes, you do, I've seen you making eyes at him in church. I expect you see him every day at the Manor now you work there. Does he like you?"

"Yes, I must admit I do like him, and he has asked me to go to the May Fair with him today. He's calling for me, later. What about you, Ruth, is there a boy you're keen on?"

"No, not really. Come on, Clarice, let me put a bit more dew on your spots, and see if we can get rid of them." She studied the ugly blemishes on her sister's face. "I hope I don't get any."

The maypole sorted, Sam and Richard made their way to The Red Lion Inn where Ned Carter was sorting through the junk in his cellar. He picked out the long trestle tables that would be used later for the villagers to sit around to consume food and drink. Though sprightly for his age, Ned was in his seventies and was glad to see the men.

"Morning, Ned. Can we give you a hand with those tables; they're pretty heavy."

"Yes, thanks lads, that would be helpful, and with the amount of food, Betsey has prepared we're going to need them. What a lovely day, though. We're so lucky after all the rain we've had."

May Day was a big event in the village of Hartford. The children had been practising their maypole dancing at the school for weeks. The end result would either be a beautifully plaited pattern of ribbons around the pole, or a tangled mess. Over the years both results had occurred, so it was anyone's guess.

Whilst they were getting the tables out from the cellar, Ned's daughter, Eveline, appeared. "Morning Sam, morning

Richard, thanks for helping Dad with the tables. Dad, don't you go doing too much now; let the younger men do the heavy lifting."

"Ah, don't fuss, lass, I'm all right. It's your mother you want to worry about; she's cooked that much food she's exhausted."

"I know, I've come to see how she's getting on. Today will be a good day for business, but I think she needs another servant to help out; will you think about it?"

"Aye, I will, and I think you're right; it's time we took things a bit easier. Trouble is servants don't pay themselves, and you know what your mother's like, no one does the job half as well as she does it herself."

"No, I know. Right, I'm going to see how she's doing, and then I'm going to visit Jane Chugg over at Hollyford Farm. I hear she's very poorly. I'll be back later to help with the hog roast, though."

Eveline went through the bar and into the kitchens at the back. Betsey was setting out pasties on large trays. They looked and smelt delicious. There were also dozens of sausage rolls. At one end of the long wooden table, a girl was cutting up ham sandwiches, and at the other end, another was preparing cut-rounds and cream with strawberry jam on top. "Hello, everyone, my goodness, this all looks tasty. You have worked hard."

"Yes, I think we're almost there now, though, thank goodness. Are you staying to help, Evie? And what have you done with the children?"

"No, I can't stay now, Mum. I've left the children with Fred this morning because I'm going over to Hollyford Farm to see Jane Chugg; she's very poorly. Have you seen her lately?"

"Yes, a couple of days ago, and she'd taken to her bed, I'm afraid. I don't know what the trouble is exactly, but she's lost a lot of weight, and she always did like her food. According to Alfred, the doctor thinks it might be a growth in her stomach, but he can't be sure. It doesn't sound good, though. I shall try to get over, and see her myself, next week.

"All right, I'll tell her, and I'll see you later. Can I borrow Bess to ride over?"

Her mother nodded, and Evie went to the stables and saddled up the old horse. She could have walked the couple of miles to Hollyford, but she didn't get the opportunity to ride often these days, and certainly not on such a lovely day. The sun was hot by this time, and Evie wished she had put on a hat. The countryside was stunning; the trees were clothed in fresh, vibrant green foliage, and the hedgerows teeming with primroses, violets, buttercups, bluebells, and red campion. In the distance, the sea was an amazing blue, and she could see three fishing boats making their way out to deeper waters.

Alfred and Jane Chugg had managed Hollyford Farm for many years and raised twelve children there. The farm was part of the Hartford Estate, and Alfred was a tenant farmer, just as his father and grandfather had been before him. The couple were in their early seventies now, and only one son, Jimmy, remained at home. He was in his late thirties, and still single. Times were hard in the countryside, with machines stealing a lot of the work previously done by farm labourers, and many young men had left for the towns in search of employment.

Recently, Alfred's youngest brother, Charlie, had returned home from a life at sea. He had travelled the world and though, he joked that he had a woman in every port, he had never married. He was a jovial man in his late forties, and Alfred was delighted when he decided to settle down at the farm. They could certainly do with his help, and having been brought up there, Charlie knew exactly what to do without being told. The two brothers were enjoying working together again.

Eveline tethered her horse to a rail outside the back door and knocked. Charlie opened the door and beamed at her. He was a tall, lean man with brown wavy hair and blue eyes, which twinkled when he smiled. His skin was deeply tanned from his travels.

"Hello, Eveline; it's good to see you again. Have you come to see Jane?"

"Hello, Charlie, yes, how is she?" As she looked into those blue eyes, Eveline's stomach did a somersault, and she turned away for fear he would see her reaction.

"Not good, I'm afraid, but she'll be pleased to see you. She doesn't get that many visitors, and she likes to hear all the gossip."

"I hope you won't be offended, but I made some chicken soup yesterday, and I've brought some for her. I know you aren't short of food here, but I thought she might like a drop."

"That's kind of you; I'm not sure if she'll eat it, but you can try. I'm afraid we're all missing her cooking since she took to her bed. We've taken on Maria Webber to help out, and she's a willing girl, but I'm afraid she isn't much of a cook."

"Oh dear, that's not good. You men need to eat plenty with all the work you do. Would you like me to show her how to make something for your dinner while I'm here?"

"If you have the time, it would be much appreciated. It was all right, when Jane was up and about, and telling her exactly what to do, but she doesn't seem to have got much idea herself. I don't think it helps that her mother died when she was born."

"Right, I'll see Jane first and ask if she wants some soup, and then I can get that on to warm and tell Maria what to do."

Eveline could see that her friend was very ill. Even though it was only a week since she had last seen her, the change was remarkable. The weight had fallen from her bones, her complexion was deathly pale, and her eyes seemed to have sunk into her face. However, her face lit up with a smile when she saw Eveline. "Hello, Evie, it's so good to see you. Thanks for coming."

"How are you, Jane? Charlie tells me you're not eating much, but I've brought you some chicken soup. Would you try a little?"

Jane shook her head. "That's good of you, Evie, but I'm sorry I can't eat anything. I don't feel hungry, and if I do eat, it just makes me sick. I can only just keep a sip of water down. I'd like Alfred to have it, though, if you don't mind."

She winced as she tried to sit up, and Evie quickly plumped up the pillows behind her. "Are you in pain?"

"Yes, I have a terrible pain, here under my ribs. It's been there a while, and I put it down to indigestion, but I can't ignore it any more. Doctor Luckett's given me laudanum, and it certainly helps with the pain, but the trouble is it puts me straight to sleep. I'll have some when you go, but I wanted to stay awake to talk to you. I'm afraid I'm not long for this world, Evie."

"Oh, Jane, don't say that. You know what they say, where there's life, there's hope."

"Aye, I know, but I've seen too many others like it over the years. It doesn't matter, I've had a good life, and we all have to go sometime. I'll be sorry to leave Alfred and Jimmy on their own, though, and, of course, they won't talk about it."

Evie sat and held Jane's hand and chatted to her for twenty minutes or so. She told her she was going to help Maria to get the men's dinner and Jane was pleased. She helped the old lady out of bed and onto the commode that Alfred had made and which housed the chamber pot. By the time Eveline got her back to bed she was exhausted and gritting her teeth to cope with the pain. Eveline went quickly to the washstand and picked up a small brown bottle. She poured a teaspoon of the reddish-brown liquid, and Jane drank it quickly, pulling a face.

"My goodness, that's bitter. Could I have a sip of water, please?"

Eveline made her comfortable, and went in search of Maria, who she found scrubbing the kitchen floor.

The girl was not lazy, for everything was spotlessly clean. Together, they looked in the larder to see what could be cooked for dinner. There was a fresh chicken that Alfred had killed the day before. He had plucked and drawn it, so all it needed was cooking. They found a suitable dish for the bird, sprinkled it with salt and put some water and fresh herbs around it. Eveline instructed Maria to stoke up the old Bodley and cook the chicken for two hours. In the cellar, there were plenty of potatoes, onions, swede, and carrots, so she helped Maria to prepare the vegetables, and told her how to cook them.

"Now, it should be ready by about one o'clock when the men come in. All you'll have to do then is make the gravy and dish it all up. You can only learn carving by doing it, so don't worry about it; they won't mind if it's rough and ready as long as it tastes good, but you must make sure the chicken is cooked through. Stick a fork in it, and make sure no blood runs out. If it does, put it back in the oven for another quarter of an hour, and then try again. I spotted some apples in the cellar so you could make an apple crumble for a pudding. I can't stay and do it with you, but if I put you going, it should be all right. It's easy. Just peel and slice the apples, and cook them gently with a little drop of water until they are soft, then add sugar until they taste nice."

Evie put some flour and butter into a mixing bowl. "Just rub that in together with your fingers until it looks like breadcrumbs, and then put the cooked apple in a dish, put that on top, and cook it for about half an hour, or until it's brown. Bit of cream on the top, and that should be lovely. All right?"

"Oh, yes, thanks, Evie. No one's ever shown me how to cook. Our Elsie's always done it at home, and I do the cleaning. She's never had the patience to teach me and, anyway, she's working at the Manor House now. Will you show me how to do a few more things next time you come? I'd like to be able to look after Mr Chugg and Jimmy and Charlie properly because I know Mrs Chugg worries about it."

"Yes, I'll come again when I can, but I must go now because it's May Day, and my mother will exhaust herself trying to feed the entire village if I don't stop her."

Evie found Alfred on her way out. "Jane's very poorly, Alfred." She looked into his sad blue eyes.

"Aye, maid, I know what's happening. I'm not blind. I don't know what I'm going to do without her, though. We've been together over fifty years."

His eyes filled with tears, and she took his arm. "I'm so sorry, Alfred. I think she needs to take that medicine regularly. I know she doesn't like to because it knocks her out, but she's in a lot of pain. Why don't you leave the farm work to Charlie and Jimmy for a few days and sit with her a bit more; I think she'd like that."

"There's always such a lot to do but happen you're right; the work will still be here when she's gone."

"I'll come again as soon as I can, Alfred. In the meantime, I'm hoping Maria will have cooked you a nice dinner."

CHAPTER 5

By the time Eveline got back from Hollyford Farm, the May Day festivities were well underway. There was dancing on the village green, an archery contest, and some arm wrestling on one of Ned's trestle tables. A group of men surrounded the opponents shouting encouragement to whichever one they had placed a bet on. Evie knew where her money would go if she was a betting woman; Francis Rudd. Although he was only a young man in his teens, Francis was as strong as an ox and well suited to his job as a village blacksmith.

Following a terrible fire two years ago, Francis had worked hard to rebuild the old smithy and was doing all he could to get the business thriving again. His father, Ben, and brother, Harry, had both perished. His mother, Matilda, had escaped unhurt, apart from the effects of smoke inhalation, but his brother, Jacob, had been badly burnt and was still not fully recovered. Jacob had always been slow-witted, and the trauma he had suffered had not helped matters. He needed constant guidance for even the simplest task. Ben Rudd had become forgetful in his latter years, and it was thought he had accidentally caused the fire in the night. Matilda, previously a jolly woman, who delivered most of the babies in the village, and also laid out the dead, was a changed woman. She continued to wear black and had not recovered from the loss of both her husband and son. Following the fire, she sold some of her land to raise the money to rebuild the smithy and provide Francis and Jacob with a livelihood.

Eveline watched as Francis, red in the face, laughed as with ease, he slowly pushed Christopher Webber's arm down onto the table for the second time. Christopher sighed deeply as he reluctantly handed over his money and walked off arm in arm with his girlfriend, Clarice. "I was sure I would beat him this year."

She tried to console him. "Never mind, there are few people who can beat Francis at that game, and I've not seen any do it yet today."

Francis looked around at the crowd and grinned. "Anyone else fancy a go?"

Eveline had seen Francis in action before and knew he could keep this up all day long. He would make a good few shillings before the day was out. Most of his opponents were from neighbouring villages and were unaware of his reputation.

However, before another contest could begin, there was a shout for young men to carry the May Queen. This year the Queen was Theresa Carter, a pretty girl of sixteen. Her long blond hair was adorned with flowers, and she wore a simple white dress. More flowers hung around her neck, and she sat on a chair lavishly decorated with greenery. Theresa was the youngest daughter of George Carter, and Ned and Betsey from the inn were her grandparents.

The young men carried Theresa shoulder high around the village. A small band preceded them, providing a reasonable rendition of local songs. Eventually, they returned to the village green, where they placed the chair on a wooden cart so that everyone could see it. Theresa stood up and cut a ceremonial red ribbon and declared the May Day celebrations officially open, although some had already started.

Eveline glanced around the crowds looking for her brother, Fred, and the six children. She spotted him at last and waved to him. Eveline had moved in with Fred a couple of years before to help him bring up his three children, Llewellyn, Rosella, and Eddie, after their mother, Lucy, had committed suicide in a lunatic asylum. The family had suffered a difficult and traumatic time. There had been two other babies, Alfie and Grace, born between Rosella and Eddie, but they had died within a few weeks of birth. It was not until Lucy was found trying to suffocate Eddie that the truth came out; she had murdered both children. Instead of going to jail, she was sent to Stockton Asylum, where all manner of treatments were tried to improve her post-natal depression and general mental health. However, none were successful, and sadly, when the opportunity arose, she took her own life.

The other three children living with Fred and Eveline were the orphan children of their brother, William, the youngest child of Ned and Betsey. William had died later in the same year as his brother Tom. A clever but wayward child, William had run away to sea as a teenager and ended up in China, where he worked for the Imperial Maritime Customs. His parents had heard nothing of him for many years until he finally came home, a widower with three children; identical twins, Matthew and Joe, and daughter, Amelia. Their mother, Lottie, had sadly perished from malaria. She had been Chinese, and they had inherited her oriental looks with their olive skin, slanted eyes, and raven black hair.

William's employers had granted him a year off work to return to England and visit his family. Ned and Betsey were overjoyed to see him, and he rented a cottage near the sea from his brother, George, and worked with Fred, in his carpentry business. Over the following months, he fell in love with Sarah Martin, a girl he had gone to school with. She agreed to marry him and return to China with him and the three children. However, when they reached London to join a ship, William was taken seriously ill and died, leaving Sarah alone with the three children. Not a maternal woman, Sarah panicked and abandoned the children at the inn where she was staying. She returned home alone, pretending she had changed her mind and William and the children had sailed to China without her.

Eventually, of course, the truth came out, and Fred and Eveline travelled to London where they found their niece and nephews in a workhouse. They brought the children back to Devon and decided the best solution was to bring up all six children together.

As soon as the story of Sarah abandoning William's children became known in the village, she was shunned by all who knew her. However, when he learnt she was pregnant with William's child, her father relented and reluctantly allowed her to return home to live. Her son, Bentley, was now two years old, but she was still ignored by all of William's family, and most of the village.

Eveline smiled at her brother. "Hello, Fred, I was hoping to get here before the maypole dancing started."

"Yes, I think that will be any time now. How was Jane Chugg today?

"I'm afraid Jane is very ill and Alfred is worried about her. I'll need to go and see her again next week. Oh, look, there's Sabina with her children." Eveline waved to her sister-in-law. "Let's walk over to the maypole and get the children organised."

The twins, Matthew and Joe, and their sister, Amelia, stood alongside their cousins, Llewellyn and Rosella. Each took a coloured ribbon in readiness for the dance, but at four, Eddie was a bit too young. Sabina joined them with her four youngest children, Edward, Stephen, Helen, and Danny.

"Hello, Fred, hello, Eveline; nice to see you both. Stephen, go and stand with Llewie and Rosie ready for the dance."

Like Eddie, Helen and Danny were also four years old and too young to dance. Although at eight years old, their brother, Edward, should have been dancing, he had been deaf since birth, so teaching him to dance had proved difficult, and he stood with the younger children.

The band began to play, and the boys and girls, standing alternately around the base of the maypole, each took hold of the end of a long ribbon. They began to dance, the boys going one way, and the girls the other as they weaved in and out and around each other. The teachers looked on anxiously, willing the ceremony to reach a satisfactory conclusion. Fortunately, this year it did, and the end result was a neatly woven pattern of red, white, and blue ribbons running down the pole, and the crowd duly applauded the dancers.

Sabina grinned at her sister-in-law. "Well, that went better than I thought it might."

"Yes, it did, and I think most of the children were ours. I remember getting in a right old tangle when I did it as a child. Shall we go and get something to eat now?"

"Yes, that sounds like a good idea. Are you coming, Fred?"

"No, not at the moment, you go with Sabina and the children and get them some dinner. I want to have a word with Dad about a job he wants me to do for him."

"All right, Fred, you take your time. Come and join us when you are ready."

Eveline could see that her mother's food was selling like hot cakes, and many villagers were sitting at the long tables eating pasties, washed down with a pint of ale as they enjoyed the occasion.

"Come on, Sabina, I don't know about you, but I'm hungry, and these children always are. Oh, look, that's lucky. I think there are enough seats for all of us at this table. What about Annie, is she coming with Selina?"

"She'll be here soon, I expect. I believe she's told you of her plans to marry Robert?"

"Yes, she did tell me in confidence because I'm going to make some dresses for her. We're going to buy the material, tomorrow. I find it hard to believe they'll be allowed to marry, though I know they were close before she married Harry."

"I know. They're adamant they will wed, but I'll believe it when I see it. I don't want her to get hurt. Robert is even talking about all of us moving into the Lodge House. Can you believe it? I mean, it would be wonderful, but I think his mother would have a fit."

Eveline laughed and was about to reply when suddenly she fell silent and pursed her lips as she spotted her sister-in-law, Sarah Carter, approaching them.

Looking uncomfortable, Sarah sat close to Eveline and Sabina with her son, Bentley. Bentley had the fair skin and curly red hair common to many of the Carter family. He toddled over to Sabina and looked enviously at her pasty. Sarah quickly went to take his hand and lead him away, but Bentley did not want to go.

He looked plaintively at Sabina. "Me want some."

Sabina hesitated, for she never could refuse a child, and this child was, of course, her nephew. Sarah scooped him up into her arms, where he kicked and screamed.

"It's all right, Sarah. Here Bentley, here's some for you." Sabina broke a corner off her pasty, blew on it to cool it, and held it out to the little boy. He immediately rewarded her with a huge smile, and said "Ta."

Sabina's heart lurched as she looked into his blue eyes, for they were so like those of his father. Suddenly she knew that William would want her to be part of his son's life.

"Thank you, Sabina; I'm sorry he bothered you. There were no other spare seats, but we'll find try to find somewhere else to sit."

Sabina looked anxiously at Eveline, knowing she might not approve. "No, sit with us if you like, Sarah. Perhaps it's time Bentley got to know his cousins."

Eveline looked surprised, but Sabina gave her a stern look, and she decided to go along with her sister-in-law.

Sarah smiled with relief. "Thank you, Sabina, but I don't want to intrude because I know how you all feel about me. I've wished so many times I could turn the clock back, and do things differently, but of course, I can't." She hung her head. "I'm so ashamed of myself, and I don't blame you all for hating me, but at the time, I panicked at the thought of caring for William's three children on my own."

"What's done is done, Sarah. I'd say it's what you do from now on that matters. Come on, join us. I think it's time to put the past behind us. What do you think, Eveline?"

Her sister-in-law looked less sure, though she too had been struck by Bentley's likeness to her late brother.

"Yes, come and sit with us, and let Bentley play with the others."

Sarah was delighted, and hesitantly at first, she joined in the conversation with the other two women. Since the truth had come out about William's death, she had led a lonely life, though she was grateful to her father for allowing her to move back home. She now dared to hope that if Sabina and Eveline would once again accept her, perhaps others in the village might follow their lead. When they had finished eating, the children all played with Bentley who loved every minute.

Sabina stood up and brushed the crumbs from her dress. "Eveline, could you keep an eye on the children while I get us all another drink? Sarah, would you like one?" Eveline nodded, and Sarah accepted gratefully. Sabina made her way across the grass to the inn, and through the bar, on her way to the kitchen.

Arthur Webber was at the bar waiting to be served, and as everyone was busy, Sabina offered to get him his tankard of ale. Arthur was a tall, lean man of about fifty, who worked as a labourer on the estate, and lived with his family in Liza Hammett's former home. He was a widower, his wife, Drucie, having died in childbirth many years before. His sons, Christopher and Dudley, were also labourers on the estate, and it was Christopher, who had recently been beaten at arm wrestling by Francis Rudd. Arthur's daughter, Elsie, was the second cook at the Manor House. She had always been a skilled cook and was now learning fast from Ethel Potts. Maria, his youngest daughter, had recently found a position at Hollyford Farm, and it was she that Eveline had helped to cook that morning. Arthur's father, Peter, also a widower in his mid-seventies, lived with his son. Peter was disabled and had lost both his hands. A former miner, he had been badly injured after an explosion and was lucky to escape with his life. He was an intelligent man who had struggled to come to terms with his disability and felt he was a burden on his family. With both Elsie and Maria now in service, life was difficult for the Webber menfolk, but they managed as best they could.

"There you are then, Arthur. You look ready for that." Sabina smiled at him.

"I certainly am, Sabina, thank you. That sun's hot today, and I rushed to get my work done this morning so that I could come here for the afternoon. Luckily, I've got a half-day off."

"I thought I might have seen your father here today. Is he well?"

"No, he's not too good. Just a bad cold I think, but he gets depressed these days. I tried to persuade him to come because I thought it would do him good to get out, but he was having none of it. His accident hit him hard and, although it was a while ago, he's never come to terms with losing his hands. There's so little he can do now. As a younger man, he loved to paint pictures but never had the time or money to spend on it, and now, of course, he can't hold the brush. It's a pity because it would be a good way for him to spend his time."

"That's a shame. Do you think he would like me to call in and see him?"

"I don't know. He can be quite abrupt and plain rude these days, but if you're willing to risk it, then it would do him good to see another face."

"That's settled then, I'll call in and see him during the week. Now, I'm going to make my escape otherwise, I'll be stuck behind this bar for hours."

By the time Sabina returned with the drinks, Annie had arrived with Selina, and as soon as she saw Sabina, the little girl went running to her granny, holding out her arms. Sabina picked her up and hugged her.

On the village green, the Morris Men had just started dancing, and the children were fascinated. The eight men were arranged in two lines and wore white shirts with coloured belts or baldrics across their chests and small bells attached to their knees. They carried short sticks which they knocked against each other. Selina loved it and joined in hopping from one foot to the other and clapping her hands.

The May Day celebrations went on well into the night, but Sabina and Annie made their way home at tea time, for the little ones were getting tired. The women sat them around the table and fed them with some bread and dripping and milk before putting them to bed.

CHAPTER 6

The next morning, Annie put Selina in the pram and went to call for her Aunty Eveline to buy the dress material. She was very excited for she had never had any clothes that were brand new. They were usually hand-me-downs from other families or adult clothes cut and altered to fit. She decided to visit Matilda Rudd at the smithy on the way. Matilda was the nearest thing the village had to an experienced midwife, and with her practised eye, she had known that Annie was pregnant before the marriage to her son, Harry. She had gone along with the theory that the baby was early, and Selina had been a small baby, so it was plausible. However, she had always hoped that the child was Harry's, though the little girl was not like him in the slightest.

Matilda was on her knees washing her steps as Annie approached, and she struggled to her feet with some difficulty, and then shuffled over to speak to Selina. "Hello, then, gorgeous, come to see your old granny, have you?"

Selina beamed and held out her arms to be picked up. She was getting rather big for the pram, but it was a bit too far for her to walk from Sabina's house to smithy. Annie left the pram and went inside.

"Have you got time for a cup of tea, Annie?"

"Yes, please, that would be lovely. I want to tell you something, Matilda, but you'll need to keep it to yourself for now."

"That's intriguing. Let me just pour the tea and give Selina a biscuit, and then you can tell me your news."

Once they were comfortably seated, Annie plucked nervously at the tablecloth, trying to think how to start the conversation. Eventually, she looked up. "I wanted you to hear this from me and no one else, Matilda. I'm getting married again."

"Why, Annie, that's wonderful news. I'm so pleased for you, but who are you going to marry? I didn't even know you were courting?"

"I'm going to marry Robert Fellwood."

Matilda's mouth dropped open. "Never, oh Annie, I wish the best for you, of course, I do, but that can never happen, surely you know that?"

"Normally, I would agree with you, but we have his parents' permission, and our engagement will be announced later this month."

"I can't believe they would allow it. I mean, why would they? You're a lovely girl, Annie, but you were a servant at the Manor House, and Robert will be Lord Fellwood one day. Oh, wait a minute." Matilda frowned and looked most uncomfortable. "Annie, I'm sorry to ask, but is Robert Selina's father? You see, I know you were with child before the wedding."

Annie blushed and looked down guiltily. "No, Robert is not her father."

"Harry was her father, then?"

"No. You're right, I was already in the family way before we married, and Harry knew that when he proposed, but he insisted on marrying me anyway, and we were happy, Matilda. I was attacked and raped at the Manor House one night after a late party. There were loads of guests, and I didn't even know who it was because it was so dark, and my attacker punched me, and I was stunned. Unfortunately for me, that once led to me being with child."

"Oh, Annie, I'm so sorry, but even so, I don't see why the Fellwoods would let you marry their son?"

"I can't say any more about it, Matilda. All I can tell you is that I now know who attacked me, and the Fellwood family would not want people to know who it was. They are agreeing to our marriage on the condition we keep it quiet. It wasn't Robert, though."

"Well, this is a strange do and no mistake." Matilda shook her head. "I always wondered if Selina was Harry's child."

"He treated her as if she was. He was a wonderful man, Matilda, and it was so kind of him to marry me and give me some respectability. I honestly do miss him."

"I shall always look on her as my first grand-daughter. Is that all right? Can I still do that?"

"Yes, of course, and I'm so sorry if this is a shock for you, but I wanted you to know the truth. Could you keep my news to yourself until it is properly announced?"

"Yes, of course, my dear and I wish you both all the best, but I think you are going to find your new life very difficult."

"Thank you, and yes, I know it won't be easy. I'm on my way to buy some material from Uncle George's shop because Aunty Eveline is going to make me two new dresses, one to go and meet Robert's parents, and the other for his birthday party, when our engagement will be announced. The truth is I'm dreading both occasions, though I am looking forward to seeing my Uncle George's face when I buy lots of new material."

Matilda laughed heartily, her blue eyes crinkling at the corners and dimples appearing in her old cheeks. "Yes, he will be surprised."

"I hope Aunty Evie can get the dresses made in time; I'll need them in a week or two."

"I'm pretty good with my needle, so if she needs some help, you tell her to come and see me. I'll gladly give her a hand, and we must have you looking your best."

"Oh, thanks, Matilda that's kind of you, and yes, I'll tell Aunty Evie."

When Annie left, Matilda waved to Selina until they were out of sight. As the old lady turned to go inside she grinned to herself at the thought of stuck-up George Carter serving Annie with his best material.

Eveline was waiting for Annie, and together they walked to the shop, Eveline holding young Eddie by the hand. George's daughter, Harriet, had worked in the shop since Mary Ann married her father, and Eveline left to look after the children of her brothers, William and Fred. She was stood behind the counter serving people, and George was checking the stock.

"Good morning, Harriet, morning, Uncle George." Annie and Eveline smiled as they approached the counter.

"Hello, what can I get for you today?" Harriet smiled. She was a little on the plump side but a pretty girl, with a sprinkling of freckles across her nose and eyes of light brown. She wore her auburn hair tied up in a ponytail with a pink ribbon.

Annie grinned. "I want to buy some material, please. Aunty Eveline is going to make me two new dresses."

Harriet looked surprised, and George appeared from around the corner. "I'll see to this, Harriet. You carry on serving behind the counter." His daughter looked annoyed, for she would have enjoyed showing the materials to her aunt and cousin.

"Our material is good quality and might be a little expensive for you, I'm afraid, Annie." The man smiled condescendingly. "We have a few ready-made cotton smocks that might be suitable?"

"No, I need enough material for two dresses, and it has to be of the best quality. Don't worry, I have the money.

Can you show me what you have, please? I would like two different colours."

George was mystified. "Of course, if you insist. The materials are over here on these shelves, but I warn you they do not come cheap."

Eveline and Annie looked through the materials and chose two fabrics, one in mid-blue and the other in a deep green. Eveline approved as she held each material up to Annie's face. "These will be ideal, Annie. The green brings out the colour of your eyes, and both fabrics will hang nicely. Now, I've worked out how much we need. I can cut it if you like, George? I think I've done this more times than either you or Harriet."

As Eveline measured and cut the cloth, George was curious. Not so long ago, Annie and her family were just one step away from the workhouse. In fact, he had enraged Sabina by offering to arrange for her youngest children to go there. He couldn't imagine where Annie had got the money to pay for the material, and for a moment, he wondered if she had stolen it, but then dismissed the thought, fairly sure his niece was no thief.

Eveline and Annie were smiling broadly as they left the shop.

"Right then, Annie, I'll get cracking on these dresses. They shouldn't take me too long with my new sewing machine. Which one shall I make first?"

"Can you make the blue one, first because I thought I'd wear that to meet Robert's parents, and keep the green one for the party? Thanks so much for doing this, Aunty Eveline. Don't forget, Matilda will help you, if you need her to."

"It's no problem, I shall enjoy it, but I'll ask Matilda if I need to. I'll let you know when I need you to try the dress on. Bye."

Annie hastened home with Selina. She had arranged to meet Robert after lunch, and couldn't wait to tell him about her shopping trip. However, she was surprised to see him already at her back door with his horse, Prince, and his sister, Sarah's pony, Jenny.

"Hello, Robert, you're early; I've not had my lunch yet. Is Sarah with you? That's her pony, isn't it?"

"No, she's not here, but she's let me borrow Jenny for the afternoon. I thought I'd teach you how to ride. Have you ever been on a horse before?"

"Yes, I've ridden Grandad's horse a few times, but he was always leading it. I've never ridden on my own."

"Well, now's your chance. I've brought some food, so if your mum will look after Selina, we could make an early start."

"Yes, of course, I'm sure she won't mind. I'm not sure I can ride on my own, though."

"I'll lead you for a while until you get used to it."

Having checked that her mother would look after Selina, Annie allowed Robert to help her onto the horse. She found it awkward to sit side-saddle and would have much preferred to sit with one leg on either side of the pony.

"I'm afraid you'll have to ride side-saddle, now you are to be a lady. I'll lead you through the woods and then see how you manage on your own once we reach the open countryside. Don't worry, though; Jenny's very placid. Would you like to do that?"

Annie grinned at him. "Yes, it sounds lovely."

Robert led her through the woods, but once they reached the open countryside, she took the reins herself. She was nervous at first, but soon gained confidence and began to enjoy herself. They trotted along together slowly until they came to the edge of the moors. Then they tethered their mounts to a tree and sat on the grass to eat the food that Mrs Potts had packed for them.

From their vantage point, they had a marvellous view of the rolling countryside around them with only one large house in sight. The gorse was in full bloom with its bright yellow flowers, and against the vivid blue of the sky, it was an amazing sight. Annie sighed as she munched on crusty bread, ham, and boiled egg and drank the cold lemonade. She thought she couldn't be happier than at that moment sat there with Robert.

As they gazed down on the large house below them, they saw a woman arrive in a pony and trap. She was accompanied by a younger woman carrying a baby. They knocked on the door, and a tall woman answered and let them in.

"That place is called Buzzacott House, and a big family used to live there, but they left last year. I used to play with one of the daughters. Nobody seems to know much about the people who live there now; they seem to keep themselves to themselves. Do you know them, Robert?"

"No, I don't know them. Anyway, never mind them, I think it's high time you rewarded me with some attention, seeing as I have taken you riding, and provided you with a tasty meal." He put his arm around Annie, pulled her to him, and kissed her gently. She lay back on the grass, and he leaned over her and kissed her more passionately. "Oh, Annie, I can't wait for us to be married; we've waited so long. When would you like to get married?"

Annie returned his kisses and murmured in his ear. "Mmm how about, tomorrow? Or could we make it later, today?"

He laughed. "If only we could. I was thinking more like August, around your birthday. You'll have to meet Mama and Papa, in the next week or two." He was suddenly serious. "Annie, you do realise that my sister, Victoria, and her husband, Frank, will be there too."

Annie's face was grim at the mention of Frank Eastleigh's name.

"Look, I know you can't stand Frank, and with good reason, but at least we know now, it wasn't he that attacked you."

"He wasn't the one that got me pregnant, but he did make a pass at me. If you hadn't saved me that day, it could have been a very different outcome."

"I know, and I'll never forgive him, but he's my brother-in-law now, and I want to make my announcement whilst all the family are together."

"Very well, but don't leave me alone with him."

"No, of course not. Our engagement will be announced next month, on my birthday. It will take a couple of months to refurbish the West Wing in the Manor House, and plan the wedding, so I think we could hold the wedding in August. Can you wait that long?"

"Yes, that will be perfect."

CHAPTER 7

Eveline had made a superb job of Annie's new blue dress, and it fitted her perfectly. To her Uncle George's further amazement, she bought some new black shoes and a ribbon for her hair. He badly wanted to know what was going on but didn't like to ask, and Annie and Eveline had no intention of telling him.

Annie was so nervous on the day of her visit to the Manor House, that she was afraid she would be physically sick. Robert collected her in the pony and trap, for she couldn't walk to the house in all her finery. Robert took her hand as she alighted and led her up the steps to the imposing front door. He could feel her hand trembling beneath his, and he smiled encouragingly at her.

"Don't worry, it will be fine. You look beautiful."

Annie had never entered the house by the front door before, and when Sid Hobbs opened it, she almost laughed out loud, despite her nerves, for he looked so surprised. The butler led them straight to the drawing-room where Charles was sitting in his wheelchair, and Eleanor, in an armchair.

Robert led Annie forward. "Mama, Papa, I'd like you to meet Anne Carter, my future wife."

Charles held out his right hand from his sitting position, for he was unable to stand. "Hello, Anne, I can't pretend we are happy about this, but Robert is determined to marry you, and we are unable to stop him, so I suppose we will just have to make the best of it."

Annie made to curtsey, but Robert, fully expecting this, held on to her arm firmly, and would not allow her to do so, and instead, she shook her future father-in-law's hand. She blushed to the roots of her hair but held Charles' gaze defiantly. "Yes, sir, I suppose we both will."

Eleanor looked at the girl coldly, incensed at her impudence. "I'm not happy about this, and I would have you know, you've come between mother and son. I will never forgive you for the situation you have placed us in."

Annie looked even more uncomfortable, but nevertheless, held the woman's gaze. "At least we both know where we stand then. For what it's worth, I'd like you to know that I love your son and intend to do my best to make him happy." The two women did not shake hands.

Robert was so angry he could barely speak. "Right, now you've all had your say, may I suggest we sit down, and ring for some tea. We must behave appropriately in front of the servants, and there are certain matters we need to discuss."

Robert rang the bell, and Maisie appeared at the door. Her jaw dropped when she saw Annie, and again, despite her nerves, Annie couldn't help but smile. Robert too smiled at the maid. "Ah, Maisie, I see you have recognised Annie, and I know you two are friends. Would you bring us a tray of tea, please, and some of Mrs Potts' best cakes?"

"Yes, sir, of course." Maisie bobbed a curtsey and ran back to the kitchen to pass on this bit of hot gossip. In no time at all, she returned with a tray.

Only when Maisie had left the room, did Robert speak as he poured the tea. He offered cake to all those present, but none could bring themselves to eat any.

"Right, now this is uncomfortable for all of us, so let's just deal with the practicalities. I've already suggested that Anne and I will occupy the West Wing. It will need to be refurbished, so when we have finished here, I'll take Anne to see which rooms she would like decorated first."

He paused, waiting for someone to comment, but as he was met with silence, he continued. "The next thing I have to get sorted out is the Lodge House, for Anne's mother and family, and, of course, Anne herself, until we marry. I can't have my future mother-in-law milking the cows and living in a farm cottage, so this must be done as soon as possible. Annie, I'm sorry, I can't keep calling you, Anne. Annie, you and I will get the key from Jack Bater before we leave today. And, of course, the third matter is that of our engagement. Victoria and I will be celebrating our twenty-first birthday in a couple of weeks, and that's the ideal time to announce it. I believe Victoria, Frank, and Caroline are expected here in the next week or so, but I have already written to them with my news, anyway. Has no one got anything to say?"

Eleanor finally found her tongue. "Just who do you intend to invite to your party, Robert? How many of our friends do you think will come when they find out you are to marry a kitchen-maid?"

"If you don't tell them, Mama, I don't think they will even realise, but I don't intend to keep it a secret. Unless Victoria feels strongly, I think it should just be immediate family and friends. I don't want too big a party because it will all be strange to Annie, and she needs time to adjust to our way of life."

At this, Charles snorted. "As if she ever will. I tell you this will all end in tears."

"That remains to be seen, but can I take it you will leave all the arrangements to me?" As he received no answer, Robert moved on. "Very well, now I hope we can all get along together as best we can. Come, Annie, I want to show you around the house." Robert and Annie took their leave, and once outside the room, Annie heaved a huge sigh of relief.

"Thank goodness that's over. Goodness me, they are furious, Robert."

"I know, but they'll just have to get over it. Come on, I'll show you the West Wing, though not the cellars, you don't need to see them again."

The West Wing had many rooms and more than enough space for the two of them. They selected a few rooms to be refurbished first, for the whole wing would take some time and a great deal of money. Annie vaguely knew the layout already, for it mirrored the other three wings of the house.

"Right, now that's settled, I'll take you to meet Sarah. Hopefully, you'll get a warmer welcome from her than you did from my parents."

They found Sarah in the music room playing the piano, the strains of Mozart giving away her presence. She didn't hear them enter the room, and they let her play on to the end of the piece, and then both applauded. "That was excellent, Sarah, well done. Can I introduce you to Annie? Annie, this is my little sister, Sarah."

Annie smiled shyly. "Hello, Sarah, I've heard a lot about you. I'm so pleased to meet you."

"Hello, Annie, welcome to the family." Sarah hugged Annie warmly. "I don't suppose you've had much of a welcome from anyone else, but if you make Robert happy, that's all I will ever ask of you."

Annie's eyes filled with tears. It was so good that someone in this house was on her side. "Oh, thank you, Sarah. That means so much to me."

"Sarah, I want to ask a favour. Would you help me to teach Annie how to behave at my birthday party? She needs to know which cutlery to use, what to drink, how to do her hair, how to dance and all that. I think I need a woman's help.

Sarah grinned widely at being called a woman. "Yes, of course, and I'll ask Jane to help." She looked at Annie. "Jane Leworthy is my governess. I'm sure she will help too. I'll tell you what, why don't you come back tomorrow morning, and join us in the schoolroom. We can take care of it all there."

"That's a good idea. Come to the kitchen tomorrow, Annie, and I'll take you to the schoolroom." Robert hugged his sister. "Thanks, Sarah, I knew you wouldn't let me down."

As Robert led Annie away, she took his arm. "Could we go to the kitchen now, Robert? I'd love to see Mrs Potts, and Maisie, and all my other old friends."

He beamed at her. "Of course, I was just going to suggest it."

When they entered the kitchen, there was a hushed silence until Annie broke it by exclaiming. "Well, is no one going to welcome me? Have you all lost your tongues?"

"Eh, lass, I don't know what to say. Young Maisie has just been telling us you were having tea with Lord and Lady Fellwood. What's going on?"

Annie laughed. "You'll never believe it, but Robert and I are getting engaged to be married. What do you think of that?"

"Oh, Annie, I'm so pleased for you." Maisie's eye's shone with happiness for her friend, and she hugged her tightly.

Molly, the tweeny, and Mrs Potts also hugged Annie, and the elderly cook wiped a few tears from her eyes. "I knew you had feelings for each other, that was always obvious, but I never thought this would happen. I can't imagine how you've brought this about Master Robert, but I wish you both all the happiness in the world."

"Thank you, Mrs Potts, now have you got any of that cake left? I could manage a piece now with a nice cup of tea."

"Bless you, lad, sit down, and I'll get the kettle on. Mrs Potts sliced up a chocolate sponge and a ginger cake. "Annie, let me introduce you to some of our new servants, though you probably know most of them already. Caleb and

Ethan are two of Jack Bater's sons and they're both footmen, and this is Elsie Webber; she's learning to be a cook like me, and her family lives near your mum. Oh, and this is Clarice Gubb; her mum, Noeleen, is married to John Cutcliffe now."

"Yes, I know them all; hello, everyone."

Robert left Annie to gossip and went to get the Lodge House key from Jack Bater. Jack, of course, was curious as to why Robert wanted the key and was taken aback when Robert told him of his plans. "My goodness, lad, that's a surprise; do your parents know?"

"Yes, they do, Jack; I've just told them. We're getting engaged on my birthday next month. I need the key now, though, because there'll be a lot of work to do to get the Lodge habitable."

"Of course, sir, I have it here. If you take a look around the house and let me know what needs doing, I'll get some of the men onto it straight away. I wish you and Annie all the best, sir. You'll make a lovely couple."

"Thank you, Jack. The other thing is that Sabina can no longer do the milking and work on the estate. It's hardly a fitting role for my future mother-in-law. Can you find someone else to do the work?"

"Yes, of course, sir, that won't be a problem at all, there are always people wanting work."

"Good, if you can arrange that as soon as possible, I'll tell Sabina. Carry on paying her wages, though, for the time being until we can sort out a more permanent arrangement."

"Very good, sir. I'm pleased for the Carter family; they deserve a bit of luck; they've had a hard time of it since poor Tom died."

CHAPTER 8

Robert had difficulty tearing Annie away from the kitchen, for she was so enjoying talking to all her old friends. Sid Hobbs said nothing, but clearly disapproved. Fortunately, Miss Wetherby, the housekeeper who sacked Annie, was out for the afternoon. Annie was glad, for she felt she had endured enough tension and unpleasantness, for one day. She would tackle Miss Wetherby on another occasion.

Robert accompanied Annie home in the pony and trap. It stopped outside her front door, and as he held out his hand to help her alight, many of the neighbours came out of their cottages and cheered loudly. Since he had collected her earlier in the day, Sabina had been besieged with questions and had told people the truth. They had been amazed at the news but delighted for Annie.

Sabina and Liza wanted to hear how they had got on. They were full of admiration for Annie, for they had not envied her, having to meet the Fellwoods, and were not sure they could have done so. Robert told Sabina that Jack would be passing her duties to another worker within days but that she would still be paid.

"Why, Robert, are you sure? It doesn't seem right to be paying me for no work."

"Just look on it as extra money for caring for Danny." He spoke quietly, for Danny was present, and, of course, had no idea of his parentage.

"I don't know what I shall do with myself all day if I don't work."

Robert laughed. "You have four small children to look after, five, including Selina, so I don't suppose you'll be bored. Anyway, I have the key to the Lodge House, so we'll have a look at it in a couple of days, you should have finished work by then."

Annie went to see him off. They longed to kiss and hold each other, but with so many neighbours watching their every move, they had to forego that pleasure. When Annie returned inside, Liza helped her out of her new dress, for Sabina had gone to visit Peter Webber.

Armed with a rabbit casserole, Sabina walked the short distance to the Webber's cottage, knocked on the door, and let herself in. Peter was sitting in a chair looking out of the window, and he smiled as she entered.

"Hello, Peter, how are you today?"

"Much the same as ever, lass, no use to man, nor beast, I'm afraid."

"Don't say that."

"Well, 'tis true. There's not much a man can do with no hands." Peter lowered his head, and would not meet her gaze, but she glimpsed tears shining in his eyes.

"It must be difficult, but you have a wise head on your shoulders, you know, and a lot of experience. I'm sure you could give good advice to younger people. Anyway, are you hungry? I've just made a rabbit stew, and I've brought some for us to share for our tea. There's enough for Arthur, and the boys, when they get home as well."

"That's kind of you, Sabina. They will be grateful. With Elsie and Maria both in service, there are no women here to do things, and we miss them, but we need the money. If you leave the stew, I'll have some later because I can't feed myself, you see. I can't do anything for myself anymore. I don't usually have anything from breakfast to tea-time because there's no one here to help me but I'm used to it."

"That's no problem because I can help you. Now, where are the plates?"

Sabina delved into the cupboards and ladled two portions of the warm stew onto plates. She had also brought some freshly baked crusty bread. She sat beside Peter and spooned the stew into his mouth and fed him with the bread, taking mouthfuls from her own plate in between. She told him all her news about Annie and the rest of the family.

"Oh, Sabina this is delicious. I've not had such a nice meal since Arthur's wife, Drucie, died so many years ago. Thank you so much. I've enjoyed your company too; you've brightened up my day."

"Good because I've got a few ideas I want to talk to you about. I wanted to put you in a good mood first, and I thought a full belly might help." She smiled at him. "Now, I believe there's not much you don't know about farming and growing things, and also mining. Am I right?"

"Aye, I worked on the land for many years until I went into mining, but then I lost my hands in an accident, so all that's no use to me now."

"Maybe not, but it could be of use to other people. How would you feel about going into the school, and telling the children how to do things concerned with farming?"

"I could I suppose, but would the teachers want me interfering?"

"I could have a word with Mr Atkins and see what he thinks. He was from Exeter before he became headmaster, and I don't think he has any practical experience of working the land. Books are all very well, but they don't beat real experience. Shall I ask him?"

Peter smiled suddenly. "Yes, all right, if you don't mind. I think I might enjoy that."

"Good, now Arthur mentioned that as a younger man, you enjoyed painting pictures, is that right?"

"Yes, I've always been able to draw, and at school, I was the best artist, but I've never had any paper or paints to use since. Why do you ask?"

"I was talking to the vicar one day, a long while back now, and he was telling me about this disabled lady he once knew who, like you, had no hands. She was born without any arms at all. Anyway, she painted excellent pictures by holding the paintbrush between her teeth and sometimes even between her toes. It sounds incredibly difficult, but she mastered it well enough to sell the paintings, and I wondered if you'd be interested in trying? I could ask Fred to make you an easel, and we could probably beg a few paints and paper from Mr Atkins in return for your help in his lessons."

Peter laughed. "You have certainly given all this some thought, Sabina. Goodness me, are you trying to reorganise my life?"

"I am that, Peter Webber, and you'd better know, I'm not a woman to give up easily."

"I can see that. Yes, I'd be willing to give it a try. Anything to relieve this terrible boredom, and I've certainly got enough time on my hands if you'll pardon the pun."

Sabina laughed, pleased he could joke about it. "Right, well, I have just one other suggestion, and then I'll leave you in peace."

"Go on, then, what else?"

"Well, you've lost your arms, from the elbow down, on the left side, and from your mid-forearm on the right, but I wondered if anyone had ever tried strapping hooks to your arms? I know it would be nothing like hands, but it might be useful for some things. What do you think?"

"How would you attach the hooks to my arms?"

"If you were interested, I thought we could talk to Seth James, the saddler, to see if he could make some sort of harness to attach the hooks firmly to your arms. Do you think they might be helpful?"

"Yes, it might help with a few things, I suppose. I could carry a bucket of water then by holding the handle and things like that." Peter looked thoughtful. "Yes, I'd like to give it a try; could you ask him?"

Sabina beamed at him. "Yes, and I'll also speak to Mr Atkins about the lessons and Fred about an easel. I'll have you busy again yet, Peter Webber, just you wait and see."

"I'm so glad you came today, Sabina. You have cheered me up. Thank you so much."

Sabina hugged the old man, made him comfortable, and then left him, promising to return when she had some news.

Sabina was keen to put her plans for Peter into action as soon as she could. She feared he might change his mind if he had too much time to think about what she had suggested. The next day she went to see Mr Atkins, and he listened carefully to her idea.

"Do you know, Sabina, I think that's a splendid idea. You're right, I don't have any first-hand knowledge of farming, and books are only so much help. Most of the youngsters I teach will end up working on the land in one way or another, so it would be helpful. Could you ask Peter to come along and see me, and we can discuss when would be a good time for these lessons. I would have thought perhaps once or twice a week, depending on how much time he has to spare."

"Oh, he has lots of time to spare. Thank you so much, Mr Atkins this will mean the world to him."

Encouraged that her plans were coming to fruition, she called at the smithy to ask Francis Rudd if he could make hooks to attach to Peter's forearms. Francis was sure it would be easy enough to do and thought it was an excellent idea. Whilst she was there, she called in to see Matilda, for the two women had been friends for a long time, and Matilda had delivered all of Sabina's babies.

"Sabina, Annie told me about her wedding plans."

"Oh, did she? We were supposed to be keeping it quiet until it's announced properly, but with Robert coming here to pick her up today, I've had to tell people. I'm glad she told you herself, though, Matilda; it's only right you should know before the rest."

"That's not all she told me." Matilda looked keenly at her friend. "She told me that Harry was not Selina's father."

Sabina looked ashamed. "I'm so sorry I couldn't tell you, Tilly. I wanted to, but Harry himself insisted no one should know. It was an awful business, and it was so good of him to marry Annie under the circumstances, and they were happy you know."

"Aye, I know, and I'm glad she told me because I've always wondered. I knew she was expecting before the wedding, and I hoped it was Harry's baby, but Selina's nothing like him. It's a sad tale, being attacked and not knowing the father of your baby, but Selina will always be like a grand-daughter to me, anyway, and Annie seems happy with that."

Sabina realised that Annie had not gone so far as to tell Matilda who Selina's father was, and she fervently hoped Matilda would never ask.

CHAPTER 9

Early one morning, Fred whistled a tune as he drove his horse and cart to a house on the outskirts of the village. The good weather had continued, and he enjoyed the hot sun on his back. The house was over two hundred years old and in bad repair, and the elderly couple who occupied it had lived there for a number of years. The roof had been repaired many times but was now leaking badly, and Fred had been asked to supply an estimate for a new one. He would complete the timber work, and then Mark Watts, the local thatcher, would do his part. As the horse trundled along the lane, Fred spotted a young woman sitting on a bank. Her face was pale as she looked up, and he noticed that she was heavily pregnant. He reined the horse in.

"Hello, lass, are you all right?"

"Yes, I'm fine, thanks, just having a rest. I'm on my way to Warkley; do you know if it's much further?"

"Yes, it's a fair step. You need to make your way along here to the village and walk right to the other end, then carry on along that same road for about two miles."

"Oh, right. It's a bit further than I thought then, but at least I'm on the right road. Thanks, Mister."

"Mind how you go then. Goodbye."

Fred went on his way, thinking it was a long way for the girl to walk in her condition. She hadn't looked too well either. If he'd been going the same way, he'd have offered her a lift, but he had to see about this roofing business first because it would be a big job, and he didn't want to lose it. He reached the house and knocked for some time on the solid front door before an old man opened it slowly, the hinges creaking for want of a drop of oil.

"Hello, Mr Carter. I'm sorry to have kept you waiting, but I don't hear so good these days, and my arthritis doesn't let me move very quickly." The man led Fred though to a room at the back of the house where his wife sat on a settee with her feet up. Fred took a seat in the spare armchair and discussed the costs of a new roof with the couple. They haggled a bit, but Fred had expected that and purposely set his price slightly high. He smiled as he came away with an agreement to carry out the work; he had achieved what he felt was a fair price, and the owners were happy because they thought they had knocked his fee down a bit. Win, win. He always felt if everyone was happy it was a good deal.

Not far from where he had first seen her, he saw the young girl sat on the ground in a gateway, her face contorted in pain as she clutched tightly at her extended stomach. There was not much doubt as to the problem.

"Now then lass, looks like you need a hand?"

She gasped. "Yes, I think the baby's coming. I didn't feel well earlier, but this has come on real sudden. It's not due for another month."

He dismounted and knelt beside her.

"Can you stand? If I can get you onto the cart, I'll take you to the inn in the village. My parents own it, and they'll help you."

"I ain't got much money, Mister. I can't pay for a room."

"Well, you can't have the child here at the side of the road, either. Come on, let's see if we can get you on the cart."

Between contractions, Fred helped the girl to her feet. To her embarrassment, as soon as she stood up, fluid gushed down her legs. "Oh no, I'm so sorry. I can't stop it."

"It's all right; your waters have broken. That's nothing to worry about, but the baby is definitely on the way now, so we need to get you some help." He lifted the girl onto the cart and make her as comfortable as he could, propped up with a couple of bales of hay he was carrying.

"Right, hold on, and we'll soon be there."

He drove the horse along steadily, trying to avoid the worst ruts in the road, and when they came to the inn he took the pony and cart around the back and ran in to find his mother. Betsey didn't hesitate, telling him to bring the girl in, and put her in one of the spare rooms. Fred carried the girl to the bedroom, laying her down gently.

"Off you go, Fred and fetch Matilda. She's the expert in these matters. Don't you worry, young lady, you're in good hands now, and there's nothing to worry about. Go on, Fred, make haste." Betsey waved her son off. "Now lass, what's your name."

"It's Charlotte, missus, Charlotte Mackie. Thank you so much." The girl gasped as a strong contraction seized her, and Betsey held on to her hand.

"That's it, Charlotte, you hold my hand, and we'll get through this together. You'll be all right. Now, how did you come to be in this state and all on your own?"

The girl looked downcast, and her face reddened.

"Now, don't you worry, lass, whatever it is, I'll have heard it all before, and I'm not one to judge, but just tell me the truth. That's all I ask."

"My family lives in Exeter, and my father is a vicar, but I've been living with a friend for the last few months. Father threw me out because of the shame I've brought on the family. I'm not married, you see. My mother's been visiting me in secret and trying to help me. There, now I expect you'll want me to leave?"

"Nay, lass, of course, I don't want you to go. Not that you can, the state you're in. You're not the first, and you won't be the last, to find yourself in this predicament, but what of the father?"

"I'd been courting Martin, my young man, for over six months when I found out I was in the family way. Then he told me he was married with three young children and had no intention of leaving his wife. He gave me some money to get rid of the child, but I couldn't do that."

Charlotte stopped again to deal with another contraction and then continued.

"I was on my way to my aunt who lives in Warkley. My mother has arranged for me to have the baby there and then get it adopted."

"Don't worry about any of that now. Let's get this baby born first."

It wasn't far from the inn to the smithy, and Fred was there in no time. "Matilda, Matilda, are you there? You're needed for a birth, Matilda."

"All right, Fred, don't knock my door down. Who's having a baby?"

"It's a young maid I found by the roadside. She was in a bad way so I took her to the inn. Mum's looking after her, but she wants your help because the baby's about to come. I don't think there's a father in the picture. I didn't see a wedding ring, anyway."

"Poor girl, she was lucky you came along, Fred."

"Aye, I'm glad I did. I couldn't see the poor girl give birth in a gateway, now could I?"

"No, of course not. Now, just let me get my shawl. Can you take me back on the cart, Fred, or are you on your way somewhere else?"

"Yes, I can take you. It'll be quicker than you walking." Matilda was still a little plump, despite all the weight she had lost since the fire, and Fred knew she could not walk very quickly.

In minutes they were at the inn and Fred helped Matilda down from his cart; they met Betsey at the back door.

Betsey grasped her friend's hands. "I'm so glad you're here, Matilda. I think the baby will be here soon. I'll see you later, Fred."

Leaving the girl in good hands, Fred went on his way. He'd not gone far when he noticed Sabina walking along the road. He stopped to say hello, and told her about the girl giving birth.

"Happens all too often, doesn't it? It's always the woman who's left with the problem whilst the man escapes any responsibility. I'm glad I've seen you, though, Fred because I have a favour to ask." She quizzed him about making an easel for Peter Webber, and he smiled at his sister-in-law.

"You're so good, Sabina, always helping someone. I don't know how you do it with all your own family to look after, and what's this I hear about our Annie marrying Robert Fellwood?"

"My goodness, news travels fast. Aye, it's true enough, though I still can't believe it. Not only that, but Robert has made me give up my job. He's still paying me and we're to move into the Lodge House when it's repaired. Can you believe that? The Carter's in the Lodge House."

"I'm pleased for Annie, and you, of course. No one deserves it more, and yes, of course, I can make Peter an easel. Not sure it will help him though; you do know he has no hands?"

"Of course, but I've heard that people can paint by holding the brush between their teeth, or even their toes, and he's willing to give it a try. He's so bored at the moment and feels useless. It will give him something to do even if the paintings aren't very good."

"I've plenty of bits of wood lying around, and it shouldn't take me long to make an easel, so I'll let you know when it's ready."

"Thanks, Fred, I'll see you then."

Leaving Fred to go about his business, Sabina walked on to find Seth James, the saddler in the village.

"Sabina, of course, I'll help. I'm fortunate enough to have two good hands. I'll need to give it some thought, though. I'll have a chat with Francis about a hook because what we make will have to fit together tightly if it's to be of any use. Probably some sort of harness to fit around his entire shoulder would be best, I should think. The hook will have to be secure. I'm not sure how comfortable it will be, though we can but try. I'll talk to Francis later, and then perhaps we can both go and see Peter and hear what he thinks. He's a clever old man, so I think we need to talk to him before we start."

Sabina thanked Seth, and went happily on her way, satisfied that her plan was coming together.

CHAPTER 10

Eleanor Fellwood glanced anxiously out of her drawing-room window and then at the ornate grandfather clock in the corner of the room. The carriage had been sent to the station to collect her daughter, Victoria, son-in-law, Frank, and granddaughter, Caroline, from the midday train, and she was impatient to see them. Since their marriage eighteen months before, Victoria and Frank had lived in London, and she had seen little of them, though she had visited a couple of times. Victoria had become pregnant almost immediately after her marriage and had not wanted to undertake the long, arduous journey to the West Country too often.

However, although she was now heavily pregnant again, she had decided to come home to celebrate her twenty-first birthday with her twin brother. Eleanor was delighted, for she had missed her eldest daughter and was looking forward to seeing her again.

Frank was from a wealthy family of bankers living in Mayfair in London. He was an ideal match for Victoria, for although the Fellwoods were no paupers, they were not in nearly the same league as the Eastleigh family. The Fellwoods came from old blood, though, and were a highly respected family, and the fact that Victoria was a beauty, was a bonus.

Charles Fellwood entered the room, pushed in his wheelchair by his valet. He didn't look at all well. His shoulders drooped, and his complexion was pallid. "Looking out of the window will not make them come any quicker, my dear."

"No, I know, but I'm longing to see Victoria and Caroline; we haven't seen the baby since she was a few months old. She won't know us."

They heard the sound of hooves on the cobbles, and the carriage swept up the drive. "Here they are now."

A few minutes later the visitors were ushered into the drawing-room by Sid Hobbs. Eleanor and Victoria embraced warmly, and the two men shook hands. Victoria turned to the nanny, who stood behind her holding Caroline and held out her arms to the child.

"Come here, darling. Come and meet your Grandma and Grandpa.

The little girl was dressed all in white and had red ribbons in her brown hair. She was a plain child considering her attractive parents, but she smiled readily enough, and when she did so it lit up her whole face. Victoria sat on a sofa and took her daughter on her knee. Eleanor sat next to her.

"My goodness, how she's grown. Is she walking yet?"

"Oh yes; the trouble is she gets at everything now. I'll show you."

Victoria put her daughter down, and she toddled around the room, pointing with her finger. She seemed quite at home until Eleanor attempted to pick her up, and then she cried loudly.

"Oh dear, I've rushed things. I forget she is not used to me. Victoria, do you want to take her and calm her down?"

"No, she probably needs changing. Nanny, could you take her to the nursery and see to her, please?"

Elspeth, the nanny, immediately sprang forward, and Caroline thankfully buried herself in her arms.

"So, how are you, Victoria? Have you kept well with this pregnancy?"

"Not too bad. I had some morning sickness for a few weeks, but since that, I've been fine, and I'm certainly better than last time. I'll need Doctor Luckett to come and see me soon; we plan to stay until after the birth if that's all right?"

"Yes, of course, darling. We're pleased to have you here, aren't we, Charles?"

Her father nodded his head and turned to Frank.

"Do you have any plans whilst you are here, Frank?"

"Oh, I'm looking forward to a spot of hunting, hopefully. I don't suppose you're able to get out on horseback now?

"No, sadly, that pleasure is no longer possible for me these days, and I'm afraid Robert isn't keen on hunting, either. Now, Victoria always liked to join the hunt, but it's hardly possible in her present condition. Never mind, I'm sure we can organise something."

"How are Robert and Sarah; will they be joining us?" Frank's eyes were full of mischief, a fact which did not go unnoticed by Eleanor.

"Sarah will be home soon; she had arranged to visit one of her friends for a couple of days before she knew you were coming today, but she'll be back for dinner. Grown into quite the young lady she has." Charles frowned. "I believe Robert has written to you about his intention to marry this girl from the village?" He raised his eyes questioningly and saw that the news was no surprise to them. "I'm sure you can appreciate how we feel about it, but he will not be dissuaded, and once he's twenty-one, we can't stop him. I've already signed the estate over to him because, since David's death and my stroke, there was no reason not to. Or so I thought." He grimaced. "Of course, I know differently now."

Victoria spoke before her husband could. "I was surprised, but I think he's been fond of this girl for a long time, even when she was a servant here. I agree it is not seemly, but if he loves her and will not be dissuaded, we must make the best of it."

Eleanor's face was like thunder. "As far as I'm concerned, she will never be welcome in this house, and I am so disappointed in Robert, I can't begin to tell you. What our guests will make of it when he announces his engagement at the party, I have no idea, and I'm dreading the occasion when I should be looking forward to it."

Her husband looked at her sympathetically. "I know, my dear. It's a difficult situation, but one I fear we cannot change."

After they had taken some tea, Victoria and Frank went to their rooms to rest and prepare for dinner. As they made their way along the landing, Frank took Victoria's arm.

"I hope you don't mind, my dear, but I've asked for a separate room whilst we are here. I know how tired you get this far on in pregnancy, and I thought you might prefer to be undisturbed?"

"How thoughtful of you, Frank; whatever suits you." Victoria gave him a knowing look. "Please remember you are in my parent's house, though, so do not do anything to make me ashamed of you."

"I'm only thinking of you, my darling, and I believe my room is only just along the corridor. I can share a room with you if you would prefer?"

"No, it suits me to have some peace and quiet at the moment. Will you escort me down to dinner? I need to rest now."

Frank nodded. "Yes, I'll see you in a couple of hours."

He strolled along the corridor to his room. Although it was mild weather, a fire was burning merrily in the grate, for the rooms were always cold and draughty in such a big old house. Maisie knelt before the fire, adding some logs. She heard him open the door, and immediately sprang to her feet.

"Why, Maisie, what a lovely surprise. I haven't seen you in such a long time; how are you?"

"I'm fine, sir, thank you. I was just seeing to your fire, but I've finished now."

Maisie turned to go, but Frank's hand shot out to grip her arm.

"Now, what's the rush? Aren't you pleased to see me?"

"If you want the truth, sir, no, I'm not. Now, please let go of my arm."

"My, how you do bear a grudge. I'm only being friendly, and there's no need to rush off. Come on, just give me a little kiss to welcome me back."

Maisie pulled her arm away from him determinedly and made hastily for the door.

"It's no good you trying it on with me, sir. I'm not interested."

"What a pity. We could have such fun together, you know, Maisie, my girl."

Maisie quickly let herself out of the door and made her way back to the kitchen.

"Oh, that man. He's no different now he's married. In fact, he's worse if anything."

Ethel Potts looked up from the bread she was kneading. "Is that a fact? We'll send one of the footmen to fetch and carry for him then; I'm not having any more trouble with you girls. Now come on, help me with the vegetables; we need to get a move on if dinner is to be on time tonight."

That evening Robert went down to dinner early, greeted his two sisters warmly, and shook Frank's hand. As boys, they had been good friends, but the last time they met they had fought. When Annie was a maid at Hartford Manor, Frank lay in wait for her when she went to the garden to pick some parsley. He pounced on her in the barn, and if it had not been for a stable lad fetching Robert, would have forced himself on her. There had been a vicious fight between the two men, with each giving as good as he got, but it had allowed Annie to make her escape.

Frank now looked at Robert with a mischievous smile around his lips.

"Robert, old man, I've not seen you for a long time. How are you?"

"I'm fine, thanks, Frank, and yourself?"

"Yes, I'm well. I hear you are running the estate now?"

They chatted for a few minutes until the gong sounded to summon them into dinner. Charles wheeled his chair himself, alongside Eleanor, Frank took Victoria's arm, and Robert held his arm out to Sarah, who smiled and took it as they all walked into dinner.

Charles raised a toast to their guests and said how good it was to have all his family around the table again.

"Father, before we start our meal there is something I would like to say, please."

Charles Fellwood looked anxiously at Robert and narrowed his eyes.

"Could the servants leave us for a moment, please?" Robert paused to allow them time to leave the room.

"You all know by now that I plan to announce my engagement at our party on Saturday, when, of course, Annie will be present. I know most of you don't approve, but she is the kindest and most beautiful girl I have ever met, and I've loved her for a very long time. I hope you will all make her welcome."

There was a long silence which no one seemed prepared to break, though Frank was looking highly amused.

"Robert, I have to say old chap, that for once your parents are right. You can't go ahead with this. It would be social suicide. I remember the girl, and she is a beauty, but not to marry. She used to work here as a kitchen-maid, didn't she?"

"Yes, you know she did, Frank. Then she married Harry Rudd, and they had a child. Her husband was killed in a terrible fire at the smithy a couple of years ago. I've been friends with her and her family for several years since I started to take an interest in farming, but, more recently, we've fallen in love. I know this has been a huge shock for you all, but I know what I'm doing and I don't care what society makes of it."

Eleanor put her hand on her son's arm. "Robert, darling, please think again about what you are doing. I'm sure she is a lovely girl, and I've nothing against her personally, but you could have your pick of many young ladies. You are an eligible young man. Since poor David died, you have thrown yourself into running the estate and have done an excellent job, but I think perhaps you have forgotten how to have fun. We could organise hunting weekends, balls, parties; all sorts of things to give you a chance to meet someone more suitable for your social position. Once Victoria has had the baby, you could even return to London with her and Frank. I'm sure you would have the world at your feet. Please don't do this."

Robert turned to his twin. "What do you think, Victoria?"

"Mama and Papa will not thank me for saying this, but I think you're right to follow your heart, Robert. If you love her, and she loves you, then how can it be wrong? I hope you'll both be happy."

Robert embraced her. "That means a lot to me; thank you so much."

He turned to the rest of the family. "Despite what you may think, I'm not stupid, and I do appreciate how difficult this will be, but I'm sure we can all adjust if we try hard enough. I'll be moving Annie and her family into the Lodge House as soon as I can get it refurbished. I've also made arrangements for the West Wing to be modernised, and Annie and I will live there after we are married. Now, can we talk of other things, because I'd like to hear all your news?" Without waiting for a response, he rang the bell to ask the servants to bring the meal.

CHAPTER 11

It was a few days since Charlotte Mackie had given birth to a daughter whom she named Doris. Betsey had taken to Charlotte, and they discovered that her granny, Gertie, had once lived in Hartford and played with Betsey as a child. What a small world. Gertie had married a soldier and moved to Exeter many years ago, but one of her children, Charlotte's Aunty Joan, lived in Warkley, and it was there that Charlotte was soon headed.

When Fred called at the inn to carry out an errand for his father, he stopped to admire the baby, and Charlotte thanked him again for taking care of her.

"Ah, it was nothing. Anyone would have done the same. I could hardly leave you to give birth in a gateway, could I?"

"Well, I'm grateful, and I'm glad you called in so I could thank you properly because I'm just about to go to my aunt's house."

"I can give you a lift on the cart if you like because I'm going that way."

"That would be a big help. Thank you so much."

Betsey embraced the young girl and sent her on her way. She hoped the aunty might let Charlotte keep her baby, for she did not want to part with the child.

Fred helped Charlotte onto the cart and handed her the baby, then stopped to speak to Robert, Annie, and Sabina, who were passing on their way to the Lodge House. They were in high spirits, and the two women couldn't wait to see inside the house. However, they took the time to chat with Fred for a few minutes, and admire Charlotte's new baby before continuing on their mission.

The Lodge House was at the entrance of the driveway to the Manor House, and in days gone by, old Tom Canning had lived there as the lodge-keeper. He had been in charge of monitoring visitors, opening and closing the gates, and ensuring undesirables were refused entry. However, as he grew older, he had not actively carried out any of these duties for many years and was in his nineties when he died. After that, it was not felt necessary to replace him, and the house had stood empty for twenty years or more.

Robert put his finger through the hole in the back garden gate and tried to push the latch upwards, but it was rusted in place and wouldn't budge. He looked around for a stick, and after a bit of manoeuvering, managed to prise it open. He had to put his shoulder to the gate to force it open, and once inside, it was clear why. The garden was not a bad size, but over the years, it had become a wilderness. Large brambles had risen to head height, and the vicious prickles tore at their clothes and faces as they tried to push their way through. Sapling trees had taken root, and there was a lot of rubbish, undisturbed for so many years. Here and there was the odd glimpse of a once-loved plant; honeysuckle and wisteria scrambled over the porch, both in full flower, and a pink rambling rose was just visible on the far wall. Stinging nettles were everywhere, and by the time they reached the back door, they were all rubbing themselves with dock leaves to relieve the irritation.

"Funny how dock leaves always grow close to stinging nettles, isn't it? It must be Mother Nature's idea of a joke." Annie grabbed another handful.

"It is, but at least they work, thank goodness." Sabina rubbed vigorously at some nasty weals on her arm.

Robert put the key into the keyhole and had to apply some pressure to get it to turn. He put his full weight behind the door to get it to open, which it eventually did, with a loud screech of protest. "Well, that's certainly going to need some oil and attention, or you'll never get in and out."

They found themselves in the dairy. The room was thick with dust, and huge cobwebs hung from the old wooden beams. The grimy windows let in little light. As they gingerly picked their way across the room, there was a loud scuttling sound in the corner, and Annie glimpsed a large rat and shuddered. Abandoned equipment and utensils littered the floor, and Sabina noticed a cheese press and butter churns that could no doubt be cleaned up. The dairy led into a large kitchen that housed a long table running down the centre. Some long benches, providing seating, were pushed under the table, out of the way.

Sabina crossed the room to another door and found it was a pantry with a tiled floor and plastered walls. There were wooden shelves near the top with slate shelves further down and a stone shelf at the bottom to keep the food cool. The small window had mesh across it to keep out the flies, and it faced north on the cooler, shadier side of the house. The pantry still contained a large mouldy old cheese that had been gnawed by rats and mice, and some jars of pickle and preserves. There was a milk jug with a beaded cloth still hanging over the top and an old bread bin with the lid hanging off. In the ceiling were hooks for hanging game. Next to the pantry was another door which Annie found gave access to a cupboard under the stairs. This was full of brushes, mops and buckets, coal and logs, and also some candles and matches.

The kitchen had a sink under the large window and an enormous cooking range on the opposite side. The floor was made of rough slabs, and the walls were lime-washed, but in several places, the rotten plaster was falling off, exposing the stonework beneath. A large swill bucket by the range still contained old peelings, and rotted food, probably collected for the pigs and poultry, but now completely dried out and like powder. Another small room leading off the kitchen housed an old copper for doing the washing and a mangle for squeezing out the water. Sabina had always shared these facilities with several of her neighbours, and her eyes gleamed at the thought of having her own. There were two other large downstairs rooms, a parlour, and a sitting room, and a hallway that led to the front door.

The sitting room had an ornate fireplace, but there did not appear to be one in the parlour, which seemed strange. Sabina commented on this, and Robert knocked the wall to investigate. "I suspect it's been bricked up, but I don't know why? I think if we knock this wall down, we'll find a fireplace behind it."

Sabina couldn't believe how much space there was. Her cottage had only two small rooms downstairs and two bedrooms upstairs. With such a large family, it had always been necessary for a few of the family to sleep downstairs, leaving even less living accommodation.

They climbed the stairs that turned a corner on the way up. The landing window looked out across beautiful countryside, and Sabina drew in her breath as she admired the view through the filthy glass. She couldn't believe that she would soon be living in such an incredible house. There were five good sized bedrooms, each with a double bed. One of the beds was still made up and the bedding was all rumpled and covered in thick dust. It looked as if it was just as old Tom had left it on the day he was carried out. All the windows had curtains, but as soon as they were touched, they disintegrated into dust.

"What a state it's in," Robert exclaimed. "It's far worse than I expected; perhaps we had better think again?"

"What, no! You're joking." The words burst from Annie and Sabina at the same time.

Sabina continued. "It's perfect; I can't believe we might live here."

"Oh, right. So, you like it?"

"Yes, of course, I like it. It needs a huge clean and a bit of work, but other than that it's amazing. Are you sure your parents will allow this?" Sabina frowned.

"It's no longer their decision. I'll get the farmhands to clear out all the rubbish and the maids to do the cleaning. Then we can get the walls re-plastered, and that chimney sorted out. I wonder if the range still works."

"Robert, could Annie and I be here to sort everything out, and help with the cleaning?" Sabina looked at Annie questioningly. "That's if you want to, Annie?"

"Of course, if that's what you want, Sabina. Annie, do you want to help; there's no need."

"Oh, yes, I'd love to help Mum get this place looking nice. In fact, I can't wait. When can we start?"

"I think we need to get our engagement party over with first, anyway. I don't want you looking tired and jaded for that, and you'll need your wits about you."

Annie's face clouded for she was dreading the party. "Yes, I suppose so. How about next week, then?"

Robert smiled. "Fine, who would you like to help you?"

"If we could have a couple of farmhands to shift the rubbish, then I'm sure Maisie, Mum, and myself could soon get this place shipshape."

Sabina left Annie and Robert at the Lodge House for some time together and walked home alone. Her mind was working furiously, and she could not hide the wide grin that spread across her face.

"No need to ask what you thought of it then." Liza smiled at her as she walked in. "It's a real treat to see you grinning like that. Not something we've seen a lot of lately."

"Well, I've definitely got something to grin about now, though I'm so afraid something will go wrong. Oh, Liza, it's such a lovely house; I simply can't believe we are going to live there. It needs a huge clean and tidy up, but I can't wait. Just wait until you see it."

"Sabina, I've been thinking about all this, and you won't need me now if you don't have to work; you'll be able to look after the children yourself. It's been a godsend living here with you since I lost Isaac, but I'll make a few enquiries about where I might be able to go. I'm so pleased for you, and I hope it works out for Annie and Robert, though I think it may be more difficult than they think."

"Yes, I think you're right about that, but Liza, there's no way you are going anywhere else to live. You will be coming to the Lodge House with us. Why we would have been in the workhouse long ago without you; do you think I'd turn you away now? You'll end your days living with me, and that's an end to it."

Liza had tears in her eyes. "Oh, Sabina, I'm so happy to hear you say that; I've been worried to death, and that's the truth."

CHAPTER 12

Robert begged assistance from his sisters to turn Annie into a lady, and they had readily agreed. A small spinet was taken to the West Wing. The room had been carefully chosen to be out of earshot of the main house, and with Victoria playing the music, Sarah and Robert endeavoured to teach Annie to dance. She soon mastered the waltz to a reasonable standard but struggled with the quadrille. She could not believe how tiring she found the lessons, and amused the others by often exclaiming, this is far worse than a hard day's work!"

Victoria and Sarah had wondered how they would get on with the former servant, but before long, the four of them were looking forward to their sessions together and truly enjoying them. Annie also needed to learn etiquette at the table, for she had no idea which knife, fork, or spoon, to use. Robert smuggled the necessary cutlery from the kitchen, and they spread a cloth on the top of the closed spinet and taught Annie what she needed to know. However, the more they taught Annie, the more nervous she became as she worried how she would remember it all.

The night before the party, Annie couldn't sleep. Cross with herself, she got out of bed to get a drink. She tiptoed down the stairs as quietly as possible, for she didn't want to wake any of the family. In the past, her parents had slept downstairs on an old double bed, for there was not enough space in the two bedrooms. However, since her father, Tom, had died from consumption, and then John and Emma from diphtheria, there was more space, particularly since Willie and Mary had gone to live-in where they worked. Now, her mum and Liza shared the biggest bedroom with her brothers, Edward and Stephen, whilst Annie and Selina, shared the other room with Helen and Danny. It was still cramped and whilst the extra space downstairs was useful, they would have all preferred to have their loved ones back.

It was a moonlit night, and she could see quite well as she went into the kitchen and poured herself a mug of water from a jug. Strolling around with the mug in her hand, she wandered into the sitting room where the dress her Aunty Eveline had made for the party, hung from the curtain rail. It was a deep green and contrasted vividly with her fiery red hair and matched her remarkable eyes. She had purchased cream stockings and gloves, and black shoes to complete her outfit. She planned to decorate her hair with matching green ribbons and let it cascade over her pale shoulders in ringlets. Around her neck, she would wear the golden locket that Robert had given her long ago, but which until now, she had kept hidden from sight. When she tried it all on, Sabina and Liza were speechless, and tears glistened in their eyes, for she looked so beautiful.

She smiled to herself as she caressed the fine material between her finger and thumb. She loved the dress and longed to wear it, but was so worried about meeting her future in-laws and Frank Eastleigh. After a few minutes, she sighed and told herself it was time to go back to bed and that worrying would make no difference at all. Quietly, she climbed the creaky stairs and crept back into her bed, relieved that no one had heard her, but sleep was still elusive.

The next morning Robert arrived in the carriage to collect Annie. Many of the villagers living in the hamlet were outside to see Annie leave her house, and they gasped in disbelief, for they hardly recognised her in all her finery. Robert, too, was taken aback by how beautiful she looked and smiled as he noticed the gold locket around her neck. He helped her into the carriage, held her trembling hand, and smiled at her.

"Don't look so worried. You'll be fine. You look amazing, and everyone is going to love you. I've instructed the servants that you are to be seated next to me and opposite Sarah, Victoria, and Frank. I know you don't care for Frank, but the girls will look after you, and I'll keep him in his place."

"There is one other thing, Annie. I haven't given you an engagement ring yet." He reached into his pocket and pulled out a small box. "I never knew my grandmother, but this was her ring. She owned a lot of jewellery, and Grandad left all the grandchildren something in his will when he died. I don't really remember him either because I was only about five or six when he died. Anyway, I hope you like it, but if not, we can buy a different one."

He carefully removed the ring from the box and placed it on Annie's finger. It was made of gold and had a large cluster of sparkling diamonds. Annie gasped. "Oh, Robert, it's so beautiful, and it fits perfectly. Are you sure it's all right for me to have this? I shall be afraid to wear it in case I lose it."

"I'm glad you like it, and yes, of course, it's all right for you to have it. Now, give me a kiss, while we have a moment to ourselves."

When the carriage stopped outside the sweeping steps to the house, Robert took her hand as she alighted and led her to the front door, which was opened by Sid Hobbs. The grumpy old man could not help but be impressed by her appearance, and to her astonishment, he smiled at her. Robert led her into the sitting room, where they were announced as they entered. Many people were already present, and all heads turned to look at Robert's future bride. Sarah immediately approached the couple, and chatted to Annie, trying to put her at ease.

Robert led her around the room introducing her to various aunts, uncles, cousins, and friends, and by the time the gong sounded for their evening meal, Annie was longing to be anywhere else. Gratefully, she sat beside Robert, thankful that she would now only have to converse with those nearest to her. However, this relief was tempered, by the worry of etiquette at the table. As Caleb and Ethan Bater served the food, they smiled encouragingly at Annie, and Caleb would have dearly liked to wink at her but knew it was more than his job was worth. The first course was watercress soup, and Annie smiled inwardly for she knew the recipe exactly, from helping Mrs Potts in the past. She reached confidently for the soup spoon and tilted it away from her as she daintily took small mouthfuls from the bowl. Robert smiled at her encouragingly.

The second course was a lightly poached salmon, accompanied by hollandaise sauce, a small amount of grated carrot and beetroot, and a potato cake. Annie took her time and watched which knife and fork Robert and Sarah selected and then copied them, pleased to think that it was the one she had suspected. Frank, seated between Sarah and Victoria on the other side of the table, was as fascinated by Annie as he always had been, and found it difficult not to stare at her. Annie was already feeling she could not eat another mouthful as the main course arrived. The guests were served with roast pork and sage and onion stuffing, apple sauce, and a medley of vegetables. The food was delicious, but she picked at it and allowed herself only the smallest sips of the delicious wines that were served with every course. Robert and Victoria had both warned her not to drink much, for she was unused to alcohol, and they knew this could be disastrous.

There were several desserts to choose from, gooseberry fool, trifle, syllabub, and, of course, birthday cake. When everyone had finished eating, Robert rose to his feet, and banged on the table with the back of a spoon.

"Ladies and gentlemen, may I have your attention for a few minutes, please? I'd like to say a few words, and thank you all for coming here this evening. As you know, it is mine and Victoria's twenty-first birthday, so I'd like to wish her a happy birthday, and thank you all for the lovely gifts you have given us." He held up his hand to silence the loud cheers and clapping and continued. "You should also know that, although we are twins, she has never failed to boss me around, and forever remind me, that she is the eldest by some ten minutes." This made the guests laugh, and they clapped again. He turned to his father. "Papa, I believe you wanted to say a few words too?"

Charles Fellwood remained seated because of his disability but forced a smile onto his face. "Yes, of course, thank you, Robert. Well, I don't have a lot to say, but may I wish our dear children, Robert and Victoria, a happy birthday and propose a toast to them." He raised his glass, and all the guests rose to their feet. "Robert and Victoria."

When the guests had settled down, Robert again took to his feet. "As some of you already know, I have another announcement to make. I would like to introduce you all to Anne Carter, this beautiful young lady at my side. She has made me the happiest man alive, for she has consented to become my wife, and tonight we are getting engaged."

Many of the guests knew nothing of Annie's background, and they raised their glasses, stamped their feet and cheered loudly. Charles slowly toasted the couple and stared hard at his wife, until reluctantly, she did the same. With a huge smile on his face, Frank rose to his feet and raised his glass.

"To Robert and Annie." He grinned mischievously at Robert as he turned to Annie and said loudly, "Annie, are none of your own family here tonight? Could they not have some time off work? Robert, I think you should have invited

Annie's mother to your party. Surely someone else could have milked the cows for one night."

Annie's eyes dropped to her lap as her face turned a bright red, and tears of embarrassment stung her eyes. Robert glared at the smirking man sitting opposite him.

"How could you be so cruel? There was no need for that." Frank did not respond, for he was too weak with laughter. Victoria looked at him furiously, and Eleanor and Charles would have been happy if the ground had opened and swallowed them up.

Robert struggled to bring his temper under control as taking to his feet, he faced the table and forced himself to smile. "Thanks to my brother-in-law, and former friend, I must now make the situation clear, though, I had hoped to leave this until a later date. I have known Annie for a number of years, and her family live in one of the tied cottages on our estate. Her father died of consumption a few years ago, and her mother has fought hard to support her children and stay out of the workhouse. Considering the hurdles this woman has had to overcome, she would put most of us in this room to shame. For a time, Annie worked here as a kitchen-maid, before she left to get married. She has one child, a little girl called Selina, and her husband, Harry, died in a fire a couple of years ago. Since I have been running the estate following David's death, I have got to know Annie better, and am now in love with her. Her mother and family are shortly to move into the Lodge House on the estate."

Throughout this, Charles and Eleanor stared stonily at their son, and Annie kept her eyes in her lap. Robert calmly took a sip of his wine and then continued.

"Now, some of you may not approve of this relationship, but you should know that I will be marrying Annie, conventional or not, so please raise a toast to my beautiful future wife." He reached down and took Annie's hand, smiled at her, and pulled her to her feet to stand beside him.

He raised his glass and surveyed the shocked faces around the table. Slowly, Victoria and then Sarah rose to their feet, lifted their glasses, and spoke firmly. "Robert and Annie." They looked around for support, and most of Robert's closest friends, including Frank, who was still smiling, also rose to their feet and joined in the toast. A few of the more elderly relatives were tight-lipped as they pushed back their chairs and left the room silently as did Charles and Eleanor.

"Right, folks, the excitement is over for the night. Perhaps I should be thanking you, Frank, for bringing all this out into the open. It's probably for the best. Come on, everyone, let's make our way to the hall, where the musicians will soon be playing, and we can relax, dance, and enjoy ourselves."

CHAPTER 13

Since Tom's death, Sabina had been helping with the milking on the estate. On six days a week, and often seven, she arose at four o'clock in the morning. On the day after Jack Bater found someone else to do her job, she woke early from habit, then realised she did not have to go to work. She found the option of being able to stay in bed a rare treat, though, in truth, she was so excited about going to clean the Lodge House, she would have been more than happy to get up at the normal time. As it was, she lay there until she heard the children stirring.

By eight o'clock, having got Edward and Stephen off to school, and the little ones fed and organised for Liza to look after, Sabina and Annie set off for the Lodge House. Robert had left the gate slightly open and sent a workman to oil the lock of the back door so they could get in easily. By nine o'clock, having helped prepare breakfast at the Manor House, Maisie joined them, and she and Annie hugged each other.

"Oh, Annie, I can't believe you are going to marry Master Robert. Am I going to have to call you Miss Annie from now on?"

Annie laughed. "No, silly; I shall always be Annie to you. When we are alone, anyway. I bet they were all surprised at the big house, weren't they?"

"It's been so funny. Miss Wetherby is very disapproving, but everyone else is pleased for you, even Sid Hobbs, and Mrs Potts, well, she's delighted. How did it go at the engagement party?"

Annie pulled a face. "Badly, I think best describes it. She told Maisie what had happened, and Maisie's eyes grew wide.

"How awful, and how mean of Frank. Did many guests leave?"

"About a third of them, I suppose, but after that, I quite enjoyed myself. At least we know now which people will accept our marriage and which ones won't. Anyway, I'm glad it's over. Now, where shall we start?"

"Sam Symons and John Cutcliffe will be here as soon as they've finished feeding the animals. Master Robert has told them to do as you say and remove all rubbish." Maisie laughed. "Fancy you having two men to order around for the day."

They made a start on the sitting room, pulling down the ancient curtains, the dust making them cough as they fell to pieces. With difficulty, they opened the sash windows wide, and let in some much-needed fresh air. Clearing the sitting room and kitchen of rubbish took them most of the morning, and they could not believe where the time had gone, but suddenly they realised they were ravenous.

"We'll have to go back to the cottage to get something to eat." Sabina stood up and eased her aching back.

Maisie grinned. "No, it's all right, I've brought a food hamper, and knowing Mrs Potts, there's probably enough in it to feed an army."

They went into the garden and found a stone bench to sit on, where they enjoyed hard-boiled eggs, ham and crusty, freshly baked bread. There was a large fruit cake as well, all washed down with ice-cold lemonade, that Maisie had stood in a bucket of cold water. With the hot sun beating down on them from a cloudless blue sky, Annie felt content.

After a short break, they continued working until the downstairs rooms were roughly swept, and all the rubbish was piled up in the corner of each room. The two men had already taken away one cartload of rubbish and were just loading up another. They were planning to have a bonfire in one of the fields to dispose of the rubbish.

Sabina flopped down onto a chair. "I'm afraid that's me done for today, girls. I'd love to carry on, but I'm exhausted; I don't know about you? Anyway, I need to get back and see how Liza's getting on; the children will be home from school by now, and I expect the little ones will have tired her out."

"I can stay another hour or so," said Maisie. "Miss Wetherby didn't say what time I had to be back, but I know Mrs Potts would appreciate a hand with the evening meal. Goodness, I'm tired, too. It's hard work, but I've enjoyed it."

Annie grinned at her. "Me, too. Robert would have got all this done for me, but I wouldn't have missed this for the world. It's been so lovely spending the whole day with you two, with no one to boss us around. Shall we come again tomorrow?"

Over the next week, the three women worked hard in the Lodge House. When the rubbish was removed, the house looked more spacious than ever. Robert called in at regular intervals, and Annie took him proudly around the house and showed him the work they would like carried out. Their priority was to investigate whether there was a fireplace in the parlour. Robert sent two workmen with pickaxes, and they hacked away at the plaster. It came off readily enough, and they soon exposed the bricked-up fireplace and set to work removing the bricks one by one. Across the mantel lay a huge oak beam, and they noticed some curious marks etched into it. Sabina shivered and looked slightly uneasy when she saw them.

"Mum, what is it? Do you know what the marks are for?" Annie looked anxiously at her mother.

"Yes, I've seen them before. They are witches' marks. In the olden days, they were scratched onto places to ward off evil spirits. In this case, presumably to stop them coming down the chimney. They were often used in haunted houses. I hope that wasn't the case here."

"Is it going to worry you, Mum?"

"No, of course not. It will take more than a few scratches on a bit of wood to stop me from moving in here, and I've never heard of this house being haunted, have you?"

Annie shook her head. "No, but it's always been empty for as long as I can remember."

The men carried on removing the bricks one by one. It didn't take long, for the ancient mortar was crumbling. As the hole got bigger, debris began to fall down the chimney. Within minutes, the room was filled with an avalanche of billowing soot, dust, and ash as the room was engulfed by centuries-old material released from its hiding place. Their noses and mouths were full of the soot making it difficult to breathe.

Within minutes, they had no choice but to vacate the room, and they ran coughing and sneezing into the garden, where they thankfully gulped in the clean sweet air. It was a good hour before the dust had settled enough to venture back in. There was a huge pile of debris by the fireplace, and Annie was glad they had not done too much cleaning before getting this job done. It would have been time wasted, for the soot and dust had gone everywhere, though, fortunately, they had closed the doors to the other rooms. As they started to shovel the dirt into sacks, they came across the skeletons of birds, the jawbone of a rat, a couple of bird's nests, and an old salt pot.

Maisie looked at the salt pot in surprise. "What on earth was a salt pot doing in the chimney?"

"I expect it was put there on a ledge to keep the salt dry. You know, it always gets damp, and then it won't pour properly. Look, have you seen this?"

Sabina picked up a bunch of what had once been white feathers, tied around the middle with a piece of string. She pursed her lips. "These were also put up chimneys to ward off evil spirits. I wonder how long ago the chimney was bricked up.

"A long time, I should think. We'll have to get this chimney swept properly before we do anything else."

The next day all the chimneys in the house were swept, and when that was done, the fires were lit to see if they drew properly. Fortunately, they did, and the house was soon far too hot. Maisie spent two days cleaning the range, which occupied most of one wall in the kitchen. It was now black and sleek, with the fire to one side and the oven on the other. After all her hard work, Maisie was delighted that the range worked, and they decided to keep it lit. Above it, a long clothes airer called a 'Sheila's Maid' stretched from one wall to another, and Sabina knew it would be a godsend for drying clothes in the winter.

Soon there was no more the women could do in the house, and they left the men to re-plaster the walls with lime mortar, replace the rotten windows and floorboards, and all the other work that needed doing before the house could be decorated and furnished.

Instead, they turned their attention to the garden and kept the two gardeners Robert had sent, to help them, very busy. Trees were felled, brambles cut back, ground dug, and hedges trimmed. After a week of hard work, the garden was clear; and much larger than they had first thought. There was plenty of room for an extensive vegetable patch, and Sabina thought she might try her hand at keeping bees, for she loved honey. She told Annie she would like to continue keeping chickens, and before she knew it, Robert had sent workmen, who built not only a chicken run but a new chicken house as well. She had to pinch herself at times to make sure she was not dreaming.

CHAPTER 14

When all the work had been completed at the Lodge House, and it was ready to be furnished, Annie and Sabina invited Betsey, Liza, and Matilda, to have a look around. It would still be a week or two until they could move in, as Robert had insisted on buying new furniture and household goods or sending spare ones from the Manor House. However, they could wait no longer to show off their new house.

The three older women were amazed at the amount of space in the house as Annie and Sabina proudly showed them around. Until she married, Annie would have the largest bedroom to herself as she now had fine dresses to store, and soon, there would be wedding finery as well. Sabina and Liza would also have a room each, something neither of them could even imagine. With Willie and Mary no longer living at home, the other two rooms would be shared by the boys and the girls, with Edward, Stephen, and Danny in the biggest one, and Helen and Selina, in the other.

Robert had sent another hamper to the Lodge House, and when the women had finished their tour of the house, they sat at a new picnic table in the garden. The earlier rain had cleared up, but Sabina insisted they sit on some old blankets as the benches were still damp.

It was a jolly meal, and the women thoroughly enjoyed their afternoon. Betsey and Matilda were thrilled for Sabina, and Liza simply couldn't take in that she would soon be living in this magnificent dwelling. Eventually, Betsey said she must get back to the inn, or Ned would be wondering what had happened to her. As she stepped away from the picnic table, she slipped on the wet cobbles, and her leg twisted awkwardly below her as she fell heavily. At once, her companions were at her side, dismayed to see her leg lying at a ridiculous angle. Betsey was pale, and the sweat stood out on her brow as she tried not to cry out with the intense pain.

"Betsey, lie still, and Annie will get Doctor Luckett. It will be all right." Sabina tried to reassure her mother-in-law and nodded to Annie, who went running off down the lane. She soon returned with the doctor, and his face was grim as he took in the situation at a glance.

"Now, Betsey, I can't pretend this isn't going to hurt because it is, but I'm going to have to pull your leg straight, and put it in splints before I can take you to the hospital. If I don't do that, you could lose your leg." He looked at the others. "Can you get her something to bite on?"

The women watched in horror as he did what was necessary. Betsey bit down on a towel and tears rolled down her old cheeks. Luckily, the procedure had taken place before Ned arrived. He helped the doctor get his wife onto the horse and cart and said he would accompany her to the hospital.

Ned returned many hours later, looking tired and upset, as he told his concerned customers at the inn what had happened. "She has to stay in the hospital overnight and she should be home tomorrow. They've wrapped her leg in linen bandages, soaked in Plaster of Paris, and apparently, it will set hard into a cast to keep her leg still while it mends. They think it should heal all right thanks to Doctor Luckett putting it into splints. It's marvellous what they can do these days."

The news of Betsey's accident soon spread around the village, and when Fred fetched her from the hospital the next day, there was quite a crowd outside the inn to welcome her home. She looked pale and drawn and was clearly in pain, but she smiled at everyone and thanked them for coming. Fred carried her inside and laid her on the bed, which they had already brought down from upstairs, and Eveline had made up with fresh sheets. Ned sat on the bed and held his wife's hand whilst Eveline went to make some tea.

"Oh, Ned, I don't know how you're going to cope with me laid up. You'll never be able to look after me and run the inn."

"It's certainly going to be difficult. I think we'll have to take on someone to help. If we could find a girl who could nurse you and help a bit with the chores, we'd probably be all right, but it's finding the right person and quickly. Can you think of anyone?"

There was a silence for a few moments until Fred spoke. "The only person I can think of is that girl, Charlotte, who had her baby here. I gave her a lift to her aunt's house in Warkley, and when we were talking, she mentioned that she used to work as a nurse at the Exeter hospital. I know she intended to have the baby adopted because she couldn't keep it and work. Perhaps she would come here for a while until you're better. You seemed to get on with each other."

Betsey smiled. "Oh, that's a good idea, Fred. She was such a nice girl, and I know her granny. Could you go over to Warkley and ask her?"

"Yes, of course, I'll go now because the horse and cart are already outside. Now, you take it easy, Mum, and I'll see you later."

It didn't take Fred long to travel to Warkley, and he hoped Charlotte hadn't already returned to Exeter. However, as he neared the cottage, he was relieved to see her hanging out some washing. She looked at him in surprise as he tethered the horse and entered the front gate.

"Hello, Fred, I didn't expect to see you again; what are you doing here?"

"Mother had a nasty fall yesterday, and she's broken her leg. She's been to the hospital, and they've put it in plaster, but she'll be laid up for weeks. We need someone to nurse her and do a few chores, and you mentioned you're a nurse, so I wondered if you'd be interested? We'd pay you, of course."

"I see, how awful for poor Betsey. I'm so sorry. It's not good to break a leg at her age, and it will probably take a while to mend."

"What about the baby? Is she still with you?"

At this, tears glistened in Charlotte's eyes, and to Fred's horror, began to trickle down her cheeks.

"No, she's not. She's gone, and I don't know where she is!"

"What do you mean? Has someone taken her?"

"Yes, my Aunty Joan. She sent me to the village yesterday to get some food and said she would look after Doris, but when I got home they were both gone. She's taken her somewhere to get her adopted. She says she didn't think I would do it. I think my father did know about the baby, and he's had a hand in this."

Fred put his arm around the girl to comfort her, for she was so upset. "I'm sorry you've had to give your baby up, Charlotte. Perhaps we could get her back?"

"Aunty Joan won't tell me where she took her, and in any case, I can't keep her and work, so it's no good. I knew I'd have to part with her, but I would have liked to keep her a little longer and, at least, say goodbye."

"Let me have a word with your Aunty and see if I can get the truth out of her. She should never have interfered."

"Thanks Fred, but it's done now and probably for the best. I kept putting it off. Anyway, I've no job to go to, and I would like to help Betsey and repay her kindness. I'd love to come and live at the inn for a few weeks. It will give me something else to think about. If you can wait until I pack my few bits and pieces, I could come with you now. I can't wait to get away from here."

Charlotte would not let Fred go into the house with her because she knew he was itching to have words with her aunt. After a few minutes, she came out red-faced, clutching a bag with her few possessions, and slammed the door shut behind her. Fred said nothing but drove the horse and cart back to the inn and took Charlotte to his mother. Betsey was overjoyed to see the girl again, and relief was written all over Ned's face. Fred left them to it and returned to get on with his day's work. He had finished the easel for Peter Webber and decided that, whilst he had the horse and cart out, he would deliver it to Sabina.

Sabina was busy packing up bits and pieces that she wanted to take from the cottage to the Lodge House and she was pleased to see Fred. "Hello, Fred, this is a surprise. How's Betsey? Is she home yet?"

"Yes, she's not too bad. I fetched her from the hospital earlier, and I've just persuaded Charlotte to come and nurse her for a few weeks because Dad would never have managed on his own. You know, the young girl who had the baby."

"Oh, that's good, they will need help, and I know Betsey liked her. Does she still have the baby?"

"No, her aunt got her adopted, and Charlotte's still upset, so this will help to distract her. Anyway, the reason I'm here is I've finished making Peter's easel, so I thought I'd drop it in. I'll get it off the cart."

He returned with a fine wooden easel that could be adjusted to several heights.

"Oh, Fred, it's perfect; he'll be so pleased. What do I owe you?"

"Nothing, you know I'd do anything for you, Sabina, and the wood cost me next to nothing. I just hope he likes it."

"I'm sure he will, Fred, but here's a shilling and thank you so much, I'll see you soon." She pressed the money into his hand and refused to take it back, assuring him she could afford it.

Peter Webber had already started giving his talks at the school, and they had gone down well. He was quite a character and was able to relate some amusing stories to the children, which kept their attention as they learned. Over his life, he had worked as a farm labourer, lime-burner, and miner, so he had no shortage of tales to tell and knowledge to pass on. Mr Atkins soon realised he was an asset to the school. The children were fascinated by the loss of his hands and wanted to know all about the mining accident in which he had lost them.

For Peter, the twice-weekly sessions had changed his life and given him lots to think about as he planned what his next talks would be about. He didn't have the luxury of being able to make any notes, but he did try to think through the topics he would talk about, though, often on the day, he went off at a tangent.

Seth James and Francis Rudd visited Peter to discuss how best to help him.

"Would a hook be the best thing, Peter? Or would something of a different shape be best?"

"Since Sabina suggested this to me, I've thought about it a lot and, if you two don't mind, I think if you can make a harness to go around my shoulders and strap onto my arms, then perhaps I could have a couple of different tools, one on each arm. My left arm finishes at my elbow, so perhaps a hook on the end would let me pull things toward me. My right arm's a bit better because I've still got most of my forearm, and that will give me better control. Do you think you could secure a fork to it? I could feed myself then, and that would be a godsend."

"Yes, what a good idea, that would be more useful than two hooks." Seth smiled at him. "Let's get you measured up then, and I'll see what I can do."

Francis joined in. "I'll make a couple of hooks, and you can decide which one is best, Peter. I think the difficult bit will be making them secure, but we can experiment and see what works best."

"I'm so grateful to you and Sabina, for thinking of this. Anything you can do will be an improvement for me."

The men were about to leave when Sabina knocked gently on Peter's door and called out to him as she entered with the easel.

"Oh, hello, lads, I can guess what you're here for. Have you sorted something out?"

They told her what they had planned, and she looked thoughtful. "That's good, and look what I've brought for you, Peter," she grinned at him, "no excuse now, I shall expect a painting for Christmas."

Peter rose and looked with interest at the easel. "Fred's made a lovely job of it. How much do I owe him?"

"Nothing, Peter. He said it was only a few scraps of wood and it didn't take him long. Now, let me adjust it to the right height for you, there I think that's about right." She stood back to survey it. "Now, have you got any paints and paper?"

"Yes, Mr Atkins has given me those over there look; a good selection."

Sabina put a cloth, a cup of water, the paints, and the paintbrushes on the table near the easel and pegged a piece of paper to it. "There, you should be able to pick the brush you want from the jar with your teeth, rinse it in the water, and dry it slightly on the cloth. I think we might need to make some of the brushes a bit shorter for you to control them better. Mind you, I have another idea, now."

She turned to Seth and Francis. "I'm just wondering if a paintbrush could be fastened to Peter's arm instead of a fork when he wants to paint. It would be much easier to control than in his mouth."

"Yes, if we make something to hold a fork, I'm sure we could adapt a paintbrush to fit as well, and then he'd have a choice."

Peter grinned. "It's incredible, thank you so much for everything you are doing for me. I'm so enjoying going to the school, and I think the children like me coming."

Sabina smiled at him. "Aw, don't be daft, it was nothing, but I'm glad it's helped. Right, I'm going to leave you to it now, but I'll be back with a stew for you, and Arthur and the boys later, and to see how you're getting on. Now that I'm not working, I've got a lot more time to do things."

When she returned a few hours later, carrying a pot of stew with big fluffy dumplings, all the menfolk were home and pleased to see her. They were gathered around the easel admiring Peter's efforts, which for a first attempt were not bad. He had outlined the scene from the kitchen window, capturing the row of cottages and the hills and trees in the background. Although far from perfect, Sabina thought it was probably as good as she could do with two hands, and although there were a few drips and smudges here and there, from a distance, it looked impressive.

As she went to leave, Arthur saw her out and took her hand in his. To her surprise, her heart fluttered in a way she had almost forgotten.

"Sabina, thank you so much. Dad was giving up on life and what you've done has made such a difference to him. That stew smells delicious and I insist on paying you for it. Here you are." He pressed a few coins into her hand and refused to take them back. "With Elsie and Maria in service, the meals you cook us are much appreciated because none of us men are much good at it. We're going to miss you when you move to the Lodge House, but I couldn't be more pleased for you. It couldn't happen to a nicer person."

Sabina was embarrassed at all the fuss but thanked him warmly, and went home happily.

CHAPTER 15

Since the engagement party, Robert had avoided his parents as much as possible and took his meals in his study. This arrangement suited him, for he was so involved in the running of the estate that, whenever he was not outside working with Jack, he was to be found poring over the accounts. He found it difficult to fit everything into his busy schedule these days but loved every minute of it.

During the early spring, he had delivered several lambs believing it essential to have hands-on experience to fully understand farming and develop his knowledge. It was now time to shear the sheep, and Robert watched for a while to see how it was done. It was important to shear the sheep before the hot summer months to prevent blowflies from laying their eggs in the moist, warm wool. If this happened, the eggs would hatch, and the maggots would start to eat the sheep and cause infection. In some breeds, if the sheep were not shorn, their fleeces would become so heavy that if an animal rolled onto its back, it was unable to get up, and magpies had been known to pick out their eyes.

"Jack, it's time I had a go." Robert had seen three sheep sheared efficiently by one of the most experienced farmworkers, and decided that the task did not even look easy. He caught a sheep, and held it between his knees and started to cut away the wool. However, the animal was frightened and sensed Robert's inexperience and nervousness, and it struggled fiercely.

"Oh, for goodness sake, keep still." Robert became exasperated as the sheep writhed and turned, making it impossible to cut the wool evenly.

"It's all right, just keep calm. You need to hold the sheep more firmly. Let it know that you are in charge. You'll soon get the hang of it; we all had to learn." Jack spoke calmly and glanced around at the other workmen, daring them to laugh. However, none of them did. They'd seen it all before and did not want to put Robert off his task, for they had the greatest respect that he was even attempting to do the same work as them. "That's it. Now you're doing better. By the time you've sheared a hundred of them, you'll be pretty good." At this, the men did laugh.

"Yes, I'm getting there, but look at the state of that fleece. It's a disgrace compared to everyone else's, and it's taken me about five times as long."

"Never mind as I say you'll soon learn."

Jack was right, and by the end of the day, Robert could shear a sheep reasonably well. He was disappointed that he was still so much slower than everyone else, and was unbelievably tired. His shoulders and back ached, and he had an even greater respect for the men he employed who did this all day long without complaint.

Robert spent as much time as he could with Annie. They enjoyed riding over the moors and Annie quickly become proficient in the saddle. She had been busy supervising the work carried out in the Lodge House and was delighted with the result. Moving day arrived at last, and the children were excited, for they had not seen inside the house. Robert sent a horse and cart to their cottage to collect their personal belongings, and Sam Symons and John Cutcliffe spent the morning loading it up.

Sabina rounded up her family. "Right, come on you lot. Say goodbye to our little house, and hop on the cart. There's just enough room for all of us to ride, I think."

Sabina and Liza hadn't been to the house for a couple of weeks, and Annie couldn't wait to show them the newly painted rooms, now all furnished with mostly new furniture.

Annie opened the front door, a wide smile on her face. "Welcome to your new home. I hope you'll like it here. She picked up Selina and carried her in and enjoyed the gasps of amazement from her siblings.

"Come on, Mum, I can't wait to show you and Liza the kitchen." She led the way, Sabina instructing all the children to stay with her and not wander off on their own.

"Oh, Annie, it's so beautiful! I can't believe we're going to live here." Sabina and Liza were reduced to tears as they opened one cupboard after another, and saw all the new pots and pans and implements in the kitchen. The larder was bursting with food supplied by Mrs Potts. Enjoying herself immensely, Annie led them upstairs and showed them all where they would be sleeping.

"Right Mum, this bedroom is for you." The room had lime-washed walls and blue curtains, her mother's favourite colour. The floorboards had been varnished and were adorned with blue rugs. The bed had a blue patchwork quilt and soft pillows, and on the sunny windowsill, Annie had placed a vase of late bluebells.

"Oh, Annie, I don't believe it. Honestly, I keep thinking I'm going to wake up in a minute." Sabina's eyes were round with wonder.

"Come on, we haven't finished yet. Next door is your bedroom, Liza. It's a bit smaller, but I think you'll like it." Again, the walls were lime-washed and the floorboards varnished, but this time the curtains, bedspread, and rugs were a pale green, and on the windowsill was a bottle-green vase of white roses.

"Annie, it looks so lovely. Thank you so much. I never, ever expected to sleep in a room as grand as this, and in my own bed. I don't know what Isaac would have made of it all."

"You deserve it, Liza. Right, now I expect you lot would like to see where you will be sleeping?" Annie turned to her brothers and sisters. "Come on then, let's see what we can find."

None of the children had ever slept in a proper bed, having made do with a palliasse stuffed with feathers or straw on the floor. Annie led them along the landing and into another large bedroom where Edward, Stephen, and Danny would sleep. There were three single beds in the room, each with a red patterned bedspread. The curtains and rugs were also a dark red, which contrasted nicely with the cream walls. In the corner was a large box of toys, and alongside it, the rocking horse, once so loved by Robert's sister, Sarah. The children gasped in amazement and ran to see what was in the box. Annie laughed.

"Yes, I thought that box might interest you. Some of those toys were Robert's when he was a boy, and he has said you can have them. Now, you have to share the rocking horse with the girls, so don't forget that. There are some lovely books on that bookshelf, so now you need to learn to read properly. Come on, you can come back and play in a minute, but let's finish the tour of the house first." Annie was thoroughly enjoying herself.

Across the corridor, a slightly smaller room held two single beds for Helen and Selina. The curtains and the bed covers were a deep pink, and the rugs were patterned with grey and maroon. Again, in one corner was a toy box, and on a shelf along the wall were six dolls. Next to the toy box was a dolls pram, a cot, and a dolls house. The two girls were wide-eyed as they made a beeline for the dolls. However, when they reached them, Helen stopped and turned nervously to Annie, whilst Selina was braver and fingered the brocade on one of the doll's skirts.

"Can we touch them, Annie?" whispered Helen. She was four years old, a pretty little girl with curly hair and blue eyes. She had always been a placid, loving child, and she ran to Annie and put her arms around her waist as she gazed up at her.

"Yes, of course, you can, but you must look after them, and not be rough. That means you too, Selina." Annie took a doll from the shelf and handed it to her daughter.

"You must be gentle, Selina. Nurse the dolly like this look, and cuddle her." Annie put the doll in the little girl's arms and showed her how to hold it and rock it to and fro. "There, now when she is asleep, you can put her in the cot, or you could take her for a walk around the room in the pram."

Selina grinned up at her mother. "This is nice, Mummy. I like this house. Can we stay here forever and ever?" Selina was much more mischievous than her Aunty Helen and had always been into everything, often running rings around poor Liza when she was looking after her. An intelligent child, at nearly three, she was beginning to settle down a bit.

"Yes, I think we can, but only if you are a good girl and look after everything. You must be careful not to break things, and not come in with muddy feet. Can you do that?"

"Yes, Mummy, I promise." Annie smiled at her daughter's solemn face.

"Come on then, let's go downstairs again, and I'll finish showing you around down there."

Annie led the way and showed them the parlour and the sitting room, where they marvelled at the chairs and sofas they would have to sit on. The furniture had been brought from the big house and was not new, but the Carter family were impressed.

When they had seen their fill of the house, Annie led them outside, where John Cutcliffe was just releasing the hens into their new home. The garden had been forked over, and onions, potatoes, peas, and beans had been planted and were already growing strongly. At the far end, where an enormous sweet chestnut tree stood, Annie had asked Fred to fix up a swing, a slide, and a see-saw. The children whooped with delight, and Selina struggled to be released from Annie's arms.

Annie turned to her mother. "Well, I don't think they'll be much trouble for a while. Shall we leave them to it and have a cup of tea? Oh, look, there's Robert. He said he would come today."

Robert came in through the garden gate and smiled at the happy scene around him. "How's it going? Do you think you can all live here all right?" He took Annie's hand and kissed it gently.

"Oh, Master Robert, we can never thank you enough. This house is incredible. I don't think I will ever stop smiling." Sabina stood before her future son-in-law with tears in her eyes.

"I'm glad you like it, Sabina, but there is something you must do for me."

"Anything, anything at all. What is it you want me to do?"

"You must stop calling me Master Robert, and just call me, Robert, please; can you do that?"

"Yes, of course, if you are sure."

Robert nodded. "Now shall we look in the larder to see what we can have for our tea? I instructed Mrs Potts to make one of her big meat pies, and there should be some potatoes and vegetables too. I suspect she might even have made one of her famous trifles and a chocolate cake. I thought on your first day it would be good to have an easy meal, and one that we can celebrate with."

When the Carter family sat down to their tea that night, they could not stop smiling, unable to believe their good luck.

CHAPTER 16

Robert and Annie had set their wedding date for mid-August, and time was moving on. Now that the family had moved into their new home, Annie felt she could turn her attention to her wedding plans. With this in mind, she asked her Aunt Eveline if she would make her dress and also bridesmaids' dresses for Mary, Helen, and Selina. She would have liked Sarah to be a bridesmaid too, but Eleanor and Charles were determined not to attend the wedding and planned to travel to London with Victoria and Frank after the baby was born.

Eveline was happy to make the dresses and went once more with Annie to George's shop. The two women asked to see all the silks and satins suitable for a wedding dress, and George's daughter, Harriet, willingly laid out everything available. When George appeared, Annie could not resist provoking him.

"Hello, Uncle George, Aunty Eveline and I are looking for some material for my wedding dress."

"I heard you were getting married. I must congratulate you on your good fortune."

"Thank you, yes, I'm very lucky, and my family is finding the Lodge House so much more comfortable than they would have been in the workhouse. Unfortunately, I'm not keen on any of these materials, so I think we'll have to look further afield. I wish you a good day."

Annie left the shop with her nose in the air and a smile on her face, and Eveline had to hurry to catch up with her. When she did so, she was laughing. "I should tell you off for what you just said to my brother, but it was so funny, I can't, and I have to say he did deserve it."

"Yes, it was a bit naughty of me, wasn't it, but I couldn't resist. He was so horrible to Mum after Dad died. The thing is, though, where can we get the material we need now?"

"Let's go to Exeter on the train, and see if we can find what we want there. What do you think? We could take Sabina with us. I think we'd have to stay overnight. It's a bit too far to travel there and back in one day and have time for shopping. Do you think Robert would take us to the station?"

"Yes, I'm sure he would, and if he'd let Maisie help Liza with the children, we could stay overnight. I'll ask him. We must get on with it, though, or you won't have time to make the dresses."

Annie went straight to the Manor House, and as usual, entered through the kitchen. She had been to see Sarah and Victoria a few times, for the three had become firm friends much to Robert's delight. Mrs Potts was pleased to see her and made her a cup of tea, whilst she sent Maisie to tell Robert that Annie was in the kitchen. Annie did not want to risk running into Miss Wetherby, or Robert's parents if she could help it. Robert arrived, beaming, and suggested they walk around the grounds. As they strolled arm in arm to the lake, she told him what had happened earlier in George's shop, and he was amused.

"I think a trip to Exeter is an excellent idea, but I will escort the three of you." He held up his hand. "I know, I can't come shopping with you, and see the new material, but that's no problem because I have some business I can attend to, and meet you all later for dinner. I don't want the three of you unprotected in Exeter, especially overnight. It's no problem about Maisie, she can spend a couple of days with Liza looking after the children; I'm sure she'll be delighted."

A few days later, Dodger took Robert and the three women to Eggleston Station to catch the first train and promised to collect them late the next day. Sabina and Annie were excited, for they had never been on a train, let alone visit the city. They were early and as they waited on the platform for the train to arrive, Annie noticed a tall woman and thought she looked familiar, but couldn't quite think where she had seen her. She asked the others if they recognised her. Sabina and Eveline didn't, but Robert said he thought she was the woman they had seen answer the door at Buzzacott House.

"Yes, of course, that's it. She's so tall she's quite distinctive."

When the train arrived, they boarded and found some seats, though it was not due to depart for another twenty minutes. Whilst they sat looking out of the window, they noticed a young woman with a baby approach the tall woman and speak to her. The young mother kissed her baby tenderly and handed her over to the older woman, who cuddled the child affectionately. The mother seemed upset as she pressed something into the other woman's hand, then turned swiftly and boarded the train. The older woman walked briskly out of the station with the baby in her arms.

The young woman moved along the train looking for a spare seat and found one close to Annie and her party. Tears were rolling down her cheeks as she sat down and searched for a handkerchief. Sabina couldn't bear to see someone so upset and went to the woman. "Is there anything I can do to help? I can see you're upset about something."

"No there's nothing anyone can do, but thank you, it's nice of you to ask. I've just had to part with my baby." The young woman sobbed as she told them she was called Jean.

"Oh dear, I'm so sorry. That's terrible. I would hate to part with any of my children. Is it a relative that has taken the child?"

"No, I've no one to help me, and I have to work, so I can't look after the child. The father abandoned me as soon as he knew I was in the family way, and I don't know where he is now. I answered an advertisement in a newspaper. It said arrangements could be made for unwanted babies to be adopted, or they could be looked after until the mother could have them back. I'm hoping to find a job where I can have the baby with me eventually. I must admit I thought the woman I met would have been younger, but she seemed caring enough."

"Do you know where she lives?"

"Not exactly, but somewhere in Barnstaple, I believe, though she is moving house next week. We agreed to meet here at the station as it was about halfway for both of us. I had to pay her to take the child, of course, but she's promised to write to me every week. When she's settled in her new home, she says I'll be able to go and see Rosie whenever I like, so at least I have that to look forward to."

Annie and Robert exchanged puzzled glances, for they were sure the woman lived at Buzzacott House, which was several miles from Barnstaple. However, they decided to say nothing as they didn't want to cause the woman more worry.

Sabina took Jean's hand. "Now, look, I'm sure your baby will be fine. As you say, the lady seemed pleased to take her, and no doubt, within a week or two, you'll hear from her. It's not so bad if you can see the baby occasionally."

"Yes, I'm sure you're right, I'm just being silly but thank you for your kindness."

Sabina resumed her seat beside Eveline and waited nervously for the train to depart. Annie, seated opposite them, and beside Robert, was also impatient to find out what it was like to ride on a train. Robert and Eveline had allowed Sabina and Annie to sit by the window, and they enjoyed pointing out various landmarks as the train chuffed along the line to Exeter.

"I can't believe how fast we are travelling." Sabina was wide-eyed. "Are you sure it won't crash?"

"No, it's safe, and the trains coming the other way are controlled by signals, so they never end up on the same track." Robert smiled at her. "Relax and enjoy the journey. Doesn't the countryside look beautiful?"

"Yes, it does, and it's so interesting to be able to see into all the farmyards and gardens as you pass. Look, some children are waving to us."

Three children sat on a garden wall, waved to the train as it passed, and laughing, the three women waved back.

All too soon the train arrived in Exeter, and once outside the station, Robert waved down a carriage. "I know an inn near here where we can stay for the night, so if we go there first, we can leave our luggage and then you can go shopping."

The carriage took them to the inn, where the innkeeper welcomed Robert like an old friend and assured him he could find rooms for all of them for the night. Robert had a room to himself, whilst the three women shared a room with one double bed and a single. The carriage then took them into the centre of Exeter, where Robert went about his business and left Sabina and Annie in the expert hands of Eveline. They agreed to meet back at the inn for a meal later.

Eveline took them to a dressmaker's shop that she knew, and before long, all three were poring over luxurious fabrics.

"Oh, Annie this one is beautiful, but I shudder to think what it would cost." Sabina caressed the shiny white satin gently.

"It is lovely, but I have been married before. Do you think I should wear cream or another colour, other than white?" Annie looked anxiously at the two older women.

"I suppose that might be more correct. How about this one?" Eveline held up a rich cream silk material.

"Oh, yes, that is lovely. Is it too expensive?" Annie looked at Eveline anxiously.

"Of course not, Robert said you were to have what you liked. I think this would hang well, and we could trim it with some of that lace." Eveline pointed to the top shelf. "Could we have a look at that lace, please?"

Mary Robbins, the shopkeeper, enjoyed their enthusiasm and was more than willing to show them any of her fabrics. She reached for the lace. "Here you are, and yes, I agree with you. That cream fabric does hang beautifully and this lace will complement it nicely. When is the wedding?"

"In just a few weeks so there isn't much time." Eveline looked at the shopkeeper anxiously. "I hope you have enough fabric because we must buy some today."

"Now, don't you worry, I have everything here you'll need. We have sequins and pearls, and ribbons and bows, so you will be spoilt for choice.

Mary Robbins was right, and it took the three women a good two hours to choose everything they needed for Annie and the three bridesmaids. For Annie, they chose the cream silk to be trimmed with fine lace and small seed pearls. For the bridesmaids, Mary, Helen, and Selina, there was more deliberation, for there were so many gorgeous colours to choose from. They finally settled for a delicate lilac material, which they thought would look good on all three children, and arranged to collect their purchases the next morning. They enjoyed the rest of their afternoon browsing around the shops and then hailed a carriage to take them back to the inn.

CHAPTER 17

Eveline continued to visit Jane Chugg at Hollyford Farm regularly, and each time she went, she showed Maria Webber how to cook another meal. The girl was a keen learner, and they both enjoyed their time together in the kitchen. One day when Eveline visited, Doctor Luckett was just leaving the house as she arrived.

"Good Morning Doctor, how is Jane today?"

"I'm afraid she's very poorly, Eveline, but she'll be pleased to see you."

"I didn't come last week as I had a bad cold, and I didn't want to risk passing it on to her, but I'm looking forward to seeing her today."

Eveline went into the kitchen and told Maria she would see Jane before they did any cooking. When she entered the bedroom, she was shocked at the change in Jane's appearance. The old lady was propped up on pillows, and her eyes were shut. Her face was ashen, and she had lost more weight. Eveline sat quietly beside her and waited to see if she woke up. After a few moments, her blue eyes opened, and when she saw her friend, she smiled weakly.

"Hello, Eveline, how nice to see you. Are you feeling better?"

"Yes, I'm fine, thanks, but I didn't want to pass my cold on to you. How are you feeling?"

"Not too good as you can see. To be honest, I just want it to be over. I'm such a burden on everyone, and I know I'm not going to get better. I wish the doctor would give me something to send me on my way."

"Now, you mustn't talk like that. You know what they say, where there's life, there's hope."

"Aye, I know, and you mean well, but we both know I won't be here much longer."

Eveline squeezed her friend's hand. "Is there anything I can get you?"

"No, I've had my medicine, and I'm not in pain. Just sit and tell me all that's going on. I like to hear all the gossip."

Eveline smiled and told her all about Annie and Sabina moving into the Lodge House, and how Annie was going to marry Master Robert. "I'm making her wedding dress myself. Luckily, it's a simple design, and Matilda Rudd is helping me. She's a good seamstress, and having a sewing machine makes all the difference, of course. We've already made the bridesmaids dresses for Mary, Helen, and Selina, so I think now it will be all right, and we'll finish in time. I was a bit worried for a while. The banns were called for the first time last Sunday, so in few weeks they'll be married."

"You tell Annie I'm pleased for her. She's a lovely girl, and she deserves to be happy after what happened to Harry; it was such a tragedy."

They chatted for a while until Eveline could see that Jane was struggling to keep her eyes open. "I'm going to help Maria prepare the dinner now, Jane, so I'll see you later.

In the kitchen, Maria was chopping up steak and kidney for a pie.

"Right then, Maria let's see how you get on with the pastry. I showed you how to make it the other day, so hopefully, you can remember what to do. I'll go to the garden and dig some potatoes and pick a few peas to go with it."

Eveline was about to dig some early new potatoes when Charlie appeared. "Hey, there's no need for you to do that. It's good of you to teach Maria to cook, but I'm not having you digging potatoes."

"Nonsense, it's not a problem, and I'm sure you've other work to do."

"Nevertheless, I'll dig them, but you can pick the peas if you like. That's a fiddly job I don't care for."

Eveline smiled, and her heart did a sudden lurch as she looked into his vivid blue eyes. She blushed and looked away quickly, and Charlie's eyes followed her thoughtfully. They both continued with their tasks in silence until Charlie straightened up and eased his back.

"There, I think that's enough teddies for today and tomorrow, and then I'll dig some more. They're better dug fresh; they scrape more easily. Have you finished picking the peas?"

"Yes, there are loads here, so it doesn't take long, but this is enough for a couple of meals. These are better gathered fresh as well."

"Come on, then, I'll carry these potatoes back to the kitchen for you."

"Thanks Charlie, but I can manage if you're busy."

"No, it's no trouble. Anyway, I've been hoping for an opportunity to talk to you. I notice you always ride over to see Jane, and I wondered if you'd like to go riding with me one day? We could go out over Exmoor; the scenery's beautiful there. Could you leave the children for a few hours?"

"I do love riding, though I have little time for it these days. I expect Sabina would mind the children for me. She never seems to mind how many children she has to look after."

"Is that a yes, then?" Charlie beamed at her, and once again those bright blue eyes made her go weak at the knees.

Eveline blushed again. "Er, I don't know ..."

Charlie put down the basket of potatoes and took her hand. "Eveline, I've become fond of you over the last few weeks, and I'd like to spend a day with you. Is there anything wrong with that?"

"Well, no, but ..."

"So, would you like to spend the day with me and go riding on Exmoor?"

"Yes I would, but ..."

"What else is there to say, then? No buts. Can I take that as a yes?"

She suddenly smiled widely at him. "Yes, you can, Charlie Chugg. I'd like that. How about next Wednesday?"

"Grand, I'll look forward to it. Now I must go because Jack Bater has said Arthur Webber and me can go ferreting in the front meadow at the Manor Farm. Apparently, it's teeming with rabbits, and they keep eating the crops. It'll be a bit of fun, and we can sell the rabbits in the village." As they reached the yard gate, Charlie put the basket down and swiftly took Eveline's hand and kissed it gently, looking at her with laughter dancing in his eyes. "If I don't see you before, I'll see you here on Wednesday, about ten o'clock then. Bye."

Whistling happily, Charlie saddled his horse and rode over to the Manor Farm cottages to meet Arthur Webber. He knocked loudly on the door and heard Arthur's father, Peter, shout to him to come in.

"Hello, Peter, how are you?"

"I'm fine, thank you, Charlie. Off ferreting, I hear?"

"Yes, that's right. Is Arthur around?"

"Aye, he's out the back choosing which ferrets to take. He's got plenty of them. Go through, lad."

"Thanks, Peter. This must be the easel I've been hearing all about then?"

"Yes, it gives me something to do, though I'm not very good. It's going to take a lot of practice before I can produce anything worthwhile. Mind you: I've plenty of time."

Charlie surveyed the painting currently clipped to the easel. It was of a nearby cove surrounded by cliffs, and seagulls wheeled in the foreground. "That looks like Raparree Beach, if I'm not mistaken. Am I right?"

Peter nodded. "Yes, I know it so well; I can picture it in my mind, though, of course, it would be better to sit there and paint it. I'm pleased you recognised it, though."

"It's good, Peter. In fact, it's amazing and far better than I could do with both hands, though that's not saying a great deal."

"You're very kind, but as I say, at least it gives me something to do. Go on now, out and find Arthur; he's expecting you."

Charlie found Arthur in his shed. He had ten cages, each housing a ferret, and one had newly born young.

"Hello, Arthur, you have a fine lot of ferrets. How many shall we take?"

"I think two will be plenty. These two here, I think, they're both jills, and they're best for catching rabbits. They're not as aggressive as the males and less likely to kill the rabbits."

"Yes, I've heard that. I'm looking forward to this. It's not often a landowner gives his permission for ferreting."

"No, it isn't, but Jack said Master Robert doesn't mind, and we can keep all we catch and sell them in the village. Be a bit of extra money, won't it? I wish all the landowners were that sensible. The rabbit numbers need to be kept down, but most of them would have you sent off to jail, or put on the treadmill, for daring to catch a few. Come on then, shall we get going?"

They put the ferrets into separate sacks and set off up the lane to the meadow. It was a large field with a slight incline and a stream running across the bottom. In one of the top corners were a large number of rabbit burrows.

"My goodness, there are a lot of burrows, Arthur. Have you brought enough nets?"

"Aye, I've plenty, and I mended several of them last night. Here, Charlie, you start pegging the nets around the burrows over that way, and I'll do the same over here." Arthur handed Charlie a handful of nets.

Half an hour or so later the nets were pegged around each of the holes in the ground.

"Right, let's see how we get on." Arthur reached into the sack and retrieved the first ferret. "This here's Tinker, and she's my best ferret. She's getting on a bit now, but a grand rabbiter she is. Never lets me down." Arthur popped her down the first hole, and then reached into another sack. "And this one here's Tinker's daughter, Titch. She's small for a ferret, and this is her first time, so I hope she'll do the business." He stroked the blond ferret, and then carefully put her down a hole.

Both ferrets vanished immediately, and for a few minutes, nothing happened. Then two rabbits came bolting out of their burrows, and straight into the nets, which immediately tightened around them. The men ran swiftly to the rabbits, peeling off the nets. Holding rabbits' hind legs firmly in one hand, and their necks in the other, they gave a sharp pull, and with a faint click, their necks were broken, and they lay lifeless. They quickly put the nets back over the burrows again. For the next hour, or more, the two men were kept busy, as one after another, rabbits shot at speed out of the burrows and into the nets. When Tinker reappeared, Arthur picked her up and stroked her fondly.

"Well, old girl, you've not lost your touch. You did a good job, today. I wonder where that daughter of yours has got to. I hope she's not going to lead me a merry dance." He put the older ferret back into a bag, and they removed the rest of the nets from around the holes. As Charlie removed the last one, the younger ferret, Titch, poked her head out of the burrow and allowed him to pick her up. However, as he carried her across to Arthur, she gave him a sharp bite on his thumb, and he cried out in pain.

"Here, take the blasted animal, she's bitten my thumb. Almost through to the bone look, vicious animal."

"Aye, they can give a nasty nip; their teeth are sharp. Make sure you give that a good wash with salty water when we get back, Charlie. You don't want it going poisonous."

They counted the rabbits that were now hung on a long stick which they carried between them. To their amazement, they had caught twenty-one rabbits.

"I think that's the most I've ever caught in one go." Arthur grinned at Charlie. "That was a nice little earner, wasn't it? Bit of fun, too. Shall we walk through the village and sell some?"

"Yes, might as well, while they're nice and fresh."

They walked through the village and found plenty of people wanting to buy a rabbit for their tea. They sold them for four pence each, which was a bargain, but after all, it had cost them nothing and people were hungry. They debated whether to call at the Lodge House because Sabina did not need to buy rabbits these days.

"What do you think? Would Sabina think it a cheek if we called?" Arthur looked anxiously at his friend.

Charlie grinned. "By the look on your face, you'll be disappointed, if we don't. Got a soft spot for her, have you? Well, I don't blame you, lovely woman, she is."

Arthur looked uncomfortable. "No, it's nothing like that, but she's been so good to Dad, and I'd like to give her a few rabbits for free. I haven't got much else I can give her."

"Come on then, nothing ventured, nothing gained."

They raised the shiny brass knocker on the newly painted blue front door of the Lodge House, and Liza answered the door. "Hello, lads, looks like you've had a good day. Selling them, are you?"

"Aye, Liza, we are, but is Sabina around? I wanted a word with her."

"Yes, come in, Arthur. She's in the kitchen making bread, but I know she'll be pleased to see you."

"Arthur, I'll go on now because I need to get back to the farm to do the milking. Alfred said he would do it tonight, but I want to let him sit with Jane. I'll take these three rabbits, and you can sell the rest, all right?"

"Yes, if you're sure, Charlie. Thanks for your help. Shall we do it again, sometime?"

"Yes, I'd like that. I enjoyed it. Bye for now."

Liza showed Arthur through to the kitchen, where Sabina was rosy-cheeked as she firmly kneaded a large lump of dough. Her hair was escaping from her bun, and she had a smudge of flour across her cheek.

"Hello, Arthur, what brings you here? Is Peter all right?"

"What, of yes, he's fine, thanks. I've been rabbiting with Charlie Chugg, and would you believe we caught twenty-one of them? We've sold most of them in the village, but I wondered if you'd like a few."

"I would indeed. I love rabbit stew, even though we've eaten so much of it over the years. It's always a tasty meal. How much are they?"

"Oh no, I don't want anything for them. You have been so good to us, Sabina, it would make me happy to give you something for a change."

"That's kind of you, Arthur, thank you. I'll tell you what then, leave a few rabbits with me, and I'll make a big pot of stew for all of us, and you as well. I'll bring it over tomorrow if you like?"

"That would be grand, Sabina. One condition, though."

Sabina looked at him questioningly.

"Would you stay and eat with us? I only see you in passing, and it would be nice to sit and have a chat with you. Dad would enjoy it, too."

"Very well, I'll see you tomorrow at tea time."

CHAPTER 18

In the early hours of the fifteenth of July, Victoria went into labour and rang the bell to summon help.

"Maisie, the baby's coming; please wake my husband, and arrange for someone to fetch Doctor Luckett."

The maid nodded and went swiftly along the corridor to Frank's room. It was two o'clock in the morning, but although she knocked loudly, she was unable to get an answer. However, the noise awoke Robert, who came to see what was going on.

"It's all right, Maisie, don't worry. I'll wake Frank. Ask Caleb to fetch Doctor Luckett."

Robert entered the room and pursed his lips when he saw that Frank's bed had not been slept in. He hurried downstairs to the drawing-room to see if his brother-in-law had fallen asleep in a chair, but as he passed through the hallway, he heard Frank enter by the front door. It was immediately obvious he was drunk and smelt strongly of cheap perfume.

"God, how you disgust me. Your wife's in labour, and you roll home drunk, and goodness knows where you've been to smell the way you do." Robert glared at the man.

Frank grinned widely. "Oh, come on, Robert, I'm only human. You must know that wives are not that much fun when they're heavily pregnant. I suppose you don't know that yet, but you soon will, my friend."

"I'm no friend of yours, but for goodness sake have a wash and sober up before you go to Victoria. She'll smell another woman on you."

"Oh, she's used to it. She doesn't seem that bothered, actually." Frank laughed. "You have a very understanding sister, old man. Anyway, there's no point in me getting in the way until it's all over. With any luck, it should give me time to get my head down for a few hours."

Robert considered preventing the man from ascending the stairs but realised it was pointless and stood to one side seething. Frank lurched past him, laughing loudly.

This being Victoria's second baby within a short timescale, her labour did not last long, and by six o'clock she held her new son in her arms. Doctor Luckett had stayed with her throughout and delivered the healthy baby. As the doctor descended the staircase, Robert approached him with questioning eyes.

"Hello, Robert, yes, good news. Your sister has a fine baby boy, and both mother and baby are doing well."

"Thank you, Doctor Luckett, may I go and see her?"

"Yes, of course, though I was rather expecting to see the father waiting?"

"Oh, he'll be here soon, I'm sure. Thanks for everything you've done."

Robert tore up the stairs and knocked on his sister's door. She was sat up in bed cradling her newborn son and smiled as Robert entered.

"Hello, Robert, what are you doing up this early?"

"I heard all the commotion in the night and waited up to see how things went. How are you?"

"I'm fine, thanks. This birth was so much easier than when I had Caroline. He's a bigger baby too, but they say the first is the worst."

Robert pulled back the shawl and looked at his new nephew. "He's lovely, Victoria. What are you going to call him?"

"If Frank agrees I'd like to call him Joshua after our Grandad."

"I like the name, and did you realise today is Saint Swithin's Day?" He looked out of the window. "It looks like it's going to be fine, which is good because you know what they say, if it rains on Saint Swithin's Day it will rain for forty days and forty nights."

"Oh, that's an old wives' tale."

"Maybe, but as we plan to cut the hay in the big field this morning, I'm pleased to see the sun shining."

"Is there any sign of Frank? I thought he might be waiting to see his new son."

"No, he was home quite late, and I've not seen him yet this morning. Do you want me to wake him?"

A sad look passed over his sister's face. "No, don't bother. He won't come until he's ready." She looked at her twin. "I'm afraid he's not exactly the doting or faithful husband I had hoped for, Robert, but at least he doesn't mistreat me. That's why I think you're right to marry for love. I realise now, I didn't know Frank nearly well enough when I agreed to marry him. All I saw was a handsome face, and I fell for his charm."

"Well, it's not good enough, and I shall be telling him so when I see him."

"You'd be wasting your time, but thanks for coming to see me. Now, go and get your breakfast. I'm hoping to have a nap; I'm tired, now."

"Yes, of course. I've got a busy day ahead, because as I say, we're cutting the hay this morning, and then I'm taking Annie and her family to the fair this afternoon. You know, it comes to the village every year, but I've never been. Have you?"

"No, of course not; we were never allowed as children, but have a good time."

"Thanks, I'm sure we will and I'll see you this evening."

Robert spent the morning with Jack and the other farmhands cutting the long grass with scythes. It was a big field, and the grass was thick, although it was the second cut of the year. Stripped to the waist, the sun glistened on their sweat-drenched, rippling muscles as their blades cut through the long sweet grass and laid it in swathes. It was essential to dry the hay quickly, for then it would be high in sugar content and more nourishing for the animals during the winter.

Jack straightened up to ease his aching back and mopped his brow, which was dripping with sweat. "It's a good year, Master Robert. The cows won't go hungry this winter."

Robert took a breather. "No, this grass should make excellent hay, especially if the weather stays good for a few days."

"Yes, and I think it will. Why don't you get off now, sir? You said you were going to the fair this afternoon, and we've done more than three parts of the field now. The men and I will easily get it finished by supper."

Robert surveyed the field. "Yes, I think you're right, Jack. We've done well this morning. Why don't you call the men in now to have their lunch break, and then you could finish it this afternoon."

Jack nodded, and Robert went to wash and get something to eat before going to call for Annie.

The Carter children were excited. They had been to the fair before, but never with Robert and they knew he would, no doubt, treat them to at least some sweets or perhaps a toffee apple. Annie answered the door herself and smiled at him happily.

"Hello, Robert, there are some rather impatient children here waiting for you. We're ready, so shall we go?"

They set off, Annie holding Robert's hand on one side and Selina's on the other. Danny held Robert's other hand, little knowing it was that of his big brother. They walked slowly, at Danny's pace, and Edward, Stephen, and Helen skipped ahead happily. Sabina and Liza said they would come along a little later.

Their neighbour, Noeleen Cutcliffe, was also just leaving her house with her five daughters. Clarice, Ruth, and Susanna, from her first marriage, were in their early teens and walked with their mother, but her stepdaughters, Daisy and Rachael, soon caught up to the Carter children and walked with them. On the way, they were joined by other villagers making their way to the fairground on the common, for it was to open at two o'clock.

A wooden archway had been erected at the entrance to the fair, and it was decorated with flowers and greenery. Across the top lay a white glove on a stick, symbolising the hand of friendship and a warm welcome to the fairground people who travelled all around the land. The mayor stood on a raised wooden platform, his gold chain gleaming brightly around his neck. A man next to him, performed a roll on the drums to silence the crowd. After a short speech, the mayor cut a red ribbon and announced the fair open.

Annie suggested they walk around the fairground to look at everything first and then decide what they would most like to spend their pennies on. They were spoilt for choice. Fairgrounds had been in decline just a couple of decades ago, but they were now popular once again. This year there were three fairground rides to choose from. One, the Dobby Horses, they had seen before. The garishly painted horses were bolted to the wooden floor and went up and down as the carousel went round and round. The children were enthralled and would have happily spent all their money there and then to have a ride.

However, they walked on past many side stalls, some selling pasties and cakes, bacon and sausage sandwiches, and others with sweets called "fairings" such as sugared almonds, gingerbread, and toffee apples. Sideshows costing tuppence a time, included the Crazy Mirrors, showing distorted images, Gypsy Freda, the fortune teller, Robert Tipney, the Human Skeleton, and Charlie, the very tall man.

The children were round-eyed as they listened to the fair hands trying to entice people inside and part with their money.

The two new fairground rides were even more exciting than the Dobby Horses, and they stood and watched in wonder. The Velocipede had bicycles, and the people riding them made the carousel turn by pedal power. With the combined effort of so many cyclists, it went surprisingly fast. The other ride was called the Sea on Land. Brightly coloured boats were bolted to the wooden floor of the carousel, but as well as revolving, the floor, which was painted blue and white, undulated as would the sea.

They continued on past a boxing booth, where several young men were waiting to try their luck at beating a large giant of a man employed by the fair. The man looked as hard as a rock, and Annie thought anyone taking him on must be mad. Next to that was a coconut shy and the children were intrigued for they had never seen coconuts before. Towards the end of the fairground were pens containing all kinds of livestock for many farmers bought and sold animals at the fair.

Robert drew Annie and the children to one side. "Right then, which ride would you all most like to go on?"

"Ooh, can we go on one?" Stephen was round-eyed as he had never for one moment expected to have a ride.

Robert nodded. "Yes, I think we should all go on a ride together, and it looks to me as if the Dobby Horses would be best for all of us. Would you be happy with that?" He could see from the smiling faces around him that his suggestion met with approval, so they made their way to the carousel and waited for it to stop. He lifted Edward, Stephen, and Helen onto three horses in a row, and told them to hold on tight. Annie sat Selina in front of her on a white horse, and Robert settled Danny on a black horse next to Annie's and then climbed up behind him. The carousel soon filled up with people, and Robert paid the man one shilling and tuppence.

Annie spotted Ruth Cutcliffe on a horse a few rows in front of her and wondered how she could afford a ride, for the Cutcliffe's were not wealthy. Selina and Danny cried out in excitement as the horses started to go up and down, and the carousel began to turn, getting ever faster. Annie grinned at Robert, as she too had never been on a ride before.

The fairground attendant was paying a lot of attention to Ruth, and Annie watched in concern, for although he was good looking, he looked quite a bit older than Ruth. All too soon, the ride finished, and Annie and Robert helped the children to dismount from their horses. Annie saw that Ruth was staying on for another ride and that the man had his arm around her shoulders. She put her hand on Robert's arm. "I'm a bit concerned about Ruth. Look, she's flirting with that fair worker, and I don't like the look of him. Her mother will be cross if she sees her."

"There's nothing you can do about it, and she can't come to much harm here with all these people around. Now, what shall we do next? Would anyone like to see the Human Skeleton, or perhaps the crazy mirrors?"

The children had seen enough starving people in their time, and so they elected to see the crazy mirrors. They were soon laughing heartily at their reflections, as in some mirrors, they appeared very, very thin, and in others short and fat. They wandered on, admiring the skill of the jugglers and marvelling at how a tight-rope walker managed to keep his balance as he walked across a taut rope suspended between two wooden posts. Annie was pleased that none of the children asked for anything. Sabina had warned them they were not to ask, and they had been good.

When they reached the coconut shy, Robert stopped. "Who thinks I might be able to knock down a coconut?"

Stephen and Danny shouted "I do, I do. Please see if you can."

Robert paid his money, but it was not as easy as he thought, and although he managed to hit a coconut, it didn't fall. Seeing the disappointed faces around him, he delved into his pocket once more, and this time he was rewarded when a large coconut wobbled and slowly fell to the ground amid many cheers.

"We'll take this home and crack it open and see what's inside. I've never tried fresh coconut before either, so it will be a new taste for all of us. I think it's time we went home now, but we'll get something to eat on the way as you've all been so good. Start thinking about what you would like. Perhaps a pasty, or a toffee apple, or some sweets?"

As they made their way to the exit, Annie saw Ruth stood between two of the tents with the fairground man. They were kissing passionately, and Annie hesitated, concerned but reluctant to interfere. Ruth must have felt Annie's eyes on her, for she pulled away and looked at Annie angrily. "What are you looking at? Never seen two people kiss before?"

"I'm sorry, I didn't mean to stare, Ruth, but I just wonder how well you know this man? Perhaps you'd like to walk home with us?"

"No, I'm fine, so please mind your own business. You're not the only one with a boyfriend, you know."

"No, of course not. I'm sorry." Annie moved on in embarrassment.

When they got back to Sabina's house, Robert drilled a hole in the coconut and drained the milk from inside. Then he smashed it open with a hammer, and they all tried a piece. They all liked it except Selina, who immediately spat it out, and pulled a face that made them all laugh.

Annie went to see Robert out. She shut the back door behind her, and they embraced and kissed. He nuzzled her hair. "Not long now, Annie. The vicar will be calling the banns again on Sunday, so soon you will be my wife. What do you think about that?"

Annie smiled. "I can't wait."

CHAPTER 19

A few days later Sabina was awakened by a loud knocking on the door. She rose in haste, puzzled as to who it could be, for it was barely dawn. Pulling her shawl around her, she ran swiftly down the stairs and answered the door. She hoped the noise had not disturbed the children, for she treasured a few moments alone in the morning with a nice hot cup of tea. Outside, in the pouring rain, stood John Cutcliffe.

"Hello, John, what brings you here so early? Come in out of the rain."

"Thank you, Sabina; it's a nasty morning. I'm sorry to trouble you, but I wonder if you've seen anything of our Ruth? She didn't come home last night, and Noeleen's beside herself with worry."

"Sorry, no, I haven't seen her, John. The last time I saw her was at the fair a few days ago."

"Aye, I think that could be the trouble. Kept going down there, she did, every day, you see. I don't know what the attraction was, but she certainly couldn't keep away, even though her mother forbade her to go there again. Then, last night she didn't come home for her tea, which is not like her at all, and we're worried because she's only fifteen."

"Now Annie did mention that she saw Ruth chatting to one of the fair workers, and she asked her if she would like to walk home with her, but I'm afraid she was a bit rude."

"Oh, I'm sorry. Youngsters, these days, I don't know. You try to bring 'em up properly, but they always think they know best. Would Annie be up yet, do you think?"

"She may be because Selina wakes early. Come into the kitchen, John, and I'll go and see."

Annie was awake, and about to come downstairs with Selina sitting on her hip. "Morning, Mum, are you looking for me?"

Sabina explained, and Annie agreed to have a chat with John.

"Hello, John, I'm sorry to hear Ruth's missing, but how can I help?"

"Sabina says you saw her at the fair with a man, is that right?"

"Yes, he was in charge of the Dobby Horses and was chatting Ruth up. Then, later, I saw them kissing, though I don't like to tell tales."

"Right, well, the fair left last night, so it doesn't take a genius to know where she is then, does it? I don't know what her mother will make of this. What did the man look like?"

"I'd say he was about thirty, with long dark hair, and he wore a brown cap. Are you going to go after the fair?"

"I think it's the only thing I can do. The fair usually goes on to Barnstaple from here, but I can't go until after work, and it's a good twelve-mile walk."

"John, I'll walk with you to the Manor and ask Robert if you can borrow a horse. Can you ride?" Annie looked at the distraught man, anxiously.

"Aye I can ride, but no, don't trouble yourself, Annie, I'll sort it out. It's not Master Robert's problem."

"He won't mind, John, I'm sure he won't. Come on, let's go and see him."

Annie would not take no for an answer and leaving Selina with Sabina, she pulled on her boots and shawl and trudged up the lane with John. The rain was easing, and it looked as if it might be a nice day after all.

"Annie, I'll have to find Jack Bater to ask for the time off to go after Ruth; I should start work in a few minutes."

"All right, John, tell him I'm asking Robert about borrowing a horse, and I'm sure he'll understand. You can make the time up, can't you?"

"Oh, yes, of course. I'll come and find you when I've spoken to Jack."

Annie entered the house through the kitchen door. Mrs Potts was surprised but pleased to see her.

"Hello, Annie, what a nice surprise. Come back to work, have you?"

"No, I'm afraid not, but it's lovely to see you, Mrs Potts. Is Robert up yet?"

"No, my dear, it is rather early, you know, barely half-past five. Mind you, he usually comes down, about six o'clock. Would you like a cup of tea, and some breakfast, while you wait?"

Annie agreed readily, for all food touched by Mrs Pott's hands, was incredibly delicious, and she was soon tucking into a big bowl of creamy porridge. Whilst she ate, she explained what had brought her to see Robert so early. Mrs Potts was right, and before long, Robert appeared, yawning, and surprised to see his future bride, so early in the day."

"Hello, Annie, is everything all right?"

Quickly she explained about the missing girl. "I wondered if we could ride after the fair with John and see if we can find Ruth. She may have gone of her own free will, but she might be regretting it now. Anyway, John wants to make sure she's all right. He's gone to ask Jack if he can have the morning off. Would you mind, Robert?"

"No, of course, not. Look, I'll have my breakfast, and then, if Mrs Potts could pack some lunch for us, we could make a day of it. John can borrow a horse, and we'll ride with him to Barnstaple to find Ruth. If that turns out all right, we can have a picnic on the way home. We were going riding today, anyway, weren't we?"

"Yes, thanks, Robert. While you eat, I'll go and find John and get Dodger to saddle up our horses. We can call and tell Mum on our way."

Before long, all three were on their way. Annie was surprised to find that John was a good rider, and he told her, that as a boy, he had often ridden farm horses bareback. They urged their horses up the last hill from where they could look down on the town and see the fair in the distance. The red and white helter-skelter, and the garishly painted roofs of the other fairground rides, were unmistakable.

"Well, at least it's here and not gone somewhere else." Annie turned and smiled at John. "Come on, I'm sure we'll soon find her now."

Barnstaple was a sizeable and prosperous town that drew farmers from far and wide to the weekly market, where livestock was sold. The fair was traditionally held on the common ground at the edge of the town and close to a park with a lake. In the centre of the lake was an island known as Monkey Island, and during the summer, rowing boats could be hired for the trip across.

They trotted down the hill and into the fairground and tethered their horses to a fence. The campsite was a hive of activity as the fair people unloaded and rebuilt their stalls and rides, hurrying to get them ready for the afternoon opening. A man hammering tent pegs into the ground stood up as they approached.

"Is there something I can do for you, folk?" He was a man of about sixty and looked as if he might be in charge. He was unshaven, and his hair was straggly, but he looked clean, and his manner was friendly.

Robert let John do the talking. "I hope you can. We've ridden over from Hartford because my daughter didn't come home last night. We think she might have run away with a man from here, the chap who was in charge of the dobby horses. Have you seen her?"

"No, can't say that I have, but that tent over there is Luke's. There he is look, just outside."

"Thanks, mate. We'll go and have a word with him."

As they approached the tent, Ruth appeared from inside. As soon as she saw her stepfather, her face reddened.

"Now then, Ruth, what are you're playing at? Your mother is beside herself with worry." John spoke angrily.

The girl hung her head and looked ashamed, and the young man left what he was doing and came striding over.

"What's going on? What do you want, Mister?"

"I want to know why my stepdaughter is in your tent. That's what I want to know. She's only fifteen, and her mother is worried to death."

"She came with me of her own free will. I never made her come, did I, Ruth?"

The girl shook her head. "No, I wanted to go with Luke, John. It's not his fault."

"With not a word to your mother, or me, and what of your job at the bakery? It's not good enough, Ruth. Now, are you coming home with me?"

The young man intervened. "No, she isn't, she wants to come away with me, and she's old enough to make up her own mind. You needn't worry, though, I'll look after her."

John looked questioningly at Ruth. "It's up to you, maid; we just wanted to know you're all right and hadn't been taken against your will. Are you sure you want to do this? The fair goes all over the country, and it will be no good if you change your mind in a few weeks and find yourself miles from home. You haven't had long to get to know this young man."

Ruth's lower lip trembled, and tears were bright in her eyes as she looked anxiously at Luke and then back to John. Annie put her arm around Ruth's shoulders.

"Ruth, you must think carefully. If you are sure this is what you want, then it sounds as if John will not stand in your way, but you'll be leaving all your family and friends, and it will be difficult for you to come back if you change your mind. It must be a hard life always on the road."

Ruth stared at her shoes for a few moments, and then raised her head and went to Luke and put her arms around him. "Luke, could you leave the fair and stay in Hartford and get a job?"

"No, I'm sorry, Ruth, it's no use me pretending. I love the fair and travelling all over the country and all my family are here."

"Just as mine are all in Hartford."

"Yes, I know, that's true. It's up to you. I'd like you to come away with me, but it's your choice. I'm afraid I can't live in one place; I'd hate it."

Slowly she withdrew her arms and walked back to her stepfather. "I think I'd better come home, John."

John nodded, and put his arm around her. "I know it's hard, but you're making the right decision, Ruth. Come on, get your bag, and then I'll give you a leg up on old Molly here, and you can ride home behind me."

Annie went into the tent with the girl and helped her pick up her few belongings. "Ruth, did anything happen between you and Luke last night? I mean, is there any chance you could be in the family way?"

Ruth blushed. "No, we haven't done anything like that. I've got my monthly, you know?"

"Well, that's a relief. Come on, let's get going."

Ruth kissed her young man, and they promised to see each other again next year when the fair called again at Hartford.

CHAPTER 20

Robert and Annie rode most of the way back to Hartford with John and Ruth. Halfway back, Ruth changed horses and sat behind Robert so as not to tire John's horse too much. On the outskirts of the village, they dismounted before going their separate ways.

"I can't thank you enough for letting me have the morning off to go and find Ruth and for using the horse, sir." John shook Robert's hand firmly. "I'll make up the hours that I owe in no time at all."

"Thank you, John, just sort it out with Jack, will you? I'm glad we found Ruth safe and sound, but we'll leave you here because we're going the other way."

Ruth climbed up behind John again, and they galloped away. Robert and Annie also remounted their horses and rode through the woods to their favourite picnic spot on the hill overlooking Buzzacott House.

"Oh, just look at that view. It's the best one for miles around. Thank goodness that early rain cleared up." Annie smiled happily at Robert. "Are you hungry?"

"Yes, I'm famished, so let's have lunch straight away." Robert took a rolled-up blanket from his saddle and spread it on the ground, which was still a bit damp. Annie removed a small wicker basket from her horse and set it on the blanket.

"Let's see what Mrs Potts has packed today. Oh, look, thick beef sandwiches and fruit cake. I love your cook, Robert, and I'm going to enjoy her cooking when we're married.

When they had eaten their fill, they lay side by side on the blanket in the hot sun and kissed passionately, until Robert suddenly pulled away from her.

"Come on; we've waited this long, we'd better get moving before we get too carried away. It's going to be difficult enough when we're married, without you finding you're in the family way before the ceremony."

"Mm, yes, I suppose so." Annie sat up reluctantly and glanced down the hill. "Look, there's that woman again. I'm sure it was her we saw at the station. You know, the one Jean gave her baby to. I wonder if she is moving house; I don't think she's been here long."

"Annie, you're so nosy!"

"I'm just curious. Come on then, where are you taking me?"

"Buzzacott woods are the start of my land, so if we ride through them, and then on around the fields, I'd like to show you some of the work I've been doing since I took over the estate."

They mounted their horses and walked them slowly through the woods, for although there was a recognisable bridleway, it was uneven, with many exposed tree roots and low branches. The woods meandered gently downhill towards a humpback bridge across a stream. Near the stream was a small makeshift hut well-hidden, between large boulders, trees, and bushes. They would probably have passed it by unseen had a man not peered out of the doorway as he heard voices.

Annie looked at the man for a moment. "Hello, Sam, I haven't seen you for a long time. How are you?"

The old man smiled at Annie with blackened, broken teeth. His straggly grey hair was dirty and unkempt, and the wrinkles on his face were full of grime. He was thin, and his clothes hung from him and were full of holes. The only tidy part of his attire was his boots.

"Hello, my dear. It's nice to see you. That uncle of yours is not around, is he?"

"No, you're all right, Sam. Are you living here?"

"Aye, for now, until someone moves me on, as they always do. I like it here in the woods, so I'd be obliged if you didn't mention my whereabouts to anyone." Sam eyed Robert anxiously. "Who's your friend, my dear?"

"This is Robert Fellwood, Sam. I'm going to marry him in a couple of weeks, so what do you think of that?" Leaving Sam to digest this information she whispered to Robert. "Can Sam stay here, Robert? I'm sure he's doing no harm?"

Robert dismounted. "Hello, Sam. I own this land, and if you promise me you'll do no damage, I don't mind you staying here as long as you like. Can you do that?"

Sam looked at Robert with interest. "Oh, aye, sir, that would be marvellous. Can you tell the manager that 'tis all right? I'm always careful to make no mess, and I only catch the odd rabbit or two, or perhaps a few fish."

"That's fine, but only you, mind. I don't want all your friends joining you."

"No, sir, I haven't got any friends really, perhaps just young Annie, here. Always been kind to old Sam, she has. Mostly, I prefer my own company."

Annie smiled. "Sam, do you know anything about that big house near here? Buzzacott House?"

Sam's face darkened. "No, not much, only that they sent me packing the other day when I tried to beg some bread. I didn't hang about either because they've got a big dog. Luckily for me, it was chained up, but the woman threatened to set it loose on me if I didn't clear off. I think she would have too; she was most unpleasant."

Robert pressed a few pennies into Sam's hand as they left and was rewarded with a beaming smile. He tried not to flinch at the old man's rank breath. As they rode off, Robert asked Annie how she knew the tramp.

"He used to come begging in the village all the time, and one day he stole a pair of boots from my Uncle George's shop. I bumped into him in the woods when I was dragging home a sack of vegetables, stolen from your garden. Poor old Sam was coughing and wheezing because Uncle George and Constable Folland were chasing him, and he would never have outrun them. I persuaded him to go through the gap in your hedge, and hide in the Manor House gardens. I hid my sack down a badger hole and picked some flowers until the men appeared, and then I said he had gone the other way."

Robert laughed. "You naughty girl, fancy doing that to your uncle."

"Oh, I can't stand my Uncle George, and I was no better than Sam because I'd been stealing as well. Thanks for letting him stay there, though, he's always getting moved on, poor old chap."

By this time, they had reached the edge of the woods, and Robert led the way down a grassy track and stopped at a gateway. "This is one of our biggest fields, but the ground was so marshy and water-logged that we couldn't do much with it. Luckily, I bought a book about farming one day when I was in Exeter, and it explained what to do. It's an interesting book by a chap called Henry Stephens, and I've found some useful information in it. Jack thinks I have these incredible ideas, but actually, they are all from the book. If he could read, I'd let him borrow it. Anyway, last year I got the men to dig deep ditches across the field, and we laid clay drainpipes to channel the water into the stream. It's worked a treat and just look at this crop of wheat we've grown. I think it's flourished because the ground here has never been planted before; we just used to let the cows graze here in the drier months."

Annie picked a sheaf of wheat and rubbed it in her hand. "Looks like it's ripe, too."

"Yes, we're going to harvest it tomorrow, and I want to be there to make sure it goes right. This is our first chance to try out the new reaper that I've bought."

"Oh, yes, of course, your new toy. I've heard the farmhands don't approve."

Robert frowned. "No, they don't, they think it will put them out of work, but it will be so much quicker than cutting it all with a scythe. It's always a struggle to get it all in before it rains. I can't wait to see the reaper working. I've bought a new threshing machine as well, and the men aren't too happy about that either."

Annie laughed at him. "I won't see much of you tomorrow then by the sound of it, but I hope it goes well."

There had been a lot of trouble throughout the country for several years, with riots breaking out in some areas, and threshing machines attacked and destroyed. Threshing normally took place all through the winter and kept many families employed. The new machines were threatening their livelihood.

"Another thing that I found out about in the book is how to rotate the crops. Until last year, we only planted two crops; wheat and barley, and then left the field fallow for a year to rest. There's a new method now named after a chap from Norfolk. He's called Charles Townsend, but people call him "Turnip Townsend".

"Why's that then, does he have a head like a turnip?"

"No, of course not, but he suggests growing turnips and using a four-crop rotation. You see, in this field, we've grown wheat this year, then next year we'll grow clover or ryegrass, then oats or barley, and the fourth year, turnips or swedes. Growing the different crops puts the goodness back into the soil, and you don't have to leave the ground fallow for a year. The best of it is, you can use the turnips and swedes to eat, or feed to the cattle during the winter. It's clever; I just hope it works. Am I boring you?"

"No, I like to hear all about it. What else have you done?"

"If we make our way back now, I'll show you the new animals I've bought."

They galloped back, laughing with exhilaration. Annie's red hair streamed out behind her, and Robert couldn't believe how skilfully she rode after such a short time. She showed no fear, and it was as if she had been born to the saddle. They took their horses to the stable and handed them over to the expert care of Dodger.

"Come on; let's look at the pigsties first. Do you remember when I came to your house to see Henry, the old boar, killed? I was so shocked, but I've got used to it, now. I remember you laughed at me because I was sick."

Annie laughed. "Yes, you were a bit delicate then, weren't you?"

"I suppose so. Now, we have two sorts of pigs at the moment. These are Gloucester Old Spots; they are hardy animals, and they produce good meat. Do you know, people say the spots on them are bruises from falling apples because they are often kept in orchards? I think poor Henry was an Old Spot, wasn't he?"

"Yes, he was. He was a dear old pig. He used to like me scratching his back for him. It's always a shame when they are slaughtered, but people have to eat. As long as they have a good life and are killed quickly, I think that's what matters."

"Yes, I agree. This is Peggy, and she's due to have her piglets in a day or two. Huge, isn't she?" Robert patted her back. "Mind you, the way her teats are bagging up with milk I reckon they could be here by morning. Looks like she's nesting too; see the straw and hay piled up in the corner? She's getting ready."

They moved to the next pigsty. "These are Tamworth pigs and a bit of an experiment. They're not popular these days, but I'm told they were bred from the Old English forest pig. My book says they are exceptionally tasty, so I thought I'd rear a few. As you can see, Suzie, here, had her litter last week."

Ten little piglets were suckling from their mother and squealing loudly as they jostled for the best position. Suzie was a large pig with a long snout, and she was brown and hairy.

"We're too early to see the cows because it's not milking time yet, but I've built up a fine herd of over a hundred shorthorns. Lovely cows they are, big and high standing, but with a good temperament and impressive milk yield. That's why I've built more shippens and taken on extra men to do the milking. There are too many cows now for the milkmaids to do the job in the meadows as they used to. Since the railway came to Devon, we can get the milk to London, and all the other big cities on the train and it makes a good profit. I'm pleased we can employ more men, too. At least it makes up for the Albion reaper taking their work away."

"I think you're very clever, and I know the men think the world of you. Now, I must go home and see my daughter. She'll be feeling neglected, though she loves her Nanny and Liza."

"Yes, all right, just give me a kiss before you go."

They went into a corner of the big barn and embraced before she ran happily down the hill to the Lodge House.

CHAPTER 21

Since Charlie invited her to go riding with him, Eveline had wondered whatever possessed her to agree. In her early twenties, she had been engaged to a young man called Jimmy, but he had been killed by an explosion in the silver mine a few weeks before their wedding. She had known Jimmy all her life and gone to school with him, and they had been inseparable. Following his death, she had withdrawn into herself, and despite several men taking an interest in her over the years, she had spurned all their advances, for none could ever measure up to her beloved Jimmy.

Since her brother, William, had died leaving his three children, and her other brother, Fred, became widowed and left to cope alone with his three, she had moved in with Fred, and looked after them all. This had given her a new lease of life and provided her with the family she never had. She was now in her forties and had never expected, or intended, to ever allow romance to enter her life again, but somehow Charlie Chugg, with his bright blue eyes and wide smile, had melted her heart. She knew if she was completely honest with herself, that her regular visits to Hollyford Farm were not only to see her sick friend but partly in the hope of seeing Charlie.

She had not dared to hope that her feelings would be reciprocated, and now that he had asked her out, she was suddenly so nervous that she didn't know if she could go. She decided to have a chat with Sabina and see what she thought. If she did go, she would need to ask her to look after the children anyway, as they were all home from school at the moment for the summer holidays.

As soon as Sabina opened the door, Eveline could see she was unwell. Her eyes and nose were red and sore, and although she smiled at her friend when she spoke, it was in a hoarse whisper which ended in a bout of frenzied coughing.

"Oh, Sabina, you look terrible, you poor thing."

"Thanks, I like you, too."

"Sorry, but you know what I mean. How long have you been poorly?"

"Since Saturday, but I feel much worse today. It's just a cold, but it has pulled me down. I'm just thankful I don't have to go to work anymore because I'd have had to go if we wanted to eat. We have a lot to thank Robert for. It's ridiculous that I worked in all weathers for years with barely a sniffle, and now, in a warm house, I'm like this. Do you want to come in? I don't want to pass it on to you."

"Oh, I'll risk it if you feel up to a chat?"

Eveline raised her eyebrows questioningly.

"Yes, I'd be glad of the company. Perhaps it will take my mind off it. Come on, I'll put the kettle on."

As they enjoyed a cup of tea, Eveline told Sabina about Charlie asking her to go riding.

"I don't know if I shall go. I mean, at my age, it would be stupid to start a relationship, wouldn't it?"

"Of course, it wouldn't. You're not old, and anyway, why should your age, matter? When are you going?"

"Tomorrow, and I must confess the reason I'm here, was to ask if you could look after the children, but I can see that's out of the question now with you looking so ill, so that settles it. I've left Fred to keep an eye on them for an hour while I came here, but I couldn't leave them with him all day. He'd never get any work done."

"Don't be silly. Of course, I'll have them, and they can play with my lot. Now they're all home from school, it's chaos here anyway, so a few more won't make much difference." Sabina suddenly grinned at her sister-in-law. "I think it's wonderful, and I hope things progress; I'd love to see you married."

"Let's not get carried away; he's only asked me to go riding. Anyway, thanks for the offer, but you aren't well. I do have one other option. I'll ask Mum if I can borrow Charlotte for the day, you know, the girl that had the baby. She misses that child something terrible, so I think she'd enjoy a day with mine. Between you and me, I think Fred is sweet on her, and I'd love him to find another woman, so it wouldn't hurt for them to see a bit more of each other."

"Is Betsey well enough to manage without her?"

"Yes, she's up and about on crutches, and her plaster will be taken off soon."

"Look, if it's a problem, come back, and tell me, and I'll have them. We can't have you missing a hot date!"

Eveline stayed half an hour drinking her tea with Sabina and then went to The Red Lion Inn to see her mother. Betsey was in less pain now and able to hobble around and do a few jobs. She was pleased to hear about Charlie, and like Sabina, was determined that Eveline would have no excuse not to go. She had long wanted to see her daughter settled and happy, but had never thought it would happen.

Charlotte was happy to spend a day with the children, and the next morning she arrived at Fred's house promptly at nine o'clock, having helped Betsey to wash and dress and have her breakfast.

"Morning, Eveline, morning, Fred, it's a beautiful day again; we're having a good summer this year." She turned to the children. "Now, I've been thinking about what we could do today. How about we pack up a picnic and go to the beach?" She was answered by squeals of delight and wide grins.

"Well, that seems to be a popular suggestion." Fred smiled at the girl. "It's good of you to come and look after the children, but you can just take it easy here in the house if you want; they can play in the garden."

"No, I'd love to take them to the beach, and I'm looking forward to it. It will be a day off for me too. Eveline, you be on your way and have a lovely time. I can see to everything, so don't rush back. Take as long as you like; I can even put them to bed, if necessary."

Eveline hugged Charlotte. "Thank you, so much; it's kind of you. Now, children, you be good for Charlotte, or there'll be trouble when I get home. Bye for now, and I'll see you later."

Fred closed the door behind Eveline. "Which beach are you thinking of going to, Charlotte?"

"I think it will have to be Rapparee because I won't be able to carry the picnic as far as Rockham, though it is a better beach. It will be fine, though, we can have fun in the rock pools and build sandcastles."

"Yes, I was just thinking Rockham would be the best one. I'll tell you what you get the picnic packed, and I'll give you all a lift there on the cart and pick you up again later."

"Oh, yes, Daddy, please take us to Rockham; it's much nicer there, and we haven't been for ages. Can you come too?" Rosella put her arms around her father's waist and looked up at him pleadingly with her big brown eyes. She was eight years old and a pretty little girl with blond hair and a peaches and cream complexion, who could twist her daddy around her little finger. "What do you think, Amelia?"

"Yes, I like Rockham beach best. Please come with us, Uncle Fred." Amelia, also eight years old, gazed up at her uncle beseechingly.

"Well, I certainly can't stay with you all day, I have too much work to do, but I don't think I'm going to be able to get out of taking you there now by the sounds of it. What do you think, Charlotte?"

"Oh, yes, I'm happy to go to Rockham. I'll get a picnic ready and some towels and spare clothes because I expect they'll get wet. Now, children see if you can find your sunhats if you have any because I don't want you all getting sunstroke, or sunburnt. Do you have any fishing nets or buckets and spades?"

Within half an hour, the cart was loaded up with the children and all they required for a day at the beach. Charlotte sat up front beside Fred and chatted to him along the journey.

"How do you like working for my mother then?"

"Oh, she's a dear and we get on well. She's been good to me and did you know she's asked me to stay on permanently even when her leg has healed?"

"That's good. Are you going to stay?"

"Yes, I am. I don't think I've ever been happier than I am now living at the inn. I get on with my mother all right, but my father's so strict he's hard to live with. I'd like to stay around here, anyway, just in case I see my baby again."

"Yes, it must have been hard to give her up."

"It's the worst thing I've ever done, and I just can't forget her. Your mother has said that if I can get Doris back, I can keep her at the inn with me, but, of course, I don't know where she is."

"Are you going to ask your aunt where she took her?"

"Yes, I'm trying to pluck up the courage to do just that, but my aunt is not an easy person to get along with. I don't think she'll tell me. She said I'd disgraced the family by having a baby out of wedlock. She won't want me to have the baby back and risk humiliating the family."

"It's not up to her. Would you like me to go with you?"

"Oh, Fred, would you mind? I'd feel so much better with you by my side."

"Yes, of course. We'll sort something out soon. Right, here we are then." Fred reined in the horse and jumped down to lift the smaller children off the cart. "You have a lovely day here, and I'll pick you up later. It's half-past ten now, so if I come back about three o'clock, would that suit you?"

"Yes, that will be long enough. Thanks ever so much, Fred."

Charlotte led the way down the beach carrying the heavy picnic basket, whilst the children followed carrying various sizes of buckets and spades and fishing nets. She found a nice sheltered spot by some rocks and spread a rug on the ground.

"Right, you can all go off and play. Just make sure you can always see me, then I'll be able to see you. I don't want to have to go home and tell your daddy I've lost one of you. Leave your shoes here with me, and go and find some crabs in the rock pools. Let's see who can find the biggest one. I'll sort things out here, and then I'll join you."

The children spent a happy hour looking for crabs and trying to catch the small fish that darted so quickly around the pools. They found several crabs, and Eddie was delighted to find the biggest. At four, he was the youngest, so Charlotte was pleased for him. He was a friendly little boy with the bright ginger hair and green eyes that were familiar characteristics of the Carter family.

"Can we go in the water, Charlotte? It's so hot, and it would be nice to cool off." Llewellyn, or Llewie as he was called, looked longingly at the gentle waves breaking onto the golden sand.

"Well, there's no one else here, so I think you could strip down to your underwear. I've brought spares for all of you so you can change afterwards. You mustn't go out too far, though, because I can't come in with you, and I can't swim. Can any of you swim?"

Llewie and the twins nodded. "Yes, we can, but I promise we won't go out too far."

"All right, then, put your clothes on the blanket, and I'll walk down to the water with you and have a paddle."

The children loved the water, splashing each other and swimming in on the waves. It was a calm day, and the tide was coming in over the hot sand, making the water a pleasant temperature.

"Charlotte, look, what's this?"

"Now, are you, Joe or Matthew?" I really can't tell."

"I'm Matthew."

"Well, Matthew, I think it's a jellyfish, and I've heard that they sting, so don't touch it."

Matthew shouted to the others. "Hey, come and see this jellyfish."

The children looked in awe at the large jellyfish. It was about the size of a dinner plate and a brownish-purple in colour. They couldn't make up their minds whether it was dead or alive but were certainly not going to touch it to find out.

"Just be careful if you see any more and don't touch them. They have long tentacles hanging down, and they sting. Anyway, shall we have our picnic now?" The children nodded their heads in agreement, for they were hungry. They sat in a circle with their towels draped around their shoulders. The sun was hot, and they soon dried out, the sand coating their legs like icing sugar. When they had finished their lunch of boiled egg sandwiches and bread pudding, Charlotte took them for a long walk along the shoreline, and they collected seashells in their buckets.

At around three o'clock, Fred arrived with the cart. The children groaned when they saw him coming down the road, for they didn't want to go home.

"Oh no, look Dad's here already."

"Never mind, perhaps we can do it again one day." Charlotte smiled at the group of children. "I shall tell your daddy you've all been good because you have; I've enjoyed the day."

As they travelled home on the cart, Fred thanked Charlotte for looking after the children.

"It was a pleasure; we've had a lovely day so any time you want me to do it again, please just ask."

"That's good to know because I have a suspicion there may be other days that Eveline will want to spend with Charlie. Anyway, I'm working at home for the rest of the day, so if you want to get back to the inn, you can." He turned to look at her. "Of course, it would be nice if you'd like to stay for tea? Eveline made a beef casserole for us yesterday, so it only has to be warmed."

Charlotte smiled happily. "That would be nice, Fred, I'd like that."

CHAPTER 22

Having left the children in safe hands, Eveline walked to the inn and saddled her horse. As she rode to Hollyford Farm, she became more nervous. When she arrived, Charlie was looking out of the kitchen window, and he waved and smiled widely.

"Hello, Eveline, it's good to see you. Fred didn't mind, did he?"

"No, of course not. Charlotte's looking after the children and she's going to take them to the seaside, so everyone's happy. Is it all right if I go and say hello to Jane before we go?"

"Yes, of course, but I'm afraid she's very poorly. Alfred's sitting with her."

Eveline had a quick word with Maria and then hurried up the stairs to see her friend. She knocked softly on the bedroom door, and Alfred called to her to come in. The room smelt stale and unpleasant, though it was scrupulously clean.

"Hello, Alfred. How are you?" Jane lay with her eyes closed. She looked even worse than she had the week before, and Eveline could see that she would not be with them much longer.

"I'm all right, lass, but as you can see Jane's very poorly. She's taking a lot of medicine because she's in so much pain, and then it knocks her out. She's barely been conscious for days, but the doctor says it's best this way. I wish it was me instead of her."

"Oh, Alfred, I'm so sorry; poor Jane. It's so hard for you too. Would you like me to stay with you today instead of going riding with Charlie? We can do that anytime."

"No, you go off and enjoy yourself. Charlie's been looking forward to you coming for days." Alfred smiled a watery smile. "You do know he's quite besotted with you, don't you?"

Eveline blushed, and Alfred grinned widely. "I see the feeling's reciprocated then, and that's good because nothing would make Jane happier than you two getting together. You go off and have a lovely day. I don't think Jane's going to wake for hours and, anyway, I'm not leaving her side. Charlie and Jimmy have done all the outside work that has to be done, and Maria will look after everything else."

Eveline squeezed his hand and smiled at him. "All right then, Alfred, if you're sure. I'll come and see Jane when we get back; perhaps she'll be awake then."

She returned downstairs to the kitchen, where Charlie was waiting for her. "Alfred insists we go out for the day although Jane is so poorly. I'll look in on her again when we get back. Maria, look after Alfred, won't you? Make sure he eats something." The girl nodded.

"Yes, of course, I will, don't worry. You two get off and have a nice ride; I've packed you up some food."

Charlie picked up the picnic bag and led the way out of the kitchen. Once outside the door he tentatively reached for Eveline's hand. "Where would you like to go? Any ideas?"

"What about Hangman's Hill? There's a fantastic view of the coast from the top. I've not been up there for such a long time, but I know a nice sheltered spot for a picnic. It's about five miles. What about you, though? Do you have anywhere in mind?"

"No, I hoped you would suggest somewhere, and that sounds perfect. I know the place you mean, but I haven't been there since I returned from the sea. Hangman's Hill it is then."

Charlie secured the picnic bag to his saddle then helped Eveline onto her horse. She smiled at him. It was a long time since anyone had looked after her in such a way, and although she was perfectly capable of mounting her horse independently, she enjoyed the attention.

Leaving the farm track behind they were soon trotting across the wild and rugged landscape of Exmoor, and when the opportunity arose, they let the horses have their heads and galloped down one hill and up the other side. Charlie reined in his horse laughing.

"You're a good horsewoman, Eveline. I thought you said you hardly ever ride?"

"No, not these days, but as a youngster, I rode a lot, and you don't forget, do you? Come on, I'll race you to the top of the next hill; that's where I think we should have our picnic." Before she had finished speaking, she kicked her horse and was off like the wind, laughing. Charlie was not far behind, but she had a head start on him, and try as he might, he couldn't catch her. At the top of the hill, she reined in her horse and dismounted, still laughing. Her hair had escaped from its bun, and her face was flushed with exertion. Her eyes danced as grinning widely, she tethered her horse to a tree. He thundered to a stop beside her.

"Hey, I hope you're not going to brag in Red Lion that you outraced me; I'll never live it down."

"I might, unless you can persuade me otherwise."

Needing no further encouragement, Charlie put his arms around her. "Hmm, I can but try then, I suppose." He kissed her gently on the lips, and as she melted into his embrace, kissed her more passionately.

At length, she pulled away and smiled at him. "I think you've convinced me not to tell tales. Shall we find a nice spot, and have something to eat? I'm starving."

They sat on a rug that Charlie removed from beneath his saddle and were soon munching on ham sandwiches.

"These sandwiches are nice, aren't they? Maria's baking is improving. This bread is as good as any I could make."

"Yes, she looks after us well. She's much better at everything since you started giving her lessons."

"She's keen to learn. It sounds like no one had taken the time to show her before. I was sorry to see how ill Jane is though, and you have to feel for Alfred."

"Yes, I know; he hates to see her suffering, and I think when the end does come naturally, he'll be sad but also relieved."

"It's a good job you've come home to live, Charlie. I know he has Jimmy to help, but I think he's glad to have you around. Don't you miss the sea, though? I know some sailors can't get used to life on land again."

"I do miss it, but I don't want the long voyages anymore. It's a hard life, and now I'm getting on a bit, I'd rather be on dry land with plenty of fresh food and water. I still go out in my fishing boat, though, and sometimes sail across to France for a few days."

"Do you? What do you go there for?"

Charlie grinned. "There are some things best not talked about, but I expect you can guess?"

"Oh, I see. Do be careful then, won't you? If you got caught smuggling, you'd go to prison, you know, or may even be transported."

"Don't you worry; it's a little family tradition started by my great grandfather who farmed at Hollyford. My grandfather and father too. Alfred never cared for the sea, so it was right he took on the farm, but I always loved going out in the boat with my father and grandfather. They taught me all I know; in every sense of the word. What I get up to is minor and hurts no one. It's just a bit of fun, and it helps to make ends meet."

They had an enjoyable day, but as they slowly trotted up the farm lane, they saw Doctor Luckett's horse tethered.

"Looks like the doctor's here. I hope Jane's all right."

Maria met them at the door. "Jane's much worse. She hasn't woken up all day, not even to take her medicine. Alfred and Jimmy are sitting with her."

Eveline frowned. "Oh dear, do you think I should go up, or not?"

"I think Alfred would like you to. I'll wait down here with Maria, though. You don't want too many up there." Charlie squeezed her hand reassuringly.

Eveline knocked, and entered the room just in time to see the doctor pulling the sheet up over Jane's face.

"Oh no, oh, Alfred, Jimmy, I'm so sorry." She hugged the old man and then his son, and they all sobbed, quite unable to speak. "At least she's at peace now, Alfred."

"Aye, she is that maid, and she's not suffering now. I couldn't wish for her to carry on as she was. Eveline, it's a lot to ask, but could you help me to organise everything? It's what Jane wanted. She said, Eveline will help you sort things out when I'm gone, Alfred, so make sure you let her."

This brought fresh tears from Eveline as she nodded. "Yes, of course, I will, Alfred, but we can talk about that later. For now, let's go downstairs and have a cup of tea. Come on." She took the old man by the arm and led him slowly from the room. The doctor gave her a thankful nod and said he would be on his way.

Eveline stayed and had a cup of tea, and she and Charlie told Alfred and Jimmy where they had been for their picnic, but inevitably the conversation soon returned to Jane and the plans for her funeral.

"Well, naturally, she'll be buried in the churchyard in Hartford, but I'm not sure about the wake. I did think we could have it here, but it would be a lot for Maria to cope with because there'll be a lot of mourners. Jane reckoned it would be best to have it at the inn, especially as it's next to the church. It would save folk having to travel out here to the farm. "What do you think, Eveline?" Alfred raised his watery blue eyes to hers.

"I think that's a good idea, Alfred. Mum thought the world of Jane, and I know she'd be more than pleased to put on a good spread. I'll fetch Matilda now, to do what is necessary for Jane. Hopefully, Fred will bring her on the cart and then he can organise a coffin. Would you like me to see the vicar to arrange a time for the funeral? I could ride out again tomorrow to tell you the details."

"That would be grand if you don't mind. Thank you so much, Evie. It's one thing less for me to worry about."

"I'd better be going now; Charlie or Fred and Charlotte will think I've run away. Don't worry about any of it, Alfred. I'll sort it all out and see you again sometime tomorrow."

Charlie went to the door with Eveline and kissed her briefly on the lips. "Thanks for coming today, Evie. I enjoyed our day out though it's a pity it had such a sad ending. I'll look forward to seeing you tomorrow."

On her way home, Eveline called in to tell Sabina about Jane, for the two women had been close. She had to pass the Lodge House, anyway.

When Sabina opened the door, Eveline could see that her friend was still poorly. "Hello, Sabina, are you any better?"

"My throat's a bit better, thanks, but this cough is driving me mad and keeping me up half the night so I'm tired. Anyway, never mind that, how did you get on?" Sabina grinned, "I want all the details."

Eveline smiled. "There's time enough for that, though I can tell you I had a lovely day with Charlie. I called in to tell you that Jane passed away earlier. She was asleep when I got there this morning, and apparently, she never woke up again. You can imagine how upset Alfred is; they'd been married for over fifty years."

"Oh, poor Alfred, but I'm glad Jane's not suffering anymore. She's had a bad time of it for the last few months. Thanks for coming to tell me."

"I was passing the door anyway, and I knew you'd want to know. I'm organising the funeral for Alfred, and I've agreed to ask Mum if we can have the wake at the inn. Now, I must go because I've been out all day, and I don't want to take advantage of Charlotte's good nature, but I'll call in again soon for a chat."

As Sabina saw Eveline out of the house, two carriages from the Manor House passed by. The first contained Lord and Lady Fellwood and Sarah, and the second, Victoria, Frank, and their two young children.

"I wonder where they're all off to." Eveline looked at her friend, questioningly.

"From what Annie tells me, they're off to London. They are only going to avoid Annie and Robert's wedding. Pathetic, isn't it? You'd think they'd want to be at their only son's wedding, but, of course, they don't approve of Annie."

"Well, it will probably be all the more enjoyable for us if they don't go."

"Yes that's true. Well, their loss is our gain."

CHAPTER 23

The next day, Eveline went to see the Reverend Rees to arrange Jane's funeral, and they agreed it should be held on the following Monday. They both felt that the sooner it was dealt with, the better. The vicar had a busy week ahead as it was Annie and Robert's wedding on the following Saturday. Eveline then went to see her mother about the wake.

"Yes, of course, it must be held here. Mind you, I'll have to get some extra help in because the Chuggs are a big family, and there will be a lot of mourners, and that will mean a lot of food. I can't stand on this leg for long, and Charlotte can't do it all. I must think who I can ask." Betsey sat down, looking thoughtful.

"Why don't you ask Sabina and Annie if they would help on Sunday? I'm sure Liza can manage the children for a few hours, and I can come too because Fred will be at home all day to look after our children. With Charlotte as well, we'll soon get it organised."

"Oh yes, of course, that would be fine."

"Good, I'll ride over to the farm now to tell Alfred the arrangements."

Sabina and Annie were happy to help, and on Sunday morning they met in the kitchen of the inn, where Betsey took charge.

"Right, Charlotte bought all the ingredients yesterday, so all we have to do is the cooking. We've got sausagemeat for sausage rolls, beef skirt for pasties, and bacon and egg for pies. Then we could bake some cakes and scones, and lastly, a few puddings. What do you all prefer doing?"

Sabina smiled. "I'm best at the savoury stuff, so perhaps Eveline and I could do the sausage rolls, pasties, and pies. Annie and Charlotte, maybe you could make some cakes?"

The two girls glanced at each other, and Charlotte nodded. "Yes, I'm happy making cakes, especially if Annie can help me."

"That sounds good then. Perhaps we should get all that done and then make a few puddings between us. I can sit and peel the potatoes and onions, and cut up the meat, so I'll do that." Betsey plonked herself down on a chair at the table, and Charlotte fetched the vegetables for her.

Charlotte was glad Sabina had suggested she work with Annie, for they were around the same age. "What sort of cakes do you want to make, Annie?"

"I don't mind, but I'm probably better at rock buns than sponges. How about you?"

"I can make a couple of sponges. If there's time, we could make some scones and cut-rounds, as well; they always go down a treat."

"Good idea. We'd better get cracking then. How do you like working at the inn?"

"Oh, I love it here, and your granny's so kind. She's offered me a permanent job, even when her leg is better."

"That's good, are you going to stay?"

"Yes, I am. I like it here, and I'm going to try to get my baby back. I hated giving her up, but my aunt left me no choice at the time. Betsey says, if I can find her, I can keep her here. Fred is going with me to my aunt's house soon, to try and persuade her to tell us where she took Doris. She's such a fierce and scary lady, I'll be glad of his support."

"Oh, well good luck. I can't even imagine what you went through, giving up your child. I'm sure I couldn't have parted with Selina. I'm glad Fred is going with you, too. He likes you, and he was pleased you gave the children such a lovely day at the seaside."

Charlotte blushed. "What do you mean? How do you know he likes me?"

"It's pretty obvious from the way he looks at you. Haven't you noticed?"

"No, not really."

"How about you? Do you like him?"

"Yes, of course, I like him. He's been so kind, and it was him that rescued me when I was about to give birth to Doris in a gateway."

"What I mean is, do you really like him?" Annie grinned at her, and Charlotte blushed again and nodded.

"In that case, I'm going to suggest to him that I'd like you to come to my wedding, and perhaps he could bring you."

"Oh no, you can't do that."

"I can, and I will, and I think he'll be pleased. It will be nice for you, anyway. The reception is going to be at the Manor House, and I can tell you the food will be amazing because Mrs Potts is a wonderful cook. We were thinking of having the reception here, but there will be too many people, and anyway now that Robert's family have gone to London, we can do what we like. Do say you will come."

"See what Fred says, and if he wants to ask me, he can. Do you think Betsey will give me the time off?"

"Yes, I'm sure she will; she's my granny after all."

By the end of the afternoon, Betsey's larder was full of pies, pasties, and sausage rolls, and the table was laden with cakes. They had also made two large trifles and dozens of scones and cut-rounds, which would be eaten with clotted cream and jam. When they had done all the washing up, the women sat around the table and enjoyed a well-earned cup of tea.

The funeral was arranged for ten o'clock, and unfortunately, it was raining heavily. Jane's six sons raised the coffin shoulder high and carried it into the church. Come the end, she had weighed next to nothing, and there was no need for so many bearers, but they all wanted to do this one last thing for their mother. Eveline had somehow found time to decorate the church with wildflowers and other blooms from various people's gardens, and it looked and smelt beautiful. She knew Jane would have appreciated it, for she loved her flowers.

The church was packed, with many people standing and some unable to get inside at all. Alfred and Jane had lived in the village all their life and everyone knew them. Poor Alfred wept throughout the service, and he was not alone. On behalf of Alfred, the vicar invited the mourners to The Red Lion for the wake, and after the burial, they all trooped across the road to the inn. With her mother still not very mobile, Eveline took charge, and rushed around, refilling plates and offering cups of tea to those who did not want ale. As the crowds began to thin, Alfred called her over.

"Come here a minute, Evie, I want a word with you. Thank you so much for sorting everything out for me; I couldn't have faced it without you. You must let me know what I owe your mother too; she's put on a lovely spread."

"I was fond of Jane and I'm going to miss her, but I'll still come over and see you now and then, if that's all right, Alfred? I'll let you know what you owe Mum, too."

"Yes, of course, you must. Mind you, I think it might be our Charlie you want to see the most." The old man smiled at her. "It would be lovely if you two made a go of it. Jane would have been tickled pink, and it would be so good for Charlie. Anyway, I wanted to ask you something. I know we had twelve children, but our daughters are all married with families of their own now, and Jane always looked on you as another daughter. Is there any chance you would consider coming to live at the farm and become my housekeeper? Maria is a willing girl, but she's young and needs someone to tell her what to do. You have been so good at teaching her to cook, and helping while Jane was ill, it would be wonderful if you could be there all the time. What do you think?"

Eveline took his arm. "Oh, Alfred, I would enjoy that, and I'd love to look after you, but I can't. You see, I live with our Fred and take care of his three children, and also William's three. He couldn't manage on his own and go out to work. Then, of course, I'm spending a bit of time with Charlie, now, and it wouldn't be right for me to live under the same roof now, would it?"

"Oh, yes, of course, you do. I'd forgotten. Never mind, but if you ever want a job, you let me know."

"I'll carry on teaching Maria to cook, but she's coming on, and I think she'll manage well. Now, if you'll excuse me, I just want a quick word with Annie before she goes. It's her wedding on Saturday, and I want her to try her dress on once more."

Sabina and Annie, loaded down with leftover food, were about to leave when Eveline caught up with them.

"Annie, wait a minute; I need to speak to you. Hold on."

Eveline hurried over. "Annie, I want you and the bridesmaids to try on the dresses once more before the wedding. Could you come tomorrow? That would give me time to do any last-minute alterations before Saturday then."

"Yes, of course, no problem."

"My goodness, you're loaded down with food. Mum's given me loads to take home, too. We made far too much; still, it's better to have too much than too little. Fred's gone to get the cart; why don't you have a lift back with us to save you carrying all this?"

"Oh, thanks, that would be a real help. Is that all right with you, Mum?"

Sabina nodded. "Yes, thanks, that will save our arms. I'll get Fred to drop me off at the Webber's house, though because I want to see how Peter is getting on. I've not seen him for a few days, and I thought I'd take him this apple pie."

Peter was delighted to see Sabina. "Aw, you never come empty-handed, do you, maid? You have a heart of gold, you do, but I expect you've been told that before? I'm glad you came, though, because I've been wanting to show you this."

A leather harness was attached to each of Peter's forearms. His left arm finished above the elbow, and on this arm, the harness had a hook embedded into it. On his right arm, which finished halfway down his forearm, there was also a harness and, inserted into this one, was a metal fork, which he was currently using to eat his sausages and potatoes.

"Oh, Peter, that's amazing! Look at you, feeding yourself. I'm so pleased for you."

Tears were running down the old man's wrinkled cheeks as he spiked a cold sausage and picked it up and bit a piece off. Despite the tears, he had a wide grin.

"Oh, my dear, you have no idea what this means to me. Just to be able to scratch my nose is amazing. I'll never be able to repay you for making all this possible. You have truly changed my life. The hook is permanently fixed to the harness, but on my right hand, I can slot in the fork or a knife or spoon, or even my paintbrush. Just to be able to feed myself makes me feel so much better. I was so helpless before."

Tears were running down Sabina's cheeks too, by this time, as she hugged the old man.

"Francis and Seth have done a wonderful job between them, and they wouldn't take a penny from me; I'm so grateful.

"How are you getting on with the harness, though? I was a bit worried it would be uncomfortable and chafe you."

"It is rubbing a bit, but I'm getting used to it, and it will wear in eventually. Arthur helps me on with it before he goes to work, and he's padded it out with some soft rags where I'm a bit sore. I'm getting quite good at changing the implements on the right arm with my teeth, though my language leaves a bit to be desired sometimes." He grinned broadly at her. "I'm going to paint you a picture, now that I've got a bit more control over the brush. You can hang it in your fancy new house then."

"I'd love to, and I can't wait to see it. Is Arthur not home yet?"

"No, he's been working overtime all week because he's asked for a few days off. He's off on a fishing trip tomorrow with Charlie Chugg."

"Oh, that will be nice for them. Mind you, the weather doesn't look too good. Is there anything I can do for you before I go?"

"No, I'm fine. Christopher will be home from work at any minute, but thanks, anyway. Please call in again soon; I know Arthur will be sorry to have missed you."

The old man winked and grinned at her knowingly.

CHAPTER 24

The next day the weather was atrocious, and it was hard to believe it was July and not February. High winds blew the torrential rain horizontally across the hills, and few folk ventured out. On the farms, the labourers brought in as many animals as they could and tried to find jobs to do undercover.

Annie wrapped cloaks around Mary, Helen, and Selina, and taking their hands, battled against the wind to walk to Fred's house to try on their dresses for the wedding. Eveline was looking out of the window and saw them coming.

"Oh, my goodness, what a day. Come in and dry yourselves by the fire. You can't put the dresses on until you are properly dry, or you will ruin them. I just hope it's not like this on Saturday."

Annie took off her cloak and shook it in the porch before helping the children to do the same.

"Goodness no, it's so rough out there, today. Still, it's nice and warm in here. You'd never think it was mid-summer. The waves on the sea are enormous."

A small frown clouded Eveline's face.

"What's the matter, Aunty Evie? You look worried. You're not planning on going to the seaside, are you?"

Eveline paused before answering. "Just a minute, Annie, I can't hear myself think. Children, why don't you go

168

upstairs and play in the bedrooms? There's no room for all of us down here. Amelia and Rosella have some dolls, and a dolls house, you girls could play with, or perhaps you could all play cards, or something?"

As the children tore off up the stairs she turned to Annie.

"I shouldn't say anything, but I know I can trust you to keep this to yourself. Charlie Chugg and Arthur Webber are going off on a fishing trip today and will be away for a few days. The thing is, it's not just a fishing trip because they are sailing to France, and you know what that means. I'm worried because the weather is so bad, and it's a long way. I'm hoping they've decided not to go."

"Well, Charlie was at sea for years, and he's an experienced sailor, so I'm sure he won't take any unnecessary risks. As regards the other business, smuggling's been going on for donkey's years, and I've never heard of anyone around here getting caught. You like him, don't you?"

Eveline blushed. "Yes, I'm sure you're right, and he is a good sailor. I must confess I have become quite fond of Charlie. Do you think that's silly for a woman of my age?"

"No, of course, not. Anyway, shall we have a cup of tea before we deal with the dresses? The children have settled down, so we might as well leave them while they're quiet."

Charlie and Arthur met at Charlie's boat at dawn. Charlie grinned at Arthur as he came on board, and they had to shout to hear each other, for the strong wind whipped their words away.

"I didn't expect the weather to be this bad today, did you, Charlie? Do you think we should leave it for another day; the sea is extremely rough."

"It is pretty awful, but we can't cancel now because the men will be expecting to meet us on the French coast in a few days. They'll guess why, if we don't turn up, but it's dangerous for them to hang on to the goods any longer than they need to. The excise men are taking far too much interest in these matters lately."

"You still intend to go, then?"

"Yes, if you're willing. It's a long trip from here to France, and I'll need your help, especially in this weather, so I can't go without you. In any case, you've asked for the time off work now. The wind's blowing in the right direction, though, so we should make good time. We'll sail along the north coast of Devon and Cornwall, then around Land's End and the Lizard, and on across the channel to France. The trip will take us a few days, but I've put plenty of food onboard, and there are several oilskins we can wrap ourselves up in. Hopefully, this storm will blow itself out in a few hours."

"All right, then, I know Ned is hoping we make the crossing because he's running out of brandy, and unless you get it for him, it's so expensive."

The first part of the journey was very rough, and even Charlie was surprised at the strength of the wind, and the powerful waves, considering the time of year. However, he loved every minute and realised just how much he had missed the exhilaration of battling with the elements. As time went by, they took it in turns to sail the boat, whilst the other got a few hours of rest. Eventually, the weather cleared up, and to their relief, the sun came out warming them. As they made their way across the channel, they could, at long last, just make out the French coastline.

"The cove we want is just around the next headland. I know the landowner, and for a bottle of brandy or two, he's happy to look the other way. It's nice and sheltered once we get nearer to land, but we just need to be mindful of the rocks; they're treacherous along this coast if you don't know what you are doing."

Skilfully, Charlie sailed the boat safely into a small cove and moored it to a nearby tree. Arthur was impressed at the way Charlie handled the boat.

"I'll just go and tell the farmer we've arrived, and then he can pass the message on. Hopefully, the men will bring the goods later when it's dark. Can you stay here, and keep an eye on the boat, Arthur?"

"Yes, of course. I'll get some food ready for when you get back."

It wasn't long before Charlie returned, smiling. "That's good. Everything is arranged, and the men will be here around midnight. We've time for a spot of fishing now, Arthur. If we get stopped on the way back, it looks better if we've got a good catch to show. Not only that, but we can sell the fish in the village."

The men spent an enjoyable few hours fishing and then settled down to get some sleep, for they knew they would have a hard night ahead of them. When they awoke, it was dark, and they ate some bread and dripping and washed it down with a mug of ale. By the dim light of the moon, Charlie kept a close eye on the cliff path, and it wasn't long before he saw four men approaching leading donkeys laden with boxes and kegs of brandy. He greeted the men warmly. They clearly all knew each other well.

"Right, Arthur, if you can help unload the donkeys and get this lot on the boat, we'll be on our way in no time."

Arthur and three of the men swiftly moved all the contraband from the patiently waiting animals into the boat. Charlie and the fourth man stepped to one side, and Charlie handed him a packet.

"Here you are, Louis, check it if you want, but it's all there as we agreed last time."

"Your word is good enough for me, Charlie; our families have been doing business long enough, non?"

"Indeed, they have, my friend, now thank you for all these goods. We'll be on our way in no time and leave you in peace. I'll send word to you when I'm coming again. Probably in about three months if that's all right?"

"Ah oui, mon ami, bon chance."

The two men shook hands and helped the others to finish loading the boat. Within minutes, Charlie deftly hoisted the sail, and the boat slowly made its way out of the cove to the open sea.

"They seem a friendly bunch for Frenchmen," said Arthur.

"Aye, they're trustworthy men, and fortunately, they speak good English. I can get by in French, but it's so much easier if they speak English. Lazy of me, I suppose. Now, we'll get moving because the French get nervous and prefer us gone, and I'd like to get across the channel through the night. I'm always happier when I'm in sight of the English coastline. Looks like we're going to be lucky with the wind too, it's changed direction just at the right time for us to make good time going home.

Back in Hartford, Annie and Eveline put the new bridesmaids' dresses on the three excited girls.

"Stand still for a minute, Selina. Just let me do up these buttons, and then we'll see what you look like."

The three little girls stood in a row, and Annie and Eveline surveyed them critically.

"What do you think, Annie, are you pleased with them? Do you think they need any alterations?" Eveline sounded anxious.

"Oh, Aunty Evie, you have done such a good job; they look amazing. Do you have a mirror?"

Yes, there's one in my bedroom. It's not full length, but they'll be able to see most of themselves. Come on, girls, come upstairs, and you can see how you look. Pick up your dresses now, and walk nicely. I don't want you to trip and rip them."

In the bedroom, the girls took turns to survey their reflections in the mirror. They couldn't believe they looked so elegant, just like young ladies. Annie swept Helen's blond hair up in her hands.

"What do you think? Should they have their hair tied up or hanging down?"

"They've all got nice hair, but it's very fine. It might be less trouble to leave it hanging down. What about if we made a headdress of flowers to rest on top of their heads? A few white rosebuds with some lavender would look nice with their dresses."

"Oh, yes, perfect; what a good idea. If there are not enough flowers in the Lodge House garden, I'll pick a few from the Manor House gardens." She grinned. "At least I won't have to crawl through a hole in the hedge now, and steal them."

"Annie, you didn't?"

"Ah, Aunty Eveline, you'd be surprised at what I did to stop the family from starving after Dad died, but the less said the better. Now, let's get you, girls, out of these fine clothes, and then I'll put my dress on, fingers crossed it fits."

Annie was equally pleased with her dress. Made of cream silk, it was a simple dress that accentuated her slim figure perfectly. She circled in front of the mirror, critically.

"What do you think? Will I do?" Her green eyes sparkled with happiness.

"You'll more than do; you look amazing. Now, girls when Annie gets out of the carriage on her wedding day and walks into the church and down the aisle, you three will have to carry this train for her to save it from getting dirty. Can you pick it up and have a little practice?"

Obediently, Mary, Helen, and Sabina clutched a piece of the fine material in their hands, and Annie led the small procession around the room.

"Thank you so much, Aunty Evie; you've done a wonderful job."

"It wasn't just me, you know; Matilda did a lot of the sewing, too."

"Yes, of course, and I haven't forgotten. I'll call round soon and thank her. At least now, we know they all fit nicely. Anyway, we had better get going. I want to call in the shop for a few things on the way home because it will save going out again later in this weather."

Annie hurried the girls along to the shop. As she passed The Red Lion, she saw her grandfather, Ned, wheeling some empty barrels out from his shed and waved to him. She crossed the lane with the children, and they stood in the shed doorway to shelter from the rain.

"Hello, Grandad, are you all right?"

"Yes, I'm fine, thank you, Annie; what weather we're having, though. I hope this rain will clear up before your wedding at the weekend. I'm looking forward to it. Who would ever have thought that old Ned Carter would be going to a wedding reception at the Manor House?"

"You'll be welcome, Grandad. Make sure you eat as much as you can."

"Oh, I will, maid, I will, I've heard about Ethel Potts cooking, but I never thought I'd sample it. I can't wait to see you happily married and settled at last; you deserve it."

Annie hugged him as he reached into his pocket and found a sweet for each of the girls.

He grinned at Annie. "I suppose you want one too, maid? Never could resist one of your Grandad's toffees, could you?"

"You know me too well, Grandad. See you on Saturday. Give my love to Granny."

"I will, Annie. We've just come back from the hospital to get the plaster taken off her leg. She's so pleased they've removed it, though I think it was a bit too soon, myself. Her leg kept itching, and it was driving her mad, not being able to scratch it properly. Mind you, she did her best with her knitting needle, and I'm sure she shouldn't have. It's marvellous what they've done, though. I don't mind telling you, when I saw how bad a break it was, I never thought she would walk again, especially at her age. She'll have to be careful for a few weeks until it strengthens."

"Oh, that's good, tell her I'll come and see her soon."

At the shop, Annie purchased some soap, tea, and flour. The bell on the shop door jangled as she was being served, and she turned to see who had come in. It was John Cutcliffe's wife, Noeleen, with her daughters, Ruth and Susanna.

"Oh, Annie, I'm glad I've seen you. I wanted to thank you for helping John get our Ruth back. Silly girl, going off like that with a practical stranger."

"Mum, he wasn't a stranger. I got to know him through the week the fair was here, and he's a nice young man."

"So, he might be, but a week's no time at all, Ruth. You should have known better than to just go off and leave me to worry about you. Mind you, he should have known better than to take you. Anyway, Annie, thank you so much, and I hope you'll be happy with Master Robert."

"It was no trouble at all, Noeleen, and I'm glad everything worked out all right in the end. How is Clarice getting on at the Manor House?"

"Oh, she's happy, thank you, and now she lives in, there's one less mouth for me to feed. I think it's hard work, though, from what she tells me."

"Good, I'm glad she's getting on all right. No doubt I'll see a bit more of her when I'm married and living there. Right, come on, girls let's get home in case the heavens open again, though I do believe it's going to dry up. Goodbye, ladies."

After waving Annie and the girls off, Eveline carefully hung the dresses in her wardrobe, thinking that as soon as it dried up, she'd get Fred to take them to the Lodge House ready for the wedding on Saturday. She would be relieved once the garments had gone, and were no longer her responsibility. She heard the back door open and called out.

"Is that you, Fred? Have you come home for your dinner?"

"Aye, it's me, and yes, I am hungry. What have we got?"

"I've made a chicken and leek pie with the leftovers from yesterday's roast dinner. It's in the oven, along with some roast potatoes that I've rewarmed, so we can have it now if you like?"

"Yes, please. I'm not working this afternoon because I'm taking Charlotte over to Warkley to see her aunty. She wants to ask her where she took the baby. It was a dirty trick sending the girl out on an errand like that and then getting rid of the child. It wasn't hers to part with."

"Perhaps she thought she was doing the right thing at the time. You know, wanted to spare Charlotte from having to hand over the child, herself?"

"That could be it, I suppose, but from what I've heard of her, it doesn't sound as if she has a kind bone in her body. I'm not looking forward to meeting her, but she'd better not mess us about because I'm not leaving without an answer."

"I think you're sweet on Charlotte, Fred."

"I must confess I do enjoy her company."

"It would be lovely if you found someone new to share your life with, Fred. What you went through with Lucy was so awful, and you stayed faithful and devoted to her the whole time, and not many would."

"Yes, of course, I did. I loved her, and she was so different before she became ill. She would never have harmed the children if she was in her right mind."

"No, I know, she wouldn't. It's difficult to understand, but it does happen. Anyway, let's eat."

Eveline called the six children in to wash their hands and sit around the table. The cousins, Rosella and Amelia, both eight years old, sat together with Eddie, the youngest, on one side of the table, and the three older boys, Llewie, Joe, and Matthew sat on the other side. Eddie wriggled in his seat and fidgeted.

"Eddie, I've told you before, now sit still. You need to behave at mealtimes, or you won't get any dinner."

"But, Daddy, Llewie keeps kicking me under the table."

Fred looked sternly at his eldest son. "Do you want me to send you to your room hungry, young man? Because I will. Why don't you behave, like your cousins, here? I never have to tell them off, do I?"

"No, Dad, I'm sorry."

Llewie looked anything but sorry and lowered his eyes to his plate. He sneaked a look at Matthew and Joe, but they were steadfastly ignoring him. Llewie found it tiresome that all three of his cousins were so well behaved; it always made him look worse than ever when he was naughty. However, he had no notion of what Joe, Matthew, and Amelia, had gone through, living in a workhouse in London before his father and Aunty Eveline had found them. They were so grateful to live with Fred and Eveline that they were careful not to put a foot wrong for fear of being sent back to London.

"Mm, Eveline, this is lovely; even better than the roast, I think, and that's saying something. You cook just like Mum does."

"Of course, I do, she taught me everything I know."

CHAPTER 25

Fred harnessed his old horse, Dolly, and hitched her up to the cart. It was a good two miles to where Charlotte's Aunty Joan lived in Warkley, so it would be quicker than walking. He patted Dolly and gave her a carrot as she nuzzled his hand. "Come on, then, old girl, no cartload of wood or a coffin to pull today. Should be an easy afternoon for you. You deserve it; you're a good girl, aren't you?" The horse munched happily on the carrot and stood quietly as Fred did up the straps. As he approached The Red Lion, Fred pulled on the reins.

"Whoa then, Dolly, wait here a minute, whilst I fetch Charlotte; she should be ready, I hope."

He went into the kitchen, where his parents and Charlotte had just finished their dinner.

"Hello, Mum, how's your leg now, with the plaster off?"

"Fine, thanks, Fred. It's such a relief to be able to scratch my leg again. Why do things always itch when you can't get at them? It's still a bit bruised and swollen look, but it's mended." She held out her foot for him to inspect.

"Oh, yes, it looks all right, doesn't it? Is it still painful?"

"It still aches, but nothing like it did. The doctor said I need to be careful for a few weeks and not walk on it too much. Mind you, there's not much chance of me doing that, the way these two fuss over me." The smile on her face took the sting out of her words.

"Make sure you listen to them, then, and make the most of it. Charlotte, are you ready to go? I've got Dolly and the cart outside."

"Yes, I'm ready, thanks for taking me, Fred. I feel nervous, which is silly because she's my aunty, but I feel better knowing you'll be with me. I think she might take more notice of you."

"Come on then, let's see if we can get some answers."

As they made their way along the country lanes to the next village, the hedgerows were full of summer flowers, and the foliage was lush and green. They saw smoke coming from the chimney of Joan Smith's cottage in the distance, and the knot in Charlotte's stomach tightened. Fred stopped Dolly at the front gate and tethered her to a post. Charlotte knocked on the front door, then opened it, and called out.

"Hello, Aunty Joan, are you there? It's me, Charlotte. Hello."

"Hold on, I'm upstairs; I'll be there in a minute."

Fred had not seen Charlotte's aunty before, and he surveyed the elderly woman as she entered the room. She had brown hair sprinkled with grey streaks and swept up into a severe bun. Her clothes were plain and dark coloured. When Charlotte introduced him, she shook his hand, but the tight smile on her lips did not reach her eyes.

"I thought you would have returned to Exeter by now, Charlotte. Is everything all right at home?"

"Oh, I didn't go back home, Aunty Joan. You know I left here to look after Fred's mother, Betsey, who had broken her leg? Well, it's mended now, but she's asked me to stay on to work at the inn, so that's what I'm going to do."

"I see, well, I hope you told your parents, you were not coming home? Were they happy about that? I thought your father wanted you to work in the church and the house?"

"I've written to mother, but I haven't heard back from her yet. Anyway, I would prefer to stay working here. Father and I never did get on as you know."

"No, he isn't the easiest man to get along with, I'll grant you that, but at least with the baby adopted, you could go home. You have me to thank for that, and you're lucky your father is willing to have you back at all."

"I'm grateful for the help you gave me, but I wish you hadn't got rid of Doris. She was my baby, and it was up to me to decide what would happen to her. By giving her away behind my back, I didn't even get a chance to say goodbye."

"You kept putting it off, and every day I could see you were growing fonder of the child. I just thought it was kinder to get the job done for you. Anyway, what's done is done. Now, would you like a cup of tea?"

"That's kind of you, but I'd better tell you the purpose of our visit and then see if the offer still stands. You see, Betsey is a kind soul, and she knows how upset I've been since I lost Doris. She has a large family, herself, and understands what it's like to lose a child. Anyway, as well as offering me a job, she says if I can get Doris back, I can keep her with me at the inn."

"I don't think that's a good idea at all. You've made the break now, and there's no point going back. No young man will ever look at you if you have a bastard to raise; surely you know that."

"I don't care about that; I just want my daughter back. I never expect to marry. I don't think I could ever trust a man again, anyway, so that doesn't matter. Now, where did you take her?"

"I'm not telling you. You're only thinking of yourself. People here know I'm your aunt, and I don't want the disgrace of a niece of mine bringing up a child born out of wedlock. Up to now, few people in Warkley know you had a child because we kept it quiet, and that's how it should stay."

All this time, Fred had remained silent, but now he stood up and confronted the old lady.

"Now, look, ma'am, you may feel this is none of my business, but Charlotte is a friend of mine, and she's been good to my mother. I'm determined to help her get the baby back, so please tell us where you took the child, and we'll be on our way and leave you in peace."

"You're right on one account, mister; it is none of your business. Now, I'll thank you both to leave my house."

Fred turned on her angrily. "No, I'm sorry, but that is not going to happen. You haven't always lived hereabouts, but I have, and I know a great many people. If you don't tell us where you took the baby, then I'll make sure everyone knows what you did. You'll never be able to hold your head up in the village again, and if I put the word out, I very much doubt anyone locally will sell you anything you need. Now, you think about it; do you want to become an outcast? Because I swear to you, I can make it happen, and I will."

Her mouth a tight thin line, and her face white with rage, the old woman scowled at him.

"I see how the land lies here, then. I'd heard you'd lost your wife; it's not difficult to see where your interests lie now, is it? You want to be careful young lady, or you'll find yourself in the family way for a second time, and I'll tell you now, I won't be helping you out, again."

Fred was furious. "You mind your foul tongue, old woman. Now, are you going to tell us what we want to know or not? Because if you're not, we'll go to the inn for lunch, and spread the word."

"Very well, if you must know, I took the child to Buzzacott House, not far from Hartford; do you know the place?"

Fred looked surprised. "Yes, I do. I know new people are living there. What did they want with the baby?"

"A mother and her daughter live there, and they advertise in the newspapers for unwanted babies to pass on to childless couples to adopt, though goodness knows why anyone would want to adopt a child. I would have thought being barren would be a godsend these days when most folks have so many children they don't know what to do with them. Anyway, I saw an advertisement in the North Devon Journal and saw the address was not far away. I think Lizzie Dymond, that's the woman's name, often meets mothers at the railway station, if they don't live locally, but I just went and knocked on the door and explained the situation, and she was happy to take the baby. It cost me five pounds, though, so I shall want that from you because no doubt she won't return it."

"Well, you took the ten pounds that Martin gave me to get rid of the baby, so it was my money, anyway." Charlotte glared at her aunt, angrily.

"I deserved the rest for taking you in and feeding you. Money doesn't grow on trees; my girl and you were always well fed here."

"I don't care about the money. Do you know if they had a couple in mind to take Doris?"

"I have no idea; I just wanted to get rid of her, and if you have any sense you'll leave things as they are. Now, please leave me in peace; you've upset me enough for one day."

"Come on, Fred, we've got what we wanted. Let's go home."

Without another word they left the house, Charlotte, knowing in her heart, it would be the last time she would ever set foot there. She would never forgive her aunt for giving Doris away. When they got outside, Fred took her arm. "Are you all right, Charlotte? I know that was upsetting for you. What an unpleasant woman she is, but at least we know now where she took the baby. It's not far either; we could go there on the way home if you like?"

"Oh, yes, please, do you mind, Fred? I shouldn't take up any more of your time."

"Don't be daft. It would be stupid not to go when it's almost on the way home. Come on."

They stopped the horse and cart outside the front door of Buzzacott House and surveyed their surroundings. It was a large house, situated in extensive grounds, but neglected with nettles and brambles, having taken over. The house was badly in need of repair, and the windows were covered in grime. Taking Charlotte's arm firmly, Fred walked her to the front door and knocked loudly. Charlotte looked as if her legs might give way at any moment, so Fred held on to her. The door was answered by a tall woman.

"Can I help you?"

Fred spoke. "Yes, I hope so. This is my friend, Charlotte Mackie. She had a baby daughter recently, and, without her permission, her aunt brought the baby here to be adopted. Charlotte's circumstances have changed, and she would like to have her baby back. Would that be possible?"

"No, I'm sorry, but as I would have told your aunt at the time, we don't keep the babies long. We arrange adoptions, and the babies go to childless couples. I can assure you we are always careful in selecting the new parents, and your baby will be well cared for. How long ago was this, anyway?"

"My baby would have been about two weeks old when she was brought here, and that was about six weeks or so ago. My aunt is called Joan Smith. Could you ask for the baby back because I didn't give my permission?"

"No, of course, not; it would be most unfair to the new parents. In most cases, they will have waited a long time trying to have a child of their own, and it would be cruel to then take the baby away."

Fred intervened. "I can understand that, but could you let us know who took Charlotte's baby, then at least, she could go and see her and satisfy herself that she is all right."

"No, I'm sorry, but it is made clear when we take the babies. We cannot give out the names of the adoptive parents because they do not want to be contacted. Now, if you will excuse me, I must get on. I'm busy."

The woman firmly shut the door, leaving them standing on the doorstep. As Fred led Charlotte away, the girl was sobbing bitterly, and Fred hugged her.

"Come on, never mind. At least she'll be well looked after. Any couple that goes to the trouble of adopting a baby, must want the child, and I'll bet they had to pay dearly for it. You can bet your life; this woman didn't arrange it all for nothing. It seems to me she's onto a good thing. She charges the women who are giving up their babies, and also the couples who adopt them. A nice little earner, I would say. I'm sorry we've come to a dead-end, but I'm sure one day you'll have more children."

"That may be so, but I'll never forget Doris; she was so beautiful, and no other child could ever replace her."

"No, I understand that. Charlotte, I don't suppose you will have heard, but I lost two babies as well. My wife, Lucy, had two children between Rosella and Eddie, and they died." He frowned. "That's not quite the whole story, she killed Alfie and Grace when they were just a few weeks old, so I know what it's like to lose a child."

"Oh, Fred, that's terrible; I had no idea. I'm so sorry, but why did she kill her children?"

"I can't pretend to understand, but she was mentally ill. We found her trying to smother Eddie, and she admitted she had killed the other two and was committed to an asylum. Luckily, we saved Eddie, and the poor girl went through hell in that asylum I can tell you; she took her own life in the end."

This time, Charlotte hugged Fred but could think of little to say to comfort him. He pulled away from her. "Come on, I'll take you back to the inn; I'm afraid we've done all we can here."

CHAPTER 26

Clarice Gubb was feeling pleased with herself. She had got all her jobs done and hoped to leave the Manor House on time for her half-day off. She knew from previous experience that Miss Wetherby would not let her go unless all tasks were completed to her satisfaction. The housekeeper seemed to take a real delight in finding fault just to delay the servants when it was their day off. With only one day's leave a month, this time was precious. Having said her farewells to the kitchen staff, she let herself out the back door and took a shortcut through the barn to the lane behind. She wished that her young man, Christopher Webber, could have the same time off as she did, but this never seemed to work out. Since working at the Manor House, she had seen Christopher every day, and they had struck up a friendship that had now become a romance. They found the same things funny, and he didn't seem to mind that she was plain-looking and suffered badly from acne. As she entered the barn, she heard her name called.

"Ah, there you are, Clarice. I was beginning to think, I'd missed you; I came to get some tools, but Jack will be looking for me if I'm gone too long. I hoped you might be leaving around now."

"Hello, Chris, you made me jump, but it's lovely to see you alone for five minutes."

He put his arms around her and kissed her on the lips. She responded, and for a few moments, both were lost in their embrace and oblivious to their surroundings.

"It's so annoying to sit with you at mealtimes and pretend we're not seeing each other. Miss Wetherby wouldn't approve if she knew, though, and neither of us can afford to lose our jobs. What are you doing on your afternoon off?"

"Mum will expect me to spend the time with her and the family. I wish you and I could spend the afternoon together, but our leave never seems to coincide, does it?"

"No, and that's why I wanted to catch you now. I wondered if you'd like to meet me later for a walk up onto the cliffs. The only thing is it would need to be quite late. What time do you have to be back?"

"It doesn't matter as long as I'm up at dawn tomorrow to do my jobs. Even if the back door is locked, I know where Jack keeps the spare key, so I can always let myself in and put the key back in the morning. Why do we have to walk so late?"

"Oh, well, keep this to yourself, but Dad and Charlie Chugg are coming home from France tonight with smuggled goods. I have to keep watch from the cliffs and signal with a lantern to let them know if it's safe to land. If the gaugers are lying in wait, Charlie will sail on to a different cove."

"Oh, Chris, I wish you hadn't said you'd do that; it's dangerous. You could go to prison if you're caught."

"It's unlikely the gaugers will be around. There aren't many of them, and they have the whole of the South West to keep an eye on. They seem to concentrate more on the South Devon coastline, from what I've heard. Nobody's ever been caught around here, but there's always a first time, and Charlie likes to take precautions. I looked for him last night, in case he was back early, but it was tonight he expected to arrive. It depends on the tides and the winds.

I'll have to wait until it's dark before I can signal. Anyway, do you want to come?"

"I don't want to get into any trouble. What time do you want to meet?"

"Would around ten o'clock be too late?"

"No, that's all right. I'll meet you on the path to the cliffs when I leave home to go back to work."

"Good, I'll look forward to it, and don't worry, I've done this a few times now and never seen anyone. Charlie is pretty generous too, so it gives me a bit more money to put by for a rainy day. I'll see you later."

He kissed her briefly and left the barn hurriedly, clutching a bag of tools.

For the second time in as many minutes, Clarice's eyes drifted to the old clock on the mantelpiece. Having so looked forward to her time off, she now found she was wishing the hours away until she could meet Christopher. Much to Ruth's discomfort, Clarice was told the story at first hand of how her sister had run off with the man from the fair. She tried to offer some support to her sister, saying that everyone makes mistakes, but her mother was having none of it.

"I keep telling her anything could have happened, and she's lucky to be here in one piece. Most men are only after one thing, and then they're off. Not you, John. I'm sure you were an honourable young man, but most aren't." Before her husband could answer, she continued. "If you girls have any sense, you will stay well away from men until you're older. Plenty of time to think of settling down and having a family, when you are at least into your twenties."

Clarice shuffled uncomfortably, knowing what her mother would think if she had any idea she was meeting Christopher on the cliffs in a few hours. Her mother had cooked a satisfying meal of pigs' liver and onions, with mashed potatoes and peas from the garden. To change the subject, Clarice complimented her on the meal. "That was delicious, Mum. Not even Ethel Potts could have bettered that."

John Cutcliffe pushed back his plate, contentedly. "She's right, love, you certainly can cook; that was tasty, thank you. Did I see an apple pie in the oven?"

"You did, and I've scalded the milk to make some cream. Shall we have it now?

Daisy and Rachael's eyes lit up at the mention of more food. There was never anything like this to eat in the workhouse. In their eyes, their stepmother could do no wrong. All the praying and attending church was a nuisance, but nothing compared to near starvation.

Clarice helped Ruth and Susanna to do the washing up, whilst Noeleen read some of the Bible to Daisy and Rachael. At long last, it was time for Clarice to go.

"Bye, then, everyone, I'll see you all in a couple of weeks when I have another half-day off. I need to get back to the Manor House now."

"Yes, all right. Mind how you go, then, it's cloudy, and that's made it dark early tonight."

Clarice waved goodbye to her mother and then, making sure she was not watching, took the footpath towards the cliffs instead of to the Manor House. She rounded a corner and jumped as Christopher stepped out from behind a bush.

"Oh, my goodness, you made me jump. Sorry, if I'm a bit late, but the family kept me chatting."

"No, it's fine, and at least it's dark, now. We have plenty of time, so shall we take the long path through the woods and then up onto the headland? The boat won't be here for some time yet, and they won't land until I've signalled."

"How will they know it's safe to land?"

"If I flash the lantern three times quickly, and then wait for a few minutes, and do it again, they know it's safe, but if I flash it once, then count to sixty, and flash it again, and keep doing that, they'll know there's a problem and they won't land."

"Very clever."

"It's simple enough, but it's worked so far."

They paused in the woods to kiss and cuddle until eventually, Clarice thought Christopher was beginning to take rather too many liberties and pushed him away. "No, you don't Chris Webber, you're not having your wicked way with me." She grinned at him in the pale moonlight. "Not that I wouldn't like you to."

"You know I'd never take advantage of you, Clarice, I love you."

That made the girl hesitate, and she looked at him seriously. "Do you, Chris? Do you love me? I'm not pretty, and I've got all these beastly spots. You could probably have your pick of all the young ladies in the village. You do know that?"

"I doubt that but it's you I want to be with, and to me, you are beautiful. Anyway, everyone gets spots, and they'll go as you get older."

She pulled him to her. "In that case, I'll tell you something, because I love you too, I love you very much."

They kissed again until, at last, he pulled away from her. "Come on, we'd better walk up to the headland, now, and get the lantern ready."

They puffed and panted as they climbed the steep cliff. At the top, there were stunted trees and gorse bushes, all growing at curious angles, showing clearly which way the strong winds blew. Christopher was sure-footed as he guided her along an indistinct path which he knew well.

"This path's been used by generations of smugglers, but it's little known to most folk, and there's thick gorse on either side, so mind your step. You'll know all about it if you fall into a gorse bush."

They reached the top and gazed out over the bay beneath them.

Clarice was out of breath. "This must be a beautiful view in the daytime. Perhaps we could come here again sometime."

"Aye, maybe. Ah, look, there she is, *The Bountiful Lady*, Charlie's ship."

"Are you sure it's the right one?"

"Oh, yes, definitely, I'd know her anywhere, and anyway, Charlie always hangs a white vest from the topmast; can you see it? It's just about visible. Now, let's just study the beach for a few minutes. The moon isn't very bright tonight, which is both a good thing and a bad thing. It means the boat's not easily seen, but then, neither are the gaugers. I think it's all right. No, just a minute, can you see something glinting over there in the rocks?"

They strained their eyes, trying to see in the dim light.

"Yes, it's difficult to see, but the moonlight is shining on something."

Just then, the clouds cleared, revealing several men hiding behind the rocks on the beach. The moonlight glinting on their rifles.

"Oh no, look, the gaugers are out! I've never seen them before. They don't usually bother coming here because there isn't a lot of smuggling locally. Anyway, listen. We must flash the lantern as I told you, but then we must get away from here, as quickly as we can because they'll have more men hidden here on the cliff somewhere, just looking for someone like me to signal. They know how it works. I think it's best if you go now, and run straight back to the Manor House before I light the lantern, then you'll be in the clear."

"No, I'm not leaving you here on your own." She put her finger to his lips. "Listen, light the lantern and signal, then put it out, and hide it. I'll put my cloak down, and if they find us, they'll just think we are up to no good as a courting couple. They'd never think I'd come here with you to signal to smugglers. You're much safer if I stay."

Christopher could see the sense of what Clarice was saying. "Are you sure? They might not fall for it."

"They will, particularly if they know my mother. She's so upright and proper and religious they'll never think her daughter could be up to no good."

"But, Clarice, if any of them know you, they might tell your mother, and then you'll be in trouble."

"I'll have to risk it, but it's better I get a telling off from my mother, than you get jailed, or transported to Australia. I think there's a hole here in the bank somewhere. I stepped in it just now, yes there, look. It's probably a badger's hole. When you dowse the lantern, stick it in there, and we'll move away from it."

Chris carefully lit the lantern, held it aloft and signalled once, then held it down out of sight and counted to sixty. He made himself repeat this ten times, whilst Clarice kept watch, to see if any men came running.

"Chris, stop now, they must have seen it, surely? We must hide the lantern, otherwise, we'll be caught."

"Yes, Charlie is bound to have been watching, he'll sail the boat away now with any luck."

He dowsed the light and thrust the lantern into the badger's hole, pulling some bracken down over it. "Come on, let's get away from this spot and find somewhere to put your cloak down and sit it out. They retraced their footsteps and hurried back down the track until they came to a clearing that looked out to sea.

"Let's sit here and look out over the bay. Oh, yes, look Charlie's sailing away. Thank goodness."

They sat side by side on Clarice's cloak looking out over the moonlit bay.

"This is romantic, isn't it? Shame to waste an opportunity." Clarice lay back and pulled him down to her.

He grinned. "You are a naughty girl, Clarice Gubb, but you're not wrong, and we get so little time alone together." He kissed her passionately.

Within a few minutes, they were interrupted when men on horseback cantered into the clearing.

"Hey, you there, get up and show yourself. What business do you have up here on the cliffs at this time of night?"

Christopher got up warily and held up his hands, for the man was pointing a rifle in his direction. "Nothing, mister, we ain't up to nothing. We were just chatting and looking at the moonlight; nothing wrong in that is there?"

"Who is that hiding behind you? Come out and show me your hands."

Clarice came out from behind Christopher with her hands held aloft. Christopher was shocked when he saw that her blouse was undone, partially revealing her breasts, and her hair had fallen around her shoulders. She looked embarrassed and hung her head. The man on the horse alighted and came towards them, swinging his lantern.

"Come here, let me see your faces. Who are you?"

Clarice's heart sank as she saw the man was a regular churchgoer and a friend of her mother. She no longer had to pretend to be dismayed.

"Why it's Clarice, isn't it? Clarice Gubb? I'm guessing your mother doesn't know what you are up to young lady, but she soon will. Look at the disgraceful state of you. You should be ashamed of yourself. You wait until I tell her how I found you. And you, lad, what do you have to say for yourself? What's your name?"

"It's Christopher Webber, sir, and we were doing no harm. We've been seeing each other for a few months now, and we were only kissing. It would have gone no further, I promise you. I respect Clarice too much."

"Aye, I can see how much you were respecting her, by her appearance. You can save your explanations for Noeleen, and I'll tell you now, rather you than me. Now, have you seen anyone else up here on the cliffs with a lantern?"

"No, sir, I swear we've seen no one else," Christopher answered honestly. "Why, what's the problem?"

"Smugglers are the problem, lad. There's too much of it going on, and it's our business to put a stop to it. There was a boat coming in tonight, that we're sure was loaded with contraband. We've had reports of it being landed in this cove before, and tonight we were ready for them, but someone signalled from this cliff to warn them. I saw it with my own eyes. Are you sure you've seen no one else? Clarice don't you lie to me and make matters worse, or I surely will tell your mother what you've been up to."

"No, sir, I swear to you I haven't seen anyone else on the cliffs tonight. The only person I've seen is Christopher. I'd be so grateful if you didn't mention this to my mother. It would upset her so much, and there's no need. I wouldn't have let anything untoward happen, I promise you."

"Aye, well, I don't think it's your mother's feelings you're thinking of, but I was young myself once, and I may not tell her. I'll think about it for a day or two. Now, both of you step to one side. I want to make sure you have no lantern with you."

The couple dutifully stepped to one side and Christopher tentatively took Clarice's shaking hand.

"All right, it looks as if your story's true, though you should know it's dangerous to come up here in the dark, with no light to guide you back. I'll send one of my men back with you. I don't want to hear you've fallen off the cliff."

"That's kind of you, sir, but I know these cliffs, and now, in the moonlight, I promise you we'll be fine. The path is clear and well-trodden from here back to the village."

"Just as you like then, I can't really spare a man, so go on your way and mind you, Clarice I shall be keeping an eye on you from now on."

"Yes, sir, thank you. Come on, Christopher, I must get back to the Manor House now."

The young couple gratefully turned towards the village and the men galloped off into the distance.

Christopher pulled Clarice round to face him. "Clarice, what happened to your blouse? I didn't undo all those buttons and your hair; how did it become so messed up? I'll be surprised if he doesn't tell your mother."

She laughed. "Oh, I undid the buttons and loosened my hair whilst I was stood behind you. I thought it would make our story more believable."

Christopher chuckled. "It certainly did. I was horrified when I saw the state of you, but I think the sight of your open blouse certainly distracted them. That was good thinking. I just hope our friend keeps it to himself."

CHAPTER 27

It had been a long journey, and Charlie and Arthur were relieved to see the dim lights twinkling on the hillsides around Hartford. They were bone-tired and longed to be tucked up in their comfortable beds.

"Not long now, Arthur and our business will be done."

"Aye, and I shan't be sorry, though I have enjoyed it. I know Christopher will be up on the cliff, but how many men will meet us on the beach? We'll need some help to unload the goods and make them safe as quickly as possible."

"Yes, don't you worry. It's all organised, and it's good we got back tonight as expected. Alfred and Jimmy will be watching the cove, and as soon as they see we are going to land, they'll be there with four ponies to take the goods away. We take the stuff to the farm and leave it there until we think it's safe to move it. We have a secret hiding place to store everything; it's been used for generations. I understand my great grandfather built it."

"Right, come on, then, Chris give us a signal. Oh, my God, there it is, look, but it's not the one we want. There must be gaugers lying in wait for us. That's never happened before. We can't land."

"What do we do now, then? It's only a matter of time before they'll come after us in another vessel."

"It's all right, Arthur, not to worry. We'll sail on to Lee Bay."

"Are you sure? The rocks there are treacherous."

"I know, but we haven't much choice. If we make a run for it now, they'll soon catch us because they have a bigger boat. They'll never think we'd try to take a boat this size into Lee Bay, and they sure as hell won't follow us. Don't worry, I've done it before because I knew this would happen one day."

"But what will we do with the goods, then?"

"Arthur, just trust me. This has been planned for, and we'll be all right, but I need to concentrate on getting the boat into the bay as soon as I can. When they see us making a run for it, they'll launch their vessel, and we must be out of sight before they see where we go."

Masterfully, Charlie turned the boat and sailed it out to sea. The men waiting on the beach saw what was happening, and the order was given to launch their own vessel as quickly as possible. Fortunately for Charlie and Arthur, the wind was, yet again, in their favour and they worked furiously to get the sails of *The Bountiful Lady* fully hoisted. Their boat was soon out of sight to the men on the beach, and Charlie immediately turned her sharply to sail into the next bay.

"Charlie, there are rocks everywhere; you'll never land it here and at this speed. We must get the sails down again."

Charlie shouted over the wind. "No, just wind in one sail, and leave the others; it will be all right."

Skilfully, he manoeuvred the boat through the choppy water of an impossibly narrow channel, and suddenly the water was calm. He turned to Arthur with an enormous grin on his face. "See, I told you, I had done it before. Many times, actually. I've practised this landing since I was a nipper and used to come out with Dad and Grandad. They wouldn't let me take the boat out alone until I had mastered landing a boat in this bay, and I can tell you it's not easy. Now, if I sail in a bit closer we'll be hidden from the eye out to sea. We'll start unloading, and then I'll tell you my other secret."

"That was amazing, Charlie. I honestly thought we would end up on the rocks."

"Oh, ye of little faith! It will come as no surprise to you that smuggling runs in my family, and I've been well trained. This bay is inaccessible by land because it's surrounded by high cliffs, so we've nothing to fear there, although it's very close to the village."

"Yes, I know, but how can we transport the goods anywhere; surely we're trapped here, unless we sail out again?"

"We'll take everything to a cave just up the beach. From that cave, there's an ancient tunnel that leads to the old silver mine, and the goods will be safe there for as long as we want. That part of the mine's not been worked for years because the silver petered out a long time ago, but the tunnels are still there. It's been a while, but I've been in the tunnel, and I know where it comes out the other end."

"Are you sure it's safe?"

"We don't have a lot of choice, do we? It was fine the last time I checked it, but there is some bad news I'm afraid."

"What?"

"Well, there are only the two of us now, and it's going to take us some time to unload everything and get it stashed in the tunnel. We're going to have to get on with it, too; I must sail out of here before the tide turns. Come on, let's get cracking."

For two hours they worked non-stop. Charlie passed the goods off the boat to Arthur, and then they both trudged up to the cave countless times from the beach. Once inside the cave, Arthur held up the lantern to look for the tunnel. Charlie grinned. "I bet you can't find it."

Arthur circled the cave unsuccessfully. "You're right, I can't see it; are you sure this is the cave?"

"Yes, here, look."

Along one side of the cave, fronds of seaweed hung from a ledge higher up. He deftly swung himself up and pulled aside the curtain of seaweed. Behind it was a large hole, which he shone his lantern into. Arthur could see that a passageway led uphill. Charlie hauled himself into the hole and pulled out a ladder.

"Here we are, the ladder's still sound. The water doesn't come up this far. Now, if you pass the goods up to me, I'll stack them out of sight, and we can get off."

It took another hour before the men had accomplished that task, and they were both so tired they could barely stand.

"Come on, Arthur, I know you're tired, and so am I, but we must sail out of this cove before the tide turns, or we'll be stuck here for hours. Hopefully, the gaugers will have given up by now, or have sailed off somewhere else. We'll have to chance it, anyway. Come on."

They sailed out of the cove without incident and were relieved to see no sign of the gaugers' boat. Charlie sailed away from the village and along the coast for a mile or two before heading out to open sea and circling back to land at Hartford. As they reached the jetty, men came running at them from all directions.

"We are impounding this boat. Come off, with your hands up."

Charlie and Arthur looked surprised. "What for? Can a man not go fishing anymore? What is it you are looking for? We have a good catch, but as far as I know, that's not against the law."

They obligingly jumped off the boat, and one of the men pushed them to one side. "Just sit down there on those rocks and wait. We have reason to believe you have smuggled goods on board from France, and we are going to search your boat. We know you've been sailing around hoping we'd be gone."

"You search wherever you like, but I'll tell you now, all you'll find is fish, so you're wasting your time."

The men took no notice, and leaving one to keep an eye on Charlie and Arthur, the others boarded the boat and went through it with a fine toothcomb. The hold was full of a good catch of fish. The man in charge came back to Charlie and Arthur.

"I expect you think you're clever, don't you, but I know you are a smuggler, Charlie Chugg, you and your father and grandfather, before you. We've been trying to catch your family for years, but your luck will run out one day, and then you'll be going to jail for a long time."

"I don't know what you're talking about, and it seems you have no proof. If it's all the same to you, Arthur and I are tired, and we'd like to get to our beds; we have a lot of fish to sell tomorrow whilst it's fresh. Goodnight gentlemen, I hope you catch your smugglers soon."

Watching discreetly from a safe distance, Christopher had been joined by Charlie's brother, Alfred, and his son, Jimmy. They watched with relief as they saw Charlie and Arthur make their way up the beach.

CHAPTER 28

On the day before his wedding, Robert was busy in the fields harvesting the corn. Jack had tried to persuade him to take a few days off to relax before the big day, but he would have none of it.

"Honestly, Jack, I'd much rather be out here working with you. The house is unbearable at the moment with so many women fussing around. Mrs Potts and the maids are baking as if they have to feed the five thousand, and Annie, Sabina, and her Aunty Eveline, are decorating everywhere with flowers. Really, it's a kindness to let me spend the day out here with you in the sunshine."

Jack laughed. "When you put it like that, sir, I can see why you'd rather be out here. This is the last field of corn to cut, and with your new reaper, it shouldn't take long."

They worked hard all morning until at lunchtime, Dodger arrived on a small cart with Molly beside him. On the cart were two hampers of food that Robert had ordered for all the workers to celebrate the last of the harvest being gathered in.

"Molly, come here a minute," Robert called the girl over. "Stay and have a bite to eat with us because I've got a little job for you to do."

"Thank you, Master Robert, but I'd better not be too long, or Miss Wetherby will wonder where I am."

"If she asks you can tell her I insisted you stay. Now, what I would like you to do is to make us our corn dolly this year. Have you ever made one?"

"No, sir, but I'd like to try. What do I have to do?"

Robert looked a little doubtful. "That's a good question; does anyone here know how to make a corn dolly?"

Several of the men spoke up, including Dodger. Robert had always got on well with the stable lad, and he singled him out. "Right, come on, then Dodger, tell us how it's done."

"Folk all have their own way of doing it, but it doesn't matter as long as you end up with a doll at the end of it. You must wait for the straw to dry out and then take some straws from the last sheaf of corn to be cut and make a doll. You should try to leave a hollow space inside its tummy because that's where a spirit will live. Then you have to plough the dolly back into the first furrow that's ploughed for the new crop next year. The spirit can return to the soil then, and it will look after the new crop."

"That sounds straightforward enough; do you think you could make some sort of dolly from the straw, Molly?"

"Yes, I'm sure I can, sir. I'll ask Maisie to help me. What happens to the dolly until the ploughing is done?"

"You just put it somewhere safe. Perhaps on the kitchen windowsill, or it could stay in the barn if Mrs Potts doesn't want it in the way."

Robert stayed for a couple of hours after lunch and saw the rest of the corn cut, but then returned to the house to see how the preparations were going. Things seemed a little calmer. The house was beautifully decorated with many flowers, and their scent filled the air. Robert went to see how Mrs Potts was getting on in the kitchen and found her sitting in her favourite chair by the fireplace.

"Now then, what's all this. Are you slacking again, Mrs Potts?"

Mrs Potts immediately made to get up from her chair, but Robert put his hand firmly on her shoulder. "Just teasing, Mrs Potts. I know you will have done the work of ten men today, already. Do you want to show me what you've made for tomorrow?"

"Yes, sir. Well, of course, there's the wedding cake; it's over there, look and I hope it's to your liking?"

The wedding cake had three tiers, the bottom one being the largest, and then each getting gradually smaller. Mrs Potts had decorated it with white icing and had piped swirls and flowers on each layer.

"Mrs Potts, it's beautiful. Has Annie seen it yet?"

"Yes, sir, and she's pleased with it. Now, come and look in the pantry and the dairy at all the other food I've prepared for tomorrow; I just hope there will be enough, but I think there will."

Mrs Potts had truly surpassed herself, and every shelf was laden with cold joints of turkey, beef, ham, and pork all waiting to be carved. There were pies of all shapes and sizes and two whole salmon. For dessert, she had made trifles and sponges, crumbles and possets, and two large cheeses were ready to be eaten with pickles and biscuits.

"Mrs Potts, it's amazing. Thank you, so much. There's enough food here to feed an army."

"I must admit I'm pleased with it all, but it's not just my hard work, you know, everyone here has pitched in."

"Yes, I'm sure they have, and I'll thank them all tomorrow. Right, now, I'd better be on my way because I'm going to meet my cousin, Percy, at the railway station. He's going to be my best man tomorrow, which is good of him because not many of my family will be coming. Do you remember, Percy? He came here quite a lot when we were growing up."

"I do that, sir. Yes, he was a nice lad. I'd forgotten about him; have you seen much of him over the years?"

"No, not much because he lives in London now, but I go and see him every time I'm there."

Robert went in search of Dodger to take him to the station in the carriage. As they passed the Lodge House, Robert asked Dodger to stop for a moment, and he went in search of Annie. She came to the door and beamed when she saw it was him.

"Hello, Robert, come in. I was hoping you would come." She kissed him briefly on the lips, shielded from Dodger's eyes by the porch.

"No, I can't stay because I'm off to the station to collect Percy. Anyway, I'm told I'm not supposed to see you this evening, but I just wanted to make sure everything is all right."

"Yes, it's fine. I tried on my dress this morning and it fitted perfectly. Aunty Eveline has done such a good job. Mary, Helen, and Selina all put on their dresses too, and they looked beautiful. I can't wait for tomorrow; I'm so excited."

"That's all right, then. As long as you're not getting cold feet?"

"No, of course not, though I'm glad your family are not going to be there. I'd be far more nervous if they were, though I'm sorry for you, that they won't come."

"Don't worry about it. It doesn't matter to me as long as you're there."

"Oh, I'll be there; there's no getting rid of me now. Have you seen all the food that Mrs Potts has cooked? And the cake; it's amazing. I don't know how she makes those flowers from icing. It's all so fiddly."

"The cake is lovely, and as usual, she's made enough food to feed the whole village, but that's all right because I want everyone to enjoy the day. Right then, I'll see you in church," he grinned and pulled her towards him and kissed her. "Until tomorrow."

Robert sat beside Dodger, for despite the difference in their stations in life they were good friends. They arrived just before the train was due, and leaving Dodger with the carriage, Robert went to find his cousin. He was one of the first passengers off the train, and Robert waved furiously.

"Percy, over here, old man. Percy, I'm here."

With a big grin on his face, a young man hustled his way through the crowd. Taller than Robert, and with mousey hair and brown eyes, he was a good-looking lad. "Hello, Robert; it's so good to see you." The two men shook hands.

"I can't thank you enough for being my best man, Percy. Not many of the family will be coming."

"That's their loss then, isn't it? Mind you, even I was a bit surprised to hear you are marrying a former kitchen-maid." His cousin laughed. "I would have loved to be there when you told Aunt Eleanor. I bet her face was a picture."

Robert grinned. "I think it's fair to say my mother wasn't happy, and that's putting it mildly. I can't wait for you to meet Annie. She's beautiful."

"I'm looking forward to it. Mind you, it's going to be difficult for you both; you are sure about this, aren't you?"

"I've never been more sure about anything; I've loved this girl for a very long time. Now, come on, let's get home because I want to hear all your news. I rather thought you might have brought a young lady with you?"

"Ah no, confirmed bachelor me; I'm not the marrying kind."

CHAPTER 29

Annie was awoken by birdsong on the day of her wedding, and she lay in bed and smiled to herself as she thought about the day ahead and how it would change her life forever. The birds always started to sing as soon as it became light, and she enjoyed listening to them, although it was so early. Her eyes adjusted to the gloomy light and moved from the window to her wedding dress, which hung on the wardrobe. It was a cream silk dress with a full skirt covered by a layer of flimsy lace, and it had a small train. The bodice had short sleeves and was also made of lace, and it fitted tightly, accentuating her small waist. She had chosen a long veil, which flowed down her back, and part of which could be pulled over her face for her walk to the altar.

The bridesmaids' dresses for Mary, Helen, and Selina hung alongside the wedding dress. They each had a full-length skirt and a simple sleeveless lacy top. They were a delicate lilac colour, and around the waistline, was a slightly darker purple ribbon tied at the back.

Annie was to carry a bouquet of pale pink roses and lavender, picking up the colour of the bridesmaids' dresses. The bridesmaids would hold small posies of white rosebuds and lavender and would wear a few white roses in their hair. They all had long hair and Sabina and Annie had practised various ways of plaiting and tying it until they found a style they were happy with and which would hold the flowers best. Annie was going to wear her long hair loose and allow it to cascade around her shoulders in its natural ringlets.

She tossed back the covers, went to the window and pulled back the curtains, praying it was going to be a dry day. However, the ground was wet and it was drizzling slightly. She frowned and hoped it would dry up before the wedding at noon. Pulling a loose gown over her nightdress, she went to the kitchen in search of a cup of tea. She was pleased to find that no one else was up, for she liked a few minutes to herself in the morning. She pulled the kettle forward on the stove and was soon enjoying a strong cup of tea which she drank sitting in the window seat.

The garden, which only a few months before had been an overgrown wilderness, was now tidy and planted with numerous vegetables and was her mother's pride and joy. Until she gave up work, there had never been enough hours in the day for gardening, but now, Sabina thoroughly enjoyed it and was learning all the time. There were two rows of runner beans, still producing scarlet flowers, and they were picking masses of beans every day. Indeed, far too many for the family to eat, but Sabina loved the fact that she could now grow vegetables and give the surplus to her neighbours. She had also tried her hand at growing potatoes and they had flourished, supplying the family since early July, and the main crop would be harvested in October. It was so lovely to be able to wander out into the garden and gather what they needed for a meal.

Annie was lost in thought as she watched the rain fall steadily on the garden and the raindrops race down the window pane. She didn't hear her mother approaching until she laid her hand on her shoulder.

"Oh, Mum, you made me jump. I didn't hear you coming."

"You were miles away; not changing your mind, are you?"

"No, of course not. Mind you, I'm half looking forward to the wedding, and half dreading it. At least the Fellwoods won't be there; that would have been far worse."

"Yes, you have nothing to worry about. I'm sure it will all go without a hitch. Now, do you want your breakfast, or are you going to have a bath and wash your hair? It will take a while to dry, so you need to do it early."

"Yes, I'll bath first, then the bridesmaids and the boys could do with a good scrub. What about you and Liza? Do you both want to have a bath? We might run out of hot water."

"No, Liza and I bathed yesterday, so we'll just wash, but there's plenty of hot water."

The Carter's had a busy morning. Liza insisted they all had a good breakfast, and she cooked bacon and eggs, with fresh crusty bread, followed by a bowl of creamy porridge.

"Goodness, Liza, we won't get into our clothes at this rate."

"Never mind that you eat up. It's going to be a long day, and no doubt lunch will be late by the time the ceremony is over, and they've taken some photographs."

By half-past eleven, the family was dressed in their new finery. Robert had insisted no expense was spared, and George Carter had ordered several different outfits for them all to choose from. Sabina wore a long, sage-green dress that matched her eyes, and she wore a cream hat. Liza had chosen a pale blue dress that also matched her eyes, and she had selected a navy hat. She couldn't stop stroking the soft fabric of the dress for she had never worn anything so fine. The younger boys, Edward, Stephen, and Danny, wore navy velvet shorts with braces, over white silk shirts, and a bow tie, but Willie, at fifteen, wore long trousers. The boys fidgeted with the high collars for they were unaccustomed to anything tight around their necks.

Mary, Helen, and Selina were longing to put on their new dresses, but Annie made them wait until the last minute, in case they spilt anything on them. The family stood around waiting for Annie to make an appearance, and when, at last, she descended the stairs, they all looked at her in wonder, for they had never seen their sister looking so beautiful.

She grinned happily. "Well, do I look all right?"

"All right? You look beautiful, my girl. I'm so proud of you, and I wish your father could see you now." Sabina's eyes were bright with tears.

"You all look incredibly smart, too. Who would have thought the Carter family would ever be dressed up in such finery. I think I just saw the carriages pull up outside. Most of you can go on in the first carriage. I need to wait for Uncle Fred, so he can give me away, and anyway, I must be a few minutes late. The bridesmaids will go with me."

Meanwhile, Robert had arrived at the church with Percy and was standing at the altar waiting nervously for Annie to walk down the aisle. He kept turning around and looking anxiously over his shoulder, much to the amusement of the waiting congregation. They were enjoying the fact that the Lord of the Manor was concerned whether a village girl would turn up to marry him. The church was full mainly of Annie's family and the local people though, there were a few of Robert's relations and friends.

About ten minutes after noon, the organ started to play the Wedding March, and Robert turned to see his bride approaching on the arm of her Uncle Fred. He gasped at how lovely she looked even with her veil over her face and as she reached him, she pushed it back over her head and smiled widely at him. The ceremony went without a hitch, and after a few photographs had been taken outside the church, the carriages took the main guests to the Manor House, leaving the rest to make their own way.

Fortunately, it had stopped raining mid-morning, and the ground was now mostly dry underfoot, though the day was still a little overcast. Several of the servants had attended the wedding, including Mrs Potts, Maisie, and Molly. It had taken some effort from Robert to persuade Mrs Potts to leave the kitchen long enough to go to the wedding, for she so wanted the food to be perfect. She had only agreed when he said she could travel back in a carriage to make sure she was there before the guests.

Robert and Annie stood at the entrance to the hall and welcomed their guests.

"My dear, you look beautiful." An old lady shook Annie's hand warmly.

Robert smiled. "Oh, Aunty Margery, I'm so pleased you accepted our invitation. Does Papa, know?"

"Yes, he does, and he doesn't approve, but I don't care because I'm old enough to do as I like." She laughed. "I would have loved to be present when you told your mother you were going to marry a servant. Now, this marriage isn't conventional, but then, neither am I and if you love each other, that's good enough for me. Mind you, young lady, woe betide you, if you upset my favourite great-nephew."

Annie smiled. "I've no intention of doing that, and I'm so pleased you came; it's nice for Robert to have a few of his own family here. There are more than enough of mine."

"Right, well, I'd better move along because I'm holding everyone up, but perhaps we could have a chat later? I'd like to get to know you better. I don't live far away, so perhaps you could call on me?"

"Yes, I'd love to. Thank you so much."

Robert intervened. "Aunty Margery you'll be able to talk to Annie during the meal because I've sat you close to her. I hope that's all right?"

"Yes, of course lad; it will be a real pleasure."

The old lady hobbled off with her walking stick, and Robert winked at Annie. "There see not all my family disapprove of you. If you can get on with Aunty Margery, she'll be a good ally for you. She's not conventional at all, and she carries a lot of influence in the family."

Next in line was Annie's, Uncle George, and his wife, Mary Ann. Annie could see that the words of congratulation stuck in his throat, and it was all she could do not to laugh.

Fortunately, Robert saved the situation by shaking George's hand, and thanking him for his help in obtaining clothes and shoes for so many people for the wedding.

"It was a pleasure, sir, and I hope I can continue to supply your household with many of its requirements."

"I'm sure we can put a bit of business your way, George, now that you are part of the family."

Annie nearly choked with laughter and whispered to Robert. "He managed to swallow his pride and dislike of me, long enough to try to get some extra business didn't he?"

Welcoming all the guests took some time, and Annie was glad Liza had insisted she ate a good breakfast for she was getting hungry. It was nearly half-past two before the guests were finally seated and able to sample the spread Mrs Potts was so proud of. Robert had insisted Annie invite as many of the villagers as she wanted, and she fretted that they might have too much to drink and show themselves up. She shared this concern with Robert, and he told her not to worry.

"You'll find that not only poor people sometimes behave badly, so don't worry about it, and anyway, I don't think any of your friends or family would let you down."

Long tables had been set out in the hall and extra servants employed to serve a large number of people. Many of the guests were unable to read or write and couldn't understand the table plans that were displayed. Robert had anticipated this, and as the guests moved on from greeting the newly married couple, Ethan and Caleb Bater took their names and escorted them to their seats. Annie and Robert had spent a long time poring over the seating plan. Normally the family of the bride would be seated amidst the family of the groom to allow the guests a chance to get to know each other. However, that was a worrying prospect given the different backgrounds of the people in this gathering. On the top table, the only guests from Robert's side of the family were Percy and Aunty Margery. Fred, standing in for Annie's father, Tom, sat next to Sabina, and the three bridesmaids, Mary, Helen, and Sabina.

Annie agonised over whether to invite Sarah Carter and her son Bentley. Since Sabina and Eveline had allowed Sarah to sit with them at the May Day celebrations, they had seen little of her, for she wisely kept herself to herself. Many in the village would never forgive her for abandoning William's children in London after his death and returning to Devon alone. Amongst these were Annie's grandparents, Ned and Betsey. Since the news had broken of what Sarah had done, and William's children had been rescued from the workhouse in London, they had refused to have anything to do with their daughter-in-law. However, it was becoming ever more difficult to ignore her because of Bentley. He was the spitting image of William as a child, and whenever Betsey saw him in the village, she became upset. With this in mind, Annie visited her granny and asked if she felt it was time to forgive and forget.

The old lady had looked at Annie, sadly. "I'll never forgive or forget what she did, but I know William would want me to be part of his child's life. Mind you, whether I can persuade Ned to accept her is another matter. I'll think about it."

"My wedding might be the perfect opportunity to get you and all the family together with her. I don't like the thought of Bentley not knowing our family; he's a lovely little boy, and I think Sarah is genuinely sorry for what she did. It sounds as if she panicked at the thought of bringing up all three of William's children on her own after he died and, of course, she had nowhere for them all to live."

"Aye, well, you can make excuses for her, but if she'd brought them back, we'd have worked something out. Anyway, I'll speak to your grandad, and I'll let you know."

So it was that at the wedding, Ned and Betsey sat with their grandchildren, Willie, Stephen, Edward, and Danny, and also Sarah and Bentley. Annie had also sat Liza on the same table to ensure her brothers all behaved themselves. At Annie's insistence, Fred had invited Charlotte, and she would have dearly liked to seat them together, but as Fred had given her away, he had to sit on the top table. Therefore, Charlotte was seated with Eveline and the six children she cared for.

It was obvious that romance was in the air, and Annie would have liked to do a bit more matchmaking, but it was difficult to achieve. She was aware that her Aunty Eveline was spending quite a bit of time at Hollyford Farm, and she was convinced this had a lot to do with Charlie Chugg. Also, though her mother would never admit it, it was clear she thought the world of Arthur Webber, and the visits to the Webber household were not all to do with cheering up his father, Peter. However, try as she might, she was unable to arrange for Charlie and Eveline, and her mother and Arthur, to sit together without raising curiosity. She just hoped they would get together after the meal.

Annie found she got on with Aunty Margery like a house on fire, just as Robert had hoped. Several different wines were served during the meal, but she carefully limited herself to one glass for fear she would show herself up. However, that one glass helped her to relax, and she suddenly realised that despite all her fears, she was enjoying herself. Once the meal and the speeches were out of the way, the tables were cleared, and the guests were able to spread out through several rooms. The band struck up, and Robert and Annie took to the floor for the first dance, which was a waltz. To the amazement of her family, Annie danced it gracefully, and Robert wished Sarah and Victoria could have seen her, for it was largely thanks to their kindness and tuition that she was able to do so.

Annie was delighted to see Sabina dancing with Arthur Webber, and also Eveline dancing with Charlie Chugg. When the ladies went to powder their noses, Arthur leaned forward and whispered to Charlie. "I didn't want to ask when the women were here, but when are we going to get the goods from the silver mine; we don't want them discovered."

"Don't you worry about it, Arthur. Jimmy and I have already been there and fetched a couple of barrels of brandy to keep Ned going at the inn, but I think the rest of it's safer where it is for a few weeks. You don't quite know who to trust these days. Don't worry, though, I'll pay you the rest of what I owe you as soon as I sell it on. I'm grateful because I couldn't have done it without you. I'll see Christopher right, too; no need to worry."

"It's not that; I'd just sleep easier when all the evidence is gone. Does Eveline know what you do?"

"Aye, she does, and I can't say she particularly approves, but she knows it's gone on for years. Anyway, we're becoming close, and I don't want to keep secrets from her. What about Sabina, have you told her?"

"No, I'd like to because we are getting on well, too, but I wouldn't want her to mention it to Annie and for her to tell Master Robert. I don't want us turned out of our cottage."

"I don't think you need worry on that score. Sabina would never betray you."

"No, I'm sure she wouldn't, but I don't want to put her in an awkward position. If we continue to see each other, I might have to give it a miss next time, Charlie."

"That's all right, Arthur, no problem. I can get someone else if I need to, but I won't be going again for a while. It was a close call this time, and the gaugers are getting better at their job. Anyway, here come the ladies."

It was likely that the party would continue into the early hours, but around ten o'clock, Robert banged on the table with a spoon and announced that he and his bride would be retiring for the night. This was met with loud cheers and raucous laughter as he swept Annie off her feet and carried her from the room.

"Robert put me down, you don't have to carry me all the way; I'm no lightweight, now I eat so much."

"Rubbish, you're still as light as a feather, and anyway, I can't bear to put you down."

They reached their bedroom, which had been beautifully decorated with pale blue wallpaper, and dark blue curtains, which the servants had already drawn. Robert gently placed Annie on the bed, lay down beside her, and propping himself on one elbow, turned to look at her.

"So, Lady Anne, here we are, alone at last. I've dreamt of this moment for nigh on four years now, and I can't believe we are finally here."

Annie giggled. "Am I really called Lady Anne?"

"No, not yet, but you will be one day. Now, I'm afraid you have promised to love, honour, and obey me, so you must do as you are told." He grinned.

"I don't think that's going to be a problem." Annie pulled him towards her.

CHAPTER 30

Annie was not the only one keen to get Fred together with Charlotte. He, too, had the same idea in mind and thought the wedding would be a good opportunity to get to know her better. However, with Arthur Webber and Charlie Chugg monopolising the time of Sabina and Eveline, he found that Charlotte was kept busy with all the children.

Once he was able to move away from the top table, he went to sit with his mother and father to have a chat, and immediately sensed an atmosphere. It was clear that Betsey and Ned were finding it difficult to spend time with their daughter-in-law. Sarah sat silently, watching her young son, Bentley, play with his cousins. Ned and Betsey sat in silence on the other side of the table.

Fred took his mother's hand. "Mum, Dad, you need to let this go for William's sake, please, for me?"

His father looked at him. "It's not so easy lad, and you'd feel the same way if this had happened to a son of yours. It's hard to forgive what happened. I wish we hadn't let Annie talk us into sitting on this table."

Fred turned to his sister-in-law. "Sarah, I know the family has ignored you since Bentley was born, but Annie arranged this to give you a chance to mend your bridges. Do you have nothing to say for yourself?"

He looked at her encouragingly.

Tentatively, Sarah looked her in-laws in the eye. "There's nothing I can say to make you forgive me, but I'd like you to know, that now I have a son of my own, I do understand how you feel, and I'm so ashamed of myself and so sorry. I don't know how I could have acted as I did, and if I could change things I would, but I can't. I panicked, and I can't undo the past, so I don't blame you for how you feel. Now look, I'll leave now, and I promise to keep out of your way. If I had anywhere else I could go with Bentley, I would because hardly anyone in the village speaks to me, but unfortunately, there is nowhere. I'm lucky Dad lets us live with him because he was just as angry as you about what I did."

She called to her son and got up to leave.

Betsey looked at Ned, and then put a hand on Sarah's arm. "Well, maid, at least you've had the grace to apologise, and, for William's sake, I think I can accept your apology and move on, but it's up to Ned here because I won't go against him."

Ned had tears in his eyes. "Aye, I guess it's time to let bygones be bygones. We're too old to bear a grudge. I know it's what William would have wanted because he did love you, and his son looks so much like him it breaks my heart."

Sarah smiled. "In that case, I think it's high time you got to know him a bit better. Bentley, come here and speak to your grandparents."

Pleased with his efforts, Fred felt he could now spend some time with Charlotte. He found her in an anteroom with at least ten children around her.

"So here you are; I was beginning to think you were avoiding me."

"No, of course not, Fred, but the children were getting a bit restless so I brought them in here to play a few games and keep them amused. It looks as if Sabina and Eveline are having a good time with Arthur and Charlie, and I didn't want the children to cramp their style."

Fred grinned. "It wouldn't surprise me if there are another couple of weddings before long. I'd be pleased about that, though. I was hoping I might get the chance to have a dance with you before the evening is over; would you like that?"

Charlotte blushed. "Yes, I would, Fred, thank you. Mind you, it's so long since I've danced, I've probably forgotten how."

"I'm in the same boat, so we'll stumble around together." He looked at the children, three of them, his own. "Now, listen, I'm going to take Charlotte for a dance, so you just make sure you behave yourselves until I get back, or there'll be trouble; do you understand? Mary, you're old enough to keep an eye on them, can I rely on you?"

"Yes, of course, Uncle Fred; you go and enjoy yourself. We'll be fine. I think we'll all go and get some more to eat. The food here is lovely."

"Yes, it is, so make the most of it. Come on, then, Charlotte, let's see if we can get around the dance floor in one piece."

As Fred whirled Charlotte around the dancefloor, she had a wide grin on her face. "Oh, Fred, this is fun. I think it's the first time I've truly smiled since I lost Doris." She faltered as tears welled up in her eyes.

"Now, come on, don't worry about that, today. Do you know I've been thinking about that woman at Buzzacott House, and she seemed shifty, didn't she? I'm not sure I believed what she was telling us; she seemed nervous. I might have another look around and see if I can find out a bit more. I'd like to speak to the daughter when her mother isn't around. Mind you, I've never seen the daughter, have you?"

"No, they never come to the village, so I don't know where they buy their food. I'd be grateful if you could have another look, though I'm afraid Doris is gone for good."

"Don't worry about it now. Are you game for another dance? This one didn't go too badly, did it?"

"No, I enjoyed it, but Fred if you keep dancing with me, tongues will wag; you know what the village is like for gossip."

"It's not going to worry me and we're both single, so what's the problem?" Fred grinned as he swept her into another waltz.

The day after the wedding, Annie awoke early, and for a few seconds, she wondered where she was. She turned and saw that Robert was already awake and studying her intently. "What are you looking at? Do I look terrible?"

He grinned. "Don't be silly; you look beautiful. It's hard to believe you are here by my side and in my bed. Did you sleep well?"

"I did, but I'm not sure about these curtains drawn around the bed; it's so hot. Comfortable bed, though. Who would have ever thought I'd be sleeping on a feather mattress in a four-poster bed? It's a bit different from my palliasse stuffed with straw."

"Is that what you slept on in the cottage?"

"Yes, of course, it's what we all slept on, though, of course, since we moved to the Lodge House we all have feather mattresses. Mum and Liza remark on it nearly every single day."

"Well, you won't ever be sleeping on straw again, Mrs Fellwood, or should I say, Lady Anne?"

Annie giggled. "I'll never get used to it you know. I'll always be Annie to my family and friends, and that's how I want it to be."

"Yes, of course. Now, are you looking forward to our honeymoon?"

"I am. I can't wait to see London. I've heard Uncle Fred and Aunty Eveline talk about it, but I never thought I'd be going. They say there are so many people there it's impossible to be on your own. I'm not sure I'll like that, but I do want to go. Can we go and see Buckingham Palace and the Houses of Parliament?"

"Yes, of course, and St Paul's Cathedral and the Tower of London. There's so much I want to show you; it's another world. I'm not sure a month will be long enough."

"Oh, it will have to be. I don't think I could bear to be parted from Selina for longer than that. What time do we have to leave today? I'd like to go and see Mum and Selina before we go if that's all right?"

"Yes, of course. There will be time if you go after breakfast, and then Dodger can take us to the station to catch the train. Anyway, it's still early, and I've given orders that we are not to be disturbed, so what do you think? How can we pass the time until breakfast?"

"Hmm, I'm sure we can think of something." Her words were cut short as he pressed his lips to hers..

CHAPTER 31

It was a beautiful morning, and Sabina had promised herself a few hours in the garden. Life was so much easier for her now than at any time in her life. She wished her husband, Tom, was alive to enjoy everything with her. She missed him now, just as much as she ever had, and although family and friends had been telling her for some time that she should move on, it was easier said than done. However, devastating as it had been to lose her husband, she had known for some time it was going to happen. To some extent, she was glad he was no longer suffering from the terrible coughing spasms that racked his body and caused him to cough up blood. Consumption was a cruel killer.

This was not the case with her children, John and Emma. They had been in relatively good health, considering their meagre diet, until they caught diphtheria and died within hours of each other. Emma had seemed unaware of the serious implications of her illness, but John knew more, and Sabina would never forget the look in his eyes as he asked her, "Am I going to die, Mum? Please don't let me die." Even thinking of it now made the tears run down her cheeks as she remembered reassuring him she would do everything she could to make him better. Burying John, aged eight, and Emma, aged six, was the hardest thing she had ever had to do, and for a long time she had thought that the crushing grief would kill her; indeed, some days, she wished it would.

Even now, when she knew she was falling in love with Arthur Webber, a part of her felt it was wrong and that she did not deserve to be happy again. Why should she be happy when her loved ones had not had the chance to live their lives? If she could have swapped places with any one of them, she would have done so in a heartbeat. Liza knew how her mind worked and had given her more than one telling off over it all.

"That's not how it works, Sabina. We don't get to choose who lives and dies, only God can do that, and we have to make the best of it. You might not like it, but there's nothing you can do about it. The worst thing you can do is waste your life worrying about it. You know full well, Tom wouldn't want that, he would want you to be happy."

Sabina knew that Liza was right. As he lay dying, Tom had urged her to marry again if she ever got the chance. Suddenly, she felt she had to go to the churchyard and talk to Tom. She had told him before he died that she would go and talk to him, and he had said he would like that. Each time she was alone with Arthur these days, she was worried might propose, and if he did, she had no idea what she would say. She loved him, and he was a good man, and she thought they would be happy, but it felt disrespectful to Tom to think of marrying another man. She walked around the garden and selected Sweet Williams, roses, and honeysuckle to put on the three graves.

"Liza, I'm going to take some flowers to the graves. Can you keep an eye on the children, please?"

"Aye, of course, I can. You take your time, maid."

It was still early as she wandered along the lane to the church, but the sun was already hot and the sky a perfect blue. The hedges were full of buttercups and celandines, and the bees and butterflies were busy collecting nectar. She pushed open the lych-gate to the church and was pleased to see the graveyard was deserted. She had come to talk to

Tom regularly since he died, and she always worried someone would hear her and think she was going mad. Perhaps I am, she thought.

"Hello, Tom, it's me, again. I don't suppose for a minute, you can hear what I'm telling you, but I told you I would come and talk to you, and so here I am. It gives me some small comfort. I've no great belief that there is a God and that I'll see you again one day, but just in case, eh? Why would God take you, who never did anybody any harm, and our two lovely children, as well? It doesn't make any sense to me. Mind you, I'd better not let the vicar hear me talking like this. Anyway, Tom, our Annie is married to Master Robert now, and one day he'll be the Lord of the Manor, and she will be Lady Fellwood. They've gone to London on their honeymoon. Goodness knows what you think about that. And guess what; we are all living in the Lodge House. I certainly didn't see that coming. Now I'm rambling on a bit, I know because I don't know how to tell you this, Tom, but I'm courting again. I'm seeing a man called Arthur Webber. He lost his wife years ago and has four grown-up children. They moved into Liza and Isaac's old cottage after Isaac died. He's a good man, Tom, and I think he's going to ask me to marry him, and if I'm honest, I want to say yes. Anyway, he may not ask me, but just in case he does, I wanted to tell you first. I hope you don't mind, and it doesn't mean I love you any less it's just that you aren't here anymore, and I'm lonely. Right, that's enough self-pity for one day, I think. I'm going to get some water for your flowers now, and just so you know, I grew these myself."

She bent over the grave and cleared the dead flowers. Then she picked up the old earthenware pot and took it with her to the stream to wash it out and refill it with clean water. She returned to the grave, and seated on the wooden cross that marked her husband's grave, was a robin. She watched it and listened as it sang to her. Tears flowed down her cheeks again. Tom had told her a saying he knew. "When robins appear, a loved one is near." She always laughed at him and told him it was a load of rubbish, but since his death, there were not many times she had visited his grave and not seen a robin.

As she approached to put the flowers on the grave, the bird flew a short distance away and sat on another cross. Sabina arranged the flowers to her liking, then telling Tom once more how much she loved him, she turned away sadly and went to put flowers on John's and Emma's graves. As she moved away, she turned back for one last look, and the robin was sitting beside the flowers she had just arranged. She shook her head in wonder and smiled. "Thank you, Tom, I know what to do now."

As she approached the Lodge House, the children spotted her coming and ran out to meet her. Selina was missing her mum and had been clingy to Sabina for the last few days. She ran to her granny, and Sabina swept her off her feet and cuddled her. Just as they were about to go through the garden gate, Sabina heard a carriage coming and told the four children to stand still at the side of the lane. They obediently did as they were told. She knew Edward and Stephen would stand still, but she put her hand out in front of Helen and Danny, just in case they took it in their heads to wander out. Although there was only a month or two between them, to look at them, it could easily have been a year. Helen was the eldest but was several inches shorter than Danny. She was petite with blond hair and blue eyes; a delicate child. Danny could not have been more different. He was a stocky, thick-set child, with dark brown, almost black, curly hair and hazel eyes. His harelip, which had made it so difficult for him to feed as a baby, did not hold him back now, and he loved his food. Sabina was pleased with his progress. When she had taken him in at Robert's request, she had not expected him to survive, and the doctor had said with his club feet he would never walk. However, as a baby, she had put his twisted legs into splints, and whether this had made a difference she would never know, but walk he did, albeit with a pronounced limp. He had no idea that

Sabina was not his mother, and at nearly four, was not yet old enough to question the fact. Sabina knew that one day he would, and then he would be told the story of how Annie had found him abandoned in the woods.

The carriage slowed to a walking pace to squeeze past the Carter family because the lane was narrow. As it passed, and Charles Fellwood saw the family lined up, his heart was in his mouth because he immediately recognised his son. He tried to distract his wife's attention by talking to her, and even taking her hand, but amongst all the fair and red headed Carter family, Danny stood out, and she could not take her eyes off him. She banged on the roof with her stick.

"Driver, stop. Stop the carriage."

"Why are we stopping, Mama?" Sarah was surprised. Her mother never acknowledged any of the villagers. Her mother didn't answer.

Dodger reined in the horses in surprise, wondering if he had done something wrong. He alighted and went to the door.

"Yes, ma'am. Is there something I can help you with?"

Eleanor stared past Dodger, first at Danny and then Sabina. "Are these your children?"

"Yes, ma'am."

"All of them?"

"Yes, ma'am. I don't know if you know, but I'm Annie's mother. I'm pleased to meet you." Sabina dipped a curtsey.

"I've not stopped because I want to meet you. I've stopped because this child," she pointed at Danny, "looks different from the others, and I'm curious."

"Yes, he does, ma'am, we've always said so, but there it is." Sabina held her ground and risked a glance at Charles Fellwood, who was shaking his head at her. Sarah saw this and was even more puzzled.

"What is wrong with his mouth?"

"He was born like that, ma'am. There's nothing to be done, but he gets by."

"Is there anything else wrong with him?"

"I'm not sure what you mean, ma'am?"

"Is he an imbecile? Is he slow-witted?"

"Oh no, he certainly is not. He's as bright as a button and quick to learn. The only other problem he has is that he limps on account of his twisted feet."

Danny disliked the intense scrutiny and began to fidget. "Mum, can I go inside now, please? I don't like this lady." He looked at Eleanor with his wide brown eyes, and she knew for certain he was her son.

"Don't be rude, Danny. Now say you are sorry, and then you can all go inside."

Danny mumbled an apology, and Sabina pushed the children through the gate. "Will that be all, ma'am?"

She looked Eleanor straight in the eye, and both women knew the truth.

CHAPTER 32

A few days after Annie and Robert's wedding Arthur went to see Fred in his workshop.

"Hello, Fred, I'm just on my way home from work, but I've been meaning to call in and thank you again for making Dad that easel. He loves it. I'm not saying he'll ever be an artist, but he's getting better at it, especially now he can hold the brush in his makeshift hand. At least it gives him something to do."

"Oh, that's good; I'm pleased to hear it. It must be awful for him to be handicapped like that. We never know what's around the corner for any of us, do we? Just shows you have to live for today and let tomorrow take care of itself. I'm glad you called in because I've been wanting a word with you ever since the wedding."

"It's not about me dancing with Sabina, is it?"

"What? Oh no, of course not. I was delighted to see you both enjoying yourself, and anyway, it's none of my business; she's a wonderful woman, though, Arthur, so don't mess her around."

"You don't have to tell me, and no, of course, I won't. Always thinking of someone else she is, and it's thanks to her, that Dad finally thinks life's worth living again. What can I do for you?"

"I want to ask a favour. I expect you've noticed that I'm friendly with Charlotte. You know, the girl that had the baby a few weeks ago? She works at the inn for Mum, now."

"Yes, I know."

"I only came to know her because I found her having the baby in a gateway, and I took her to the inn. Eventually, she went with the baby to her aunt's house in Warkley. I thought that would be the last I saw of her, but then Mum broke her leg, and I asked Charlotte if she would come back to the inn to look after her. She'd worked as a nurse before she had the baby, you see. When I saw her in Warkley, she was upset because her aunt had sent her to the village on an errand, and whilst she was gone, she had taken the baby somewhere for adoption."

"That's awful, but how can I help?"

"It turns out my mum knew her granny, and not only that, but Mum gets on with Charlotte, and she's offered her a permanent job, even though her leg's mended now. Mum's told her she can keep the baby at the inn if she can get her back; my mum's a real soft touch sometimes."

Arthur looked puzzled as to why Fred was telling him all this.

"Sorry, Arthur, I'm rambling; I'll get to the point. I took Charlotte to see her aunt, and we persuaded her to tell us where she took the child. It wasn't easy because she doesn't want Charlotte to have the child back. She says it will bring more shame on the family, and it's best to leave things as they are. Eventually, she told us that she took the baby to Buzzacott House. Do you know where I mean? It's that big house on the edge of Exmoor."

"Aye, I know it. I don't know the people that live there, though."

"No, neither do I, but I took Charlotte there, and we asked about the baby. The woman told us that she takes the babies for a fee, and then arranges for childless couples to adopt them, no doubt for another fee. She said the baby had gone, and she couldn't get her back."

Arthur still looked puzzled. "So, what do you want me to do about it?"

"I'm just suspicious, I suppose. The house was neglected, and it looked filthy from the outside. You'd think with people coming to swap babies they'd keep it nice and tidy. The woman wasn't at all friendly, and she seemed shifty to me. It's a long shot, but Charlotte's desperate to get her daughter back, so I wondered if you'd go with me to have a snoop around; I'd feel better if I had company. I can't explain it, but I just feel something's not right. I thought if we go when they're out, we could have a good look around, and they'd be none the wiser."

Arthur grinned. "It sounds harmless enough, but what we need to know is when they are likely to be out, isn't it? We can't just go wandering around their property and then find they are in. They'll have the police after us. They'd probably think we were planning to rob them."

"Yes, I know. Annie says the old tramp who used to hang around the village is living nearby in some sort of ramshackle hut. Sam, I think he's called. Apparently, Master Robert said he didn't mind him living there. According to Annie, poor old Sam has already fallen foul of the woman living there. I thought if I rode out and asked him about their comings and goings, he might be able to tell us a regular time when they are likely to be out. What do you think? Are you game?"

"I wouldn't mind going with you, but it's difficult for me to get time off work. I'm not self-employed like you, so I can't come and go as I please, and I've recently had a few days off to go to France with Charlie Chugg. I can't ask again so soon. Sunday is the only day I get off, so unless they go to church, I might not be much help. I'll tell you what though, I'm seeing Charlie tonight, and he can come and go as he likes on his brother's farm. I'm sure he would go with you. Take it from me, he likes an adventure, does Charlie."

Fred grinned. "I've heard he does. Yes, ask him if you don't mind. Tell him there'll be a pint or two in it for him. I'll ride out and see Sam tomorrow, and find out if he knows of a good time to go. You won't say anything to anyone, will you, Arthur?"

"You need to ask?"

"No, sorry, of course, I don't."

The next day, despite some heavy drizzle, Fred saddled up his horse and rode towards Exmoor. It was a shame it was so misty because he knew that all around him, the scenery was beautiful, and he didn't get many opportunities to enjoy it. By trade, he was a carpenter, and the mainstay of his business was making coffins, for all too many people died young of this or that ailment. He could turn his hand to most jobs, but when he had the time, he liked to make furniture and keep it in stock to sell. Ideally, he would have loved a shop to display it all but didn't have the room. Fortunately, a lot of business came his way by word of mouth, for he was well-known for his good craftsmanship. He couldn't complain. He made a good enough living to support himself and his sister, Eveline as well, as his three children and those of his brother, William. They didn't go hungry, and the children were fairly well clothed, though trying to keep them in shoes was a challenge. He was grateful to Eveline, for he could never have managed without her.

When his wife, Lucy had been alive, she had been unable to cope with the children, and it had been so difficult to keep an eye on things in the house and work enough hours to support them all. Then, with all the fuss over Sarah, abandoning William's children in the workhouse in London, Eveline and he had gone to find them, and he had come up with the idea that she could move in and look after all of them. It had worked out well, and Fred knew the arrangement suited Eveline, too. However, he wondered how much longer it would last, for he knew that Charlie and

Eveline were becoming an item, however much she might deny it. Only a blind man would not have seen they were a couple in love when they danced at Annie's wedding. Ah, well, he thought to himself, she deserves to be happy, and I wouldn't deny her. At least, the children were not tiny babies, anymore.

He enjoyed his ride despite the wet weather, for he seldom took to the saddle. Usually, he was taking wood or tools to or from a job, and for that, he needed his horse and cart. When he came to the woods on the edge of the Manor House land, he looked around for Sam. The undergrowth was dense, and he meandered along the track keeping an eye out on either side. He didn't want to shout out for, he thought Sam probably valued his privacy and might hide. In the end, he found him by following the smell of cooking. He followed his nose through the trees to where he found the old man sitting by a fire. A large pot was suspended above the fire, and the smell from whatever he was cooking, was surprisingly tempting. He climbed down and led his horse forward.

"Hello, Sam, I'm Annie's, Uncle Fred. Would you mind if I stop to speak to you for a few minutes?"

"I'm not doing any harm, and Annie's young man said I could stay here as long as I like; I ain't doing no harm, mister."

"No, I can see that Sam and I'm not here to make trouble for you. I just want to talk to you about something."

"Well, there's usually trouble when people want to speak to me, but I've just been here minding me own business for weeks now. I ain't stole nothin'."

"No, really, there's no trouble. I'm just hoping you can help me with something. Sam, what are you cooking? It smells delicious."

"Aye, it does, doesn't it? 'Tis some trout I caught earlier, and I've sprinkled a few wild herbs on them. Me mother taught me to cook when I was a nipper. Sam, she said, if you can cook, you'll never starve. And she was right, I can make a tasty meal out of next to nothing. Knew what she was talking, about did my old mum."

Fred smiled at the old man. "It just so happens I have some fresh bread and cheese in my saddlebag. Would you like to share your fish, and my lunch, and we could eat together? Your cooking has made me hungry."

"That sounds like a good idea, young man, and if you're a friend of Annie's, then you can't be all bad. Mind you, her other uncle; he must be your brother; I've no time for him. A nasty piece of work he is for all his religion."

"That's got to be our George you're talking about, and I don't disagree with you; he's not the easiest man to get along with, nor the kindest."

"You can say that again."

Fred went to get his lunch, and the old man vanished into his hut and came out with two plates. He poked about in the coals of the fire with a stick and pushed out a tin with a lid on. Deftly, he removed the lid, and inside were some small potatoes. He raised his eyes to Fred. "Don't ask where I got 'em, but I don't eat much."

Fred grinned as Sam slid some potatoes and one fish from the cooking pot onto each plate. Fred broke off a piece of bread each and a lump of cheese, and the two men settled down to their meal.

"Here you are, I've only got one fork, but you can have it. I learnt to eat with my fingers long before I learnt to use a fork." Fred took the implement gratefully.

For a few minutes, they munched away in silence.

"Do you know, Sam, I think this is one of the most delicious meals, I've ever eaten. I don't know what herbs you've put on the fish, but it's lovely."

The old man grinned showing all his decayed teeth and much of his last mouthful of food. "Aye, I told you my mother knew how to cook. This bread and cheese is good, too. Now, what do you want to know?"

"Annie mentioned that you'd fallen foul of the people living in Buzzacott House, and I wanted to know if you see much of them. It seems they take in babies from people who don't want them or can't keep them and then pass them on to people who do. All for a price, of course. The baby of a friend of mine was taken there a few weeks ago, and now she wants her daughter back. We asked the woman who lives there, but she said the baby was adopted. I think she was hiding something, and I'd like to have another look around, preferably when the house is empty. Do you know if they are ever out on a regular day each week?"

"A horrible woman, she is. I went there once to beg a crust of bread on a day when the fish weren't biting, and she threatened to set her dog on me. A great brute, he is. I think she would have too, so I haven't been there since. It's difficult for me to know what day it is, but she goes out together with her daughter about once a week."

"Do you know what day of the week, it is?"

"No, not really, but they go on the horse and cart, and I think they go into the next town for their shopping, so I expect it's on market day; that's what most folks do. Anyway, they go off with the cart empty and come back with shopping on it and food for the horse. They don't go in the direction of Hartford, so they must go to Eggleston. Is that any help to you, Fred?"

"Yes, Sam, I think it is. Do they go in the morning or the afternoon?"

"About mid-morning usually, and they don't come back until a couple of hours after dinner."

"Sam, I'm grateful to you, and when I next pass this way I'll bring you a loaf of bread and some more cheese. Would you like that? I've got an old tarpaulin at home that I don't use anymore. Would you like it to cover the roof of your hut? It might make it a bit more waterproof. I can give you a hand to get it up there."

Fred was treated to another glimpse of Sam's rotten teeth as the old man grinned at him in thanks.

CHAPTER 33

Not a word was spoken in the carriage as it made its way along the tree-lined avenue that led to Hartford Manor. The enormous oak trees had been planted many years before by a long-dead ancestor who could never have lived long enough to see them in all their glory. They cast dappled shade across the lane, and as intended, successfully hid the old house from sight until the last bend had been negotiated and then it was revealed in all its splendour. Hartford Manor was a beautiful building, which had been virtually rebuilt in the late eighteenth century after a fire. Old manuscripts found in the library proved that a house had stood on the site for hundreds of years.

Sarah wasn't sure what the problem was, but from the icy atmosphere which had pervaded the carriage, she knew something quite serious had upset her mother. She debated whether to ask, or even introduce an innocent topic of conversation, but one look at her parents' faces persuaded her that it was better not to interfere. It was with some relief that she alighted from the carriage when it arrived outside the Manor House, and the footman opened the door for her. Now she did risk turning back to her parents.

"Mama, Papa may I go for a ride, please? It's not the same in London riding around the park, and I'd love to take

Jenny out for a gallop over the moors. It's so good to be home, and it's a lovely day."

Her parents looked at her distractedly as if they had forgotten she was there. Her father smiled weakly at her. "Yes, of course, just make sure you tell the stable boy where you are going, please, and be back in time for our evening meal."

"Yes, Papa, thank you." She raced off to her room to change her clothes, delighted to be out of the carriage and free to do as she pleased.

Eleanor stepped down from the carriage and headed straight for the house, tight-lipped and grim-faced, ignoring the servants who stood in a line waiting to welcome their employers back home. Two footmen lifted Charles out of the carriage and placed him gently in the waiting wheelchair. He bade them push him over to Sid Hobbs, where he spoke a few words to him, permitting the servants to resume their duties. As the servants ambled back into the house, one or two whispered to each other. "Blimey, did you see the face on her Ladyship? I wonder what's upset her." Sid Hobbs silenced them with a stern look.

The footmen took Charles to his downstairs room, and his valet arrived to make him comfortable. He was tired, for it had been a long journey home, and his body ached. He closed his eyes and hoped to get some rest before answering the questions from his wife that he knew were inevitable.

However, this hope was not fulfilled when twenty minutes later, Eleanor came into the room. Charles opened his eyes tiredly. "The journey has exhausted me, my dear, and I feel quite unwell. Would you mind if we spoke later when I've had a rest?"

"I'm sorry, Charles, I know you're tired, and so am I, but this cannot wait. I need to know, though I think I already do; is that child our son?"

Charles sighed deeply. "It's no good me telling you otherwise, is it, when you already know the answer? Yes, that was our son. I'm sorry Eleanor, I hoped you would never see him again but, of course, I could not foresee the future. I had no idea the Carter family would ever move into the Lodge House; how could I?"

"When the child was born, I asked you to get rid of it. To send it far away to be looked after so that I would never have to see it again. It was so deformed, and you knew it reminded me of my younger brother. I begged you to do that. Why did you not do as I asked?"

"It was more difficult than you think. I didn't know anyone who lived far away who would take a deformed child. More than that, it needed to be someone who could wet nurse it. The doctor didn't think the baby would survive on cow's milk, so it had to be a woman feeding her own baby. What did you expect me to do with the child? Throw it down a mine shaft, or into the local pond? I've heard it happens, but I didn't think you meant for me to do that when you insisted I get rid of it."

"No, of course, I didn't, but I thought Doctor Luckett would help you to arrange something. I thought he would have colleagues all over the country who could help. I've always thought the child was miles away from here being cared for by someone, and now I find he's been living in the village all along. Everyone must know, and we must be the laughing stock for miles around. How could you disgrace us like this?"

"No, that's where you are wrong. When Robert came into your bedroom and saw his deformed brother, he was upset, and it was too late then to tell him the story that child had been stillborn as we intended. He was keen on this servant girl even then and had befriended the whole Carter family. He told me Sabina, the mother, had recently given birth and would be able to feed our baby. He offered to ask her if she would take the child. She had recently lost her husband with consumption and had eight children of her own. The family were near starvation and he thought if I paid her, she would look after our baby, and that is what she agreed to do. Doctor Luckett told me the family was poor but clean and tidy and that she was a good mother. He thought the child would be cared for as well there, as anywhere, and so that is what we did. Robert took the baby and handed it over to the servant girl, and she pretended she'd found it in the woods. It's not uncommon for these things to happen when girls get in the family way, and the story was accepted by local folk. Few people know the truth, and they know better than to tell anyone, or I'd make their life very uncomfortable."

"Is this why you agreed to Robert marrying that girl?"

"Yes, he threatened to tell you about the boy, and I didn't want that to happen. However, in truth, I would have had no say in the matter because he is of age, and we had already signed the estate over to him. You may want to blame me, but I couldn't have stopped him, anyway."

"You must have known I would eventually see the boy if they lived in the Lodge House; we pass it every time we go out."

"Well, again, I didn't know they would move there, and there was nothing I could do to stop it."

"So, is that all your secrets or do you have any more? Is there anything else I should know about?"

Charles grimaced inwardly but kept his face composed. "Of course not; what else could there be?"

"I don't know, Charles. We've never been madly in love, but I did think we were always honest with each other. Now, I'm not so sure."

He reached out, and she allowed him to take her hand. "I'm sorry, my dear, I know this has been a terrible shock for you, but nothing needs to change. From what I hear and from the way the boy looked, he is well cared for and is thriving. He may never know it, but at least he has his brother in his life, and you can rest assured Robert will see that he never wants for anything. What did you think of him? Apart from his deformed lip and the fact he limped, I thought he looked quite normal. He looked intelligent, didn't he, and the woman said he is."

Eleanor drew her hand away. "That's all very well, but as a mother, how do you think I'm going to feel when I drive by in the carriage and see a son of mine playing in the road with all the local riff-raff?"

"I'm sorry to say this Eleanor, but perhaps you should have thought a bit longer before rejecting him, so quickly, and so finally. I wanted to keep him to see how he progressed, and now I think he would have been fine."

"That's easy to say now, but at the time, the doctor thought that as well as his physical disabilities, he would also be an imbecile. I saw enough of what that entails with my brother, Sydney. It was heart-breaking to see, and I didn't want to watch a child of mine suffer like that."

"No, I know, and I do understand, but I don't think this child is an imbecile; when I looked into his eyes, I thought he looked normal. Anyway, it's too late now; what's done is done, and we must just make the best of it."

"Well, the family will have to move. I'm not having them living there right under our noses. That woman was looking down her nose at me. How dare she? A commoner like her! As soon as Robert is back from honeymoon, he will have to make other arrangements."

"I don't think he will, my dear, and we can't make him. Perhaps we could have another driveway made in the other direction. Then you would not need to go that way. Now, I'm sorry, but I must rest." The old man laid his head back and closed his eyes. He was relieved when he heard his bedroom door close.

Difficult questions were also being asked in the Lodge House. Edward had only been four, and Stephen two, when Annie appeared with the newborn baby, and the tale she had found him in the woods. They had never considered that Danny was not their brother. Sabina was glad her two eldest children, Willie at fifteen and Mary at thirteen, now lived in with their employers. They knew the truth and may have given something away to Lady Fellwood, though they too knew the subject was not for discussion.

Stephen, now aged six, was curious. He pulled at Sabina's skirt. "Mum, what did the lady want? Why did she look at Danny?" The other children pricked up their ears, keen to hear the answer too.

"I think she was just taking an interest now that Annie has married Master Robert. Danny does stand out because he has dark hair, and you all have red and fair hair." She ruffled Danny's dark curls. "And, of course, he is so handsome. Anyway, Liza, I believe you made some scones this morning, didn't you? Shall we have some with jam and cream for our tea?"

Liza came swiftly to the rescue. "I did, so you children sit up to the table, and I'll put the kettle on." Sabina looked at her gratefully over the children's heads and heaved a sigh of relief.

CHAPTER 34

Charlie agreed to go to Buzzacott House with Fred and they knew that Friday was market day in Eggleston. Charlie helped Jimmy and Alfred with the milking and then rode over to call for Fred at nine o'clock. They knew it was no good arriving too early at the house until the two women had left for their day's shopping. Eveline was delighted to see Charlie and cooked both men a hearty breakfast of sausages, bacon, and eggs with large doorsteps of fresh bread and field mushrooms.

"My goodness, that went down well. You certainly can cook, Eveline." Charlie contentedly pushed back his empty plate. "You're a lucky man getting meals like that cooked for you every day, Fred. Maria is getting better at her cooking all the time, mind, but she's got a way to go to match you, Eveline. I don't think we'll need any dinner."

"I must remember to take a loaf of bread and a chunk of cheese for Sam because I promised him. I need to load up that old tarpaulin on the horse too. If you could give me a hand, Charlie we can get going then. By the time we've put the tarpaulin on Sam's roof, I should think the women will be well out of the way."

Eveline started to clear the table. "Just be careful what you're doing, you two. You don't want the police after you for trespassing. I don't see what good this will do, Fred. I'd rather you left well alone."

"Don't you worry, we're only going to have a look around, and no one will even know we've been there. Now, we'll see you later. Bye"

The men loaded up the horses and galloped off in the direction of Exmoor. It was a nice dry day, so this time, Fred was able to enjoy the views of the countryside all around him. It didn't take long to reach Sam's hut, though, once again, they smelt the smoke from his campfire, before they saw him. They dismounted and tied their horses to a tree, and Fred began to unload the tarpaulin as Sam appeared, trudging up the hill from the stream below.

"Hello, Sam, how are you?"

"I'm all right, Fred, thank you. Who's this?" Sam looked warily at Charlie.

"Oh, this is Charlie, he's a good friend of mine. You don't need to worry about Charlie. He's come to help me put this tarpaulin on your roof, and we've brought some nails to keep it in place. Would you like us to do that for you?"

"Aye, I'd be grateful. It leaks badly when there's a heavy downpour, and then I get so cold. I've got a makeshift ladder here that I made; that might help."

The tarpaulin was heavy, and the two men struggled to lift it onto the roof, then they took it in turns climbing the rickety ladder and nailing it down.

"There, that will be better, Sam, and now it's nailed down it shouldn't blow off in the wind. Oh, I've just remembered, I've got some bread and cheese in my saddle bag for you. In return for that delicious fish, you cooked for me the last time I saw you."

"I'll cook some more for you if you like. I caught some trout earlier this morning, so it's all fresh. It's a real pleasure for me to have a bit of company. I don't see many folk and that suits me fine because they often bring trouble, but you're different, Fred. I like you."

"That is tempting, but my sister cooked us a plateful of bacon and eggs before we came out, so we'll give it a miss today. Thanks for the offer, though. Now, Sam, have you seen the women from the house pass this morning on their way to market?"

"Aye, they went by not ten minutes before you showed up."

"Did they speak to you?"

"Nay, they wouldn't speak to me. And come to that, I don't want to speak to them so that's all right."

"What time do you think they'll be back, Sam?"

"I don't know what time it will be, but it's usually late in the afternoon, so not for a while yet. Are you going to the house?"

"Yes, we want to have a bit of a nose around, but we don't want them to know."

"I'll tell you what; if they pass before you come back, I'll give you a warning so you can scarper."

"That sounds good, but how will you do that?" The old man grinned. "I'll show you."

He vanished into the hut and came out carrying a hunting trumpet. He put it to his lips and blew hard, managing a long, but not very tuneful, note.

Fred and Charlie grinned. "That's perfect, thanks, Sam. I'm not even going to ask how you came by a hunting trumpet, but that would be helpful. We'll see you later. It shouldn't take us long, anyway."

They left the horses tied up near Sam's hut and walked back to the road. They didn't see a soul, for it was an isolated spot, and few folk came that way. They did not have far to walk until they came to a pair of large wrought iron gates, which were wide open. In better days, the gates must have been a grand entrance to a house of some note, but the years had not been kind. One gate was leaning on its side, and both were rusty and had not been painted for years. The driveway was full of weeds, and there was a deserted atmosphere as they made their way to the house.

"Creepy, isn't it, Fred? I don't think I'd like to live here, though, with some attention, it could be a lovely place again. It must be years since this undergrowth was cut back, and it makes it so dark and gloomy. I can see why you wanted some company. I wouldn't be comfortable coming here on my own."

They went to the front door and tried the handle and found it was locked. The large windows on either side of the door were covered in grime, and it was difficult to see in. Fred was careful not to make too many obvious marks but went to the side window and rubbed off some of the dirt so he could peer in. Both of the rooms that they could see into were sparsely furnished, with no sign that babies were being cared for. Charlie went around the side of the house, where he came to a wooden door set into a high fence. He tried the handle, and that too was locked.

"We're not going to be able to see much Fred unless we can get over this fence, and it's pretty high. I don't know why they need a fence like this out here in the middle of nowhere. It doesn't look that old, either. What do you think, shall we climb over?"

"Yes, I'm game, if you are. The front garden is fairly small for a house this size, so I think most of the land must be out the back. Is there something we can stand on?"

They searched around and found an empty barrel, and rolled it over to the fence. "We must remember to put it back when we go."

Charlie took a rope from his waist, tied it around the barrel, and threw the other end over the fence. "You may think I've done this before." He grinned. "I always like to make sure I've got a way out if I'm going into a tricky situation."

Fred looked at him in admiration. "You think of everything, Charlie. You're a handy chap to have around. Here goes then."

Fred hauled himself up and over the fence, followed swiftly by Charlie. The back garden was huge and overgrown. The neglected feel to the property continued, and they made their way to a window that looked into a kitchen. Here, there were more signs of someone living there, but the room was dirty, with unwashed dishes stacked high near the sink and what looked like a pile of laundry. They tried the handle to the back door, but again, it was locked. They found this surprising, for few folk bothered to lock their doors locally, and for a house this remote, it seemed unnecessary. They didn't get the chance to explore further, for suddenly, a large dog appeared, baring its teeth and growling at them.

"Don't run, Fred! If you run, it will chase you, and I think it means business. I've got a stick, so you just back away slowly and get over the fence. I'll keep it busy until you're over, and then I'll make a run for it. Gingerly, Fred retreated to the fence whilst Charlie brandished the stick at the dog. However, as soon as it saw Fred start to climb the fence, it ran towards him, barking. Charlie lunged at it and whacked it across the rear haunches. The dog yelped sharply and turned his attention to Charlie, leaving Fred time to get to the top of the fence.

"Come on, Charlie. Run for it, and I'll help you up."

The dog held on to the stick with its large yellow fangs, and Charlie slowly edged backwards towards the fence. Battling with the stick in one hand, he grabbed the rope in the other but had to turn his attention to getting over the fence. Immediately the animal saw its chance and sunk its teeth deeply into Charlie's leg. He screamed in pain and kicked viciously at the brute's head. The dog held on, but a second kick, sent it spinning away, yelping and with Fred's help, he managed to get onto the fence. The two men virtually fell down the other side, and Charlie bent to survey the damage to his leg. He had a nasty bite which was bleeding profusely.

"Bloody animal! Talk about vicious. Now, why would they need a nasty dog like that, out here?"

"Come on, Charlie, I'll put this barrel back where we found it, and then we'd better make ourselves scarce. There's nothing else we can do, anyway."

Leaning on Fred, Charlie limped his way back to Sam who was waiting for them. "How did you get on? Oh, what's wrong with your leg? Did the dog get you? I thought I heard barking."

"Yes, damn the brute, he's had a right go at my leg." Charlie rolled up his trouser leg to reveal a deep bite. The blood was running freely down his ankle and over his boots.

"You'd better let me see to that, or you could end up losing your leg. Sit down and take off your boot and sock, so I can see what I'm doing. I know a thing or two about medicine. Living the life I do, I've had to take care of myself, and my mother didn't just teach me to cook. Fred, can you fetch a bucket of clean water from the stream, please?"

The two men were amazed at the efficiency of the old man as he made Charlie plunge his whole leg into the icy cold water. He went to his hut and came out with a package of white powder, which he added to the bucket.

"Don't worry, it's only salt, so it won't hurt you, but it will clean the wound, so give it a good soak. I've seen that dog, and trust me, you don't want your leg to become infected. I've seen what can happen many a time over the years."

Eventually, when he let Charlie take his leg out of the cold water, they could see that the wound was clean, and the bleeding had almost stopped. Sam vanished into his hut again and came out with an old tin and some rags. He passed the tin to Fred. "Here, Fred see if you can get the lid off that, will you?"

Fred prized off the lid to reveal some greyish-green ointment inside.

"I haven't had cause to use this for a long time, fortunately, but it's made of all sorts of herbs, and is good to help wounds to heal. We'll put a bit of that on, and I'll bind your leg tightly with these rags."

The old man worked swiftly, and before long, Charlie's leg was bound, and Sam allowed him to replace his clothing and boots.

"There, now if I were you, I'd ride home and rest that for a few days. It should be all right now but keep an eye on it, and if it starts to go red around the wound, you'd better go and see a doctor; or come back and see me. I think I know nearly as much as any doctor, or I wouldn't have lived as long as I have. What did you find at the house, anyway?"

"Not much really, but it's run down and neglected. I think if you want folk to come and buy babies, you would need to make it a bit more welcoming. And why would you need a high fence and a vicious dog like that? It doesn't make sense. I don't feel inclined to go back, though. I think we need to ask Constable Folland to make a few enquiries and see what he can find out. He can go to the house officially to ask a few questions. Anyway, Sam, thank you so much for your help. No doubt, we'll see you again, soon."

The two men returned to their horses and galloped back to the village.

CHAPTER 35

Annie was having the time of her life in London, though she missed her daughter and the rest of the family. Until she met Robert, she had never been further than the neighbouring villages and had been amazed at the number of people and shops in Exeter when she visited on the train. However, that experience had done little to prepare her for the sights of London. Every street was teeming with people, all apparently on important business, for they hurried past with no time to stop and chat. Everywhere she looked, people were trying to sell something to make a few pence. Flower girls, matchstick girls, and shoeshine boys, carters selling fish, meat, and vegetables, and even people acting, or singing and dancing, with their caps out in front of them, hoping for a few coppers.

Annie was spellbound but saddened by the number of homeless people wandering around aimlessly trying to find something, anything, to eat. What upset her the most were the ragamuffin children, all as thin as rakes, but as ready as the next man to pick your pocket and rob you. In Hartford, although many lived at subsistence level, there was usually a small amount of help available from the Overseers of the Poor. Even neighbours would often assist if one fell on particularly hard times. Here, no one seemed to care for the plight of the orphans and poor people. It was all Robert could do to stop Annie from handing out all her money to the children that constantly begged.

"Annie, you mustn't show your money in public, or you may be attacked. It doesn't matter how much you hand out; there will always be a crowd wanting more. I know it upsets you, and it is awful, but we can't save them all."

"No, I know, but it's so sad, and don't forget I know what it's like to be hungry. It's not right, we have so much, and they have so little."

He took her hand and led her firmly to the waiting carriage.

"What would you like to do now? Shall we go back to the house and have some lunch, and then go somewhere else this afternoon? You haven't been to St Paul's Cathedral, yet and that's worth seeing. Or we could take a boat trip down the Thames? What do you think?"

The honeymoon couple were staying at Percy's house in Grosvenor Square, a wealthy district in the Mayfair area of London. Fortunately, Percy was broadminded and cared not the slightest that Robert had married a servant girl. He was much of the mind to live and let live. His late father, Algernon, was Robert's maternal uncle and by far the wealthiest member of the family. Percy had lost his mother several years before, and Algernon had died five years ago. Until his father's death, Percy had dated young women and made a pretence of his intention to marry one. He hated leading the girls on but knew his father would never understand his sexual preference for young men and didn't want to risk being disinherited. However, now that his fortune was safe, as long as he was discreet, he could do as he liked.

Grosvenor Square, or Little America, as it was sometimes known, was a beautiful area of London. Percy's house had a basement, four floors and attics, and was sumptuously furnished. Outside, an extensive park with tall trees provided a safe and pleasant area for the residents to enjoy walking or riding in.

"Why is it called Little America?" Annie asked Robert.

"Apparently, John Adams, the second president of the United States, lived at number nine at one time. He was an ambassador here."

"I see." Annie had no idea what an ambassador was but decided to leave it there. "There is one thing I'd like to do while we are in London."

"What's that, then? Shopping for presents for all the family?" Robert grinned at her. "That's fine if you'd like to."

"No, well, I would like to do that, but not today. You once told me about your friend, Stephen Turner, who was at Westford School with you, do you remember?"

"Yes, of course. He's a good friend. I hoped he would come to the wedding so you could meet him, but he's working in Europe, and couldn't get back. So, what about Stephen?"

"Well, you told me that his father is a famous Harley Street surgeon, and I wondered if he could do anything for Danny. You know about his lip or his twisted feet. Of course, it would probably cost a fortune, so if it's impossible you must say so."

Robert looked at her in surprise. "That's an excellent idea. I always intended to do that, and never got around to it. I know his parents, so I think they will see us. It might be best if we go to his father's surgery because I can't quite remember where they live in London, though I know they have a house in Devon. We'll get some lunch and then go to Harley Street. If he can't see us today, I'm sure we can make an appointment."

Later that afternoon, the carriage stopped outside the Harley Street premises in Marylebone, and Annie and Robert made their way up the steps. They stepped into a waiting room where an elderly woman sat behind a desk.

"May I help you?"

"Yes, I hope so. I'm a friend of Doctor Turner's son, Stephen, and I wondered if the doctor could spare me a few minutes of his time?"

"It's unlikely if you don't have an appointment; the doctor is busy."

"Is it possible you could at least ask for us, please?"

"If you'd like to take a seat, I'll mention your presence to Doctor Turner when he is next free. May I ask your names, please?"

"Yes, of course. Tell him it's Lord and Lady Fellwood, thank you." The receptionist looked suitably impressed, whilst Annie stifled a giggle.

"Oh, Robert, that sounds so grand. It doesn't sound like us at all.

"Well, it's close to the truth. The titles will be ours one day. Might as well make use of them."

They waited for nearly half an hour before they saw an elderly man limp out of the door in front of them and go to the receptionist to make another appointment. That done, the woman smiled at them, then knocked on her employer's door and went in. After a few minutes, she held the door open and said the doctor could spare them a few minutes.

Robert entered first and was greeted by an elderly, distinguished-looking gentleman with white hair and a beard. He shook Robert's hand warmly. "Robert, my boy, how nice to see you. I can't think how many years it is since I last saw you. It must be four or five at least since you came to stay for a week or two in Devon. How are you? Is this your lovely wife?"

"Hello, sir, it's good to see you too, and yes, it is a few years. Please may I introduce Anne, my wife. We're on our honeymoon in London."

The doctor took Annie's hand and leaned over and touched it with his lips. "My dear, it is good to meet you; I'll have you know you have married a fine young man."

"Thank you, sir, yes, I already know that."

"I'm sure you do. Now, I expect you know that Stephen is still working in Italy?

"Yes, sir, how is he?

"Oh, fine, fine, as far as I know. He came home last Christmas, but we haven't seen him since, though he writes occasionally. We're planning to go and see him this Christmas. Now, is this just a social call, or is there something I can help you with?"

"It's a bit of both really, sir. I wanted to look in and say hello whilst we are in the city, but I would also like your advice. Anne has a younger brother, who was born with a hare lip and club feet, and I wondered if there is any treatment you could suggest that would be helpful. I know that if nothing can be done, you will be honest and tell me so, whereas some doctors would just be after our money. I wouldn't want the child to suffer any unnecessary treatment."

"That is a sad statement, but probably true. How old is the child?"

"He's four, sir. He struggled to thrive as a baby because feeding him was difficult, but he manages to eat most things now. He walks, but with a bad limp."

"Do you know what caused the deformities? I mean, does it run in the family?"

"No, sir, not as far as we know."

"Is he mentally impaired?"

"No, sir, he is intelligent, and able to speak, though not clearly."

"I see. It's difficult to say without seeing the child for myself because every case is different. I do treat patients with deformities with increasing success. Possibly we could break and reset his ankles so that his limp would be improved. With his hare lip, I would need to see him and examine the inside of his mouth because it depends on how extensive the deformity is. Is the child here with you in London?"

"No, sir, he's in North Devon. I was just seeking your opinion as to whether it is worth me making further enquiries."

"Yes, I would say it is. As you know, I have a property in North Devon where my wife, Clara, prefers to live. She doesn't like the city, and the countryside is much better for her health. Stephen lived there in the holidays when he attended Westford School. I go there as often as I can, and Clara occasionally joins me here in London. I shall retire there, eventually. Now, young lady, would you like me to take a look at your little brother?"

"Yes, sir, I'd be grateful, but how can we arrange that? Would we have to bring Danny to London?"

"That would be one way of doing things, but I am going to Devon for a few days next month, and I'd be more than happy to take a look at him whilst I'm there."

Robert intervened. "That is extremely kind of you, sir. If you think something can be done, we would also need to have some idea of the cost, if possible."

"One step at a time. I can't promise he can be helped until I see him, but I'm more than happy to take a look. Now, I must see my next patient, but would you like to come to dinner this evening? Then we can talk about it further and hear each other's news. I had no idea you had taken over the Hartford Estate from your father. Is he in good health?"

"Yes, sir, he's fine, but since he had a stroke, he's found it all too much to manage. Anyway, we would love to come to dinner this evening. Where do you live?"

"Here, of course. My surgery is only on the lower floor. Would you like to come back at seven o'clock this evening, and we can eat together?"

"Yes, thank you. We'll see you, later."

As Annie and Robert walked away from Harley Street, Robert took her hand. "That went well, didn't it? Are you happy to go to dinner with him, tonight? I couldn't very well refuse."

"Yes, of course. He seems nice, and it was kind of him to say he will see Danny."

"Good, what do you want to do now? Shall we get a carriage, back to Percy's house, and relax before we need to leave for dinner, or is there anywhere else you'd like to go?"

"There is one more place I'd like to visit if it's all right with you."

"Of course, where do you have in mind?"

"Highgate Cemetery. It's where my Uncle William is buried, and I know Gran would be pleased if I visited. I liked him too, so I'd like to go, anyway. The only trouble is I've no idea where the grave is, and I think it's a big cemetery."

"We can go and have a look. Is there a headstone?"

"Yes, there should be, my Uncle Fred paid to have one put there, but no one has visited since. The landlady that William and Sarah stayed with, showed Uncle Fred where the grave was because she went to the funeral. I never thought to ask him, or Aunty Eveline, where the grave was before we left home."

"We might be able to find the vicar or someone to ask. I'm not exactly sure where Highgate is, but we'd better get a carriage because I don't think it's within walking distance."

It was a good job they hailed a carriage because the cemetery turned out to be over four miles from where they were and too far to walk in the time they had available. They entered the imposing gates to the cemetery and started walking down the first path, keeping an eye open for William's grave. It was a hauntingly beautiful place, with old trees covered in ancient ivy and many ornate graves, some with sculptured angels adorning them. It was very peaceful. The cemetery had been opened some forty-odd years before when the graveyards in central London were becoming overfull and considered a health risk. There had been a lot of burials since then, and they looked around to find someone to help them find the grave they sought. The only man they found, other than visitors like themselves, was a labourer digging a grave. He asked how long ago the burial took place and was able to direct them to the more recent excavations. They thanked him and continued going methodically up and down the rows of tombstones.

After half an hour or so, Annie gave a yell. "Robert, here it is! I've found it."

He hurried over to join her, and together they surveyed the granite tombstone and read the inscription.

"In Loving Memory of William Edward Carter who died on 14 June 1881, aged 36 years.
A native of North Devon and of the Imperial Maritime Customs, China.
Rest in Peace."

Annie had tears in her eyes. "I'm so glad we found it. I'm sure he would be pleased that one of his family took the trouble to visit."

"Yes, I expect he would. What did he do in China? It sounds impressive."

"I'm not sure, but I know he was regarded as very clever, and he had a good job. They kept it open for him for a year to allow him to come home and see his family. I'm glad Uncle Fred put that he was from North Devon too because he's a long way from home. At least, I can tell the family he has a nice gravestone."

"Yes, now if you've seen enough, I think we'd better get a carriage back to Percy's house and get ready for dinner with Doctor Turner."

They retraced their steps down the path and waved their thanks to the gravedigger as they passed.

CHAPTER 36

Charlie's leg was throbbing as he galloped back from Sam's hut with Fred. They rode to Fred's house as it was nearer than Hollyford Farm, and Charlie was more than glad of an excuse to see Eveline again. She was busy making pastry and had flour all over the table, and her forearms were covered in it. Her face was flushed with the heat of the kitchen, and wisps of her slightly greying hair had escaped from her bun. Charlie thought she looked beautiful. Hearing them come in, she looked up from her task.

"Hello, I'm glad you're back. How did you get on?"

"Yes, all right; we didn't get caught, anyway, but there was a huge dog there, and he's taken a chunk out of Charlie's leg."

"Oh no, Fred, I told you not to go. Charlie, I'd better have a look at your leg and bathe it."

"No, it's all right, you finish making your pastry. Old Sam bathed it for me and bandaged it up so the wound's clean. He put some sort of ointment on it, which he says will stop it festering, so I think it's best left alone for now."

"Oh, well, I hope he knows what he's doing. Dog bites can be serious if they get infected. You must keep an eye on it."

"Sam certainly seemed to know what he was doing, and he's had to look after himself for years so I trust him. He's a nice man when you get to know him. I don't know how he came to be living like he is, but I think he prefers it."

"How about you, Fred? Did the dog bite you, as well?"

"No, luckily for me, Charlie took the brunt of it. It's a nasty bite though, so Eveline's right you must take care of it."

"I'm making this pastry for a pie for tea, but I have some nice crusty bread, cheese, and pickled onions if you're hungry? Charlie, if you would like some too, it would give you a chance to rest your leg for a while before you ride home."

"That's kind of you, but you've already cooked me breakfast, and I'm not hungry. I wouldn't say no to a cup of tea, though."

"Fine, sit yourself down then, because I want to hear what happened. You don't mind if Charlie stays do you, Fred?"

"No, of course not. I was grateful for your company this morning, Charlie, and I don't like to think what would have happened if I'd faced that dog on my own. He was vicious. Please stay for a cup of tea by all means. If you don't, Eveline will only be cross with me."

Eveline blushed furiously and slapped her brother on the arm. "Behave yourself, Fred Carter, or you'll get no dinner later."

As they drank their tea, they told Eveline all that had happened that morning.

"It does seem strange as you say, but I don't see what you can do about it. I mean, they aren't breaking any laws, are they? If they want to neglect their house and have a wild dog roaming in their garden, then it's their business."

"Yes, I know it is, but if they are taking in babies and selling them on, then surely they'd want the place to be a bit more welcoming? And why live in the middle of nowhere with a dog like that? It must be difficult for people to find, particularly mothers with no easy way of getting there. I think it's suspicious, and after lunch, I'm going to find

Constable Folland to see what he thinks. There's nothing to lose, anyway."

Eveline looked thoughtful. "I don't think many mothers go to the house. When I went on the train to Exeter with Annie to get her wedding dress material, there was a woman at the station who took a child off her mother. Annie and Robert were sure it was the same woman they had seen at Buzzacott House when they were out riding; she's quite distinctive because she's unusually tall. Anyway, the mother of the child then got on the train. She was very distressed about parting with her child, and Sabina went to comfort her. You know what a soft heart Sabina has, and she couldn't bear to see the young girl so upset. Jean, she was called. She told us that she'd seen an advertisement in a newspaper. It said babies could be found adoptive parents or looked after until the mother could have them back. The tall lady had arranged to collect the child at the station as it was a convenient meeting place for both of them. Jean said that the woman was moving house and that when she had, she would write to Jean to let her know the new address so she could visit the child. She didn't want her baby fully adopted, she wanted to pay to have it looked after until she could find a way to have it back."

"That's interesting; if she collects the babies from the railway station, it wouldn't matter what state the house was in. Mind you, if they look after babies there, surely we would have seen nappies on the line, or some sign of children? Would they leave the babies on their own whilst they go into Eggleston on market day? It just doesn't make sense."

Having finished his tea, Charlie pushed back his chair and winced as he put his weight on his leg, which had stiffened up. "Right, I must get going, or Jimmy and Alfred will be complaining I've left all the work to them today. Now, Eveline since you have fed me so well today, I must insist on repaying the favour. Would you like to come to the farm one day soon, and have some lunch? Maybe we could go riding again?"

"That would be nice, Charlie, and now all the children are back at school, I can get away for a few hours. Would you mind if I did that, Fred?"

"No, of course not, why should I mind? You take good care of all of us, Evie but you have your own life to lead. I'm glad you're friendly with Charlie. You go to the farm whenever you like. Even if the children are not at school, I've plenty of work to keep me busy in the yard for a day. In any case, now they are bigger, they can more or less look after themselves, as long as I'm around to keep an eye on them."

"Good, how about tomorrow then, Eveline?"

"Would you mind if we made it the day after? I can make some food ready for everyone's tea, then. It will save me doing it when I get home. I'm not organised enough to do that for tomorrow. I think your leg might be painful tomorrow too. If it is sore, we needn't go riding; I'll just come for lunch."

"Good, I'll look forward to it. Bye then, Fred, I hope you get on all right with the policeman, but whatever you do, don't go to that house on your own, will you?"

"No, I won't. If I can repay the favour and help you out with anything, Charlie, you only have to ask, you know that, don't you?"

Charlie grinned. "Ah, now, there's a thing; I thought you'd never ask."

"Go on, then. How can I help you?"

"Let's just say I have some goods that need moving from the old silver mine. I've got Arthur Webber, and my nephew, Jimmy, lined up to help, but you know what they say; many hands make light work. Could you spare me a couple of hours on Saturday?"

"Yes, of course. Where do you want it taken to?"

"Some to Eveline's dad at the inn, and the rest to the farm. Alfred has a good storage place. Not a word to Constable Folland, mind."

"No, I understand, and my lips are sealed. All right then, where shall I meet you?"

"Is ten o'clock, just inside the entrance to the silver mine, on Saturday all right?"

"Fine, I'll walk out with you because I'm going to find Folland now. See you later, Eveline."

Fred saw Charlie off on his horse and then walked into the village. Constable Folland lived at the far end in a small cottage. His wife, Ada, was in the garden picking peas. "Hello, Fred, how are you?"

"I'm fine, thanks, Ada, is Wilfred around?"

"Yes, he's in the kitchen, not long finished his lunch. Let yourself in, will you? I want to finish picking these peas for tea."

Fred strolled along the path to the back door and knocked before opening the door and calling out. "Hello, Wilfred, are you there? It's Fred Carter. Can I have a word, please?"

Wilfred was still sat at the table with a cup of tea in front of him.

"Oh, hello, Fred, yes, come on in. Not seen you for a long time. Is anything wrong?"

"I'm not sure, Wilfred, but I want to talk to you about something."

"Sit down then, lad. I'm a good listener. Have to be in my profession."

Fred told him all about Charlotte's baby and the woman at Eggleston station and then about his and Charlie's activities that morning.

"You do know I should arrest you for trespass, Fred Carter? It's a bit of a risk you telling me all this, you know. By rights, I should arrest you and Charlie, and make sure you are up in front of the magistrates. Good job I know you both so well, isn't it?"

"I know it puts you in an awkward position, Wilfred, but that's a chance I had to take. What do you think? Does it sound suspicious to you?"

"It certainly seems odd, but I'm not sure what you want me to do? I mean, from what you've told me, you've no proof the woman has broken any laws."

"Could you just go and talk to her and see what she has to say? I mean, what's happening to these babies? I've no proof, Wilfred, but I think something's not right at that house. It can't do any harm, can it?"

"No, I suppose not. All right, I haven't got much on tomorrow, so I'll ride out and have a chat. What's the woman called; do you know?"

"No, I don't know anything about her, but I think she has a daughter living there with her. Thanks Wilfred, please let me know how you get on."

CHAPTER 37

The next day, true to his word and on what should have been his day off, Wilfred saddled up his horse and rode towards Buzzacott House. He stopped on the way for a chat with Sam to find out what he made of the situation, but as soon as Sam saw the policeman coming he was off as fast as his legs would carry him.

"Sam, stop. There's nothing to worry about; I just want to talk to you." He hurried after the old man and soon gained on him, for Sam was not that nimble.

"Sam, you can't get away from me, so please stop."

The tramp turned and eyed the policeman suspiciously. "I ain't done nothing wrong, and Annie's young man said I could stop here as long as I like."

"That's fine, Sam. You're not bothering anyone here. Can I just talk to you for a few minutes?"

"Aye, well, I don't suppose I've much choice. What do you want to know?"

"Fred Carter has asked me to have a look around Buzzacott House, and I wondered if you know the people there?"

"Not really. There's a woman and her daughter, but I ain't seen no man about the place. They've made it clear I'm not welcome, so I keep away."

"Do you ever see people calling at the house?"

"Sometimes. A few young women with babies. They seem to bring them, and then leave without them, but I don't know what happens to them. The woman goes out quite a bit with the pony and trap, mostly into Eggleston, but I've only seen the daughter go out with her once a week to the market. Perhaps she stays home and looks after the babies. They've got a vicious dog out the back; he bit Charlie's Chugg's leg almost down to the bone. That's all I know, mister."

Leaving Sam in peace, Wilfred knocked on the door of the big house. The sound from the tarnished brass knocker echoed for some time before a woman eventually answered.

"Can I help you?"

"Good morning, ma'am, my name is Constable Folland, and I'm the policeman from Hartford. I'd like to come in and ask you a few questions, if I may?"

"Surely we can talk here? I don't like people coming into my house."

"No, I'd rather come in, if you don't mind. I've had reports of babies being brought to this house, and I need to ask you what is going on?"

"Very well, you'd better come in." The woman led the way and escorted Wilfred into the front drawing-room. The heavy curtains made the room dull, as did the grime on the windows. The room was furnished with dark, heavy furniture and had not been dusted for some time. "Please sit down."

"First of all, what is your name?"

"It's Lizzie Dymond."

"Can you tell me why women bring babies here?"

"I have indeed looked after a few babies for various friends of mine, just temporarily, you understand. As I'm sure you are aware, many young girls find themselves in the family way these days with no means of supporting a child. Unfortunately, when a man find out a baby is on the way, he often vanishes without a trace. I used to be a nurse, and sometimes my ex-colleagues contact me to ask if I can look after a baby for a short time until the mother can make better arrangements and take the child back. Usually, I only look after a baby for a few weeks, and then it goes back to its mother."

"Do you have any babies here at the moment?"

"No, it doesn't happen often."

"Do you charge for looking after them?"

"Yes, of course, I can't do this for nothing."

"Do you also arrange full adoptions?"

"Yes, I have done once or twice, and in those circumstances, the child is always better off living with a couple who wants it, and can provide for its needs. Why do you ask?"

"Do you remember an elderly woman from Warkley, who brought a baby girl to you several weeks ago?"

"Yes, it was the daughter of her niece, I believe. The girl had no means of supporting the child, and the aunt felt she was doing her a favour in getting it adopted."

"Is the child still here?"

"No, a couple in Exeter had been waiting for just such an opportunity, and I was able to deliver the child to them within days of receiving it. A good outcome for all concerned. They were overjoyed."

"Can you give me the details of the adoptive parents, please?"

"No, I'm sorry. I'm not trying to be difficult, but as I explained to the child's mother when she turned up here the other day, I don't pass on any details of adoptive parents. My discretion is part of the deal, and I keep no records for precisely that reason. They pay me in cash for my trouble, and that is the end of the matter."

"You must remember where you took the child?"

"No, I met them at the railway station. I never want to know where a child is going, and then I can't divulge any information even if I wanted to. It's better this way and gives the adoptive parents peace of mind."

"Do you live here alone?"

"No, my daughter, Thurza lives here with me."

"Do you have a husband?"

"No, he died some years ago."

"May I see your daughter please?"

"I don't see how that is relevant, but yes, I suppose so. I must tell you she is slightly slow-witted."

The woman rose and went to the door. "Thurza, can you come here a moment, please? A gentleman wants to speak to you."

A dark-haired girl in her thirties appeared. She looked nervous and was unwilling to look Wilfred in the eye.

"Hello, Thurza, can I ask you a few questions, please?"

The girl looked anxiously at her mother and then down at her feet and said nothing.

"I'm sorry as I said she's not quite right; never has been. Strangers make her even worse. I'm surprised she even came into the room. Come here, darling. There's nothing to worry about."

The woman crossed the room and put her arm around her daughter. "Is this necessary, constable? We have done nothing wrong, other than look after a few babies for close friends, and your visit will unsettle my daughter. She will probably keep me awake all night after this. I'd like you to leave now."

"Yes, ma'am. I can see she is uncomfortable. I'm sorry to have troubled you, but you understand we have to be seen to follow up concerns."

"Yes, of course. I do hope I have been able to put your mind at rest, that we are just living here quietly and minding our own business. The remoteness of this spot would not suit everyone, but it is ideal for my daughter as she is so nervous of people."

Giving Wilfred no opportunity to see anything of the rest of the house, she firmly showed him to the door.

Wilfred galloped back to the village and called in to see Fred, who was putting the finishing touches to a fine table he had been working on for weeks.

"My, that's a lovely piece of furniture, Fred. Should fetch a pretty penny. Is it for anyone in particular?"

"It would make me a handsome profit, it's true, but I didn't give my niece, Annie, and her husband, Robert, a wedding present, and I thought this might be acceptable. It's difficult to know what to buy when your niece marries into the gentry, and I don't have a lot to spare. I've been rushing to get it finished because they'll be back from their honeymoon soon. They're going to live in the West Wing of the Manor House, and I thought they might like this. I hope so, anyway."

"You've made a fine job of it; I should think they'll be delighted."

"Fingers crossed, but if they don't want it, I can easily sell it. I'd like to make more furniture, but most of my time is taken up making coffins and doing other woodwork for folk. Mustn't grumble though, I've always got plenty of work, and that's a godsend."

"Have you ever thought about taking on an apprentice? Then you could put more time into your furniture making. You're good at it."

"Yes, I have been thinking about that for a while, but my eldest son, Llewie, is ten so I've been waiting for him to be big enough to learn the trade. He helps out a bit already, but I'd like him to stay at school as long as possible. Not something I was able to do, but we all like to make a better life for our children, don't we? Anyway, how did you get on at Buzzacott?"

"I had a word with the old tramp, and he said he'd seen some women leaving babies there. I had to smile because back along, some boots were stolen from your brother, George's shop, and we were sure Sam stole them. We chased after him, and I don't know how he got away, but we never caught him. Anyway, today, his clothes are all rags and tatters, but he has on a good pair of boots. I'm pretty sure I know where they came from, but I can't prove it now."

Fred smiled. "Well, I know it's not right, but I expect Sam needed them, and to be honest, George could afford to give him a pair of boots. Not that he ever would, of course; he counts every penny, always has. So, what about the woman at the big house?"

"Yes, I went there, and she didn't want to let me in, though she did, eventually. Only into one room though, and it was pretty dirty, but that's not a crime. She admitted she takes in babies, either to look after for a short time until they can return to their mothers, or for full adoption. She said she used to be a nurse and that previous work colleagues sometimes contact her to see if she can help. It all sounded all right. I asked about your friend, Charlotte's baby, but she said the child was adopted by a couple in Exeter, and she wouldn't tell me who they were."

"No, she wouldn't tell us either."

"She said she doesn't keep records so that the adoptive parents' can't be traced. She even hands over the children at a railway station, so she doesn't know their home addresses. She says that is the deal she offers, and it provides the adoptive parents' peace of mind. I suppose I can understand that because if you've taken in a child and got attached to it, you wouldn't want it taken away again. Not so good for the natural mother if she changes her mind, of course, but then I don't think circumstances would allow that to happen often."

"Does she have babies there now?"

"She said, not, and I certainly didn't see any evidence of any or hear any crying. Her husband died years ago and she has a daughter living with her, who doesn't seem quite right. I asked to see the girl and she came into the room, but she looked uncomfortable and wouldn't speak to me. Her mother said it suits them living in the middle of nowhere because the girl is nervous of strangers, and that did seem to be the case."

"We're no further forward, then?"

"I don't think what she's doing is illegal, and unless we find evidence that she was mistreating these babies, there's nothing more to be done. I'm sorry, Fred, but I think Charlotte will have to accept that her baby is gone for good, though by the sound of it, to a family who will love her and bring her up as their own. That must be some comfort, surely?"

"Yes, I suppose so. Thanks for making enquiries, Wilfred. I'm much obliged."

CHAPTER 38

Annie fidgeted in her seat and couldn't wait for the train to pull into Eggleston station. She leaned against the window trying to see how far away they were.

"We won't get there any quicker, you know. You might as well relax and enjoy the rest of the journey." Robert smiled as he took her hand. "It won't be long now before we're home. Dodger should be waiting with the carriage, hopefully."

"I know, but I can't wait to see Selina, and Mum, and everyone. I've never been parted from Selina before, and I feel so bad leaving her."

"She'll have been fine with her Granny, and anyway, she'll love the presents you've bought her. I should think all your family will be pleased with what you've bought them."

"Yes, they will. It's so lovely to be able to buy them presents. Thank you, Robert. We spent so much money; I can't believe it. Probably more than Dad would have earned in a lifetime."

"Well, you're a lady now, Anne Fellwood, so you're able to spend money now and then. Not all the time though, we must make sure the estate pays its way, so we'll need to be a bit careful now for a while. I'm planning on making more changes to the way the estate is run. We have to move with the times, and I'm looking forward to it."

"I'm not looking forward to seeing your parents again."
Annie frowned.

"No, I know, but you won't have to see much of them.
The West Wing refurbishment should be finished by now.
There's even a separate entrance we can use, so we don't
have to see my parents at all."

"I don't want to stop you from seeing them; they're
your family, after all, but I think they would rather not see
me, and the feeling is mutual."

"If they can't, or won't, accept you, then I don't plan on
seeing much of them. I despise my father every time I see
him for what he did to you, and I'll never forgive him for
that. They have their own servants, so they're well cared for,
and they've still got Victoria and Sarah and their
grandchildren, so they're all right."

As the train slowed and the countryside became more
familiar, Annie's excitement grew. "Oh, look, there's
Dodger, with the carriage. Not long until we're home now.
Do you mind if we go to the Lodge House before the Manor
House?"

"No, of course not. I thought we would probably stay
and have a meal with your family before going to the Manor.
Dodger can go on ahead with the carriage, and the servants
can unload our luggage and sort it out, and we'll walk there
when we're ready. Annie, have you thought about Selina? I
mean, do you want her to come and live at the Manor House
with us?"

"Yes, of course. She's my daughter. That's not a
problem, is it?"

"No, not to me, but have you talked to her about it?"

"No, not yet. I thought it could wait until we got back
from our honeymoon. Why?"

"I just want you to be prepared, in case she doesn't want
to come. She's always lived with your mother and all the
other children, and she may not be comfortable leaving
them all. It may be best to take it slowly and just let her
come for a few hours at a time."

"Oh, yes, I suppose so, though I hope she will want to be with me."

"She probably will, but she's not seen you for more than a month. Anyway, here we are, home at last."

They alighted from the train and made their way over to Dodger and the waiting carriage whilst a porter dealt with their luggage.

"Hello, Dodger, it's so good to see you." Annie smiled at the stable boy.

"Yes, Annie, sorry I mean, ma'am, it's good to see you, too. Did you have a good time in London?"

"We did, thank you. Is everyone well at home?"

"As far as I know, ma'am. Shall we get going now, sir?

"Yes, please, Dodger, can you drop us at the Lodge House and take the luggage onto the Manor House, please? We'll just take these bags in with us."

As soon as the carriage pulled up outside the Lodge House, the entire Carter family, and Liza, came spilling out of the door to greet the newly married couple. To Annie's disappointment, Selina clung to Sabina's skirt and looked shyly at her mother.

"Hello, darling, do you have a hug for me?" Annie held out her arms.

The child hesitated, but after encouragement from Sabina, she moved towards Annie and was soon gathered into her arms. "Have you been a good girl for your Granny? I missed you so much. Did you miss me?"

Selina nodded and clung to her mother.

"She's been as good as gold, but she has missed you, especially the first week or so. Anyway, did you have a good time?" Sabina hugged her daughter.

Edward, Stephen, Helen, and Danny all gathered around Annie, trying to hug her. "We had a great time, but let's go inside, and I'll tell you all about it. I might just have some presents for you all, too."

Once inside the house, Annie delved into her bag and found gifts for them all; thick shawls for Sabina and Liza and warm winter coats for all the children.

"There, hopefully, you'll all be warm this winter. I think the coats will be too big, but I thought it was better that way than too small and you'll soon grow into them. Do you want to try them on?"

The children did just that, and although a little on the large side, the garments were perfect.

"Now it just so happens I did find a few toys as well, so let's see what we have here. They are all wrapped up, so just let me find them and then you can unwrap them. Why don't you all sit in a circle, and take it in turns to open your present? It had better be the youngest first, so that's you, Selina. Here what do you think this is?"

The five children sat cross-legged on the floor in a circle, and Annie handed each of them a gift wrapped in pretty tissue paper.

Selina looked at her mother for permission and then tore off the paper excitedly. "It's a dolly, look, Granny, I got a dolly. Thank you, Mummy."

The children unwrapped their presents in turn; Helen also received a doll, Danny, some alphabet building bricks, Stephen, a spinning top, and Edward, a toy train. The children were overjoyed, for not many presents came their way.

Liza clapped her hands. "Right now, how about some tea? I've got a chicken in the oven, roasting with some parsley stuffing and potatoes, and it should be ready just about now. Who's hungry?"

"Oh, Liza, I've missed your cooking, and I'm really hungry, so yes, please, let's eat." Annie hugged the old lady.

Over a simple but enjoyable meal, Annie and Robert told them all about London and also their visit to Stephen Turner's father. Sabina looked a little apprehensive.

"Do you think he can make things better for Danny?"

"We don't know yet, but at least he will take a look. Is that all right with you, Danny? Will you let a doctor have a look at your feet and your mouth, to see if he can fix them?"

The little boy nodded. "Yes, it would be nice if I didn't limp so much. Some of the boys at school tease me because I can't run."

"We'll see if we can make that a bit better then, but we can't promise, so don't be too disappointed if it can't be done." Robert smiled at his younger brother.

Soon it was time for Annie and Robert to go to the Manor House. She hugged her mother. "I'm not looking forward to this."

"You knew when you married Robert what it would entail, so hold your head up high, and take no nonsense from anyone. You'll be fine, and from what Robert's been saying, you needn't see his parents often at all. What about Selina?"

"Is it all right if I get settled in first and then take her for a visit, and see if she's happy to come and live with me? I want her to, but I don't want to upset her."

Annie picked up her little daughter and hugged her. Selina, I have to go now, but I'll be back again in the morning; is that all right?"

"Don't go away again, Mummy."

"No, I promise I'll be back tomorrow to see you. Why don't you take your new dolly to bed to cuddle tonight?"

"All right, then."

CHAPTER 39

It was almost dusk as Robert and Annie walked the half-mile or so to the Manor House. It was a pleasant walk along the tree-lined avenue, and they meandered through the gardens on their way to the West Wing. Although the summer was nearly over, the roses were still in full bloom, and in the early evening, their scent could be smelt in the air. Hand in hand, they strolled through the walled vegetable garden, smiling as they traversed the path where a few years before Annie had crawled in torrential rain, dragging a sack of stolen vegetables behind her.

Moving on, they passed through orchards of apples, pears, and mazzards. The mazzards were long gone, picked by the gardeners and made into pies, or bottled for the winter by Mrs Potts, but the apple and pear trees were heavily laden with ripe fruit. They walked on, enjoying the last rays of the sun until they reached the lake and sat on a seat, watching the trout jump to catch flies. It was an idyllic spot, and so quiet and peaceful, after all the hustle and bustle of London. Robert put his arm around Annie, and she laid her head on his shoulder.

"Oh, Robert, it's so good to be home, isn't it?"

"Yes, it is. I enjoyed London, but I wouldn't want to live there. I'm looking forward to going around the estate with Jack tomorrow to see how things are doing."

She lifted her head, and he kissed her gently on the lips.

"Come on, shall we go and see our new home?"

She nodded, and they made their way to the new entrance in the West Wing. At Robert's request, no new servants had been employed. He wanted Annie to choose her own household staff, so they let themselves in by the front door, and took a look around their new home alone.

The painters and decorators had done an excellent job and everything looked bright and new. In the hallway the tiled floor had been scrubbed until it was immaculate and covered here and there with thick rugs. The oak panel work had been re-varnished and the few brass ornaments that were dotted around gleamed in the last rays of sun that shone through the sparkling windows.

"Oh, Robert, it's so beautiful," breathed Annie, "doesn't it look lovely?"

"Yes, it does. Who would have thought the dilapidated old West Wing could look so amazing? Let's look at the other rooms. See, the drawing-room is next."

Slowly, they made their way from room to room, taking in all the sumptuous furnishings. Comfortable chairs, vibrant tapestries, and beautiful new curtains adorned each room. Having explored the drawing-room, study, parlour, and dining room, they made their way up the magnificent staircase. On the first floor were six bedrooms, all of a good size, and all decorated according to Annie's wishes. In the master bedroom, the lower half of the walls were panelled with ancient oak, now highly polished. Above that, the walls had been replastered and painted a pale green. The carpet was a darker green, as were the curtains, including the ones that adorned the large four-poster bed in the centre of the room. Everywhere they looked, there were vases of flowers from the garden and hothouses. Beautiful roses and lilies, and the scent was intoxicating.

"I can't believe we'll be living here, Robert. This must have cost a small fortune."

"It did cost a lot of money, but they've done a good job, haven't they? The poor old West Wing was in a terrible state, so it was necessary. Anyway, the estate has made good profits since I took over. The bank manager, Mr Billery, approved all the expenditure, and he likes my ideas for the future. Nothing will need doing for a long time now, but we need to get busy in the next few days employing some servants to look after everything. I thought you would like to choose who works here, yourself."

Annie looked at him in delight. "Really? Can I choose the servants?"

"Yes, of course."

"Could I take some of the old servants that I used to work with?"

"That may not go down too well, but if they want to come here to work, I don't see why not. Who do you have in mind?"

"Definitely Mrs Potts, and Maisie and Molly. They were all so good to me when I worked here, and especially when I was attacked. Miss Wetherby will have a fit if I take them from her, though."

"Good; serves her right. Look, I'd better go and see my parents and let them know we're back. I'll mention to them that you would like those three servants to work here, and I don't suppose they'll mind. They might not want to lose Mrs Potts, but I'll see what I can do. We might have to share them until replacements can be found, but that's all right, isn't it?"

"Yes, of course, I don't want to cause any trouble, but it would be so lovely to have my friends working here."

"That's fine, but you must remember you are the lady of the house now, and not a kitchen-maid. Are you sure it wouldn't be difficult for you?"

"No, it would be a real comfort to me to know I have people close to me who I can trust and who care for me."

"Very well, then, will you be all right if I leave you for a while?"

"Of course, I'd like another look around, but then I might go to the old kitchen and see my friends. I won't say anything about them changing jobs though until we know if it's possible."

The door from the West Wing to the main house had, at Robert's request, been bricked up, and the only access connecting the two dwellings was on the lower floor where the kitchens were situated. He knew this would make it easier for some staff to service both households. He went down the old staircase, through the new kitchen which was to serve the West Wing, and down a passageway to the kitchen of the main house.

Mrs Potts looked up from her favourite chair by the fireplace. "Why, hello, Master Robert, how nice to see you, sir. I forgot you could come in that way now. Are you pleased with your new accommodation?"

"Yes, it's all looking lovely, thanks, Mrs Potts. How are you?"

"I'm fine, sir, and how is Annie? Oh, dear, I must stop calling her that. I'm sorry, sir."

Robert grinned. "Don't worry about it, Mrs Potts, I don't think Annie is going to worry what you call her, you know she thinks the world of you. She's fine, thank you, and we had a wonderful time in London, but I'll leave her to tell you all about it."

He heard footsteps on the stairs and turned. "Oh, hello, Hobbs, could you let my parents know I am here, please?"

"Of course, sir. They are in the dining room. Would you like to come with me?"

The butler entered the dining room and advised the Fellwoods that their son was waiting to see them.

Robert entered the room and noticed that his father was looking frail. He had lost weight, and his face had an unhealthy pallor. His mother did not look particularly pleased to see him.

"Hello, Mama, Papa, how are you both?"

"Your father is not too well, but I am fine, thank you. Where is Anne?"

"She's looking around the West Wing. The workmen have made a lovely job of it and you wouldn't know it was the same place. She feels awkward and didn't think you would want to see her. She intends to keep out of your way as much as possible. With the new entrance to our quarters, you will probably barely see her at all, so hopefully, we can all dwell peacefully and get on with our lives."

His father shifted uncomfortably in his chair. "That sounds like the best plan, but there is something we must talk to you about."

Eleanor took over the conversation. "When we returned from London, we came past the Lodge House where you have installed that family and the children were playing outside. It was quite obvious that one child was the odd one out. The whole family have bright ginger or fair hair, and there was one child with dark locks. As we passed, I noticed that he limped, and when he turned around, I could see his mouth was deformed. If there was any doubt in my mind that he was my son, it was dispelled as soon as I looked into his eyes. It was like looking into the eyes of David. Do you deny he is my son?"

Robert looked aggrieved and glanced at his father. "No, I can't lie to you, Mama. He is your child. At the time you wanted nothing to do with him, and we had to find someone who could breastfeed him, and who we knew would take care of him. Sabina, Annie's mother, had recently given birth and was feeding her daughter, Helen. Whatever you may think, Sabina is a good woman, and she dotes on her children. I knew that no one would care for him better. The only problem was that you wanted him taken far away, where you would never see him, but that was difficult to arrange. Of course, at the time, I had no way of knowing that Harry Rudd would be killed in a fire or that Annie and I could ever be together. When that happened, it made sense for the Carter family to move into the Lodge House. I'm sorry if seeing him was a shock to you; I am."

"It disgusts me that you used this information to blackmail your father into letting you marry the kitchen-maid. I'd rather he had told me the truth and put a stop to this ridiculous marriage."

Robert looked again at his father, who gave an almost imperceptible shake of his head. "That's not quite true, Mama, though Papa did not want you to find out about Danny. Neither of you could prevent me from marrying whom I like. We've already discussed this. The estate is in my name, and I'm over twenty-one, so I had no need to blackmail anyone, though I did keep quiet about Danny rather than upset you."

"Well, they'll have to move. They cannot continue to live on my doorstep where I shall probably see the child every time I go out in the carriage. How do you think it will make me feel seeing him every time I pass?"

"I don't know, Mama. I really don't. I never understood how you could part with him as you did, especially knowing how much care he would need. I'll tell you now it's thanks to Sabina's patience and care, that he survived at all. He had great difficulty feeding, and he didn't thrive for a long time. At the same time, she had to care for all her other children and work on the farm to earn money; to be honest I don't know how she coped with it all. If anyone deserves to live in the Lodge House and enjoy a better standard of living, it is Sabina Carter, and she will not be moving."

His father looked at him worriedly. "Robert, I can see your mother's point of view, and I can also see yours. This woman, Sabina, has done her best for the child. The only solution I can see is to build another driveway in the other direction, and we could use that one. What do you think?"

"I think it would cost a great deal of money and is unnecessary. I'll give it some thought, but I don't think it's practical. A new driveway would have to be of considerable length to join up to the other lane that goes into Hartford.

I'll discuss it with Jack Bater and see what he thinks. There is one more thing I need to tell you about Danny, seeing as you now know he is your son. When we were in London, I went to see Stephen Turner's father. You may remember I was at school with Stephen, and we stayed at each other's houses in the holidays sometimes? His father is a highly-respected surgeon and physician, with premises in Harley Street. Stephen is working in Europe, but Annie and I spent a pleasant evening with Doctor Turner, and he has agreed to take a look at Danny to see if he can improve his mouth and feet. He has a house near Cullompton, where his wife lives most of the time because she dislikes London; he intends to retire there when the time comes."

"That is of no interest to us, Robert, we do not intend to become involved with the child, but if his quality of life can be improved, then that would be a good thing." His father looked at Robert intently. "Just out of interest, is the child intelligent, or lacking, mentally?"

Robert grinned. "Oh, I can tell you that he does not miss a thing; he is a clever and altogether lovely little boy. I'm fond of him and glad I'm in his life, though, of course, he has no idea I'm his brother. Now, there is one other matter that I need to speak to you about. I have purposely waited until Annie and I returned from London before engaging any servants to look after us in the West Wing. We need to get on with this now, so we will be seeking new servants within the next few days. Would you have any objection, if some of the current staff came to work for us, and the new people worked in the main house? Annie is friendly with Mrs Potts, and two kitchen-maids, Maisie and Molly, and she would like them to work in the West Wing. We wouldn't take them until suitable replacements had been found, of course."

Charles Fellwood spoke quickly before his wife could voice her views. "I can't see a problem with that, can you, my dear?"

"I don't mind about the kitchen-maids, but Ethel Potts is an excellent and reliable cook, who's been with us for many years, and I'd be sorry to part with her. It's whether we can find someone of an equal standard."

"I suspect Elsie Webber, the girl that Ethel has been training, would probably be able to step up, but it depends what Mrs Potts says; she will know best. Are you happy for me to have a word with her, and also Miss Wetherby, of course?"

"What about Miss Wetherby, do you want her to manage both households?"

"No, I haven't spoken to Annie about a housekeeper yet, but I suspect she will either want to manage things herself or take on someone new. Miss Wetherby was rather unkind to Annie when she worked here." Robert could not believe he had nearly divulged the real reason his father had not objected to his marriage.

"Very well, you may ask the servants involved. Of course, they may not want to change."

"Thank you, I'll do my best to sort it out satisfactorily for everyone. Now, I'll bid you goodnight; I'm tired after the journey back from London."

CHAPTER 40

Since dancing together at Annie and Robert's wedding, Fred and Charlotte's feelings for each other intensified. Fred visited the inn more often, usually with the excuse of making sure his parents were all right, but Betsey was not fooled for a moment.

"We're seeing quite a bit of you, Fred, not that I'm complaining mind."

"Well, what with you breaking your leg and Dad getting on a bit, I like to make sure you're both all right. I don't suppose George does much for you?"

His mother smiled at him. "You tell yourself that if you want, Fred. I don't see much of George, it's true, but I think we both know the reason you're here so often, and at the moment, she's hanging out the washing. Why don't you go out to see her? In fact, when are you going to make an honest woman of her? You're both single, and your feelings are easy to read."

Fred grinned. "Am I that obvious? It's true, I do think the world of Charlotte, and I think she feels the same way."

"What are you waiting for then?"

"She's not got over losing her baby yet, and for me, it feels like I'm betraying Lucy to think of marrying another woman. I've only known Charlotte a few months, anyway."

"That's rubbish, Fred Carter, listen to yourself. The best thing for Charlotte would be for her to have another child, and as for Lucy, she's been dead and gone over three years now. She would not have wanted you to be miserable and lonely for the rest of your life. If I've learned one thing in my time, it's that you have to grab happiness when you get the chance. Life's too short to waste time. You deserve to be happy, Fred, and so does Charlotte."

"Maybe, but it's not so easy, is it? There's Eveline to consider. I don't think it would work with both women trying to run the house. Evie's been so good to me, I couldn't ask her to leave, and then, of course, if we married, Charlotte would have to leave the inn, and you need her here to help you."

"I think Eveline would be the first to tell you to follow your heart. She'll want you to be happy, Fred. She could always come back here to live. As long as she was here to look after them, she could move back with William's three. As for Charlotte, yes, of course, I'd miss her, but there are always people looking for work, and I'd soon get someone else, and if Eveline was here, she would lend a hand like she used to. Anyway, I wouldn't be losing Charlotte because she'd be my daughter-in-law. It's up to you, of course, Fred, and only you know your true feelings, but I would like to see you happy again."

"Aye, well, I'll think on it, and I'll go out and see Charlotte now. I might ask her out for a walk later; would that be all right with you?"

"Yes, of course, and don't hurry back."

Fred went up the steep steps to the back garden, where Charlotte had nearly finished hanging out a basket of washing.

"Hello, Fred, I didn't know you were coming here, today."

"I just called in to see if Mum and Dad are all right, but I wondered if you'd like to come for a walk, later? Mum says you can take the afternoon off, and it would be nice to have some time to ourselves."

Charlotte blushed. "That would be lovely, Fred. What time do you want to go out?"

"I'll call for you about two o'clock, if that's all right, with you?"

"Yes, fine, I can help Ned out at lunchtime first. It's busy, then. See you, later."

Fred duly called for Charlotte, and as they left the village behind, he took her hand. They headed towards the open moorland. The sun was shining, and the heather was still in full bloom, creating a beautiful purple haze as far as the eye could see.

"This is a lovely walk, Fred, my favourite, I think. Oh, look, there's a squirrel. Did you see it? It just vanished up that tree."

"Yes, I just caught a glimpse. They move so fast, don't they? I quite like them, but Dad says they are just dirty rats with fluffy tails."

"Have you heard any more about that woman at Buzzacott House?"

"No, I've not been back there since Charlie got so badly bitten. Thank goodness his leg is healing. Old Sam's ointment certainly did the trick. Despite what Wilf Folland said, I still think they are up to no good. I might go and see Sam again, and ask if he's noticed any more comings and goings."

"You might as well let it drop, Fred. I think Doris is gone for good. I know I must put it behind me, but 'tis hard."

Seeing tears glistening on her cheeks, Fred stopped and pulled her to him, leaning with his back to a tree.

"Don't cry, Charlotte. I can't bear to see you so upset. At least from what we heard, Doris is being well looked after, and that's something, surely?"

"Yes, of course, it is, but I'll never stop wanting her back."

Fred wiped her tears away with his thumbs, and then kissed her eyes, nose, and finally her mouth. "There's something I want to ask you, Charlotte. I don't know if it's too soon, but I know I love you, and I hope you have feelings for me? Charlotte, will you marry me?"

Charlotte gasped, then smiled widely. "Do you mean it, Fred? Do you really want to marry me?"

"Yes, of course, I wouldn't have asked otherwise, would I? Do you want to think about it?"

"I don't need to think about it, Fred. There is nothing I would rather do. I love you, too."

"Oh, Charlotte you've made me such a happy man, and I didn't think that would ever be the case again. Thank goodness, I came across you in that gateway all those months ago."

"Fred, how would we manage, though? I mean, your mother needs me, and then there's Eveline to consider. Her home is with you, and I'm fond of her, but I'm not sure it would work with both of us living there."

Fred looked sheepish. "Actually, my mother came up with a solution."

"You've discussed this with Betsey?"

He wouldn't look her in the eye. "Not intentionally, but she told me it was time to make an honest woman of you, and the more I thought about it, the more I thought she was right."

Charlotte laughed. "What are you a man, or a mouse, Fred Carter? Did it take your mother to make you propose to me?"

"Yes, I suppose it did, if I'm honest. I've been thinking about it for some time, but I didn't want to rush you because I know you're still sad about Doris. Mum said that if we did marry, Eveline could go back to living at the inn like she used to, and maybe take Joe, Matthew, and Amelia with her. I wouldn't mind if the children stayed with us, and I don't suppose you would, but it would be cruel to take them all away from her; she's loved looking after them."

"That sounds like a good plan. Come on, let's climb to the top of that tor, and then go back and tell Betsey and Ned. Then we need to talk to Eveline and see what she thinks. The last thing I want to do is upset her."

Betsey was amused to hear that Fred had proposed so quickly. "My goodness, lad, you soon acted on that advice. Even I didn't see that coming. Still, good for you. I'm pleased, and I hope you'll be happy together."

Charlotte's eyes were shining with excitement. "Thank you, Betsey. If it wasn't for you, I wouldn't even be here, so it's you that's made this possible. It sounds as if it's thanks to you that Fred proposed at all, and I couldn't wish for a nicer mother-in-law." She hugged the old woman.

When Ned heard the news, he shook his son by the hand and kissed Charlotte on the cheek. "I'm glad for both of you; you already have somewhere to live, and with Fred's three children to look after, that should help to take your mind off your baby."

"Mum, Dad, just one thing. Please keep this to yourself for now because we are going to tell Eveline, and I want her to be the first to know. I just hope she won't mind."

"I think you may find she is half expecting it."

Eveline was delighted for them and said she had started to feel in the way, so it was something of a relief.

Charlotte hugged her. "Are you sure you don't mind? I'd feel terrible if you felt I had pushed you out."

"No, it's fine. I know you'll make Fred happy, and that's all I want. I've loved looking after all the children, but it's a busy job, I can tell you. If Mum's happy for me to live at the inn with William's three, then I think that's a good solution. If I do that I can help out and keep an eye on Mum and Dad too because they're not getting any younger. The children may miss each other, but they'll see each other at school, and we all live near to each other, anyway. Shall we leave things as they are until after the wedding, and then I'll move to the inn with the children?"

"Yes, that sounds like a good plan. We haven't had time to even think about when the wedding will be, and we'll have to talk to the vicar, but I don't see any point in waiting, do you, Charlotte?"

"No, the sooner the better for me. I still can't believe it; this has happened so fast."

CHAPTER 41

Eveline had become a regular visitor at Hollyford Farm. She went on the pretext of visiting Alfred, but after each visit she found herself counting the hours and days until she could go again. As she neared the farm, she steadied the horse to a trot. Charlie appeared from the barn, carrying a bundle of hay high on a pitchfork over his shoulder. He grinned widely, and her stomach did its usual somersault as she looked into his blue eyes, and she mentally reprimanded herself for behaving like a lovesick schoolgirl.

"Hello, Evie, it's good to see you. I was hoping you'd come today. Let me just put this hay in the shippen for the cows, and then I can speak to you."

She dismounted and tethered her horse, smiling at him as he reappeared. He took her hand and drew her into a corner of the barn. He pulled her into his arms and kissed her passionately. "I've missed you, Evie."

She smiled happily at him and returned his kisses until they heard Alfred enter by the back door of the barn, and they hastily pulled apart.

The old man chuckled when he saw them. "No need for you two to worry on my account. I'm glad to see you're getting on so well." He went on his way, still grinning to himself.

"Oh, Charlie, what must he think of me. Allowing you to kiss me in a dark corner of the barn! What a way to behave."

"Don't be daft. He doesn't care. I think we've made his day. He'll be teasing me about this for days to come."

"Let's go to the kitchen so I can check your leg because I'm not sure you're looking after that bite."

"It's fine, there's no need."

"Nevertheless, I'd like to make sure. Dog bites can be serious."

"Oh, come on, then."

They found the kitchen deserted, but they could hear Maria moving around upstairs. Charlie sat in the only comfy chair and Eveline perched on a stool in front of him, took his foot in her lap, and peeled away the layers of cloth.

"Right, let's have a look. The dressings will need replacing, anyway. These are the same bandages I put on the other day, aren't they? You've not even looked at it."

Charlie looked sheepish. "No, I haven't, but it isn't bothering me, and it would if it was infected."

"Oh, my goodness, it's still nasty, isn't it? You're right, though, it's not inflamed and it is healing nicely. You have a lot to thank Sam for; I'd like to know what he puts in his ointment."

"I'll ask him next time I see him, but I don't know if he'll tell me."

"I've got some news to tell you. You'll never guess what, but Fred has proposed to Charlotte, and she has accepted. It's all a bit sudden, but anyone can see they think the world of each other and I'm pleased for them. Mind you, it will mean big changes for me."

"That's great news; I'm glad for them. They've got on since day one, haven't they? Must have been love at first sight. What do you mean about the big changes for you?"

"Well, I can hardly carry on living in Fred's house when they're married, can I? I'm sure we would get on all right, but Charlotte will want to run her own house without me watching her every move. To be honest, I've been feeling in the way, lately. It's been obvious they want to be alone."

"What will you do, then?"

"It's all sorted. As soon as they are married, or probably just before, I'll move back to the inn with William's three children. It will work out well because that will leave Charlotte with Fred's three to look after, and I'll still have Joe, Matthew, and Amelia. I'd miss them if I had to give them all up now. It will be good for Mum and Dad to have me around again, too, because Charlotte will no longer work at the inn."

"I see; you seem to have it all worked out, which is a shame because it doesn't quite fit in with my plans at all."

"What do you mean? It won't affect you at all."

"Ah, well, you don't know what my plans are, do you?"

Eveline looked puzzled and then startled as Charlie sank to one knee and cried out in pain as he remembered his dog bite. He grimaced and quickly swapped legs.

"Ouch, ah, that's better. Sorry, I forgot about my sore leg."

He took her hand, "Eveline Carter, will you marry me?"

"Are you joking, Charlie? Or are you just saying this because I have to move out of Fred's house? Because I will be fine at the inn."

He pulled her towards him. "Of course, I'm not joking, now will you answer me, or do you want to think about it and cause me days of anguish?"

"Oh, Charlie, do you mean it?"

"Yes, of course, I mean it; I love you, Eveline. I've been wanting to ask you for a long time, but I couldn't see a solution to your domestic arrangements. I couldn't ask you to let Fred down, but it sounds as if that problem is solved now. What do you say?"

She put her arms around him and gazed into his vivid blue eyes. "Oh, Charlie, I love you, too and yes, I'd love to marry you."

Laughing, he pulled her to him and kissed her happily. "That's amazing. I'm such a lucky man. Let's get married tomorrow."

"Whoa, steady on; you really have swept me off my feet, but there are still William's children to consider. Mum and Dad can't look after them on their own, and it wouldn't be fair to expect Charlotte to take on all six, though I suspect she would. I can't abandon them; I love them like my own, and I'd never let William down. It's unlikely Sarah would take them because there's no room in her dad's house."

"They can come here with you, of course. I'd never ask you to give them up. There's loads of room here on the farm. Alfred and Jane had twelve children, and I'm one of ten, so it's nothing new here to have a houseful. More than half the bedrooms are empty. Do you think they'd be happy to come here?"

"Oh, yes, they'd love it. After spending months in that workhouse in London they're grateful for anything. I don't think they've got over that ordeal yet. Perhaps they never will. Sarah does have a lot to answer for. Do you think Alfred and Jimmy would mind if they came here, though? I mean, they aren't related to them, and it will be three extra mouths to feed."

"I'm sure they won't mind, but if they do, I'll get a job somewhere else with a tied cottage. It's not a problem. People around here know I'm a good worker, and I can turn my hand to most things. Shall we go and tell Alfred and Jimmy now? I can't wait to tell somebody."

Maria was laying the table for dinner when Charlie and Eveline walked in hand-in-hand and grinning widely. Alfred and Jimmy had come in from the fields and were scrubbing their hands at the sink. Maria glanced up.

"Hello, Eveline, would you like to eat with us? It's roast pork and there's plenty of it. I'd love you to have some to see if you think my cooking has improved."

"Yes, please, that would be lovely, and if the smell is anything to go by it will be delicious."

Charlie waited until they were all seated. Maria, too, for she was treated as one of the family. "We've got some news to tell you."

Jimmy and Alfred glanced at each other and smiled. "I think we can guess, can't we, Dad? Go on, then, tell us."

"I've just asked Eveline to marry me, and she has agreed. What do you think of that?"

Alfred took her hand. He had tears in his eyes. "This would have made Jane so happy. I wish she was here. She thought the world of you, Eveline, and she hoped this would happen; she told me so. I couldn't be more pleased. What about all those children you look after, though? I asked you to come here as housekeeper longer ago, and you said you couldn't leave them.

"No, well, things are changing at quite a pace at the moment. Our Fred is marrying Charlotte Mackie. I don't suppose you know her, but she's a young girl who's been working at the inn. She will move in with Fred after they are married and will look after his three and we need to sort out what will happen to my other two nephews and niece. They were my brother, William's children."

"Aye, I remember William, and the news they were abandoned in London; it was a terrible business. You're not sending them to live with his widow, are you? Not after what she did?"

"No, though, she is sorry about it all now." Eveline glanced at Charlie, her eyes pleading for him to help her out.

"Alfred, if it's all right with you and Jimmy, I'd like the children to live here with us after we're married. Would you mind?"

"Mind, no, of course, not. It would be wonderful to have children in the house again. This table needs a few more seated around it. What do you think, Jimmy?"

"Yes, that's fine with me. I was more worried you might say you were going to leave the farm, and Dad and I wouldn't want that. We need your help."

"This girl, Charlotte, is she the one who gave up a baby for adoption a few months ago?"

"Yes, that's right, Alfred. I went with Fred to Buzzacott House to see if we could find out anything about where the child had been taken to. That's where I got bitten by that brute of a dog. Charlotte still frets over her daughter, and Fred would love to get the baby back for her. We still think there's something fishy going on there, and I don't think Fred will rest until he gets to the bottom of it. If you two can manage this afternoon I thought I'd ride back with Eveline, because by rights I should ask Ned if I can have her hand in marriage, even though she's already said yes. I'd better do things right." He turned to look at Eveline. "I'd like to go and see Sam today because I'd like to thank him for looking after my leg. Is that all right with you?"

"Yes, that's fine with me. Maria, this pork is perfectly cooked. If there's enough left, perhaps we could take Sam a pork sandwich?"

After they had eaten their fill, Eveline made a pork sandwich for Sam, cutting thick slices of fresh bread and spreading it generously with butter. "There, I think he'll enjoy that."

They galloped off towards Buzzacott Woods, where they knew they would find Sam.

"That's strange, Sam usually has a fire going, but I don't see any smoke and I don't think he ever lets it out if he can help it. I wonder if he's decided to move on. I thought he'd stay there for the winter because his hut is waterproof now. Anyway, let's go and see."

Charlie led the way through the thick wood to a clearing where Sam's hut was all but invisible if you didn't know it was there. There was no sign of the old man, and the hut door was shut, whereas it had always been open when Charlie had visited before. He carefully climbed down from his horse, putting his good leg down first to take his weight.

"Hello, Sam; are you there?" Charlie pushed the door open. As his eyes grew accustomed to the dimness, he could see a body huddled on the pallet Sam slept on. His fears grew as the old man showed no sign of movement, and he felt for a pulse on the old man's neck. To his relief, Sam stirred and then panicked as he realised someone was bent over him.

"It's all right, Sam, it's all right, it's me, Charlie. Are you poorly, or just having a nap?"

Sam opened his eyes and gazed at Charlie. He didn't recognise him for a few moments, but as realisation dawned, he gave a weak smile. "Oh, hello, Charlie. I was fast asleep. Just a minute and I'll get up."

With some difficulty, the old man swung his legs to the floor and pushed himself to a sitting position, groaning loudly. He sat there for a few minutes as if summoning the strength to stand.

"Sam, what's wrong? Are you hurt?" Charlie could see the tramp was thinner and even more unkempt than usual.

"Aye, I'm not too good. That's why I was resting. Hold on, and I'll come outside. There's not much room in here."

Charlie led the way from the hut and signalled to Eveline to dismount from her horse. He turned back to talk to Sam and gasped in shock. Sam's hair was crusted with blood, and there were dark purple bruises and weals all down one side of his grimy face. He swayed dangerously as he made his way towards where the fire should be burning merrily.

"Sam, what's happened? Has someone beaten you?"

"No, I'm all right; I fell over the other day and bumped my head, but I'm on the mend. Oh, now, my fire's gone out." The sight of the cold, grey ashes seemed more than the old man could take, and suddenly tears coursed down his wrinkled cheeks.

Charlie quickly pulled forward the tree stump which seemed to be Sam's favourite seat. "Here sit down, Sam and tell us what happened."

"Nothing happened. Like I told you, I fell over."

Charlie persisted gently. "I don't think you did, Sam. Your injuries don't look like the result of a fall. They look as if someone beat you with a stick. Tell me who did it, and I'll give them a hiding they'll never forget."

Sam smiled but shook his head. "No, I don't want you getting into trouble. How's that dog bite?"

"Still sore, but thanks to you, it's healing nicely. That's why I'm here; I wanted to thank you. I might have lost my leg if it wasn't for you. That ointment was good stuff, Sam. This is my friend, Eveline, she's Annie's aunt, and she'd like to know your secret ingredients."

"Aye, I'll be bet she would; well, if you come when I'm better, my dear, I'll show you how to make it. I've always kept it a secret and told no one else, but maybe it's time I did. I may not be around a great while longer."

Eveline sat next to the old man. "Hello, Sam, I'm pleased to meet you again. I've seen you before when you came to the inn."

Sam squinted at her out of his left eye which wasn't swollen shut. "Oh, yes, I remember you. You gave me food more than once if I remember rightly."

"Yes, I did, Sam. I've brought some food for you today too. Have you eaten?"

"No, I haven't eaten for days. I've been too sore and poorly to move from my bed."

"In that case, see if you can manage a few mouthfuls of this pork sandwich. It's nice and fresh and tender too. Here you are." He took half of the sandwich from her gratefully, and slowly nibbled at it, gingerly trying to avoid his split lip.

"Charlie, could you get the fire going for Sam, please? I can heat some water then and bathe his injuries when he's finished eating. Perhaps we could make a hot drink for him too. Do you have any tea, Sam?"

"No, I don't have any tea, but there is some dried mint in that tin. I could have a cup of that. You too, if you like."

Whilst he ate his sandwich Eveline went into the hut to find some rags and then sat beside him. Charlie got the fire going and went to gather more firewood.

"Sam, tell me who did this? I won't let Charlie go after them, but tell me. How many men were there? Did they steal much?"

At that, the old man did smile. "Nay, 'twasn't men. To my shame 'twas a woman. Fancy me getting beaten up like this by a woman, 'tis a sad state of affairs."

"So, who was it, and why did they beat you like this? Oh, wait a minute, was it the woman at Buzzacott House?"

"Aye, you're a smart maid. I was doing no harm. Mind you, I was spying on her, so I suppose she had some cause. I saw another woman bring a baby to the house and I knew Fred and Charlie wanted to know all about that, so I followed her and hid in the bushes. The girl handed over her baby to the tall woman and then made off back the way she came. Unfortunately for me, I sneezed a couple of times, and the woman heard me. She passed the baby to her daughter and came running over to find out who was there. As soon as she saw me, she set about me something vicious with a big stick she was carrying. Beat me black and blue, she did. I'm bruised all over. She said if she ever saw me near the house again, I'd be sorry and she'd set the dog on me. I don't want Charlie going there and saying anything to her because it's me that will suffer for it when he's gone. If I could move on, I would, but my hut's here, and I'm not fit to travel. I might roam again when I'm better, but my hut's nice and cosy now, and young Fellwood did say I could stay, and that doesn't happen often."

"Oh, Sam, I'm so sorry. What an awful thing for her to do."

"Aye, she showed no mercy, even though I was screaming. She's a big woman too, almost as strong as a man, and there's not much to me these days. Just a bag of old skin and bones."

"Sam, will you let me bathe your wounds and put some of your ointment on them?"

He nodded. "Yes, all right. I haven't felt well enough to see to them myself or to go and get food or firewood. I feel better for that pork sandwich, though. I think you and Charlie might just have saved my life between you."

By this time Charlie had a good fire going, and the water was soon hot. He made Sam some mint tea, and Eveline bathed his wounds and daubed ointment on them, but he refused to undress and let her see his other injuries. Charlie fetched a supply of firewood and stacked it near the fire.

"Sam, we'll come again tomorrow to see how you are. There's enough firewood there to last you until then, and we'll bring some more food and clothes. The ones you have on are covered in blood. Will you be all right on your own until then?"

He nodded. "I will now and thank you so much for your kindness. To tell you the truth, I'd given up and was just waiting for the end to come, but perhaps it's not quite my time yet after all."

"Of course, it's not. We'll see you tomorrow, Sam."

Charlie and Eveline galloped back to the inn, where Ned was delighted to accept Charlie's request for his daughter's hand in marriage. Betsey was overjoyed at the thought of both her daughter and her son getting married.

CHAPTER 42

Robert and Jack Bater strolled around the farm, discussing the work that needed doing. Jack was delighted Robert took such an interest in the work on the farm. A lesser manager might have disliked the interference from his employer, but Robert had studied farming in detail and was able to tell Jack newer and better ways of doing things despite Jack's considerable experience. Together they made a great team, and the profits were better than they had been for many a year.

"I thought perhaps we could plant this field with winter wheat, Jack. I've read that Squarehead Master gives a reliable crop. Have you grown it before?"

"No, not that variety. We usually sow Yeoman or New Harvester, but it's good to try new things. I've heard Squarehead is excellent for thatching too."

"That's what I thought. We'll have the grain and also the extra income from selling it for thatching. Perhaps we could start the ploughing towards the end of next month?"

"Yes, we've got all the hay in now, so we can do that. It'll take a week or two to get the ground ready because I like to leave it to settle for a few days after ploughing before we drag it to break it down."

"Then is it ready to sow the seed?"

"Yes, I usually sow winter wheat around the middle of November. It gives it a better chance to germinate before the ground turns too cold, and with your new seed drill, it will be so much easier than it used to be with the seed fiddle. My goodness, I've walked miles in my time walking up and down, up and down a field, scattering seed. Makes your arms ache too."

Robert grinned. "It's an amazing invention, and I'm glad it will save you some leg work. We have a lot to thank Jethro Tull for."

"Who's Jethro Tull?"

"He invented the seed drill sometime back in the 1700s. I don't know why my grandfather or father never bought one. Probably they were more expensive back then, and my father certainly didn't like to spend money, but it's so much more efficient than using a seed fiddle. Once the seed's sown and we've put the roller over it, we'll lose far less seed to the birds."

They walked on to the next field where a crop of mangelwurzels was looking healthy.

"These are a good size this year, aren't they? Are they ready for harvesting yet, Jack?"

"Yes, but there's plenty of time; I plan to get the men on to that in the next day or two. We might get them in then before the next rain."

"I'm happy to help. What do we have to do?"

"Oh, you just pull them with your left hand, like this, and chop off the leaves with a knife with your right." Jack demonstrated. "Then we come along with a horse and cart, and pick them up, and store them in the barn. Hopefully, they'll feed the cows and pigs for most of the winter."

"What happens to the leaves?"

"We just plough them back in. Puts a bit of goodness back in the soil. Shall we walk on to the orchards now? I want to look at the apples."

They entered the orchard and surveyed the many rows of fruit trees. Some of the fruit had fallen to the ground in the recent winds.

"What sort is this one, Jack? I know little about apples."

"That's a Russet. Lovely apple; keeps well for eating until April if you store them carefully, and some people think it makes the best cider of all. We have four rows of them. The next lot are Coxes Orange Pippins. Again, nice apple, with the orange and red skin." He picked one off the nearest tree. "Nice yellow flesh and very juicy, nice to eat, but also good for cider. Then we come to the largest and oldest trees and these are Bramleys. Not an eating apple, but excellent for apple pies, and having sampled many of Mrs Potts pies, I'm sure you know that."

"Yes, I have. What do we do with all these apples?"

"We sell some in the Pannier Market in Barnstaple each week, store some for use in the house during the winter, and the rest we make into cider. Cider has become popular in recent years, and I think we should make more of it this year. We used to only sell it locally, but now we can send produce on the train to London, I think we should make a lot more. We use it to pay people too, especially the casual labourers that we need from time to time. Mind you, I never give them any until they've finished the work."

"That sounds like a good idea. Do we mix the apples to make the cider?"

"I thought this year we might make a separate batch from each variety, and then one combining all three, and see which sells the best. What do you think?"

"Yes, another good idea. Now, you can probably put my mind to rest over something that old Arthur Potts was telling me the other day. I think he was just teasing me because I know nothing about it, but he was enjoying a drink from a stone flagon of cider, and he said it was good because of the rat he put in it. Surely not?"

Jack laughed. "I'm afraid it's true, sir. We usually put in a dead rat or two."

"Oh no, I can't believe it. Why would you do that?"

"It can be any sort of meat. I did once hear of a farmer whose best pig went missing, and they never did find the animal. The cider that year was exceptionally good, and

298

when all the cider was gone, there were the bones of the pig in the bottom of the vat. The poor old sow must have toppled in while drinking the fermenting juice and drowned. The farmer swore it was the meat of the pig that made the cider so good. Mind you, it wasn't an exercise he wanted to repeat because pigs cost too much. That's why most farmers chuck in a dead rat or two."

"But how does it make it taste better; it's disgusting."

"Cider is corrosive because of its high acidity, and it dissolves the meat off the bones. It's the protein in the meat you see, it feeds the yeast and speeds up fermentation. In any case, it's all gone before you drink it. All adds to the taste, as they say."

Robert grimaced as they walked on across the fields to continue their tour.

Annie didn't think she had ever been so happy. To finally be able to openly express her feelings for Robert filled her with joy. However, although she had lived at the Manor House for a couple of weeks now, she was finding it difficult to settle in. She had seen nothing of her in-laws, for which she was grateful, though Sarah had come to see her a few times and had admired the new furnishings, hardly believing the West Wing was the same dilapidated place she had explored as a child.

Annie had taken Selina to her new home several times, but the child was not content there. A beautiful bedroom had been prepared for her, with all sorts of toys, but she was not to be swayed. She was happy to visit and spend time with her mother but always wanted to go home to Granny. Annie was upset by this but could understand it because she, too, felt out of place. She was no longer one of the servants, yet did not fit the life of a lady. She was unused to having time to herself and found it difficult to fill the hours when Robert was out with Jack, where he loved to be.

So far, the servants from the main house had also looked after the needs of Annie and Robert in the West

Wing, but this was causing problems, and it was clear the matter must be addressed. Having put the matter off until now, Annie determinedly rang the bell, and when Molly appeared, asked her to bring tea and cakes for two. When Molly duly reappeared with a loaded tray some twenty minutes later, Annie told her to ask Mrs Potts to come and see her. Annie welcomed the old lady into the room and bade her sit down.

"This is a change of circumstances, Mrs Potts, isn't it? I'm used to you telling me what to do, and now we have to get used to me doing the opposite." Annie smiled at her. "I need your help with something."

"Of course, my dear. I've always had a soft spot for you, and of course, Master Robert, so if there's anything I can help with, you only have to ask."

"I know it's put extra pressure on the servants, looking after the main house, and us here in the West Wing. Having done the chores myself at one time, I appreciate only too well how difficult it must be to carry all our meals here from the main kitchen, let alone cope with the rest of the work, so I need to make changes. I need to employ our own servants, and Robert has decided to leave this to me. He's spoken to his parents, and they are willing for me to choose some of the existing servants, and they will employ new ones. I wondered if you would like to come to the West Wing and work for me. What do you think?"

"Yes, of course, I'd be delighted to cook for you and Master Robert. Would any of the maids be coming with me? It would be hard work to train new ones from scratch, particularly at my time of life."

"If you want to be employed as the cook here, then that's fine because I love your cooking, but I had another idea. How about if you became the housekeeper, in charge of all the servants in the West Wing, like Miss Wetherby is in the main house? You know everything there is to know about running a kitchen, ordering the food, and keeping accounts. Would you like to do that? It would be a bit more money for you, and I thought it may be a little easier than being on your feet all day cooking."

"That would be nice, and I appreciate the offer, but who would be the cook?"

"Well, you'll know better than me, but Maisie has worked for you now for several years, so would she be ready to step up as cook? You'd be on hand if she wasn't sure of anything, and you've always got on together, haven't you? It would be more money for her, too."

"That's a good idea, and the girl does deserve it; she's always been a hard worker. Yes, I think that would work. What about the main house, though? Who would be the cook?"

"It would be up to Miss Wetherby, but I thought maybe Elsie Webber could take that on?"

"Yes, I'm sure she could. I've been training her for over a year now, and she was experienced before she came here. Are you going to ask any other servants to come and work for you?"

Yes, I'd like Molly as a kitchen-maid, to assist Maisie and possibly Ethan or Caleb Bater to become a butler. Which one do you think would be the most suitable?

"They're both fine young men, but Ethan is the oldest, so by rights, it should probably be him."

"I'll take your advice, thank you, Mrs Potts. I'm going to talk to Miss Wetherby and advise her she will need to look for new servants, then I'll speak to Maisie, Molly, and Ethan. We'll have to do this gradually because we can't leave the main house short of servants, but hopefully, within a week or two, we should be able to get it all in place. We may need to employ one or two new servants here, but I think we'll see how this works out first. Now, let's enjoy our tea and cakes, shall we?"

CHAPTER 43

Robert was pleased to hear that Annie had made arrangements to sort out the staffing.

"Well done. It can't have been easy, especially the meeting with Miss Wetherby."

"No, it wasn't, but I was determined to establish my authority where she was concerned, and I have to say she took it well. I was surprised."

"She knew it was no use to argue. Not now you are married to me; she daren't."

Annie grinned. "I quite enjoyed it. Anyway, Mrs Potts and the others are pleased with their new positions, and Miss Wetherby already knew of people waiting for an opportunity to work here, so the new servants are going to start next week."

"That's excellent because we'll be giving our first little dinner party the week after. I had a letter from Doctor Turner this morning saying he's returned to Devon for a couple of weeks, and he offered to come here and see Danny. I thought we could invite him for dinner, and ask him to stay overnight with his wife, and then take him to see Danny the next day. I think Danny would be more comfortable seeing him at the Lodge House than here, don't you?"

"Yes, without a doubt. Goodness, I'm not sure I'm ready to host a dinner party, though. Will it be just the Turners?"

"It can be, but I'm tempted to ask Sarah and Aunty Margery; would you like that?"

"Yes, I think it would help if Sarah was here and Aunty Margery seemed to be on our side at the wedding, didn't she? She asked me to visit, but I haven't done so yet. Is it far to where she lives?"

"No, not far; perhaps ten miles or so. Why don't you visit and invite her to dinner?"

"I can't just arrive unannounced, can I?"

"There isn't time to write first. I'm sure she won't mind and, if she's out, or can't see you well, so be it. You can just leave the invitation. Would you like me to go with you?"

"No, I think I'll go alone. I have to get used to all this, Robert and I think Aunty Margery will be a good ally. Can you write the invitation to dinner, though? Your writing is far better than mine."

The next day Dodger drove Annie to Enderby House, where Robert's Aunty Margery lived alone. She had lost her husband several years before, and they had no children. Annie would have liked to ride up front with Dodger and have a chat along the way, but she knew this was unacceptable, so she sat inside the carriage. She enjoyed the journey, looking out across the fields and into peoples' gardens as they drove by, but couldn't help thinking that Dodger had a better view than she did.

The stable boy drove the carriage carefully up the impressive drive to the large house. He helped Annie from the carriage, and as she made her way up the steps, the door opened, and the butler came out to greet her.

"Can I help you, ma'am? I saw the carriage arrive from the window."

"Yes, thank you. I would like to see Lady Margery if she can spare the time. Please ask her to accept my apologies for arriving unannounced."

"Of course, ma'am. I will see if she is willing to receive you. May I take your name, please?"

"Yes, please tell her Anne Fellwood would appreciate a few moments of her time. Thank you."

The butler showed Annie into the drawing-room, and she seated herself near the window. She did not have to wait long before the old lady swept into the room with her arms held wide.

"Annie, my dear, what a lovely surprise. I'm so glad you came; I wondered if you would."

"Thank you so much for seeing me unannounced. Robert didn't think you would mind, and there wasn't time to write. I'm sorry, but I'm not sure what to call you? Should I call you Aunty Margery too?"

"You are welcome here any time, my dear, and yes, of course, you should call me Aunty Margery. So why the hurry to come and see me?"

Annie explained about Doctor Turner and his wife and the reason for their visit. "We wondered if you would like to come to dinner, and perhaps stay the night? It would be lovely to show you all the improvements we've made to the West Wing. I suppose you must remember it from your childhood when you lived there?"

"It wasn't used even then, though it was in better repair than in recent years. I'm glad it's had a new lease of life, and yes, I'd love to come to dinner. I know Clara Turner, so it will be good to catch up with her. It's strange your little brother should have a hare lip. I don't think Charles would remember, but his Uncle George had a hare lip, and he died young. Mind you, I think Charles would only have been about eight when George died. Joshua, Charles' father, was the eldest, so of course, he inherited the estate. I had a few other brothers and sisters, but they have all passed on now, and I'm the only one left. I take it Charles and Eleanor are not invited to your dinner party?"

"No, they wouldn't come anyway, but we are going to ask Sarah. She's been so kind to me and we get on well." Annie was keen to keep the conversation moving forward, for she did not want Aunty Margery to read too much into the fact that the hare lip seemed to run in the Fellwood family. She was a sharp old lady, and Annie didn't want her putting two and two together.

"Oh, that's good. She's a lovely girl and I always enjoy her company. How are you getting on living at the Manor House?"

"Well, I've engaged my own servants. I worked with some of them at the Manor House when I was a kitchen-maid; they are my friends, and I need them around me. They understand that my station has changed, and they are respectful, but I know I can rely on them, and that's important to me just now. This dinner will be something of a test for them as well as me because they are only starting next week, and the dinner is soon after."

"Can I give you a bit of advice?"

"Yes, of course, I'd be grateful."

"On the day they start, go into the kitchen yourself and welcome them, and tell them you are relying on them. Seek Mrs Potts advice about the menu for your dinner party and keep it simple. She has years of experience, and she will know exactly what to serve. I'm sure it will be a splendid evening, and I'm looking forward to it already. You will be amongst friends, and you mustn't worry about any of it. Now, I hope you have time for lunch before you depart?"

"Yes, I'll do that, and lunch would be lovely, thank you."

A week later, Annie and Robert waited on the doorstep of the West Wing to welcome the doctor and his wife. Aunty Margery had arrived earlier in the day and had gone to her room for a rest. Robert squeezed Annie's hand reassuringly and whispered. "It will be fine. They are nice people, and you look beautiful."

The couple alighted from their carriage and mounted the steps. Doctor Turner did the introductions.

"My dear, this is Robert and Anne, though I believe she is known as Annie to her friends, so I suggest that is what we call her if she doesn't mind?" He looked at Anne enquiringly.

"Oh, yes, Doctor Turner, of course, that's fine." She smiled at the elderly couple, and responding to firm pressure from Robert, resisted the urge to bob a curtsey.

"Good, now we have established we are friends, you can't continue to call me Doctor Turner. I am Geoffrey, and this is my wife, Clara. She's been longing to meet you, Annie."

The grey-haired lady on his arm smiled at Annie. "It's a pleasure to meet you, my dear. Thank you so much for inviting us. I haven't been too well lately, and we haven't socialised much, so this is a real change."

"Oh, I'm sorry to hear that. Are you better, now?"

"Yes, I'm fine now, thank you. Geoffrey tells me you have invited Lady Margery. I'm so pleased because we've known each other for years, and will have a lot to catch up on."

"Oh, that's good. My aunt mentioned to Annie that she knew you. Now, we'll get you settled into your rooms, and then, by all means, join us in the drawing-room, if you like, or you could have a rest if you prefer. Dinner will be at seven o'clock." Robert led the way down the hall, where Molly was waiting to show the couple to their room.

Despite her nerves, Annie thoroughly enjoyed the evening, for the other three women present were determined to make her feel comfortable. Mrs Potts had chosen to serve a starter of leek and potato soup, with fresh crusty rolls, followed by roast beef and all the trimmings. "You'll find you can't go far wrong with that." Mrs Potts had told her. The new housekeeper was right, and the meal was delicious. For pudding, there was a choice of apple pie, lemon posset, or bread and butter pudding, and Robert was able to entertain his guests with his new knowledge about his apple orchards.

When the party ended the guests went to their rooms, and Sarah took a shortcut to the main house through the kitchens. "You did well, Annie. No one would have known you weren't born a lady." Sarah hugged her as she bade her goodnight. "See you soon."

The next day after breakfast, Robert and Annie took the doctor to the Lodge House to see Danny, leaving Clara and Marjorie to enjoy the morning together, strolling around the gardens. Annie told Robert about Aunty Margery's comment about hare lips, and they were both glad she was not going to see Danny, because for sure she would have picked up a family resemblance. It was a dry morning, and the three of them decided to walk the short distance to the Lodge House. Sabina and Liza were waiting anxiously with Danny, having sent the rest of the children outside to play in the garden.

The doctor did his best to put Sabina and Liza at ease and then turned his attention to Danny.

"Now, young man, I've come to have a look at your mouth and your feet. Is that all right with you?"

Danny nodded nervously.

"I'm not going to hurt you, so there's nothing to worry about, and if you're a good boy, I might find you a special treat when I'm finished. How does that sound?"

Danny grinned, making the split in his upper lip even more prominent.

The doctor laid him on the table and looked into his mouth. "Thank you, Danny. Now, can I have a look at your feet? Good, let's take off these boots then, so I can have a proper look. That's it."

The doctor moved Danny's ankles this way and that and then asked him to stand up and walk slowly around the room. "That's fine, Danny. Thank you. Now, I promised you a treat, and so I've brought you a small present. Do you like sweets?" Danny nodded. "Yes, I rather thought you might. Here you are, then. There's a special lollipop for you because you've been such a good boy, and here are some toffees that you might like to share with your brothers and sisters. Would you like to go and play with them in the garden?"

The little boy limped off happily. Delighted that only he had a red lollipop, and pleased to be able to share the toffees with the other children.

Liza brought in a pot of tea and some cakes, and the doctor waited until they were all settled before he spoke.

"Right now, the good news is that I think I can help Danny with all of his deformities, though it's a pity I didn't get my hands on him when he was a baby. It's always better to treat these things as soon as possible. How old is he, now?

"He's four, sir."

"I thought he must be about that. You have done a good job of looking after him, Mrs Carter. I expect he was difficult to feed when he was born, wasn't he?"

"Yes, it took a long time to feed him because he couldn't suck very well. He struggled for the first six months of his life, and of course, I was feeding his sister, Helen, as well at the time, so I didn't have much milk to spare."

"I see; I didn't realise he had a twin."

"Oh, no, sir, he's not my child; he's a foundling. Annie found him abandoned in the woods, and because I had milk I agreed to take him in. I couldn't see him starve."

"That's even more commendable. Well done. Tell me has someone already treated his feet?"

"Just me, sir. I saw how they turned in, one worse than the other, and I bound them tightly with splints for several months. He didn't seem to mind, and I thought it might encourage them to grow straight. At the time, I didn't think he would ever walk, but he manages as best he can, though, of course, he does limp."

"You did an excellent job, Mrs Carter. That is precisely the treatment any physician would have suggested. Now, I can help Danny with his mouth and his feet, and I suggest we tackle the problems one at a time because the procedures will cause him some discomfort. However, with modern treatments, this is considerably minimised, compared to how it used to be. This is thanks to two men, who between them, have revolutionised surgery. Thanks to a man called James Simpson, we now use a gas called chloroform to anaesthetise patients. It puts them to sleep while we operate. This saves a lot of pain though, Danny will be a bit uncomfortable when he wakes up. We also have to thank another man, Joseph Lister, for initiating the use of carbolic acid. We sterilise our equipment in this and also use it on the wounds. In both cases, it reduces the chance of infection. Now, I'm not sure if you needed the history lesson, but I'm trying to reassure you, that I can correct Danny's deformities without causing him too much pain, or risk to his life."

Robert looked at Annie and Sabina. "That sounds positive to me. What do you think?"

"It would be wonderful for Danny if he could eat properly and not limp. Children can be so cruel, and he gets teased at school. Where would the operation be done?"

The doctor turned to Sabina. "It would be best done in London. My surgery there is well equipped, and I could keep an eye on him for a few weeks after the operation. Maybe you could come to London with him, and stay with us?"

Robert put his hand on the doctor's arm. "There is just one thing, Geoffrey. I must ask, how much will the operations cost? I'm willing to pay, but I do need to know how much is involved?"

"There will be no cost, Robert; it will be my pleasure to help such a lovely little boy. I'm not short of money, and I always carry out a few operations for free every year. I prefer to charge the extremely rich patients who come to see me in Harley Street. All too frequently, there is little wrong with them that more exercise and a little less port, would not cure. Maybe you could organise the transport for Danny and his mother? Now, the operation on his mouth will be the more complicated procedure because it involves his palate, though it's not the worst case I have dealt with. I suggest we do that one first, perhaps after Christmas, if that suits you? I'm quite busy for the next couple of months."

"Oh, that is good of you. Are you sure? I'm happy to pay something."

"No, really, it will be a pleasure. Now, shall we get the young man back in, and see what he has to say about it?"

Danny and his siblings returned to the room where the doctor explained to Danny what he was going to do.

"You will be asleep, Danny, whilst I repair your mouth, but it will be sore for a few days after. I'll be able to give you some medicine to ease it, though. Would you like me to fix it?"

"Yes, please. Can you do my feet, as well?"

"Yes, I can, but we'll do your mouth first, and let that get better, and then we'll think about your feet. Is that all right, with you?"

Danny nodded happily. "Yes, please."

"Good, then I will say goodbye for now, but I will see you in London after Christmas, and we'll get it all sorted out. Robert, I'll leave you to make all the arrangements, if that's all right?"

"Yes, of course. Thank you so much, Geoffrey. I've always wanted to get this done for Danny. Thank you for making it possible. Come on, we'll walk back to the Manor House now and get some lunch. Goodbye, Sabina."

CHAPTER 44

Since Sam's beating, Charlie and Fred had made a point of keeping an eye on the old man. This was partly due to Eveline insisting they do so, but also because they were still suspicious of Lizzie Dymond at Buzzacott House. They could see no reason for her to beat the old man if she had nothing to hide. Sam was still recovering from his injuries. The bruises on his grimy face were now purple and yellow, but his eye was now open, although it was still bloodshot. He was glad to see Charlie and Fred, for he enjoyed their company, and since Eveline had been involved, she had sent him food regularly, and he was beginning to look the better for it. She had even sent him a parcel of old clothes, and he had not looked so tidy or been as warm for many a year.

A couple of weeks after Sam's beating, Charlie was helping Fred with a difficult roofing job not far from Sam's hut, and they decided to call in and see him. As they trotted side by side, they discussed their wedding plans.

"Not long now, Charlie before we both get hitched. Have you been married before?"

"No, I've always travelled too much to get tied down, and that's always suited me. I'm ready now, though, and I'm looking forward to marrying Eveline. I'll take good care of her, Fred; you don't need to worry."

"I'm not worried, Eveline's a strong woman, and she can look after herself. Mind you, I've heard about you sailors with a girl in every port; she won't stand for that, you know."

Charlie laughed. "No, there'll be none of that, I can assure you; I'll be faithful. It's nice of your Annie to offer to have the reception at the big house, isn't it? It'll cost a pretty penny, and I'm happy to pay my share. It will be good to have the extra space, seeing as we're having a double wedding."

"Yes, I know. I've offered to pay as well, but I doubt Robert will take anything. He's enjoying being part of a real family. I don't think he's ever known much affection from his own. I'm glad we're having a joint wedding. It makes sense, seeing as it would be pretty much all the same guests at both ceremonies. Are you planning on going on honeymoon?"

"No, not straight away. Eveline wants to get the children settled in at the farm before we think of going anywhere. Maybe one day, we'll manage a day or two away, but not for a while, not until they would be happy staying with Alfred, Jimmy, and Maria. How about you and Charlotte?"

"No, same thing. I can't afford to take time off at the moment because I'm busy, and anyway, it's the same with my three children. They know Charlotte, of course, and they get on well with her, but they're bound to miss Eveline looking after them every day, so we want to take it slowly. Both William's children and mine have been through enough upheaval already."

"I can't believe how well it's all worked out. Anyway, here we are, there's the smoke from Sam's fire. When I see that from a distance I think he must be all right."

"He should be, what with Eveline feeding and clothing him, and us getting firewood for him; he's never had it so good."

Sam heard the horses' hooves and came out of his shed, beaming his familiar toothy smile. "Hello, lads, nice to see you again; I look forward to your visits. Sit yourselves down. I'm just cooking some fresh fish, and I know you're a bit partial to that; would you like some?"

"It does smell delicious, so it's hard to say no, but we don't want to take your food away."

"Nay lad, there's plenty more trout in that stream, and I've nothing better to do than catch them. I've nothing to go with the fish, though."

"I can help you out there, Sam, because Eveline has sent you two loaves of bread and some cheese. I'll just get it from my saddlebag."

As the three men ate their food, the conversation inevitably turned to Buzzacott House and the woman who lived there. "She's not bothered you since, has she, Sam?"

"No, I've kept away, though it was a close shave, yesterday. I went near the house picking herbs because that's where the ones I wanted grow, and she came out carrying a bundle. I dropped straight to the ground in the bushes and lay still on my belly because the last thing I wanted was for her to see me and beat me again. I'm only just getting over the last lot. I had to lie there quite a while, and I was worried I would get the cramp."

"Why was she there so long; what was she doing?"

"She had a spade with her, and she dug a hole and put the bundle into it so I suppose it was some rubbish, or perhaps a dead cat or something. Anyway, the ground was hard and full of thick roots, so it wasn't an easy job, but she kept at it. I waited until she had gone back into the house before I dared to move, and then, of course, it took me a while to get my stiff old joints moving before I could get up. At least she didn't see me, though, thank goodness."

"Today's Friday, so it's market day at Eggleston. Did you see her go out with the horse and cart?"

"Aye, she passed early this morning. No sign of the daughter, though, so she must be in the house."

"I'm not worried about her. Shall we take a look at what she buried, Charlie?"

"Yes, we can if you want, but it's probably a smelly old cat or her kittens. What else would she be burying? I hope it was that beastly dog."

"Nay, lad, it wasn't the dog. The bundle wasn't big enough; she'd struggle to carry that great brute. No, I reckon it will be a cat."

Sam took them to a glade just outside the garden wall, and they could see where the earth had been disturbed. Sam wouldn't stay with them but returned to his hut. "I'll leave you to it. I don't want to risk her coming back and seeing me. She might beat me again, and I'm not sure I'd survive another hiding. You should be all right, though; she isn't usually back until later in the day. I'll keep watch and blow my horn if I see her coming along the road."

Using Sam's spade, Fred gently dug away the soil. He got down about six inches and could see some blue material showing. "Whatever it is, she didn't dig down far. Mind you, these tree roots make it hard going. There I can pull the bundle out now, I think."

Fred pulled at the material and it came free of the hole. "Right, let's have a look. Oh, my God, no!"

Both men gasped in horror as a child's tiny foot fell free of the material.

"Oh, Charlie, it's a baby. Oh, please God, don't let it be Doris."

Fred's face was as white as a sheet as he peeled back the patterned curtain material and exposed the naked body of a small baby. It was so emaciated, it was impossible to tell how old the child was, but one thing was clear, it was the body of a male child. There were no obvious signs of injury.

"What do you think happened to it? There are no injuries. Do you think it just died, and she wanted to get rid of it? What a terrible thing to do. The poor child deserved a decent burial."

Charlie pulled anxiously at Fred's sleeve. "Fred, I've got a horrible feeling there might be more. Look, the ground is disturbed here in other places." Both men felt physically sick. "Let's not look for any more; let's get Wilf Folland. He needs to sort this out, not us. He can't ignore this. Wrap the child up, again, and we'll take it back to Sam's." They scraped the soil back into the hole, and Fred carried the tiny body.

"I knew they were up to something, but even I didn't suspect this. I just hope we don't find Charlotte's baby here too. It would truly break her heart."

They left the child's corpse near Sam's hut, and he promised to keep an eye on it. Even the tramp had tears in his eyes when he heard what they had found.

Charlie and Fred galloped back to the village and told Wilfred what they had found. He was flabbergasted. "I can't believe it. Do you think they murdered the child? I mean, why would they, if they could get it adopted and make money? It doesn't make sense."

"Wilfred, what do you want to do? Shall we go back and explore the house, and see if there are any more babies?"

"Yes, I think we'd better, but what about the dog? Perhaps we'd better wait until the woman is in?"

"I think it would be best to have a look around while she's out of the way. The daughter is there, so she can let us in the front door."

"I'm not sure she will. She didn't seem quite right to me when I saw her."

"I know what we'll do."

The two men looked at Charlie. "What?"

"We've still got some laudanum that the doctor gave Jane when she was so ill and in a lot of pain. It used to put her to sleep quickly. How about we soak some meat in it, and feed it to the dog? It won't take long to ride to the farm first; I know where the medicine is. I kept it in case I ever have toothache, again."

The policeman took charge. "Yes, I think that's justified in this case. If the girl will answer the door, so be it, but if not, we'll dope the dog and go in through the back. If I get questioned about it, I'll say we did it in case there were any other babies in danger. I can't see anyone arguing with that."

With several pieces of pork soaked in laudanum, the three men rode as fast as they could back to Sam, where they showed Wilfred the body of the child. Although he had been warned what to expect, he was shocked when he saw the sad little corpse. "Even if this child died from natural causes, deaths have to be registered. You can't just bury bodies in the woods. This woman has a lot to answer for. Come on."

Wilfred knocked loudly on the front door, but there was no response. "Are you sure there's someone in there?"

"Yes, Sam said she wasn't on the pony and trap with her mother, and I think I just saw a curtain twitch in that window. Shall we see if we can get in the back?"

Fred led the way to the back of the property and wheeled over the old barrel they had used before, to get up and look over the fence. Immediately they could hear deep-throated growls as the dog spotted Fred.

"It's here, and it's not happy. Charlie pass me the meat."

Fred threw a piece of meat over the fence, and the dog immediately gulped it down hungrily. Fred kept throwing the meat until it was all gone.

"He doesn't seem to mind the taste, mind you, he looks half-starved. No wonder he fancied a piece of your leg, Charlie. There's no sign of him going to sleep yet. Oh, wait a minute, he looks a bit unsteady."

Within a few minutes, the dog keeled over and was fast asleep. The three men climbed over, with Fred and Charlie hauling Wilfred over between them, for he was an older man and carried more weight.

"Well, I won't be coming back this way, and that's for sure." Wilfred was red in the face and gasping for breath with the exertion.

They tried the back door, and luckily, this time, it was unlocked. They called out as they walked through a scullery and into a large, untidy kitchen, but no one answered. Dishes were piled high in the sink, and there were mounds of dirty washing. They wandered through another room and then into the front room, where the girl was sat near the window tightly cradling a sleeping child. She looked terrified.

"It's all right, lass; we're not going to hurt you. We just want to talk to you."

"My mother's not here."

"No, we know, but that's all right. We just want to talk to you about the baby."

"It's mine. This one is mine. I'm keeping this one. Mum said I could."

Slowly, Wilfred sat down on a chair near her. Did you have the baby yourself, Thurza? That is your name, isn't it?"

"Yes, that's my name, but Mum says I mustn't talk to strangers."

"I'm a policeman, Thurza. You met me the other day, so it's all right to talk to me. May I just see your lovely baby? Is it a boy or a girl?"

Gently he pulled the shawl away from the baby's face and was relieved to see the child was breathing, though it did not stir. It looked malnourished, and it was impossible to tell how old it was.

"What a lovely baby. What is it called?"

"It's called Thurza, like me."

"How lovely. So, it's a little girl then, is it?"

"Yes, of course, it is. She's tired now. She needs to sleep. She needs lots of sleep. Mum says so."

"Are there any other babies here, Thurza?"

She frowned hard. "I'm not allowed to talk about the babies. Please go away. Mum will be cross." She looked frightened. "Please go. Mum might give me the stick if she finds you here. Please, go now, before she comes home."

"I'll make sure your mum doesn't hurt you, Thurza, I promise, but you do need to tell us about the other babies. Where are they?

The girl sat in stubborn silence, rocking to and fro, once more in a world of her own. Wilf put his hand on her arm, and she flinched as if she had forgotten he was there. "Leave me alone; I'll tell Mum, and she'll beat you."

"No, she can't do that, Thurza. I'm a policeman. Now, you must take me to the other babies, or I will have to take you off to jail. Where are they?"

The girl got to her feet unsteadily, and still hugging the child to her, silently led the way from the room and into the hallway. She walked to a door under the stairs, opened it, and led them down some dimly lit stairs. In the basement, a little light came through two grimy windows. As their eyes adjusted to the gloom, the men looked around the filthy, sparsely furnished space.

"There are no babies here, Thurza. Why have you brought us here?" Where are the babies?"

"They're here. Look, over there on the bed." She led the way to an old double bed in the far corner and pulled back a shawl that was covering three small bodies. "There they are, look. They'll soon be angels, but I'm keeping Thurza. Mum said I could." She looked at them, defiantly."

The men gazed at the babies in disbelief. "Are they alive?" Fred was the first to move and picked up the nearest child. It was warm but floppy and unresponsive. "This one is, but there's something wrong with it. Here take this one, Charlie."

Fred picked up the second, and then the third child, to find they too were alive, but in the same condition.

"I don't know what's wrong with them, but they are alive."

Wilfred inspected the three children. "I think they're drugged. I've heard about this; people drug them to keep them quiet. It saves feeding and looking after them. They use stuff called Godfrey's Cordial; it's got morphine in it.

He turned to the girl who was standing silently watching all they did.

"Thurza, why aren't you looking after these babies too?

"Mum won't let me. Mum's an angel-maker. She sends most of them to heaven to be with Jesus because he wants them more than their mothers did. She's a good person. They don't suffer, and they don't cry. They just go to sleep."

They heard a key in the lock of the front door and a voice shouting "Thurza, where are you?"

CHAPTER 45

On hearing her mother's voice, Thurza panicked. "Oh no, it's my mother. She'll kill me for bringing you down here. We must hide." She ran to the corner of the room and crouched behind the bed, a terrified expression on her face and tears running down her cheeks.

Charlie pushed past her and ran straight up the stairs. Lizzie Dymond was standing at the open door to the basement, and as soon as she saw Charlie, she slammed the door shut, and he could hear her fumbling with a key.

"No, you don't. He twisted the handle and pushed hard. The door moved an inch or so, but she was putting all her weight behind it on the other side. She was a strong woman, but no match for Charlie, and he soon had the door open. As soon as she realised she could not lock him in the basement, she ran swiftly for the front door, but Charlie was too quick for her and grabbed her from behind. She kicked and fought like a wildcat, scratching at his face and trying to bite him.

"Stop it, stop it now, or I'll make you! You're not going to win, so stand still."

She ignored him and continued to fight with all her might. Charlie did his best to hold her, but when she bit him on the hand and finally pulled free, he slapped her hard across the face, and she fell to the ground stunned. By this time, Wilfred and Fred had joined in, and together, the three men pulled her to her feet, sat her on a chair, and tied her to it.

"Lizzie Dymond, you are under arrest for the neglect and murder of, I don't know how many babies. I will be making arrangements to take you to Barnstaple jail. Do you have anything to say for yourself?"

"Where is Thurza? Did she let you in? I told her not to answer the door."

"No, she didn't, so don't blame her. We came in the back way. Now, what's wrong with those babies downstairs? Have you doped them?"

"I'm telling you nothing."

"Fred, can you ride to the village, and come back with a couple of carts, please? Charlie and I will stay here and wait for you. We'll need some women to look after the babies on the way home. If they've got any spare nappies and clothes, that would be useful. Those babies are soaking wet."

"Yes, Wilfred, of course. Charlie, is that bite all right? She's drawn blood."

"Aye, I'm all right, but I've had just about enough of getting bitten in this house. First the dog, and now a madwoman. I hope neither of them has rabies!"

Fred galloped back to the village. He could scarcely believe what they had found. He wondered if any of the surviving babies could be Doris. "No use worrying about that now, Fred Carter." He said to himself. "Pull yourself together, man, and do what you must do." He hitched the cart to his horse and went to find his sister. Eveline was in the garden, picking in the dry washing.

"Hello, Fred, you're back early. Tea won't be ready for a while."

"No, I'm not here for tea. I've come to ask for your help." He told her what they had found at Buzzacott House.

"Oh no, Fred, that's awful. Is Doris there?"

"I don't know. She might be, but the babies are in such a state it's difficult to know, and of course, I only saw her once. Anyway, we need to get back there as soon as we can and get those babies attended to. I thought we could take our children to the Lodge House and ask Liza to keep an eye on them all. It's asking a lot of a woman of her age, but I want to take Sabina with us. I did consider fetching Charlotte from the inn, but I can't take her to that house. We'll need to get Doctor Luckett to have a look at the babies and see if they can be saved. I have my doubts, and I don't want Charlotte seeing them until we know if they will live."

Eveline rounded up the six children and put them on the cart. "We're going to the Lodge House, where you can play with your cousins for the afternoon, and you must be good for Liza because she is an old lady. If you're naughty I will hear about it, and there will be trouble. Do I make myself clear?" Six heads nodded. Eveline could be strict when she wanted to be.

At the Lodge House, Sabina and Liza were astonished to see Fred and Eveline arrive with all the children but more than happy to help when they heard what had happened.

"Liza are you sure you'll be all right with all these children?" Sabina looked at her anxiously. "You can go with Eveline if you like, and I'll stay and look after them."

"No, I'll be all right. It's a dry afternoon, and they can play in the garden. There's plenty here for them to do. I'm too old and stiff to be jolted about on a cart, all the way to Buzzacott. You'll cope better with the babies than me. I don't want to see them, poor little mites."

Leaving Liza with the eleven children, they went to the smithy to find Francis Rudd. They could hear the blacksmith hard at work long before they saw him. The sound of Francis hammering on his anvil was a common sound in the village. Sure enough, there he was, sweat dripping from his brow as he took mighty swipes at a lump of metal as he hammered it into shape. When Fred pulled up in the cart, he went out to meet him, mopping his brow.

"Hello, Fred, ladies, is everything all right? You look a bit flustered."

Quickly Fred told him what had happened and asked if he could help. "We need two carts, you see, Francis. Wilf Folland wants to take the two women straight to Barnstaple jail because there's no jail here in Hartford, and they certainly need locking up. In fact, I hope they throw away the key. If you could do that with Wilfred, we can bring the babies back here. Can you leave the forge for a few hours?"

"Aye, I'll make the fire safe, and then go and tell Mum, or she'll wonder where I am. You go on with the women, and I'll follow when I'm ready. I know where it is. I'll be there as soon as I can."

Wilfred heard the horse and cart coming along the track and went out to meet it.

"Ah, there you are, Fred. Hello, Sabina, Eveline. Thanks so much for coming. The girl is still in the cellar with the baby she was holding. She won't come upstairs, she's that frightened of her mother, but she'll have to now, and we need to take the baby away from her too. Would you ladies like to see if you can persuade her to part with it?"

They went into the house where Lizzie was still tied to the chair. Sabina went over to her.

"You evil bitch; I hope you hang." She slapped her hard across the face. "That's for all the mother's whose hearts you've broken, and especially our Charlotte's."

Wilf took her arm. "Come on, Sabina. Leave her alone; I'll make sure justice is done. Oh, there's Francis, outside with his cart. He didn't hang about, did he? Charlie, can you stay here and keep an eye on her?"

Fred led the way down the stairs to the cellar with Wilfred, Eveline, and Sabina following. "You're not going to like what you see, I'm afraid."

Thurza was still crouched behind the bed, peering out to see who was coming. The child in her arms was whimpering. Sabina went to her. "Hello, Thurza, my name's Sabina. Can I see your baby? I like babies. I have lots of my own." The girl held the baby tightly and turned away from Sabina.

"Come on, look, your baby is crying. Does it need feeding? Shall we get it some milk?"

The girl looked up. "There's none left unless Mother got some. Go away and leave me alone."

"Thurza, your baby's poorly, and we need to take it to a doctor to make it better. Will you let me do that for you?"

"Babies don't get better. They turn into angels and go to heaven. Mother told me, but I like this one, so Mother said I can keep her for a while."

"Thurza, the doctor can make this baby better. Will you let me take her to the doctor? You don't want this one to become an angel, do you?"

"No, I like this one. She's pretty."

"Come on then, let me have a look at her. I can see you've looked after her. You're a good girl, Thurza."

Sabina smiled at her reassuringly.

"All right then." Reluctantly the girl handed the baby over to Sabina.

"Thank you, now we'll take her upstairs together."

"Is my mother up there?"

"Yes, but she won't hurt you, Thurza. We've told her you didn't let us in. Come on, I'll go first."

Sabina took the child from the girl and looked at it sadly. It was thin and weighed next to nothing. She led the way up the stairs, and Wilfred followed. As soon as Thurza saw her mother tied to a chair, she tried to bolt back down the stairs.

Wilfred stepped forward quickly to block her path. "Now, it's all right, Thurza. We had to keep your mother quiet because she was fighting us, but we haven't hurt her. We're going to take you both for a ride on a cart, so you come outside with me, and you can get on it first. Charlie, I'll get Thurza settled, and then I'll come back to help you with this one."

Leaving Thurza with Francis, who had stayed on the cart, Wilfred returned to the room. He looked down at the woman. "Now are you going to behave yourself? You'd better because you're going nowhere with us three men to deal with you. It will be easier for you if you come quietly because it wouldn't upset us too much to give you a good hiding."

The policeman untied the ropes that were holding her to the chair but left her hands tied behind her back and pushed her out of the door. Once she was loaded onto the cart, he tethered his and Charlie's horses to the back of the cart and turned to Sabina, who was at the door holding the baby.

"Sabina, Charlie and I will ride back on the cart with Francis, so we can keep an eye on these women. We'll call on Sam and collect the body of the dead child. That will have to go to Barnstaple. You, Fred, and Eveline do what you can to make the babies comfortable and then bring them back to the village. Would you mind taking them to your house for the time being? I want to get these two locked up in Barnstaple, and then I'll come and see what's to be done about the babies. I'll fetch Doctor Luckett on the way and bring him to have a look at them."

"Yes, that's fine, Wilfred. We'll see you, later."

"Just a minute, Wilfred. What about the dog? We can't leave it here to starve, and it's too dangerous to let it go."

"Would you mind putting it down, Fred? It's a shame, but it's so vicious, I don't see any alternative. See if you can find a gun in the house. If not, one of us will have to come back to see to it."

Fred and Eveline brought the other three babies upstairs, and together with Sabina, they set about changing all four into dry clothes, for they were saturated in urine. As they peeled off their wet clothes, which no doubt some heartbroken mother had lovingly dressed them in, they were saddened to see how emaciated they were. The three little girls and one boy were heavily drugged, for apart from the odd whimper, they lay limp and lifeless, barely breathing. The little girl that Thurza had been so fond of had fared slightly better. She wasn't as thin as the others, and she had been changed more regularly.

"Oh, look at their poor little bottoms. They are so sore. It's a wonder they aren't screaming."

"I don't think they can at the moment, but I don't know what they'll be like when the drugs wear off. We need to get them to Doctor Luckett as soon as possible, and see if he can do anything for them."

"How old do you think they are?"

"It's impossible to tell, isn't it; they are so starved. Fred, how old would Charlotte's baby be, now?"

"I think she was born in early May, so I suppose she'd be about six months old by now. Do you think any of these babies could be Doris? They don't seem big enough."

"Doctor Luckett might have more idea, but the first thing is to try to save them, then worry about who they belong to. No doubt the police will search the house for any records and, of course, the woman will know if she can be persuaded to talk."

Eveline sighed and brushed away a few tears. "Right, that's all four changed. Fred, do you want to deal with the dog while we get the babies on the cart? That's if you can find a gun. Mind the beast doesn't bite you."

Fred searched the rooms for a gun and finally found a rifle on top of a cupboard in the kitchen. It was fully loaded. Cautiously, he opened the back door and peered out to see if the dog had regained consciousness. It was just stirring and getting shakily to its feet. Swiftly he went over to it and shot it in the head. "There, you'll never bite anyone else, but at least you didn't suffer." He wondered whether he should bury it but decided it was more important to get the babies back to the village. No doubt the police would be coming to investigate, so they could deal with it. He'd seen enough unpleasantness for one day.

CHAPTER 46

Liza saw Sabina and Eveline step down carefully from the cart with the babies in their arms and opened the door for them. "Oh, poor little dears. Do you think they'll live?"

"I don't know, Liza, but could you warm some milk? We'll see if they'll feed. I think there are some bottles and teats in that cupboard near the sink." Sabina put the two babies she was carrying in one of the armchairs. "Eveline, put the other two in that chair if you like."

"I've already found the bottles and washed them, and the milk is ready to go on the stove. We only have two bottles, though, and one teat. I would have gone to the shop to get some more, but I couldn't leave all the children."

"Have they behaved themselves?" Eveline asked anxiously. "You look tired, Liza, but thank you so much for looking after them."

"Oh, yes, they've been good, but I'm afraid at my age it doesn't take much to tire me out."

"Fred, there are some bottles in our kitchen, but I'm not sure about teats. Would you mind going to fetch them, and buy some teats from the shop?

"Yes, of course, I will. I'll do that, but then I must go and tell Charlotte what we've found. It will upset her, but she'll never forgive me if I don't, and she has to know sooner or later."

Fred returned with the bottles and teats, and Sabina and Eveline coaxed the babies to feed. The little girl that Thurza had favoured, soon sucked hungrily at the teat, and Sabina heaved a sigh of relief. "I think this one will live. She wants to anyway, and that's half the battle." She looked at Liza and Eveline, who were cradling the other two little girls.

Eveline smiled. "That's good. This one is sucking a little bit but still sleepy. How about yours, Liza?"

"No, this one seems too sleepy. I think I'll leave her a bit longer and try the boy. Mind you; he looks in a worse state than the girls." She picked up the tiny child and put the bottle to his lips. He stirred slightly and opened his mouth. "Oh, yes, I think he might take a little drop."

They heard a knocking at the door, and Sabina told Stephen to open it. "It's Charlie, and the doctor, and the policeman, Mum. Shall I let them in?" Stephen yelled from the doorway.

"Yes, of course."

The three men trooped in, and the doctor went straight to the babies. "Goodness me, how could anyone let babies get into this state? Don't give them too much milk. That could do more damage than good because they aren't used to it. Just give them a little drop and often. I think we'll probably need to mix some morphine with it and wean them off it gradually. We won't give them any yet, and see how they react, but no doubt they will miss it if we stop it completely."

"Have you come across this problem before then, doctor?"

"Sadly, yes. The mixture most commonly used is called Godfrey's Cordial or Mother's Friend, and lots of families use it to make the children sleep so they can work. The parents have to get some sleep to work the long hours they do, and this keeps the children quiet. It's mostly just morphine mixed with treacle. Unfortunately, children quickly become addicted to it. It's not a problem here in Hartford because we only have one shop, and thankfully,

George refuses to sell it. I used to work in a big town, and the shops there sold it by the jugful. Over time, the treacle separates from the morphine, so the further down the barrel you get, the stronger the dose becomes. I've known one dose to kill a child; it's pretty lethal. Apart from being malnourished, is there anything else wrong with them that you know of?"

"They've been asleep all the time, even when we changed them because they were soaking wet. There are no wounds on them, but their bottoms are very sore from lying in soiled nappies."

"I can give you some ointment for that. If you can leave them in a warm room with their nappies off and let the air get to their skin, that will help. What's going to happen to these babies? It will be hard work looking after them once the drugs wear off. Are they going to the workhouse because I can't see them getting the right care there?"

Wilf Folland interrupted. "That was my next question. I'm grateful to you, ladies, for what you have done, but this isn't your problem. I'm afraid I will have to take them to the workhouse because there is nowhere else. Unless the hospital would take them, doctor?"

"Yes, it would, but the hospital is struggling to cope with several cases of measles, and if any of these babies caught that, they would likely perish. Probably the workhouse is the better option, though a poor option, it may be."

Before they could further discuss the babies' future, there was another knock on the door, and Stephen ran to answer it. It was Fred and Charlotte, and she didn't wait to be invited in. Pushing past Stephen, she ran into the room and put her hand to her mouth. "Oh my God! Is one of them, Doris?"

Fred gently put his arm around her. "We don't know, Charlotte. Wilf, is it all right if Charlotte has a look to see if she thinks any of them is her daughter?"

"Yes, of course. Take your time, my dear."

Charlotte looked at each of the female babies in turn. "None of them look big enough to be six months old."

"No, but they've been starved, so naturally they are small." Doctor Luckett took her hand. "Think carefully, did Doris have any distinguishing marks on her body, like a mole or a birthmark?"

"No, there was nothing like that." Charlotte took each baby in turn and looked closely. She kept returning to the one Thurza had favoured. "I think this one is Doris. Her features look familiar, and her hair is blond like mine. I think the other two will be dark-haired. I'm pretty sure she is Doris. May I keep her?"

All faces turned to the policeman. "Well, now, she needs looking after at the moment, and if you are willing to do that, then I'm grateful. However, I have to make more enquiries about all this and search the house to see if there is any evidence of who these babies belong to. If we find this baby girl belongs to someone else, we would have to give her back if they wanted her, and I don't want to upset you further. Maybe you shouldn't become attached to her until we know."

Gently Fred tried to take the baby from Charlotte. "Wilf's right, Charlotte. It would be best to leave this to someone else until we know for sure. I couldn't bear for you to have to give her up a second time."

Charlotte looked down at the child and then around the room. "I understand what you're saying, but I am convinced this is Doris. Anyway, if there is evidence to the contrary, I will hand her back, I promise, but I want to care for this child. If she goes to the workhouse, she may not live long enough to go to any parents. I would rather look after her, even if I do have to give her back."

"Very well, as long as you understand the situation. So that just leaves the other three. If you ladies can wrap them up, I'll take them with me to the workhouse when I leave."

Eveline and Fred exchanged glances, and he gave an almost imperceptible nod of his head. Eveline then looked at Sabina for confirmation of what she was thinking.

Sabina spoke up. "It's all right, Wilf, we'll look after them, at least until you find out who they belong to. Eveline, if you can take one, I'll look after the other two because I have Liza to help me, and no doubt when Annie hears about all this, she'll help too."

"That's kind of you, ladies, and I'm sure these babies will stand a much better chance of survival in your tender care." Wilf looked relieved. "Now, I was just going to tell you what will happen next. The two women are locked up in the Barnstaple jail where I suspect they will be in for a hard time when the other women find out what they are in for. Few women like to hear of babies being mistreated."

"What about Thurza, is she locked up with her mother?" Sabina looked anxious. "She's frightened of her, and I don't think Thurza understood what was going on. She's simple-minded."

"I'm afraid she's in with her mother at the moment because there's nowhere else for her to go, and they'll need to stick together in there. Tomorrow, I'll take two officers with me, and we'll search the house for any information about the babies, and we'll also dig in the woods to see if there are any further bodies. What about the dog, Fred? Did you shoot it?"

"Yes, luckily, it was still too groggy from the laudanum to attack me, and I shot it before it knew what was happening, so it didn't suffer."

"We'll bury it when we go there tomorrow, then. Thanks for doing that; not a nice job. Now, I'll leave you, good people, for now, and I'll be in touch soon. Are you coming, doctor?"

"Yes, there's no more I can do here, and the babies are in good hands. Here is a small bottle of morphine for each of you ladies. If the babies are fretful when they wake up, just put a couple of drops in their bottle, and that should help. It's difficult to know what dose to give them because we don't know what they've been having and we mustn't overdose them. I'll visit each of you in the morning to see how things are. I bid you all goodnight."

CHAPTER 47

A few days later, Charlie went to see Sam. When they found the babies at the house, there was no time to tell the old man all that had happened, and Charlie thought he deserved to know. Sam had been involved in the investigations concerning the babies, and no doubt, he would be delighted to hear that the woman and her daughter were safely locked up and could do him no further harm. However, Sam was better informed than Charlie, for he had been speaking to the police.

"They called here and asked me a few questions, and I showed them where that baby was buried. A nasty business all of it. They told me the pair of them were locked up in jail. I should think they will hang. I hope so, anyway."

"I'm not sure the daughter deserves that, Sam. She seemed a bit simple to me, and she was scared to death of her mother."

"I'm not surprised; I was too. Great bully; she was built more like a man than a woman. Did you know they found two more bodies?"

"No, I didn't. Oh, that's awful, but I'm not surprised. It looked like there had been more digging. When they've finished investigating, Wilfred is going to come and tell us what's happening."

"How are the babies that you found? Will they live?"

"We think so, though it's touch and go with one little girl. The one Charlotte is looking after, the one she thinks is Doris, is doing well. She was better looked after than the others because Thurza, the daughter, had taken a liking to her, and I think she got most of whatever milk was available. Eveline is looking after another little girl, and Sabina, Annie's mother, is looking after two of them, a boy and a girl. It's that baby girl that is struggling, but if anyone can nurse her back to health, it will be Sabina. Mind you, those women have their work cut out. Now the drugs are wearing off, those babies are crying night and day. Doctor Luckett keeps raising the dose of morphine, but he has to be careful in case he overdoses them. I think it will take a long time for them to recover completely if they ever do. Anyway, I'm not just here about that, Fred and I wondered if you'd like to come to our weddings? You know, Fred and Charlotte, and me and Eveline are all getting married? It's on Saturday, and we would like you to come. The reception is at the Manor House, thanks to Annie and Master Robert."

Sam laughed. "Eh, lad, I wouldn't know how to behave at a do like that, and what would I wear? They won't want a smelly old tramp like me going to the Manor House. Whatever next. I'm tickled, to have been asked, though and no mistake."

"If you'd like to come, you can have a bath at my house, and we can find you some tidy clothes. You'd be all right, Sam. I can make sure I get you a seat near someone you can talk to. You deserve a treat for helping us to rescue those babies."

"You're so kind, Charlie, but surely you don't want me there?"

"Yes, I do, Sam, and so does Eveline and Fred. If you would like to come, you can ride home with me now on the cart. What do you say?"

"How many days is it until Saturday?"

"Today is Thursday, so it's the day after tomorrow. If you come back with me today, you can have a good scrub tomorrow, and I'll sort you out some clothes to wear. Alfred has some he can't get into anymore, and he won't throw them away, but I think they'd fit you."

"But where would I stay until Saturday? I can't walk back here to my hut; it's too far for me these days."

"I've been thinking about that. There's a loft above the old stables that we don't use nowadays. In the past one of the grooms used to live there, and it's quite pleasant. Nice and warm all year round above the animals too. You can stay there if you like. In fact, if you want to do a few odd jobs around the farm, you can stay there as long as you like. We couldn't pay you, but we could feed you. Would you like to live there, or do you prefer to be on the road? I know some people do."

"I've been on the road all my life so I don't know anything else, but it is becoming more of a struggle the older I get. Are you sure, Charlie? I don't want to be a nuisance, and I can't remember the last time someone wanted me anywhere. Usually, they can't drive me away fast enough."

"I've talked to Alfred, Jimmy, and Eveline, and they are all happy for you to live there. As I say, we can't run to another wage, but we could find you enough food, or you can still catch fish and rabbits."

Well, 'tis kind of you." Sam looked thoughtful. Then he grinned. "I'll tell you what then. I'd like to give it a try. I can always come back here if I don't like it, can't I? What about all my stuff that's here, though?"

"We can take most of it on the cart today; that's why I brought it. If you bring what you need the most, we can always come back another time if you decide to stay. It's pretty deserted here, so I doubt anything will get stolen."

Sam hadn't much in the way of possessions, and it didn't take Charlie long to load what he needed onto the cart. As they travelled back to the village, Sam occasionally burst out laughing.

"What are you laughing at Sam?"

"I'm that tickled to think I'm going to the Manor House. I wish my old mum was still here, she'd surely pee her pants, laughing.

When they reached the farm, Charlie took Sam up into the loft. "What do you think, Sam? Could you be comfortable here?"

"Sam looked around him in wonder. "My goodness me, yes. Look, there's a bed and even a table and chair. What more could I want?"

"I'll fetch your bits and pieces, and then I'll get you something for your supper, and tomorrow you can have a bath."

The next day Charlie put the old tin bath in front of the kitchen stove and helped Maria to fill it with hot water. He then told her she could have a few hours off to go into Hartford.

The girl grinned. "I don't suppose he's got anything I haven't seen before, Charlie. I've had to clean up Grandad times enough since he lost his hands."

"Yes, I suppose you have, Maria, but Sam may not see it like that. I think putting his body in water is going to be quite a shock, let alone have a lovely young girl like you watching. You make the most of it and enjoy a few hours off." She went off laughing as he went to fetch the old man.

"Come on then, Sam, take your clothes off and get in. I've put some old clothes there you can wear for today, and then some better ones for the wedding tomorrow. There's no one around. I've sent Maria to the village, and Alfred and Jimmy are out in the fields. Do you want me to leave you to it?"

"It doesn't matter to me, lad. I've nothing to hide."

He stripped off his clothes and gingerly lowered his thin, grimy body into the hot soapy water, some bruises from his beating still showing. "My goodness, that feels lovely. I can't remember when I last had a bath. In fact, I'm not sure I've ever had one since I was a nipper. I used to swim in Shebworthy pond now and then in the summer months when I was younger."

Fred handed him a cloth. "Here you are, use this with the soap, and give yourself a good scrub. If I wash your hair, would you like me to cut it for you, and shave you?"

"You can if you like. Do you know what you are doing, or will it be a basin on my head? That's what my mum used to do."

"I should be able to make a fairly good job of it. When I was at sea for months on end, we often used to cut each other's hair when it got too long and the weather was hot."

Charlie snipped away at the thick grey hair and then at the long and matted beard before he fetched a cut-throat razor to finish the job. "Now, keep still, Sam, I don't want to nick you."

When they were both satisfied that he was clean, he stepped out of the bathtub carefully and dried himself on the rough towel Maria had left for him.

"You get dressed in those clothes, Sam, and I'll get rid of this bathwater. Good heavens, the water is filthy. I'll have to clean the bath afterwards or Maria will grumble at me. Leave your dirty clothes there, and I'll get Maria to wash them."

"I'm sorry about the dirt, Charlie, but you did insist on bringing me here. Do you have any scissors that I could cut my toenails with? They've been troubling me for a long time, and now they are nice and soft they should cut easily."

"Yes, here you are."

Charlie busied himself emptying and cleaning the bath, and then he took it out to the washhouse and replaced it on its nail on the wall. He returned to the kitchen just as Sam was tucking his clean shirt into his trousers and pulling on a coat.

"Good Lord, Sam, no one will know you! Come with me. There's a mirror in Alfred's bedroom."

The two men went up the stairs, and Sam surveyed himself in the mirror. "Will you look at that? I've never seen myself in a full-length mirror; I look almost respectable, don't I?"

"You certainly do, Sam. Now, don't get dirty until after the wedding. There are a few other people who will want to bath before then, including me."

CHAPTER 48

Fred and Charlie fidgeted as they waited nervously at the altar in Hartford Church. Fred's brother, George, was his best man, and Jimmy was Charlie's.

"I hope they're coming; they're late," whispered Charlie.

"Of course, they're coming. Brides are always late. It's what they do," hissed Fred, trying to look relaxed.

"I didn't think Eveline would put me through this, I ..."

Before he could finish his sentence, the organ started to play the wedding march, and both men turned to look down the aisle. With wide smiles on their faces, Charlotte and Eveline stood one on each side of Ned, who proudly escorted them down the aisle to give them away.

Eveline was dressed in a full-length white dress with a long train and embroidered bodice. A beautiful lace veil, one of Charlie's many spoils from France, hung over her face, and she carried some late pink roses from the Manor House greenhouses. Charlotte's dress was cream, again full-length, but much plainer, though it suited her slight figure. She too had a veil over her face and carried a bouquet identical to Eveline's. There were no bridesmaids. They had decided there were so many girls in the family who were eligible that it was easier to have none. That being the case, they handed their bouquets to Betsey as they reached their future

340

husbands. Both brides lifted the veils from their faces, and the Reverend Rees began the service.

Everything went without a hitch, and before long the happy couples were seated in a carriage to take them to the Manor House. As was traditional, they waited in the hallway of the West Wing to welcome each guest.

First in the queue were Annie and Robert with William's children, Joe, Matthew, and Amelia, Fred's children, Llewellyn, Rosella, and Eddie, as well as Selina. Sabina and Liza followed with the Carter children, Willie, Mary, Edward, Stephen, Helen, and Danny. Robert whispered to Annie. "Goodness, Annie, you do have a lot of children in your family."

"There's more yet. Here comes Uncle George and his lot."

Annie's Uncle George shook Fred's hand, then Charlie's, and lightly kissed the hands of his sister, Eveline, and Charlotte. As he bent over Eveline's hand, she whispered to him. "George, be nice to everyone today." She looked into his eyes. "Please, be nice, no preaching." He smiled at her. "Don't worry, I'm on my best behaviour. I won't show you up. You look beautiful, Evie; I'm so pleased for you."

Charlotte had not invited any of her family, for they had not supported her in her hour of need. She would have liked her mother there, but that would have meant asking her father, and she felt she was better off without him and his opinions. However, there were plenty of relatives on Charlie's side for he was one of ten children. Having been at sea for years, even Charlie had not met some of his nieces and nephews and he had to rely on Alfred to make the introductions.

Although strictly speaking, the wedding was nothing to do with Robert's family, he had asked Sarah and Aunty Margery, both of whom, were now firm friends of Annie. He had decided against asking his sister, Victoria, as it would have meant her travelling from London with two young babies, and Annie preferred not to see her husband, Frank, if it could be avoided.

All the furniture had been removed from the dining room to make way for several long tables to accommodate all the guests. The great hall in the main house would have been far more suitable for so many people, but Robert knew his mother would be horrified at the thought of people from the village being entertained in her house, and so they had decided to make do with what they had. It just wasn't worth the upset.

Together, Annie and Eveline had worked out a seating plan, for they knew it was important for people to sit where they felt comfortable. Families were sat together, of course, but they weren't sure where to seat Aunty Margery and Sarah, or for that matter, Sam.

They had giggled together as they considered the options. "It's difficult, isn't it? I mean, how many weddings have a titled lady and a tramp to accommodate."

"It would be funny to sit Sam on George's table, don't you think? He's convinced Sam stole those boots from his shop, and he'll never forgive him."

Eveline laughed. "No, I don't think we'd better do that. Anyway, George is the best man for Fred, so he'll be on the top table. So will Jimmy, Ned, Betsey, and your mother. What about if we sit Sam with Liza and the children? Liza won't mind and she'll keep an eye on him."

When it was Sam's turn to shake hands with the newly married couples, Fred looked at him in amazement. "My goodness, Sam, I didn't recognise you. What has Charlie done to you?"

In truth, Fred had not been sure who the old man was until he smiled his toothy grin, and that gave the game away. There was not much Charlie could do about that.

"I know, I've not been so clean for many a year or had such lovely clothes. What good people you all are. I can't believe I'm here at the Manor House for my dinner; I never thought this would happen." He smiled a thoughtful smile. "I keep thinking I must be dreaming. Thank you so much."

"It's you we have to thank, Sam. You helped a lot in saving those babies."

Charlotte shook his hand warmly. "Yes, thank you so much, Sam. It's good to meet you at last; I've heard a lot about you." She winked at him and whispered in his ear. "I know what it's like to be hungry and have nowhere to go, so you enjoy yourself and eat as much as you can; you deserve it."

Eventually, all the guests had been welcomed and shown to their designated seats. Annie and Eveline had decided against displaying the seating plan, for many present could not read and write. Instead, the footmen escorted people to their seats just as they had for Annie's wedding. Aunty Margery and Sarah sat with Annie and Robert, a good distance from Sam although he now looked respectable. Selina, William's children and Fred's children also sat with Annie, and she just hoped they would behave.

Maisie had been nervous about catering for such a large party, and this was her first big test since being promoted to the position of cook. However, she still had Ethel Potts in the background to advise her, and all went well. The meal started with chicken soup or salmon, followed by roast pork and all the trimmings. A whole pig had been turning on a spit in the kitchen for hours and was incredibly tasty and tender. There were several desserts to choose from, followed by cheese and biscuits.

During the meal, Annie told Aunty Margery and Sarah about the babies they had found in Buzzacott House, and they were horrified.

Aunty Margery nodded her head. "I have heard about this before. When I was younger, I lived in London and was involved in charity work, though my husband didn't approve. These women take in children, either to look after in the short term until the mother can have them back or in some cases to arrange a full adoption. Mind you, most do their best for the children, and doctors are often involved. Unfortunately, you always get a few who are only in it for the money, and they don't care what happens to the children. It's very sad. Where are the babies today?"

"A lady in the village, Matilda Rudd is looking after them so that all the family could come to the wedding. Matilda is an old lady now, but she still delivers many of the babies in the village. We know they will be safe with her."

"How are they doing? Are they all expected to live?"

"Yes, it was touch and go, especially with one little girl, but it's been a couple of weeks now, so Doctor Luckett is hopeful they will all pull through. They are taking a little milk and often, but the most difficult thing is weaning them off the morphine. Without it, they cry all the time. We're reducing it gradually, but it's going to take a long time, and it's hard work looking after them."

"What will happen to them?"

"We're not sure yet, we're waiting for the police to tell us if they've traced any of the parents. My mother is looking after a boy and a girl, and my Aunty Eveline, another little girl. If they have to give them back, it won't be too bad, but we're hoping and praying that the baby Charlotte is looking after is her daughter, Doris. If she has to give that child back, it will break her heart. It would be like losing her all over again."

Once the meal was over, the guests left the dining room to allow the servants to remove the tables and make room for dancing later. The guests circulated, and Sabina was able to sit with Arthur Webber and his father Peter. She was glad Peter had agreed to come but had been concerned about how he would manage to eat the meal. She wondered if he was confident enough to eat in public with the newly made attachments to his arms. However, she needn't have worried because he coped admirably well, having opted for salmon instead of soup, which would have been more difficult.

Under the table, Arthur took her hand and squeezed it. "There's no denying both brides look beautiful today, but not as beautiful as you." He whispered in her ear.

"Ssh Arthur, someone will hear you."

"Doesn't matter if they do, does it? We're both unmarried, so why shouldn't we be courting?"

"Is that what we're doing then, courting?" She grinned at him.

"I would have thought that was obvious by now."

"I can't stay too long today. Matilda is looking after all four babies and they are hard work. It's good of her to do it, and I don't want to leave her on her own for too long."

"She'll be all right for a while, and I know she'd want you to stay and have a few dances with me. You will, won't you?"

"Yes, just a few."

Looking up, Sabina was surprised to see Robert's Aunty Margery at her side.

"Hello, I don't think we've met, but I'm Robert's Aunty Margery, and I believe you are Annie's mother? Sabina, isn't it?"

"Yes, ma'am; it's lovely to meet you." Sabina got up to curtsey to the old lady.

Margery pushed her back down. "No need for any of that. I don't stand on ceremony. I've always been the black sheep of the family, but now I am so old I can do what I like. I wanted to congratulate you on your lovely daughter. I know Charles and Eleanor disapprove of her, but I can see she makes Robert happy. Now, these must be Annie's brothers and sisters; will you introduce me, please? I'll know who she is talking about then. We've become good friends, and it's always good to put a face to a name."

Sabina introduced all of her children, staring intently at each one as if trying to communicate by telepathy, the necessity to be polite. She needn't have worried, for all the children had seen that stare before, and anyway they wouldn't upset Robert for anything.

Margery put her hand on Sabina's arm. "Sabina, could you tell me who that gentleman is? The one who is sitting with the older lady. Is he her husband?"

"Oh no, that's Liza. She's a widow, and she lives with me and the family at the Lodge House. The man she is with is called Sam. He's an old tramp who's lived rough in the village for as long as I can remember. The reason he's here is that he was camping near Buzzacott House, and he helped Fred and Charlie when they were curious about what was going on there. Charlie is letting him live at Hollyford Farm now, in a loft above the stables. I'm pleased for him because he's getting on a bit now. I don't know his story, but he always seems like a nice old man. I've never seen him so clean, though. Why do you ask?"

"Oh, no reason, but he looks familiar. I guess I must have seen him in the village over the years."

The old lady turned her attention to Arthur and Peter. "And who do we have here, then? More relatives?"

"No, this is my friend, Arthur Webber, he works here on the estate, and this is his father, Peter."

Margery shook Arthur by the hand. "I'm pleased to meet you, Arthur. What do you do on the estate?"

"I'm just a farm labourer, ma'am."

She turned to Peter. "I've heard everything about you, Mr Webber from Annie. I'm impressed at how well you are managing your disability. Some men would have given up; you should be proud of yourself."

"Why, thank you, ma'am. It's all thanks to Sabina. She got people to make me this harness, and now I can use all sorts of implements. I've got a knife, fork, and spoon that I can use and even a paintbrush. Sabina's brother, Fred, made me an easel, and I pass the time, painting. I'm not very good, but I'm improving."

"That is interesting, Peter. May I call you, Peter?" He nodded. "Well, Peter, I like painting too, so perhaps I could see your paintings sometime."

"Why yes, ma'am, of course; it would be a pleasure. There is one hanging in the hallway here. Annie insisted on buying it, though I don't think it was worth anything like what she paid me for it. She was being nice to me, I think."

"In that case, would you take me to see it, Peter?"

"Yes, of course, ma'am. If you follow me, I'll take you to it."

As Peter and Margery walked out to the hallway, Arthur and Sabina looked at each other in surprise. "I didn't see that coming. What a lovely old lady; not a bit snobbish, is she? Do you think she fancies my dad?"

Sabina slapped him. "Behave yourself, Arthur Webber. Now, the band is starting up, so are you going to give me that dance you promised?"

CHAPTER 49

The time following the wedding was a busy one for Annie. The newlyweds could not afford a honeymoon, but to let them have some time to themselves, she had offered to have William and Fred's children stay at the Manor House for a week where she would look after them. She was delighted when Selina agreed to come as well, and the little girl seemed happier in the house with the company of the other children. Finally, she slept in the bedroom Annie had lovingly prepared for her, albeit shared with Amelia and Rosella. The twins, Joe and Matthew, and Llewie and Eddie, all shared another room. Annie had arranged for the children to have lessons with Sarah's governess, Jane Leworthy, instead of going to the local school. The children found this a novelty, and Jane was delighted to have her classroom full of children for a change. Sarah moved from pupil to deputy teacher for the week and also enjoyed her new role.

Annie was also looking after Charlotte's baby, Doris, and the little girl that Eveline had been caring for. Eveline had named her Martha, though she was trying not to become too attached to her, in case she had to hand her back. Annie enlisted Molly's help for the week, particularly with the babies, who were taking up far more of her time than she had anticipated.

She was surprised one morning when Ethan came to ask if she would receive Aunty Margery. "This is a lovely surprise, Aunty Margery; how nice that you have come to see us. I'll call for some tea."

"That would be lovely, my dear. I hope you don't mind me turning up, unannounced?"

"No, of course not; you're welcome here any time. Mind you, I am busy this week because I'm looking after Selina and all Fred and William's children, and also two of the rescued babies. The children are no trouble at all. They're happy playing in the gardens and with all the toys in the nursery, as well as having some schooling from Sarah's governess. What with that, and enjoying Mrs Potts' cooking, they have no reason to be naughty. It's the babies that are taking up the time of myself and Molly, and she still has to help in the kitchen quite a lot of the time."

"That's why I'm here. Robert mentioned that you were looking after all these children, and I wondered if I could help. I'm only sitting at home with nothing to do, and I've always loved children, though I was never blessed with any of my own. Would you like me to stay and help for a few days? You'd be doing me a favour because I get bored at home with too much time to myself."

Annie was surprised. "Yes, that would be lovely. You're welcome to stay; we have plenty of room. You don't have to help with the babies, though."

"No, really; I'd like to. There is one other thing I want to do while I'm here, though. I want to go and see that man who paints, Peter Webber. He showed me the painting in your hallway and I like it. It's a seascape and he has caught the light amazingly well. I like to paint too, but I've never produced anything as good as that, and I'd like his advice. I want to ask him to paint me a picture. It's remarkable how he can paint as well as he does when he has no hands. He's an inspiration to us all and I'd like to help him sell more of his paintings. I suspect your mother, Sabina, is rather fond of his son, Arthur? Am I right?"

Annie smiled. "She's not admitting it, but yes, I think you're right. I'd like to see her settle down with Arthur. It's several years since she lost my dad, and she's still a young woman. I'll ask Molly to keep an eye on the children this afternoon, and we could take the babies for a walk in the pram and go to the Webber's house. Would that be too far for you to walk? It's only in the village near the church. The fresh air might make the babies sleep better tonight, too."

"That sounds like a good idea. I'll get my servant to bring my luggage in then. I brought a few changes of clothes, just in case you were happy for me to stay. Where is Robert this morning?"

"Oh, he's out and about with Jack Bater, our farm manager. Robert loves looking after the estate; he was born to do it, and he's made lots of improvements. He's thinking of introducing shooting parties here next year. He says they bring in a lot of money, so he and Jack are discussing breeding pheasants."

"That's a good idea. On my estate, we have shooting parties and I understand they are lucrative, though I leave it all to my manager, I'm afraid. You do need to make sure the money is coming in these days because estates like this seem to get ever more expensive to run."

Margery stayed the whole week, and Annie enjoyed her company, as well as her help. However, she had to admit to herself, that she would not be sorry to hand the children and the babies back to Eveline and Charlotte. Charlotte had moved to Fred's house and Eveline to Hollyford Farm, and both women appreciated the time to make a few changes to their new homes. Annie asked Selina if she would like to stay at the Manor House, but she wanted to go home with the other children. "I do like it here with you, Mummy, but I don't have anybody to play with. Can you come, and live with Granny, again? That would be best."

Annie explained that would not be possible now she was married to Robert, but Selina did agree to come and stay for a couple of nights again soon, so Annie felt that at least she was making progress.

A few days after all the families had returned to their respective households, Wilfred Folland visited Sabina.

"I have some news, now that our investigations at Buzzacott House are complete, and it would be easier to tell everyone all together."

She agreed to invite everyone involved to the Lodge House, and so Annie, Fred and Charlotte, and Charlie and Eveline all waited in Sabina's parlour for the policeman to arrive. Charlotte was anxious, for she feared losing the baby for the second time. Fred held her hand and tried to comfort her but, he too was nervous. Eventually, they heard a knock on the door, and Annie answered it and showed Wilfred in.

"Hello, everyone. Thanks for organising this, Sabina; it's so much easier to see you all together. I have a lot to tell you. Following the discovery of the babies at Buzzacott House, I went there with my colleagues, and sadly we recovered another two bodies of young infants, buried close to where you found the first child. I suspect they were not buried in the garden because the dog would have dug them up. Incidentally, we buried the dog in the same hole, so thanks for dealing with that, Fred. We searched the house from top to bottom for any records that might help us to identify the babies, both dead and alive, but we found nothing. However, we sent a photograph of Lizzie and Thurza Dymond to several police stations throughout the country, and they were recognised in several areas. It seems they have been doing this for several years and kept moving on to avoid getting caught. We also put their photographs in the newspapers to see if any mothers recognised them, and two have come forward."

Charlotte gasped, and Fred held her hand tighter and put his other arm around her. Wilfred picked up on her anxiety.

"You will be pleased to know, Mrs Carter, that the little girl you are looking after, is indeed your daughter, and so you can keep her."

"Oh, thank God!" Charlotte burst into tears of relief, and Fred held her tight.

"The two mothers who have come forward gave up a boy and a girl to be looked after but wanted them back at a later date. They didn't want them fully adopted. Lizzie Dymond met both of them at the railway station and assured them she would write as soon as she had moved to her new address. Of course, she never intended to do so, and they never heard any more. This seems to be how she got her money. The mothers paid her to take their babies, and she just let them die rather than spend time and money looking after them."

"Do you know which ones are their babies?" Asked Eveline.

"It's going to be difficult to know. I think we'll have to bring the mothers here to see the living babies and establish whether they can identify them. The two bodies we found were both of little girls, so the boy does likely belong to the mother who has come forward. They both want them back."

"What about Lizzie, has she told you anything?"

"Yes, she's been co-operating because she wants to avoid the death penalty, though I don't think she will. She admitted that the baby Thurza had taken a liking to, is yours Mrs Carter, but she didn't want to upset her daughter by making her part with it. She said when she first started this business, she looked after the babies properly and found new parents for those destined for full adoption. However, as she became older, it all got to be too much trouble, and she realised there was an easier way to make money. She admitted she's been drugging the babies to keep them quiet and need little care. It seems she couldn't quite bring herself to kill the infants, but she had no problem in letting them slowly starve to death."

"Where is she now? Is she still in Barnstaple jail, and what about Thurza?"

"Lizzie has been sent to Exeter jail and will stand trial for murder after Christmas. I think it is more than likely she will hang, and rightly so. There was another famous case back in 1870; you may remember it. It was in all the papers. A woman, called Margaret Walters, was hanged. She was known as the Brixton Baby Farmer. That's what they call these women; baby farmers. As for Thurza, I'm not sure if it might not be better for her if she hanged too, but she's been sent to an asylum because it's clear she has mental problems."

Fred shuddered. "She'd be better off hanged; I can assure you."

"It's not for us to say. Now, can I arrange for the mothers to come and see the babies, please? It seems more than likely that the baby boy does belong to the mother who has come forward, and the other mother says her daughter had a crooked little finger. She says she was born like it. Do either of the babies you are looking after have a deformed finger?"

Eveline looked mightily relieved as Sabina said. "Yes, the little girl I'm looking after does have a crooked finger, and I'm also looking after the boy, so you'd better tell the mothers to come here."

Eveline took Sabina's hand. "I'm so sorry, Sabina, did you want to keep them?"

"No, I've become fond of them, but I've had nine of my own, and watched three of them, die. Mabel as a newborn baby, and then John and Emma as young children. I can do without further heartbreak and worry because although they are beginning to thrive, I don't think they are out of the woods yet. These two have also been hard work, or maybe it's because I'm getting older. Are you happy to keep Martha, though, Eveline?"

"Oh, yes, I've never had any of my own, and I'm too old now. I love William's three, but none of them were babies when I started looking after them. Is it all right if I keep the baby, Wilfred? It's what Charlie and I have been hoping for."

"Yes, we've finished our enquiries, and I'm grateful to you ladies for looking after them. I know it's been hard work, and it's thanks to your efforts that they've survived. I didn't think they would. Sabina, I'll let you know when the babies' mothers can come, but it should be in the next day or two. Now, I'll leave you folk to get on and bid you all good day."

CHAPTER 50

Within weeks of their marriage, Annie found she was vomiting every morning, and remembering how she had been, when expecting Selina, she knew the cause. For the first few days, Robert was concerned about her, but when she always felt better during the day, and particularly when she ate, she assured him that she was not ill but pregnant. They were both delighted but decided to keep it to themselves for the time being. She was getting used to living at the Manor House now and had felt more comfortable since her previous workmates had joined the staff in the West Wing. She knew they had only her best interests at heart and felt she was amongst friends. Sarah and Aunty Margery had become regular visitors, and Annie was fond of them. Both ladies were helping Annie to pick up tips about behaving and feeling like a lady. They didn't criticise when she got something wrong but simply told her how it should be done, and she was grateful to them.

Each week she entertained Sabina, Betsey, and Matilda and enjoyed ringing the bell and ordering tea and cakes. They all laughed together about how their station in life had changed. The two babies Sabina had cared for had been returned to their grateful mothers. She missed them, but not the sleepless nights, and was glad she now had time to spend with her eldest daughter. Charlotte's daughter, Doris, was now seven months old. She was still small for her age and not yet sitting independently, but growing stronger every day. For the first few weeks it was difficult to get any response from her at all, but she was beginning to come out of her shell and show her personality. The first time Charlotte heard her chuckle, she thought her heart would burst with happiness, and began to believe that the little girl would eventually recover from her awful ordeal. Martha, the child that Eveline and Charlie had adopted, was also improving. It was not known how old she was, for she was so weak and emaciated when they found her that even Doctor Luckett had little idea. He thought she was probably about five months old, and like Doris, there was no response from her for several weeks. However, she was growing stronger and, recently, they had managed to get one or two smiles from her, which was heartening. Both babies were nearly weaned off the morphine, needing only a drop or two in their bottles at night to soothe them.

Annie had recently asked Aunty Margery to join the ladies for their weekly get together and, despite their different backgrounds, the five women got on extraordinarily well. The visits had done Matilda the world of good, for since losing her husband, Ben, and son, Harry, she had found it difficult to take any interest in life. Knowing that Selina was not her grand-daughter made her all the more grateful that Annie was keeping her in her life.

Aunty Margery was as good as her word and had visited Peter Webber several times. They enjoyed each other's company and loved to discuss his paintings. He gave Margery advice on how she could improve her techniques, and she commissioned him to paint a seascape for her. The painting now hung in her drawing-room and was her pride and joy. She insisted on paying him, and he was astounded at the amount of money she gave him. He protested that he was more than happy to give her the painting because he enjoyed her company, but she would have none of it. Each time she entertained guests at her mansion, the painting was admired, and Peter now had commissions for three more paintings. Sabina visited Peter regularly and was thrilled at how his painting career had taken off.

"It's all thanks to you, Sabina. When I think about what my life was like, before you came to see me that day, and how it is now, I can't believe the change. I'm truly a different man. I used to dread waking up to another boring day, but now I'm so busy, the hours fly by. I can never thank you enough."

With Christmas not far away, Annie asked Robert if she could invite all the family for lunch on Christmas Day.

"Yes, I'd like that. Who are you thinking of inviting?"

Annie smiled as she put her arms around him from behind his chair and nuzzled his ear. She kissed his neck. "That's the thing. Do you mind how many people I invite?"

"Oh dear, I know when you are trying to get around me for something. How many are you thinking of?"

"I want to invite all the family, but I've counted them, and it would be forty-three people. Would that be all right?"

"Goodness me. How do you get to that number?"

"Well, we're so happy now, and I want to share it with everyone. I've never got on with my Uncle George, but even he seems to be improving, and I was so glad to hear that he doesn't sell that awful Godfrey's Cordial in his shop. Perhaps he's not too bad, so I'd like to ask him, Mary Ann, and the two babies, as well as my cousins Theresa, Francis, and Harriet. I've always got on all right with them. Then, if no one objects, I think it's time to include Sarah and Bentley. It's time everyone put the past behind them, and this could be just the occasion to make it happen."

"I've no problem with any of it, but just make sure Sabina and Betsey don't mind. Who else?"

"Uncle Fred and Charlotte, and Charlie and Aunty Evie, and all their children. Then there's Mum, Liza, and my brothers and sisters. I thought we could ask Charlie's brother, Alfred Chugg, his nephew, Jimmy, and Sam. Do you know, I don't even know his surname?"

"Is that it?"

"No, not quite." She looked at him pleadingly. "They aren't family, but I'd like to ask Matilda, Francis, and Jacob Rudd. For a long time, they all thought Selina was Harry's child, and they still treat her like she is. Do you know what your parents will do for Christmas?"

"I've not seen much of them, but I know father's not been well. They don't socialise much anymore or travel. Why you're not thinking of asking them, are you? They won't come."

"No, I don't want them here, but I'd like to ask Aunty Margery and Sarah. I don't want to make things any more difficult than they already are, though."

"I would imagine that if Mama and Papa cannot travel to London, then perhaps Victoria and Frank will come here with the children. We could ask Aunty Margery and Sarah, and leave them to decide if they would like to come. I think I know where they would rather be. Seating all those people for a Christmas dinner will be a bit of a challenge, but we managed it for the wedding, so it should be all right. I'm going to leave you to break the news to Maisie and Mrs Potts, though."

"Yes, it will be a lot of work for them, and I'd be happy to help." She held up her hand to stop Robert. "I know, I know I can't do that now I am the lady of the house, but perhaps we could get in a few extra people to help, and we must make it up to them in some way. They serve us well."

"Of course, they do; they all adore you, and so do I, now come here and kiss me. Now, that you have wound me around your little finger yet again."

"I thought it would be a good time to announce our news. Doctor Luckett says everything is fine, and the baby will be born towards the end of June. Oh, sorry, there are two more people we need to ask."

"Who now?"

"Arthur and Peter Webber. Arthur and Mum are spending a lot of time together, and I think your Aunty Margery has fallen for Peter Webber."

"Never, she's far too old for all that. She must be over seventy."

"Well, maybe not romantically, but they have become fond of each other, and I know they will enjoy spending time together."

"Very well, then. It should be a lovely Christmas, but there is one condition."

"What's that?"

"I'm busy on the estate with Jack, and that's what I prefer to do, so I'd like to leave all the arrangements to you. Is that all right?"

"Yes, of course. I'd like to do it."

Annie wasted no time in making preparations for her Christmas party. Having consulted Aunty Margery and Sarah, she had some invitations printed. "It is how you should handle these things, my dear, and it's all a learning curve for you. One day, and before too long, no doubt, you'll be entertaining the gentry, and you must know how to do things properly." Annie couldn't see that happening any time soon, for she and Robert had not received one single invitation anywhere the entire time they had been married. However, this did not trouble either of them. Once the invitations were printed, she delivered them herself, and they were greeted with delight. Her Uncle George's mouth almost dropped open, but he recovered his dignity just in time.

"Why, Annie, this is so kind of you; are you sure you want us there? I've not always treated you and your family as I should." He looked sheepish. "I'm sorry, I am. I'm a silly stuck up old fool, sometimes, but I'm truly glad things have worked out so well for you and your family. Tom would be so proud of you."

"Thank you, Uncle George, and yes, I do want you to be there at Christmas. There is just one thing I would ask."

He looked at her quizzically.

"Please be nice to William's children. I know you don't like the fact they are half Chinese, but they can't help it, and they are William's children. If you aren't nice, I think Aunty Eveline or your mother will slap you."

He laughed. "Yes, fair enough, and I think you're right, they will."

"Good, thank you. Mrs Potts will be in to see you soon to place a big order of food. I must go now because Christmas is only a few days away, and the time seems to be slipping away fast."

CHAPTER 51

Carol singing was a tradition in Hartford that went back to the olden days. Some of the carols were unique to the village, for they had never been written down, and the next generation learnt them by listening to their elders. For several nights leading up to Christmas, the villagers would all pile onto a cart or two and travel miles to the surrounding villages singing their carols and collecting money for the workhouse children. Quite often, they would travel and sing all night long, often not getting home until the early hours, when they would grab a couple of hours sleep and set off for another full day's work.

Each outlying farm that they visited would supply them with refreshments. It was often bitterly cold travelling around during the wintry nights, and they were glad of a chance to warm themselves by the fire and enjoy some food and drink.

It was late on Christmas Eve when Robert and Annie heard the carol singers outside. They opened the door and listened to the crowd sing a couple of carols and then invited them in. John Cutcliffe had always been a good singer, and even the straight-laced, Noeleen could not object to him being out all night singing carols for charity. However, as he passed Annie and Robert on the way into the house, they both gasped. His hair had been virtually all cut off, and one eyebrow was missing. Seeing their surprise, several of the villagers started to laugh.

"What's happened to John?" Annie asked Sam Symons.

"Ssh, he doesn't know." Sam tried to keep a straight face. "I don't know what Noeleen's going to say when she sees him."

"How does he not know?"

"We've been out singing since late afternoon, and, of course, everywhere we go, we get given a drink of something. He's had one too many, and he fell asleep at the last place. A couple of the lads gave him a haircut and shaved off one eyebrow for a lark. I don't know how he slept through it the way everyone was laughing."

"I thought he'd given up the drink?"

"He has, but his willpower deserted him tonight, and he's had several. Of course, now he doesn't normally drink, it's had more effect than usual."

"Oh dear, I'd better stop him having any more. He'd better not be hungover for Christmas Day, tomorrow."

"Too late for that, ma'am; best let him enjoy himself while he can. I wouldn't like to be in his shoes when Noeleen gets her hands on him."

On Christmas morning, the West Wing looked beautiful. On Annie's instructions, a huge Christmas tree stood in the hall adorned with shiny glass baubles and little candles. Boughs of mistletoe, holly, and ivy were hung around the walls. In the dining room, the same long tables used for the wedding had been assembled and were covered with snowy white tablecloths. The crockery and cutlery, supplied by Aunty Margery, gleamed in the late winter sun, and in the centre of each table stood an ornate arrangement of blooms from the hothouses.

Robert put his arm around Annie as they both surveyed her handiwork. "It looks amazing. You have done a wonderful job, Annie. You should be proud of yourself."

"I've had a lot of help from Sarah and Aunty Margery. I don't know what I would have done without them both these last few months. I wish Selina had stayed here with us last night, so I could give her some presents this morning, but she didn't want to, and it's no good making her."

"I can understand how she would miss the other children because that's what she's always known, but she's getting better about coming here now, isn't she? She stayed the night recently, and I'm sure as she gets older, she will want to come more. I suspect when she has a new baby brother or sister, she will be quite keen to come here."

"Yes, I expect you are right. I just hope she doesn't get jealous of the new baby. We must make a big fuss of her when it arrives."

Robert grinned. "More than usual, you mean?"

"Oh, I know I spoil her, but I'm so glad I'm able to. Listen, I think I can hear our guests coming. The Carters always were a noisy lot."

All the guests arrived more or less together, and for a while, it was chaos in the West Wing as they were all served with tankards of ale, or a glass of wine, and some nibbles. Eventually, the gong sounded for lunch, and everyone took their seats. The meal, prepared by Maisie and Mrs Potts, was outstanding, for they had gone to a lot of trouble. With oxtail soup and freshly baked rolls to start, followed by roast goose and all the trimmings, many guests were full before pudding was even mentioned. Robert banged on the table with his spoon.

"Can I have your attention, please, everyone? I hope you have all enjoyed your meal and I don't see how you could not have done as it was delicious. I've asked Maisie and Mrs Potts to join us for a few minutes because I want to thank them for their tremendous efforts. Can we hear it please for Maisie and Mrs Potts?" Everyone cheered and toasted the cook and the housekeeper, who had both become red in the face and escaped as soon as they could.

Now, you'll all be relieved to hear I'm not going to make a long speech, but I do have a couple of things to say. First, I'd like to thank Annie for organising all of this today, and I think you'll agree with me that she looks every inch a lady." There were loud cheers. "Now, before we raise our glasses to Annie, we do have one other bit of good news to tell you, and that is we are expecting our first child in June. So, can I ask you to raise your glasses to Annie and our new baby?"

Everyone in the room rose to their feet and toasted Annie and Robert's announcement. When the noise had settled down again, Robert continued.

"Good, thank you very much, now I hope you all have room for a pudding because I think Maisie and Mrs Potts have made several. Thank you."

Arthur Webber stood up. "Would you mind if I also say a few words, sir?"

"No, of course not, Arthur. Please do."

"Thank you. Well, ladies and gentlemen, I don't think any of you will be surprised to hear that Sabina and I have become close over the last few months. She probably saved my father's life, not to mention two babies, and you all know what a wonderful person she is, so you don't need me to tell you. Anyway, I'm delighted to tell you that she has agreed to become my wife. So, can I ask you please to raise your glasses to Sabina? Thank you." Amidst loud cheers, everyone congratulated the happy couple.

When the meal was finished, the family left the tables, so they could be cleared away to make room for dancing. This gave the guests a chance to circulate and chat with each other. Sabina and Arthur were talking to Annie and Robert when Aunty Margery joined them.

"Do you mind if I join you?"

"No, of course not, Aunty Margery; did you enjoy the meal?"

"It was simply magnificent, my dear. If I wasn't so fond of you both, I would offer your cook and housekeeper a big rise in salary to come and work for me."

"Oh no, please don't. I don't know what I would do without them."

"Now, there is something I must ask. It's been troubling me since the double wedding. Who is the old man talking to Charlie and Eveline? Over there, look."

"Oh, that's, Sam. I think I told you once before, he used to be a tramp, but he lives at Hollyford Farm now."

"Do you think you could introduce me to him, please?"

Annie looked surprised. "Yes, of course, but may I ask why?"

"I keep thinking I know him, but I can't place him, and it's plaguing me. What is his surname?"

"I'm afraid I don't know. He's always just been Sam. I'll call him over, and you can ask him."

Robert went to fetch the old man. "Sam, can I introduce you to my Aunty Margery. She seems to think she knows you."

Sam smiled happily. "I'm very pleased to meet you, ma'am."

"Hello, Sam, may I ask what your surname is, please? I'm sure I know you from somewhere, and I can't think where."

Sam's toothy smile grew even wider. "No, you don't know me, ma'am, but I know why you think you do. My surname is Fellwood, ma'am. In fact, I am your nephew." The shock on everyone's face made Sam burst out laughing.

"My father was your elder brother, Thomas. He was next in line to Joshua, Charles' father. As you know, there were a lot of children in the family, and I believe you were the youngest, so there was a big age gap." Aunty Margery nodded. "Thomas fell in love with a gypsy girl, called Jane, when they were only teenagers, and she gave birth to a baby boy. I was that baby. Naturally, Thomas was told to never see her again, and the gypsies were forced to move on, but instead of doing as he was told, Thomas ran away with them and never came back. He married Jane before I was born because he wanted me to have the name Fellwood.

365

Unfortunately, he was killed in an accident when I was only two, and my mother brought me up alone. I travelled with the gypsies for years until my mother passed away, and since then I've fended for myself." He reached into his pocket and drew out a gold locket. "You may remember my father from this photograph? My father gave my mother this locket, and she treasured it all her life. There's a picture of him on one side, and my mother on the other. No matter how hungry I've been, over the years, I've never been tempted to part with it." He passed the locket to Margery, and slowly she nodded her head.

"My mother always told me that I was the spitting image of my father. I can't tell you what it has meant to me to finally eat at a table in the Manor House."

"Oh, Sam." With tears in her eyes, Aunty Margery hugged the old man.

AUTHOR'S NOTE

I hope you enjoyed reading this book as much as I enjoyed writing it. If so, I would really appreciate it if you could leave a short review on Amazon or Goodreads.

An honest review is the highest compliment you can pay to any author and it would mean so much to me.

If you would like to find out more about me and my books, and keep up to date with new releases, please visit https://marciaclayton.co.uk/ and join my mailing list.

Thank you.

Marcia

The Rabbit's Foot

Book Three in The Hartford Manor Series

Mr Edward Snell was more than a little curious when Robert Fellwood, the heir to Hartford Manor, and his elderly aunt, the Lady Margery, begged an audience on a Saturday morning. However, being such valued clients, the solicitor was happy to oblige. As his clerk showed the visitors in, he was intrigued to see them followed by an old man who, though respectably dressed, had something of a vagrant about him. The crisp suit in which he was attired could not disguise his weather-beaten face, or his missing teeth.

Robert introduced his Uncle Sam and explained he had come to claim his inheritance. The solicitor was old enough to remember the extensive search for Thomas Fellwood when his father, Ephraim, died in 1840. However, that was some forty-five years ago and the young man had never been found. Yet, here was Sam, who claimed to be Thomas Fellwood's son and, even more surprising, was the fact that the Fellwood family appeared to have accepted him as such.

The Rabbit's Foot is an intriguing and compelling novel with many unexpected twists and turns. Set in the small village of Hartford, it tells the tale of how an old man, who has spent his life with barely a penny to his name, suddenly finds himself rich beyond his wildest dreams. However, there is only one thing that Sam Fellwood truly wants and that is to be reunited with his son, Marrok, whom he abandoned at the age of five. Will Sam find the happiness that has eluded him for so many lonely years?

Lightning Source UK Ltd.
Milton Keynes UK
UKHW042330020222
398095UK00003B/69